Flight

Rise of the Thunderbirds

Lianne Miller

Lianne Miller
publisher@liannemiller.com
www.liannemiller.com

Publisher's Note: This is a work of fiction. Names, characters, places, and incidents are a product of the author's imagination. Locales and public names are sometimes used for atmospheric purposes. Any resemblance to actual people, living or dead, or to businesses, companies, events, institutions, or locales is completely coincidental.

Edited by Christina M. Frey, Page Two Editing
Cover Design by Steven Novak, Illustrator

Flight–Rise of the Thunderbirds (Book 1)/ Lianne Miller — 1st ed.
ISBN: 978-0-9963768-9-1
ISBN: 0996376895

TABLE OF CONTENTS

Dedication

To the myths and legends that awaken the Spirit's desire to dream while teaching the lessons that keep hearts pure and set us free.

Author's Note

It was my intent to share some aspects of Native American culture, but in a generic fashion, and in a manner that fictionalizes some, but not all elements of a culture and lifestyle that can vary greatly from tribe to tribe. No ceremonies or tribal spiritual practices—aside from those somewhat vaguely known by the public—were divulged, out of respect for the people who hold these acts, beliefs, and practices as sacred.

The Hachaath lived on Vancouver Island, British Columbia, and were part of the Nootka tribes that inhabited the Pacific coast area, including northwest Washington. Contact with Europeans led to an outbreak of smallpox, which is believed to have led to the extinction of the Hachaath.

No tribe should be forgotten and lost to time.

Breaking Ties

"Hurry, we have to hurry!" the tall, winged man calls to his sister and brother, trying to ignore the fear and dread rising within himself.

His sister stares at him, disbelief rippling through the shock on her face. "The decision was made?"

"The kings' messengers are spreading the word now. The permanent seals activate at sunset. We have to go!" The urgency in his voice matches his quick stride as they begin the sprint toward the nearest veil a mile away.

Their Enethuran family chase after them, not understanding that the Seelinaran royal courts are breaking ties and sealing the veils, that this world is no longer safe for those belonging to the sister world of Seelinara. All fae must return—but humans are to remain behind. Knowing this will destroy the foundation of love and happiness they've shared with these people, the three fae turn to face those they're leaving forever.

A hint of grief carries in the first brother's solemn admonition: "For many seasons we have lived among you. Our magic will remain with the people, and the storytellers will teach the children of our time here and remind you that the guardians will walk among you again one day. They will protect you. Do not fear them, for they will be like us. They will need you long before you will need them. Follow the oracle's instructions to hide and guide them well until the thunderbirds must rise again."

Each fae exchanges tearful hugs with their human spouse and their hybrid children before stepping back a few paces to gaze at their loved ones one final time. Then their wings flex as the words are spoken to activate the veil, and the thunderbirds step backward through the shimmering portal, sealing the fate of two worlds.

CHAPTER 1: NATE
A Day in the Life

Light and sound explode into my head, assaulting bloodshot eyes that don't want to focus. I roll onto my stomach and blindly reach for the bottle of bourbon on the nightstand by the bed. Not nearly enough left. Lifting my head I dump the last burning swallow down my throat and let the bottle drop to the floor. The loud clink when it rolls into the leg of the bed frame jolts the ache in my brain. I lie there facedown, unmoving, trying to decide if the pitiful amount is going to burn through the fog clouding my brain or numb it back into oblivion. It's the former, and with it the start of a horrendous hangover.

Propped up on my elbows now, I lift my eyelids one slow blink at a time, and the red shaded vision goes with them—but not the incessant *thump, bang, thump-bang* hammering my head. It takes me a second to recall where I am. Then I realize it's not just my head; someone is pounding on the bedroom door.

"Damn it, Nate, come on, man. We're going to be late again." It's a voice I know too well and don't want to hear right now because of what I know will come next. "I can't afford to lose this job because of your shit. If you're not out here in the next minute, I'm leaving without you." Yep, he's proving my point once again.

Grimacing, I close my eyes again and cradle my head a moment before I sit up and reach for my jeans. Then my body shifts into motion, my legs swinging over the edge of the mattress, and I become uncomfortably aware that my jeans are not on the floor, where I usually drop them. No, they've bunched my shorts into a stranglehold around me—not a pleasant way to wake. Rafe is still beating on the door. "Fuck, bro, keep your damn panties on!" I shout. "Give me a minute, will ya?" I need to scrub the taste out of my mouth and hit the head.

"You've got one minute, asshole." Rafe stomps away from the door, his fading footsteps an unpleasant reminder of how tough the day ahead will be.

My sluggish brain flickers to life, and I realize that not only did I pass out fully clothed again, but I didn't even take my boots off. My gaze spins around the room. A blur of dark paneled walls, the beat-up dresser, and a tattered rag rug on the worn wood floor fight for my attention. I can't even blame this one on a wild party. No, it was all me. I went out with the intention of finding a little action—fighting or fucking, I really didn't care—but all I found was the bottom of a bottle when neither panned out. It wasn't for lack of trying. I unleashed my charm on a filthy-cute little blonde, but her giggly girlfriends wouldn't give me five minutes alone with her. Bunch of hyenas. It was too bad, too; she had a fine-looking ass and a decent rack.

Yeah, this is going to be a miserable day. I don't know which will be worse—the nonstop *thwack, thwack, thwack* of hammers or the constant buzz of the power tools, not to mention the incessant bitching Rafe will do. For a second I entertain the thought of going back to bed to sleep it off, but he's not the only one who needs this job, and jobs are hard to come by. The economy is bad enough, but escalating political rhetoric, the whispers of war, and our own sketchy backgrounds further complicate job opportunities. I groan as I reach for a rubber band and stumble over my feet on the way to the door. My clothes smell like the bar, so I snatch a clean T-shirt from the dresser as I pass it. In the bathroom I load toothpaste on my brush, stuff it in my mouth, and head out—I'll brush my teeth and braid my hair in the pickup. Thank fuck it's Friday.

The engine of the pickup revs as I slam the door to the house; Rafe's impatient, as usual. I barely get a leg in the cab when he peels out on the dirt driveway. One look tells me he's about to unload again. He doesn't disappoint.

"You've got to stop doing this shit, Nate. Times have changed ... it's not like when we lived off the land, when you could be as stupid as you wanted." He glares at me. I scowl back. "We have to blend in, and your bullshit is costing us one job after another."

I lean out the window to spit the toothpaste, then draw a mouthful of water from the bottle to rinse and spit again. "Shut the fuck up. I don't need this from you again today."

Rafe punches the dash but doesn't relent. "You know we need paper trails now, and we already look like a couple of job hoppers. Throw in your hung-over ass, and everyone thinks we're the stereotypical lazy, drunken Indians."

Yeah, he's not helping my headache one bit. I swear he whines worse than some women on the rag. I've heard this bullshit complaint from my brother before, and I'm well aware outsiders see me as some caricature of what they think Indians are like. Of course I don't give a flying fuck what they think about me, and it's not like I'm trying to confirm their ignorance of Native people. I have bigger problems—I won't waste my time trying to change a mind that is already made up. Moot point. I'm doing what I can to escape a future that I may be destined for whether I want it or not, and the booze keeps me from losing my fucking mind. Rafe and I know the truth of why I am the way I am, and that's all that matters to me. But it doesn't mean I'm going to take his bullshit either. "Just drive so we can get this day over with."

Rafe slams the door when he gets out at the job site, a useless gesture meant to emphasize his displeasure with me. His buddy Devlin waves us over to the scaffold he's standing on. The anger on Rafe's face melts into a genuine smile as he greets Devlin. That's another difference between us—what's the point of having friends if I'll need to end the friendship before they discover we're not normal? Walking away from people I like is bad enough, but I have no desire to reexperience the heartache of leaving someone behind whom I befriended and cared about. The few friendships I've had in my long life were more than enough to teach me that lesson. Even now I sometimes catch myself wondering how they fared, whether they lived to old age, and if they had families to see them on their journey. The shadows of their ghosts haunt me, and I don't need to add more unsuspecting souls to that group. Rafe, though, doesn't seem bothered by it; he makes friends everywhere we drift. He's even managed to keep some older friends long-distance after we moved on. That shit ain't for me. I just need to kill time, cheat life, grow old, and die.

"They loaded the roof an hour ago, and I need both of you on top laying shingles today," Devlin says. He gives me a disapproving look—he knows I'm in rough shape, and I can tell he's reluctant to send me up there. If he knew a fall from that height wouldn't kill me, he'd probably pitch me off the roof himself. Sometimes I wish he would—it'd break up the monotony of this routine.

I buckle on my tool belt. "I'm not that hung over. I can roof." Without waiting for a reply, I start up the ladder.

A couple minutes later Rafe climbs over the edge, carrying a box of roofing nails and an insulated bag of bottled water. I grab a water and head over with the nearest roll of underlay—each tacker-hammer strike feels as if I'm beating on my own skull. Rafe is right ahead of me, laying the drip edge. But we focus on the job, and I know that I won't have to hear any more of his shit about my life ... for now, anyway.

By the end of the day, we have most of the roof finished, and I'm more than ready to go home, hit the shower, and go out. We're about to get in the pickup when Devlin jogs over. "Hey, I'm putting together a team for the pool league. Round robin. You guys in?"

"Sure thing." I look at Rafe and know he'll go, if for no other reason than to keep my ass out of trouble.

Devlin says, "Great. Stop by Griz Country Bar tonight at seven to meet the guys and get a copy of the team roster and schedule."

Rafe swings by a drive-through on the way home—he's making sure I eat something before I start drinking tonight. I watch him shove a few fries into his mouth as he drives. He's doing what he's always done, taking care of me when I don't give a shit, and sometimes I'm amazed he stands by me—no matter what I've done, he's never abandoned me. "Hey, bro ... I know I'm being an asshole again, but thanks for sticking with me," I tell him.

He glances at me and snorts. "Yeah, I'm thinking it's a chronic condition. You need to get your shit together, man." Rafe shakes his head. "Can't keep going on like this, bro."

It just gets old, knowing there's hundreds of years ahead before I can get out of this shit life. I look out the passenger window. I don't want to get into another argument, not now.

"We've been too long off the rez and away from the people," he says.

I silently disagree with him on this point—we're still outsiders, even among other Natives, because we're not from the same tribe or rez. Most people, while friendly enough to talk to, keep their walls up.

Rafe says, "I think we should hit some of the pow wows, go for a sweat, spend time with the elders—it'd do you some good."

I give a half shrug. "Maybe I just need to get laid."

Rafe laughs now and claps me on the back. "You're not alone in that department. Tell ya what ... if we don't find a couple of chicks while we're doing this pool league, let's hit a rez or two and see if we can find some there."

"Yeah, no thanks. You can chase the split-tails on the rez if you want. I don't want to get near any of them with a seven-foot spear." Don't get me wrong—some of the most beautiful women on the planet are Native American. I just can't risk being around them.

"What makes you so sure that the one"—meaning the woman I must avoid at all costs—"is on the rez or hanging out at pow wows?"

He knows the answer, and I shouldn't have to explain it to him for the millionth time. Our father's dying words warned us of one who would forever change our lives, and the surefire way to derail my plans to end this life is to mix it up with that gal and get stuck with no way out. Over the centuries the elders and seers taught us what Father never explained: our curse is thanks to a gene from some legendary grandfather who lived eons before we existed. Whatever triggers the gene's activation is unknown and a rare event, but when it happens it more often than not afflicts boys rather than girls. Our cousins escaped the curse and have long since taken the journey—their Spirits are free. Ours are not.

Resentment of the normal lives they were blessed with burns through me. Our aging process has been slowed to a snail's pace, but immortality will only strike its unwelcome blow the moment we complete the bond with our soulmates. I have no desire to live forever, and I will go out of my way to avoid crossing paths with the woman who can damn me to that fate.

The irony isn't lost on me; most people look for ways to cheat death. Not me. I'm seeking to cheat an immortal life while Rafe throws his arms wide open to embrace it. Whoever said twins think and act alike were wrong—we don't always want the same things in life. We can be as opposite as night and day and still share a unique bond.

Rafe looks at me now, and my jaw tightens—he wants to argue this point again and I don't. This is a family curse tied to the people's legends, and I'm convinced that Mrs. Right-but-oh-so-wrong-for-me will be Native. Rafe won't admit it, but even he knows our soulmates are Native, and it's why he always searches for his among them. "Not going to go there," I tell him. "I'll stick with the rest of the split-tails—got it?"

Rafe shakes his head slowly, only this time he looks sad and defeated. Shit. I'm stomping on his dreams again. Rafe wants to find his soulmate, to do this together, and I don't. Never have, never will. Still, I hate it when I hurt him, and I know I'm being an ass. It doesn't matter that we'll likely reconcile our differences—we usually do—I can't risk pushing him out of my life. He's all I have, and we need each other to get through the centuries ahead of us. That is, until he finds his mate—the defining moment that will lead to our permanent separation.

Yeah, it's not fair for me to expect him to wait until I'm gone to find his mate. By then it will be too late for him too. I can't condemn him to that end any more than I'll seal my own fate. Fuck, this curse is hard to live with.

"Sorry, bro," I say. "I know you want to find your woman and live forever, and I'm not making it easy on you." I can tell by the set of his jaw that he's upset—my apology isn't going to cut it. We're the only family we have, and he's made it quite clear he doesn't want to lose me either. The truth is, neither do I, but someday he'll have to; until then I can at least help him find part of his dream. "I have an idea, if you want to hear it."

"What is it?"

"How about we divide our weekends? One weekend we stay away from the rez so I can chase whatever comes my way, and the next weekend we hit up a pow wow or go kill time on the rez and you can look for your dream girl." I cringe inwardly at the idea. It scares the shit out of me to consider the day when Rafe stops aging and

I go down that slow path alone. But eventually he will go on without me, and until that day I'll need him to see me through to old age and death ... and to bury my body.

Rafe pulls into the drive, parks the pickup, and actually smiles at me. "Deal!"

It's my turn to shake my head as I make for the bathroom, trying not to think about the agreement we just struck. I've a feeling that I'm going to end up on the losing end after all. I open the shower tap to get the water hot while I take my braid out and brush my hair, then step into the shower. It's been decades since my hair was short—I tried it for a while to assimilate because it was expected of us, but I still hold traditional beliefs and have deep respect for the people and our heritage. Once society became more accepting of Native men with long hair, I grew it out again, and now it's past the small of my back. It boosts my Native pride to feel connected to the deeper meanings the outside world doesn't know or understand about our beliefs and lives.

Rafe pounds on the door, complaining about me not leaving him any hot water. It'd be nice to stand in the spray a little longer, but we do need to get ready to go. I pull on a pair of jeans and a T-shirt and lace up my boots. I'll finish getting ready in my room, though I only need to braid my hair and put on some cologne. I never dress up to go to the bar. While that may attract a split-tail or two, it sucks having button-down shirts ruined if I get in a fight—which is an enjoyable and fairly common occurrence for me. The only drawback is that T-shirt sleeves aren't long enough to cover the scars on the back of my arms, and that invites gawking. Not that I can't handle it, but it gets old lying about my supposed tattoos.

A half hour later we pull up to Griz Country on our bikes and back them at an angle to the curb before we go inside to find Devlin. Sometimes I still miss the days when a good horse was the best means of transportation, but our Harleys are a decent substitute. The bikes are nearly identical, like us, with the only difference our shifter preference. Rafe has a standard hand-clutch foot shifter, while mine is a suicide shifter—fitting, all things considered.

Devlin is waiting at the back of the room near the pool tables. I grab a couple of beers at the bar, and Rafe and I join the others. Quick introductions are made—we're a five-man team. The other two dudes I've seen around but can't say I know them. I'm thinking this might be okay, but then the one called Brad seems to take issue with us.

"Hey, chief, weren't you the stupid blanket-ass who got the shit beat out of him over at Great Escape last weekend?"

And we're done before we start, and no, it wasn't me—I win all my fights. I set my beer on the table without breaking eye contact and take a step toward him. My hands curl into fists; looks like it's a fight night, and I'm more than happy to oblige this jackass. "You got a problem with me or just Indians in general?"

He points to Rafe. "Maybe it was this one, then. Can't tell any of you apart."

Wrong thing to say. While I may flip my brother shit, no one else gets to walk on him like that. "Fuck you!" I draw my arm back and nail the son of a bitch square on the jaw—I hear bone break and a tooth flies out of his mouth. He goes down to the floor like the sack of shit he is.

The bouncers are on us immediately, and between them and Rafe, I'm shown the door. They inform me that I'm banned for a month. Great. It's not the first time I've been eighty-sixed from a bar—and I doubt it will be the last. I look down at my knuckles and notice two are cut and swollen. That will either add to the collection of scars or it won't. I shake my hand out and curse my half-full beer still left inside. It's too early to go home, and since it wasn't much of a scrap, I'm up for some female company for the remainder of the night. "You want to go on over to the Mint Bar and see if we can find a little action?" I look across at Rafe as he straddles his bike.

Rafe, for once, isn't upset with me—he may be the calmer of the two of us, but he doesn't like that shit any more than I do. If people saw even one-tenth of what we've seen in over five hundred years, there'd be no racism on this planet.

He nods. "Yeah, getting laid sounds a heck of a lot better than the bullshit that happened in there."

The Mint Bar is busier than usual for a Friday night, and when we walk inside it's easy to see why—they have a live band. Rafe and I have to shout over the crowd to hear each other. With beers and shots of bourbon in hand, we make our way to a table near the dance floor. Man, the split-tails are hot tonight. Out on the floor a few women are dancing with men, but most huddle in small groups together. The latter is my target. While some girls seem to get off on dancing like that, there's always one who'd rather be grinding against a man.

I knock back the shot and take a long pull from my beer before I walk toward a group of girls who are looking us over with curiosity and even interest instead of fear or disgust. Rafe is right next to me—he wants to work the twin angle to our advantage. Must be desperate to get laid. I flash him a knowing smirk.

It's no surprise to me when Rafe moves in on a gal with a medium fake-bake complexion and long black hair that looks like it came from a bottle. That's one more thing I don't understand about women. They are beautiful—stunning, even—in a natural state. Don't they know how ugly they look with their hair colored, gooped up, coated with hair products? And then there's the makeup caked several layers thick on their faces. What's worse is waking up next to one of those chicks when they don't wash the shit off—scary and ugly thing to see when my eyes first open in the morning. It's another reason I try not to fall asleep with my bed dates and usually leave right after we're done having sex.

Even though the girl doesn't look Native, she fits Rafe's type: long dark-brown or black hair, bronze complexion, dark eyes. Not me. I'll take anything as long as she doesn't remotely resemble someone with our heritage—it's safest for me to cheat life that way. Blonde, redhead, brunette ... white, brown, yellow, or black, it really doesn't matter. As long as she's got a smoking-hot body, I'm good to go.

And near Rafe's girl I see something that appeals to me—a sexy little redhead with a stacked rack, dancing as if she doesn't have a care in the world. I sway to the music to get her attention. She freezes midmotion and looks up at me, then at Rafe, and then she darts a quick glance toward her friend. Both gals are doing the double take that means they realize we're identical twins, and the way they smile at each other signals we've hit the easy score tonight.

I'm at least a foot taller than the redhead gyrating her hips and moving closer to me—she's only five two or five three, which means I have a bird's-eye view straight down her top to her front bra clasp. Man, I'd like to bury my face in her rack. I dance closer, allowing the barest hint of contact between us, and her smile grows bigger. "See something you can't resist, sweetheart?" I say with a wink.

She takes the bait and leans into me as I grip her hips. Within seconds she's grinding against me, and my dick goes hard. Unlike some split-tails who pretend not to notice when that happens, she presses tighter to me. It's clear what she wants, and I plan on giving it to her. When she turns and rubs her ample tits against my chest, I'm certain I won't be going to bed alone tonight. She just doesn't know it will have to be her bed. I never let girls know where we live—I don't need anyone hunting me down later or stalking me and demanding more.

Over the next few hours we laugh, tease, dance, and drink. She tells me her name, but a few minutes later I've already forgotten it. I'm only interested in one thing, and I already know that after tonight I won't see her again.

Within seconds of that thought, she reaches up to cup a hand around the back of my neck. "Do you want to get out of here?"

"What do you have in mind?"

She glances at her friends. "My apartment is within walking distance if you'd like to come on over."

Oh, hell yeah. I bend down and brush my lips against her ear. "I'd like that, our own private party."

While she's collecting her purse, I let Rafe know that I'm going to be busy for a couple of hours and will see him in the morning. He just smiles and nods. By the way the black-haired gal is wiggling on his lap, I suspect he's not going without tonight either.

The redhead and I walk the few blocks to her apartment, stopping occasionally to kiss and grope each other. I swear this chick would do me on the sidewalk if I encouraged her. I need to get her home before we embarrass ourselves in public—her hand has already been down the front of my pants twice. It's been a while since I've had a gal this open and brazen, and I already know it's going to be a fun time.

When we arrive at her apartment, she doesn't waste a second locking the door behind us and shoving me into her bedroom. We're shedding clothes as fast as we can, and then she strips the rubber band off my braid, gushing about how she loves my hair as she finger-combs the long strands. It's not the first time a girl has gone gaga over my hair—some women want it loose when we have sex, though others are content to leave it alone. I really don't care either way, but if it adds to their desire to please me, I'll let them do whatever they want with it—short of cutting it off, of course.

From the way this split-tail is acting, there's no need for foreplay—she's ready and wanting. I grab a condom out of my wallet. Not that I need to worry about diseases, but it makes the ladies feel better, and it prevents passing on the cursed gene to an unwanted child. Her eyes follow my every move, and when I join her on the bed, she's already lying there with her legs wide apart ... an open and eager invitation. I crawl between her thighs and take a nipple in my mouth, teasing it with my tongue as I cup her other breast in my hand. A lustful moan escapes her. Trailing kisses upward to find her mouth, I align my body with hers. She grabs my hips and pulls me closer, slamming me firmly against herself with every thrust. Her uninhibited eagerness builds the excited tension between us, and I fucking love every second of it. I slip a hand between us while she groans with pleasure—yeah, she's what I expected, fun and predictable.

Within minutes I have her at the edge, and the way she's moving and screaming sends me to the precipice too, but she falls before I do. Breathing heavily, I try to ignore the dead fish she turns into. I really hate it when chicks do that. They grumble about men failing to please them, but so many just up and quit the moment they orgasm. It's rare I find a gal who will wear a man out to enjoy as many as she can. Still, I don't stop; I pull her tighter to me as my hips pound against her, and even without her help I find my release after a few more strokes. Then I relax and let my full weight settle on top of her while I take a moment to come down from the somewhat satisfying high.

I kiss her once more before I roll away from her and crawl off the bed. She rises onto her elbows, uncertainty reflecting in her hesitant smile. "Where ya going, hot stuff?" Her tone is seductive. Pathetic. And it's too late for it to work on me—I've already learned she's selfish in bed. Not my kind of lover. Now, if she'd made more of an effort, I'd consider a second round, but she does not deserve one, and I'm not going to be the cuddle toy she tosses out come morning. I wink at her. "I've got my ride waiting for me."

She sits upright, as if someone doused her with ice water. "What? You're just going to leave, just like that?"

I bend over her and press another kiss to her lips. "It was fun, sweetheart. Thanks."

She's getting angrier by the minute, so I dress as fast as I can. I'll never understand split-tails. They act all hot and bothered one moment and turn ice cold and cruel the next. Without looking back,

I let myself out of the building and breathe a sigh of relief. That could have gone much worse if she wasn't so stunned by my departure. I remember a few other mad-as-hell split-tails I've walked away from in the past—screaming and hollering as they chased me down, begging me to come back. No thank you, don't need that shit. At least I won't be passing out drunk tonight, which means tomorrow may be tolerable. It'd be a good day to go for a ride with Rafe—though I won't know until morning whether he's wrapped up in his gal for the rest of the weekend or if he's one and done like me.

My Brother's Keeper

Man, my brother is a dickhead. It amazes me sometimes how twins can be polar opposites, and staring at Nate's text message proves it once again. I'm still lying here with Randi, who's asleep curled into my side, while he's already ditched his bed date. Why am I surprised? I get that Nate's never going to accept what we are, but this destructive phase is wearing beyond thin. Myself, I'm ready to accept my role as a guardian, to reach my full potential. The idea of immortality is somewhat scary, but I'm thrilled at the thought of being more than human and fulfilling our purpose of offering protection and help to those who need it most. The hardest part for me, aside from the wait, is the unanswered questions. So much has been lost to time; even the elders know little about the guardians who came before us, other than that they disappeared a few generations before Nate and I were born. It leaves me wondering if the immortality part is even real ... an extremely long life span is still mortal if death is at the end.

If we're not one, then we are the other, but so much of what we are remains a mystery even to us. We've learned little since the first signs appeared when we were boys, but the proof couldn't be ignored: after the fever broke, our bodies were left with featherlike permanent scars in shades of black, tan, and brown. My marks cover the back side of my shoulders and upper arms and run down my entire back; then they appear to fold, layering over my hips and ass and down the back of my legs, stopping just above the bend of my knees. My brother's scars are identical to mine. They've never faded or gone away, and others assume, I suppose because we're twins, that we have matching tattoos. The only tat we have in common—a red-tailed hawk—represents our clan, and it's located between our elbows and wrists on the inside of our arms. His is on the right, mine on the left.

I look at my watch, knowing I should get on home—Nate keeps texting me. He wants to go on a ride today, but I'm not ready to leave Randi's bed. Her head is resting on my chest, and she's snoring quietly. I push a strand of hair away from her pretty face. She's nice enough, and I'd like to see her again, but I already know she's not the one. Like with all the women before her, I have no sense of connection, let alone the compulsion to remain with her. Shouldn't I feel something if she's my soulmate? But I can't bring myself to be an asshole like my brother. While I may sleep with a gal right after we meet, I like to give her a few weeks of fun before I break it off. I can't just fuck and run like Nate does or ignore a chick as if nothing happened if I see her the next day. Yeah, he can be heartless.

And it bothers me, because he wasn't always like this. In fact, this side of him didn't surface until long after we learned what our future holds. I remember the fever that changed us and how afterward our family moved from one tribe to another to hide what we'd become. They couldn't reveal that we had stopped growing like normal kids, that for every three years other children aged, we gained just one month. It took thirty-six of their years to mark one year for us, and in that first long year of our new lives, we watched our parents age from young adults to elders. Long before we turned twelve, Mother had taken the journey, and Father finally revealed the truth to us as his frail body prepared to free his Spirit to join her and the Ancestors.

I've never forgotten that final conversation, and my mind replays it now, bringing the familiar ache deep inside. "Sons..." My father was struggling to breathe but managed a faint smile. "I must tell the story of what you are. It is time ... There are no more days for me to protect and guide you. Grandfather Sun will rise again without me."

My brother looked as scared as I felt. We had begged for this truth for years, and at last Father was ready to tell us, but only because he couldn't hide it anymore—because it no longer mattered whether we were too young or immature to handle knowing. It was then that our father's impending death hit me, and I feel the ache and sense of loss acutely even now.

"In the last world, magical beings lived among us, and some remained even after the birth of this world. But when this world was born, a barrier formed between Mother Earth and her sister Seelinara. The magic ones lived in that sister world, though some knew how to travel between them. Grandfather was one who knew."

I remember staring into the milky cloudiness of his dying eyes and wondering why he was telling us this story; we'd heard it before. There had been many stories of the deaths and rebirths of our world, of the beings that once existed but were no more. We had no way of knowing when or where this story really began or how many generations passed between Grandfather and Father. We didn't have extra labels—great or great-great, once or twice removed, first or second—to identify family relationships. We were simply sister, brother, mother, father, daughter, son, grandmother, grandfather, granddaughter, or grandson regardless of the generations in between.

Father, though nearly blind, seemed to sense my uncertainty. "We must accept that this is how the Creator intends our worlds to be. Never question who you are." Even then, without full sight, his

penetrating gaze saw through me; he understood what I was thinking. I looked down and nodded again.

"Grandfather came to this world seeking a wife. It took many
seasons, but he found her, and they had many children. Not all became as you are; guardians are chosen exclusively by the Creator
and the three sisters of fate. We never knew it would happen to one
of you, let alone both of you."

This part of the story I had never heard before, and it unnerved
me then, but I've come to accept it, embrace it, even, as something
that was always meant to be. "Sons, your Spirits have magic," Father
said. "Many moons beyond several lifetimes will pass before you become men ... warriors ... guardians." His voice became almost inau-
dible as he murmured, "Thunderbirds."

He swallowed and reached for our hands. "Many will come and
then cross to the lands of our Ancestors in that time. You must always seek the elders and healers among the people to help you on
your journey."

I remember the way he licked his pale, cracked lips, bringing no
moisture to them. My brother grabbed a water bladder and held it
carefully to Father's mouth while Father wetted his parched tongue
and throat.

"Only the Creator knows if you will journey beyond this life or
walk forever above the Red Road." His weak grasp tightened briefly
around our fingers. "All are born, live, and die—this is one part of
the great circle of life. Only the Spirit walks the Red and Blue Roads,
but a few are given a different journey and walk forever in the space
separating the two."

Unfortunately it would be decades before I discovered what his
statement meant. That moment came for me at age seventeen, when
I finally realized that generations of people would continue to come
and go before Nate and I found our true place in this world. We're
getting closer, I know, but we're still not there.

My father rasped out, "You must go back to the people. Find the healer to help you on your journey."

Tears ran down my face then, and my brother's cheeks were wet too. We weren't ready to be alone in the world. We had learned to trust our parents and their judgment and wisdom, and we seldom disobeyed them. I wanted to rebel this time but knew I couldn't. So I choked on my words, already knowing the answer to my question: "Where will we find them?"

"The Creator will guide you. Your dreams will lead you to the one meant for you—follow them. When she stands by your side, you will rise to protect the people for all time." My father's body tensed, and his breathing changed to labored panting. Even now I feel the pain in my chest too and wince at the memory of him gasping and fighting for enough breath to say his final words. "When ... I drop my robe ... you must ... fly. Do not ... bury me. You need ... the people ... the people need ... you ... Never forget ... your Spirit-twin."

Dropping the robe was a common expression among a few tribes, one that signaled leaving the Red Road and beginning the Spirit journey. One, by the account of our dying father, that my brother and I may never take. If our aging hadn't already practically stopped, we would have been in our mid-forties when he died. Instead we were trapped, almost frozen in the bodies and minds of eleven-year-old boys. I was so terrified that I was unable to speak, merely nodding while my brother, braver than I, pledged, "We won't forget, Father."

We did as Father instructed when his last breath slid weakly over his lips—we fled. Yeah, in time we found our tribe and even returned to them on a few occasions until the day we discovered them gone. We learned from one of the Nootka clans that the Hachaath had been wiped out during a smallpox outbreak; the handful of survivors had joined other bands. Left with no choice, we sought friendly tribes that believed in and told stories about the thunderbirds. We still do. But even among them, we can never stay long—in part because Nate doesn't want to be there.

I'd like to say that we stopped running once we found the people, but the truth is that Nate's been running ever since Father took the journey. And I've followed my brother, unwilling to lose the only family I have. This life is lonely enough with just the two of us, and time always forces us to leave those we care about behind. Hell, even now I find myself plugging the holes of our existence with whatever I can manage for friendship—regardless of the inevitable sadness that comes with loss, these friendships keep me grounded, sane, and remind me of the greater purpose for our being here. Our lives aren't supposed to be about us but for those who will need us someday. That one thought is what quells my anger at Nate in his worst moments. Well, that and the good man I know he's capable of being when he's not in one of these moods.

It's true—in favorable years Nate can be a better person than I am. I've seen it in the way he'll tend to a wounded animal or secretly give to the needy, and I've caught him sitting with the dying in hospitals or nursing homes when no one else is there for them. He's also hunted down more than one woman-beater and given them a hefty dose of their own medicine, along with the threat of death if they ever touch a woman the wrong way again. His mood shifts are even more contrary and show in the extremes between his goodness and the abrasive give-no-fucks attitude. But as much as we can be opposites, our bond as twins won't allow me to believe we're meant for different destinies. A part of me will never stop dreaming of a day when we stand together in the role we were born to fill.

For now, the feather-shaped marks remain the biggest part of the mystery. If the legends are true—the thunderbirds once lived among the people—then the marks on our backs must be something more than just scars to prove our identity to tribal elders. Nate thinks I'm nuts and claims it's wishful thinking, and he equates it to the mark of Cain—a true sign of our curse, as he calls it. Most of the elders agree with him to a point. Without conclusive proof, it's impossible to know which version is true, but we can't all be right, can we?

Some of the earliest legends tell of men putting on wings to fly, while others indicate the thunderbirds are not men at all—they're large birds, the size of grown men. The elders maintain the marks are more symbolic than anything and that thunderbirds only live in the legends and old stories. I'm not sure what to believe, but instinct tells me the thunderbirds existed at some point before they were lost to time. Why else would Father claim we are somehow tied to them? I know he spoke the truth. But why feather scars? It doesn't make sense, and I can't shake the niggling feeling there's more to it. There has to be, or what is the point of our lives?

In some respects it doesn't matter to me either way. And there is the most glaring difference between Nate and me: I'm eager to rise to the challenge, whatever it may be. He is less than willing—he's downright avoiding it. I accepted the path the Creator chose for me when we were young, and I like to think we're pretty damn lucky now. The ages we've seen come and go are unimaginable to those who only live in short segments of time, and I can hardly wait to see what our future holds a year or a thousand years from now. While I'm still uncertain how our soulmates are supposed to tie into all of this, just the thought that I will have a good woman at my side for eternity, one the Creator meant only for me, is enough for now. She will ground and balance me by bringing strength to weakness, joy in sorrow, wisdom to foolishness, and reason to brash thought—which I need when I'm feeling lost. She must be beautiful, perfect, my hope when I despair. A sweet bonus.

That, of course, is a future Nate wants no part of, and his resistance to the possibility of a mate and immortality leads to these destructive bouts once or twice a century. Usually his recklessness and carelessness result in accidents that severely injure him. I don't know if he's getting tired of being busted up, hurting, and healing or if each difficult period nudges him just a little closer to acceptance. All I know is that I'm thankful we get breaks from his self-destructive bullshit once in a while. I couldn't take it if he was always at his worst—I would part ways with him regardless of the loneliness it would bring to my life.

It's tough having sympathy for him when his own sheer stupidity hurts him for the umpteenth time. I've lost count of the number of wagons, cars, trucks, and motorcycles he's wrecked while driving too fast or drunk. It's thirty-two, I think. But that isn't as bad as his numerous attempts to end his life—which scared the absolute shit out of me until he stopped trying to kill himself centuries ago. That was his first reaction to the realization that we might live forever: drowning, cutting his own throat, diving off a tall cliff, refusing to eat or drink, running into a forest fire ... oh, and let's not forget, ladies and gentlemen, Nate challenging wild animals and being gored by buffalo, mauled by grizzly bears, and attacked by badgers or wolves. Hell, I've forgotten the number of times he tried to end his life, but every one of them failed. Thankfully those days are behind him ... replaced by these cycles of his not giving two fucks one way or the other.

It's these cold, heartless years that bother me the most—I know my brother has a good heart, and he can be so much better than this asshole who drinks, fights, and screws around. Nate knows how to treat a woman right, but when he loses respect for himself, he goes through one woman after another, sometimes several a night, and I learned a long time ago that it does no good to cock-block him. Nate simply finds a way around me, or we end up in an all-out fistfight that only postpones what he set out to do in the first place. He's run this gamut more than once.

And Nate's drinking and penchant for fighting make everything worse. Although he'd never act deliberately, he has come close to killing other men in meaningless fights. He's narrowly dodged a few lengthy sentences, too, from injuring men who never stood a chance against him but were too stupid to walk away from his challenge. Yet he's seen more than his fair share of time in city or county jails for drunk and disorderly conduct. Booze is the constant, with women and fights his go-to distractions. Man, it's been rough keeping his ass out of the clink—I'm amazed he's avoided hard prison time, but I like to think he's smart enough to know where to draw the line.

Prison would expose our unnaturally long lives, and that's something we must avoid. I can't fathom how people would react, but my gut instinct tells me it wouldn't be good—with my luck we'd end up locked in a secret laboratory where they'd run tests on us for eternity. How could they hope to figure out what we are when we're still trying to discover that ourselves?

Randi stirs, bringing me back to the present, and I lift her chin toward me. "Hey, babe, I've got to get going. If you don't have any plans tonight, we can hang out or go for dinner or a movie or dancing at the bar again."

She looks up at me through sleepy eyes and reaches for her cell phone—she wants me to add my number to her contact list—then rolls over to go back to sleep. I enter my information, silence her phone, and send a text from hers to mine. In turn I send a reply: "thanks babe, call me." I leave the message open on her screen so she'll see it when she wakes up.

Nate is waiting for me when I get home; he's already packed a lunch, and no surprise, it includes a half rack of beer stuffed into the saddlebags on his bike. We take a secondary highway to a dirt road that leads into the mountains. From there we hike up to the saddle—there's a meadow on top with a stunning bird's-eye view of the valley below. I can still picture the valley as it was before the area was settled. While we've adapted to the changing times, including choosing new, more modern first names once a century, something about unpopulated regions calls to us. At times I miss the quieter centuries before industry and high technology came along—the long walks, horseback rides, and years of isolated living. We still hunt and fish, but it's different now with all the regulations and restrictions. If there were one thing I could change about our long lives, I would want the ability to go forward or backward in time so that we could enjoy the best each period offers.

But today is starting off well. We haven't argued yet, which is rare when Nate's in destructive mode. I glance tentatively at him. "You going to see that redhead tonight?"

"No, once was more than enough." He shrugs. "I know you'll go back to that split-tail you were with—you always do. Why do you waste your time?"

I pluck a leaf off a bush and let it drift to the ground. "We'll never agree on this. But yes, I'll see Randi for a while."

We fall into silence until we reach the meadow. I've got something else on my mind, and now—while we're alone and Nate's sober—may be the best time to bring it up. Devlin doesn't run a full crew in the winter when his business slows down, and Nate and I are on the layoff list since we were the last ones hired. Watching for his reaction, I say, "You have any idea what you want to do for work this winter?"

"I guess it depends on whether we stay here."

We've only been in this town for two years, and it will be another few years before people begin noticing we're not aging like they are. A bonus—for me—is the proximity to two different reservations. I've always felt that our destined mates are within the Native American community somewhere; my only uncertainty is what race our soulmates will be. Still, I'm more than ready to find my gal. I'm tired of being alone with Nate. "I'd like to stay put ... thought I might apply for a job over at the rail yard or"—I struggle to keep a smile off my face—"manage your career while I pimp you out as a male stripper. We can bill your show as Rez–Erection."

The look on his face is an indescribable mix of shock and in-credulity—priceless. "You're really funny, asshole."

"Why not? Half the gals in town have already seen you naked." I like pushing his buttons, getting him all riled up. "They'd turn out in droves to get another chance at you. We'd make a killing."

"Fuck off. You know how I feel about showing my scars." Nate scowls and mumbles under his breath about stupid curse, idiot brother, and why me.

I can't keep a straight face any longer and burst out laughing. His eyes narrow and then he lunges, tackling me to the ground. We grapple for a few minutes, but like most of our wrestling matches, it ends in a draw. I flash him a smile as I sit up. "Sometimes you're just too easy, bro." I laugh again and shake my head. "Do you really think I'd want to see your naked ass in public? Trust me—I see enough of it at home."

"You're a real comedian." Abruptly he turns the conversation to our plans for the night ahead. Nate wants to avoid the Mint Bar—he doesn't want to run into the redhead from last night—and he suggests going over to the Hideout on the outskirts of town. That puts me in a bind for when we go back later. Randi sent a text message minutes after we left home—she'd like to go dancing again. "I'm meeting that gal from last night at the Mint."

Nate doesn't pause so much as a heartbeat. "So? We'll stop by the Mint, you go in and get your gal, and then we'll go on over to the Hideout."

I'm not sure Randi will go for it, but I don't want him getting drunk and ornery alone. When we reach the highway I pull over, kill the engine, and give Randi a call. "Hey, babe, you up for a ride on my bike tonight?"

"I thought you were coming to the Mint?"

"Yeah, about that ... bit of a change of plan."

She's suspicious, and I'm trying like hell not to tell her my real reason with Nate right next to me, listening to every word. He hates it when I babysit him. Randi warms to the idea—I breathe a small sigh of relief—but then she sets the fuse on fire. "Does your brother want to take Tamara?"

I look over at Nate. "Want to take Tamara?"

"Who the fuck is that?"

Turns out Randi heard him, and next thing I know, it's my pride she's trying to nail to the wall. "I can't believe he just said that! Is his memory as short as his dick? He went home with her last night—what a jerk. Oh, this is rich ... unbelievable. So tell me, because you're twins and all, do you both practice the three *f*'s?"

I about choke—it's not a phrase I've heard in a long while, and I'm surprised she even knows it. *Find 'em, fuck 'em, forget 'em.* Nate is not short of memory; he's just being an ass. Shit. Could this get any more messed up? Now I have a split-second decision to make, thanks to my dirtbag brother. He's still scowling at me with his arms folded across his chest. Knowing it will mean another fight with Nate later, I say, "No, that's just him. Never mind the ride—I'll meet you at the Mint in twenty if you want."

Nate has his bike started and is peeling out before I even get my phone back in my pocket. I watch him flip me the bird and ride away. Damn it! I hope he keeps his ass out of trouble tonight; the last thing I want to do is bail him out of jail. I start my bike too and take off down the highway. Even though Randi isn't the one, I sure hope she makes this decision worth it.

The moment I walk into the Mint, I know I'm going to pay for what Nate did to Tamara—she, Randi, and two other gals are glaring daggers at me as if it were my fault. I hate this shit. Chicks and their head games. I square my shoulders and smile at Randi as I approach, hoping they understand it wasn't me regardless of how much I look like Nate. No such luck. First Tamara spouts off and then Randi joins her, and a minute later the other two friends jump in to tell me what man-whores me and my brother are to treat women this way. They're not entirely wrong—while I may not follow the three *f*'s, as Randi put it, I usually dump a girl within a few weeks. It looks as if I won't have to worry about going through the motions with Randi. If she were the one, I'd smooth things over and make it right, but she's not, and there's no reason for me to make the effort.

My jaw clenches, and I motion between Randi and me. "This isn't going to work. Sorry, babe ... I'm outta here."

Now she looks shocked. If I had to guess, I'd lay odds that she thought she and her friends could dump all over me and at the end of the night she'd still take me home. Hell no, I don't play those games. Without another word I leave the bar, deleting her number from my phone as I go outside. I hear her yelling behind me, but I start my bike and head home, my mood ruined.

Lying in bed two hours later, I wonder for the millionth time when and where I will finally find my soulmate. Unlike Nate, I don't need to dive into the bottom of a bottle of booze, and I'm not interested in picking up chicks for one-night stands. But the more time passes, the more isolated I feel, as if I'll always walk this path alone.

Nothing is ever accomplished by looking back; the only thing I can do is go forward. I've seen vague, blurry images of her in my dreams, though I wish I knew her name or could see her face clearly and get a hint of where she might be ... *when* she might be. I can't imagine my future without her, and in my mind's eye I can see her standing by me as we tackle whatever destiny throws at us. Tonight I will seek another dream of her, which will have to do until I find her and we're together.

Once more I pray that the Creator will send her to me soon—I'm ready to get on with my life. I just wish Nate were too.

CHAPTER 3: NATE

Repeat Lesson

Leaving Rafe on the side of the road, I run up through the gears, pulling the throttle wide open, and within minutes I'm back in town and speeding straight through to the outskirts on the other side. For a Saturday night the Hideout is dead; I down one beer and leave. Anger is burning through me after that shit phone call with the split-tail Rafe banged earlier ... it ruined a good day spent with my brother. I head over to an old dive called Charlie's, but this place is dead too, and again I leave after one beer. It must be the band at the Mint pulling people away from the other bars.

On my way back through town I stop at the Great Escape—there's usually a rough crowd there, bikers, mostly, and I'm in the mood for a fight. I know someone will eventually oblige me. I'm on my fourth beer with a whiskey chaser when a tall blonde sits on the stool next to me and starts flirting. Her back is to the bar, and I can tell she's already a bit tipsy, but I buy her a drink. She almost falls off the bar stool as she leans over and plants a quick kiss to my cheek. Given the caliber of women in this place, I'm surprised she doesn't do more than that. But then she pitches forward, stumbling, nearly falling down. That explains it. My arm juts out, steadying her, and then I turn on my stool to face her as she steps forward and moves between my legs, draping her arms around my neck.

Just as my plans for the night begin to change, I get that fight I was looking for when I first arrived. It seems this split-tail is here with a boyfriend, and he's not one bit happy with my hands on her ass or the way she's pressing up against me.

He pushes her back and takes a swing at me as I try to bail off my stool, duck the hit, and get on my feet at the same time. Instead I trip on the stool she knocked over when he shoved her away, and I go down to the floor. The fucker doesn't wait for me to get up—he puts the boots to me and lands a few kicks to my ribs and face before I can roll clear. I manage to get upright, but just as I return a little punishment, the bouncers step in and separate us. They toss me out first, and I know the drill—they'll wait until I leave before they show him the door.

I wipe blood from my nose and start up my bike. It's too early to go home; I'm banned from Griz Country, and the only other bar in town that I haven't been to tonight is the Mint, and I'm not going back there. Racing out onto the highway, I make for the next nearest town. There's only one bar there, but it will do.

When I arrive, the place is half-dead too, and the patrons are most likely locals—my two favorite pastimes are off the activity list in a place like this if I'm going to avoid jail. Worse, after a few rounds the bartender cuts me off and refuses to serve me another drink. While I may be drunk, I'm not totally shit-faced, but I figure I might as well go home. There's no arguing with this dude—he won't change his mind.

As I head out, a niggling inner voice tells me that I need to reassess how drunk I am—I've already nearly driven off the shoulder twice. But I'm just a few miles out now, and if I can keep it between the lines, I'll be home in ten minutes. The last bend before town is in sight. Two miles beyond it is my exit, and a few blocks from there an empty bed awaits me.

Next thing I know, I'm on the ground, hurting like one sorry son of a bitch, and there's an EMT leaning over me. She says something, but I pass out before I can process her words. When I come to again, I'm lying in a hospital bed with my left leg elevated in a cast, and I have one very pissed-off brother staring down at me.

"What ..." My voice cracks—my throat is too dry to speak. Man, there isn't one pain-free spot on my body. I feel as if I've been put through a meat grinder.

Rafe grabs a paper cup off the tray next to me and shovels a few ice chips into my mouth. "Just shut up, bro. You fucked up again. Last night you lost it on the bend before town, went into the ditch and flipped your bike. Paramedics said they found you crumpled next to a tree—blood smear and missing bark on the trunk, so they're sure you hit it. Cops think you were going at least a hundred." I'm not sure if he's disgusted or relieved—his somber expression suggests a bit of both. "Your bike also hit a tree, and it's toast ... no fixing it this time."

Fuck. I can't afford to replace my bike right now, and I'm fairly certain I'll end up with a DUI out of this one. Up until now all my wrecks have been in remote areas—mountain roads, middle of the desert, open land on different rezes—and by the time the wreck is reported or I'm located, it's too late to prove I was driving drunk. There'll be no getting out of this one ... I'm screwed, and not in the way that I like.

I try to lift my head to take stock of my injuries, but I can't move it. There's some type of weird contraption on my head and neck. Now I'm starting to panic a little. What else is broken or torn up or missing? Rafe seems to understand and sits on the edge of the bed, explaining that I've broken my left leg, pelvis, a few ribs, cheekbone, and neck. I've got a skull fracture and some internal injuries too, but apparently they did surgery, removed my spleen, and stopped the internal bleeding.

"You'll be back in surgery to remove the rigging on your pelvis before they release you from aftercare, but the leg hardware and the halo on your head will be there a few months." He looks over his shoulder at the door, then turns back to me. "Given the spinal injury, they believe you're paralyzed from the chest down, but they won't know for certain until they do additional tests."

That's the least of my concerns. I learned a long time ago that my body heals itself in time, and I know paralysis isn't possible any more than accidental death. Before I can respond to this development, Rafe says, "You can't go making a miraculous recovery and start running around here in the next couple weeks like this never happened. They expect it may take a few days before you regain feeling or movement even if you're not paralyzed, which we know you're not."

"Fuck. Shit." I clench my eyes shut a moment. "Damn it. Are you sure my bike is totaled?"

"Yeah, man, it is. Both wheels are bent, the gas tank and seat are gone, and the frame is twisted and broken. The engine will need looking at—it may be beyond repair." He pulls out his cell phone to show me photos of what's left of my bike, and it's clear that he wasn't exaggerating.

Son of a motherfucking bitch. I want it to be a bullshit nightmare, but I know the truth—it's a big middle finger to myself. Fuck me all to hell. Can this life get any worse?

A nurse walks in, checks the IV bag, and asks me how I'm doing. Like shit, I tell her, and she just nods and offers pain meds if I need them.

When she leaves the room, Rafe and I discuss the next step. This screws up everything. I hate pretending I'm a normal human when it comes to broken bones, but I have no choice or they'll realize something is wrong with me. Which means that aside from losing my bike, I'll be out of a job by the time they remove the hardware from my pelvis, neck, and leg.

Yeah, throw another log on the fire until everything around me is burned to ash. Come on, bring it on—let's torch this pathetic existence. Add the potential DUI, and I could be back in jail for a bit—though Rafe says I deserve to be there for my stupidity. I'm about to argue that point when a doctor comes into the room to go over my injuries, the procedures and tests they want to do, and general expectations for healing time and physical therapy. I tell him that I'm a quick healer and don't expect to be off my feet long. Of course he looks at me like I don't know what I'm talking about—he's the expert, after all—and he ends the conversation with a quip about how time will tell. Yeah, you stupid son of a bitch, it will.

Rafe hangs out a little longer before he takes off too, which gives me way too much silence for pondering how I fucked up this time. I know we're supposed to stay hidden from the world and that I'm being reckless with our secret, but sometimes I'd just like to get it out there so we can stop pretending—we're freaks, so get over it, and let's move on. Rafe would have a stroke, but ask me if I give a shit now. Hell, maybe someone could find a way to kill us, or at least me, and put me out of my misery. The one thing that keeps me from stepping over that line is the possibility that I'm wrong and that revealing what we are could make our lives far worse than I can imagine.

If Rafe was pissed before about my drinking and running around, he's going to be a nightmare now, especially if he has to take a second job to cover our expenses while I'm out of work. He'll just love that on top of chauffeuring my ass around for a year until they return my license. No, Rafe will want to move back onto the rez until this is behind us, and if I'm paroled instead of sent to jail, I won't be in a position to refuse. I think I'd rather sit in jail. Last time he got me on the rez to heal, I was stuck there for three of the longest weeks of my life. I don't even want to think about how long it'll be this time. It's not the people in general; I can't afford the chance that the woman I must avoid will finally cross my path. Yeah, just what I need ... months of nothing to do but fight off rez chicks trying to crawl into my bed. Fuck me.

CHAPTER 4: NATE

Inescapable

Patches of blue sky break through the gray clouds, and people crawl along in rush-hour traffic, seemingly oblivious to the darkness hovering over them ... and over me, for that matter. How long will I have to keep up this charade? It's only been a few days since my accident, but because I've had no complications, they moved me yesterday to this aftercare facility to convalesce and begin therapy. I'm already tired of lying down, but they believe it's too soon for me to move around with the pelvic and neck injuries. Rafe expects me to play along for the three to four months the doc says the leg rods and pins and the halo ring brace on my neck are supposed to stay on. Fuck that shit—the most I'm going to give this is one month, maybe two if I can stand it that long. Then regardless whatever bullshit excuse Rafe has, it's going to be a miraculous recovery.

Rafe found me a good attorney for the DUI, but the most she did was file paperwork with the court to get me a public defender. She knew we couldn't afford her services. I told Rafe we should have offered her sex in return. He didn't find that funny—though actually, I was as serious as a heart attack. The replacement attorney is on the phone with me now, and it sounds as if he'll enter a not guilty plea and then get the court to postpone my hearing until after I'm released. I'm not really sure the guy knows what the hell he's talking about. He sounds like a damn moron.

I hang up the phone, thinking about the wreck. I still can't believe my bike is totaled, and I have no idea when I'll be able to replace it. For a few centuries we didn't need to worry about money at all; living off the land and moving from tribe to tribe provided what we needed. But this last century has changed things, and we're finding it difficult to play by society's rules and earn a living. There aren't a lot of jobs on the rez, and it's a challenge to find a job off the rez with a sketchy background like we have—not to mention the fun of making up facts and falsifying records since we're several centuries old. We have a plan to save enough cash to go into business for ourselves someday, but this accident is going to set us back, thanks to the bullshit medical bills. What little the insurance pays won't be enough to replace my bike either. So far that's my biggest regret—I liked that bike.

Then there's Rafe's plan to relocate me to the rez, which isn't going to happen if I have anything to say about it. If I can hold out here for two months and then get the judge to sentence me to prison for the full six months a first offense can entail, the rez will be off the table. If the judge is like those I've encountered before, he'll be harsh on me due to my heritage and the fuck-it attitude I intend to give him. Yeah, if I can play this right I'll have eight or nine months to avoid Rafe's bullshit trap, and by the time I get out, I'll be ready to go back to work. The hardest part will be the time here, pretending to be injured.

I grab at the halo and give brief thought to ripping the damn thing out of my skull. I'd like to pull its rods off to scratch under the cast or just pry that off too. I'm not sure which is worse, the rigid, restrictive framework around my head and pelvis—neither was removed before they transferred me to the aftercare facility— or the itchy feeling under the cast. The leg, they claim, must remain casted due to the multiple breaks aside from the ones they used pins and rods to fix. At least the pelvic scaffolding will come off sooner than the rest. Wish I could say the same for the dry spell I'm suffering—I'd give anything for a case of bourbon to help kill the time and get me through the days ahead. Shit, this is going to be a long two months.

Six weeks later they send me back to the hospital to remove the hardware from my pelvis. I'm not going to miss that damn contraption—nothing worse than scaffolding sticking out of my body, and I'm tired of lying on my back. When I come out of surgery, though, I notice that my pelvis is once again in pain. The doctor explains that the surgery to remove the external fixator had complications due to my advanced healing, which they didn't expect, and this may slow my rehabilitation. I'd love to tell the asshole I told him so, and that it'll be the same with my neck and leg, but I don't bother. It doesn't do any good to argue with Dr. Fucking-know-it-all that I'm a quick healer.

Within a day or two of starting physical therapy, I'm already bored with pretending to struggle and hurt. I have to remind myself that I'm on the backstretch now, halfway to being a totally free man again—I only need to get through court and my jail sentence, and then I'll put this whole mess behind me. I settle into the new routine and make deliberate, appropriate progress each day, but as my release date nears, time slows down, and I'm sure it's mocking me. I can't even charm a nurse into having sex with me. I've taken to counting the hours until I'm out of here.

On my final day in the facility, I'm sent for x-rays of my leg and neck; once more the doctor is amazed by the extent of healing, but he's reluctant to remove the halo ring brace or the cast before the minimum time passes. That means waiting another four to six weeks, which adds to my sour mood. Shit, I want this over with—

I haven't had a drink, a woman, or a fight since the night of my wreck, and I'm way overdue for a little fun.

Rafe goes through the motions of helping me into the pickup and then drives us straight home. I'm already pissed that bars are off-limits, but when I discover there's no booze of any kind in the house, I about fucking lose it. One bullshit drink, the one I've looked forward to for weeks, and it doesn't even exist? "What the fuck, Rafe? I need a drink."

"No, you don't. This has gone on long enough. We're going to keep you sober and out of trouble, and we're moving back to the rez."

His defiant look tells me he's prepared to argue this with his fists if necessary. So am I. "No way, man," I tell him. "I'm not living on the rez again."

His hands curl tighter, and I hear the anger in his voice. "We have to be out of this house at the end of the month—that's five days away. You don't have a fucking choice! Devlin kept me on as long as he could, but my last day was yesterday, and I had to take what I could find for work. The smokehouse at the jerky factory on the rez was the best option for supporting us until your DUI disaster is behind us."

Shit. Somehow I need to bridge the gap between the move-out date and when the judge sentences me for the DUI. The problem is that my court date is still two weeks away, leaving me nine days with no place to live. I'm confident enough my plan will work—it has to—that I guess I can lie low on the rez for nine days. I've endured longer than that. "Fine, but after my court date I'm not going back for a good long while."

"We'll see," Rafe mumbles under his breath. It makes me wonder what the hell he's up to.

I'm zero for two ... no booze, and I'm moving to the rez. I need something to lift my spirits. "Any chance we can go to the bar so I can pick up a split-tail, at least?"

"You don't fucking get it, do you?" he bellows at me. "No bars, no booze—period. As far as women are concerned, you need to find a new way to meet them, and you're going to treat them with respect again. If you weren't so pigheaded, you'd give the gals on the rez a chance. Might even find one you like."

Oh, hell no—we're not going there. After getting out of the medical facility, I thought this nightmare was almost over. Now I can see that the next two weeks are only going to pile on top of the shit sandwich I've been chewing on the last few months. I know my brother too well; he won't back down, and he'll fight me nonstop if I resist. Fuck! And I'm zero for three. At least there's one thing I can win on—the cast on my leg is coming off. Now.

Rafe asks where I'm going as I head for the hall, but I ignore him. In the utility room I grab a pair of bolt cutters out of the toolbox and get to work freeing my leg. My brother follows me and leans against the doorjamb, but I think he knows better than to fight me on this. I pretend he's not there. Don't get me wrong—I love my brother, but part of me wants to beat him with this damn cast once I get it off my leg.

Of course, he's probably thinking the same thing about me. How the hell did we manage to get through more than five centuries together? I'm still shaking my head at that thought when the cast falls away. Underneath, my skin is pale and dry, and the metal sticking out of my shin is a harsh reminder that this isn't over yet. Unfortunately I'm stuck with the hardware in and outside my leg until they remove it.

"Come on—let's get dinner going." Rafe nods in the direction of the kitchen. "I started some dough before I picked you up, and it should be ready by now. After the crappy menu you've had, I thought you might like some fry bread and canning jar stew tonight."

I follow him to the kitchen, appreciating his consideration of the awful food I've had the last two months. Typical Rafe. He can't ever allow me to stay pissed off at him—no, that's too easy. Instead he humbles me by the way he always looks out for me, even when I'm being a complete asshole. "Sounds good. Thanks, bro."

The rest of the evening goes by without any more arguing, and it seems to set the tone for the next few days. When we take the first load of boxes out to the trailer Rafe rented on the rez, I'm not sure what to expect. It turns out the singlewide two-bedroom mobile home is by itself in a field and well away from the town. It's obvious he chose the location to keep me away from the bar and the one store that sells booze, but I see at least one benefit to the location: I can avoid people as much as possible while I'm here.

One day before my court date, and I'm sitting in the attorney's office, going over my DUI charge. I'm thinking they scraped the bottom of the barrel for this guy. I swear the man's a sloth. He thinks, moves, and talks slowly, and he seems uninterested in anything but getting rid of my case as soon as possible. My anger rises as he and Rafe try to back me into a corner over the plea deal. I want to plead guilty and allow the court to sentence me to the full six months if they'll drop the additional alcohol treatment after my release. "I know they provide the program during incarceration, and I can complete it inside," I say for the seventh time.

"You don't understand, son. This is your first offense, and the judge tends to go easy on first-time offenders. The most you'll get if you accept the plea agreement is twenty-four hours in jail, a six-hundred-dollar fine, and the loss of your driver's license for a year. Outside treatment is a once-a-week commitment, which means you'll be free to go on with your life."

I wish he'd stop calling me son—if he knew how many years we've lived, he'd never use that term. "I don't want their damn plea deal."

"Knock it off, Nate. You've got to stop running." Rafe glares at me. "This is going to be costly enough, and if you don't do the deal, I may have to shell out a thousand bucks for your fine."

"I'll pay you back. I told you that."

The attorney must be getting tired of the argument too. "We have to appear in front of the judge at ten tomorrow morning. Rafe, try talking some sense into your brother tonight, and we'll meet here at eight, maybe settle this plea before the appearance."

And just like that he dismisses us, opening his office door and telling his secretary our next appointment time. I want to knock the man on his fat ass. Rafe notices my shift in mood and keeps himself between me and the attorney, his arm preventing me from going around him. From frustrated to pissed in two seconds flat—I want to rip off his damn arm and use it to club some sense into the lawyer. But Rafe shoves me out the door instead.

The next few hours fly by, and before I know it I'm sitting in a courtroom with my attorney, who is saying we need a recess because I'll accept the plea agreement. Hell the fuck no! I didn't agree to that, and I'm not signing anything. I leap to my feet. "Your Honor, that is not how I plead. I don't want that lousy deal." I've been in jail before—being an Indian off the rez in the 1800s, a few assaults last century, and one drunk in public a decade ago. One stint behind bars was five years. In any event, jail is far less risky than living on the rez—at least when I'm behind bars, I don't have to worry about crossing paths with the wrong damn woman. Hell, I'd go back for another five years if it meant avoiding that fate.

The judge scowls at me and then looks between me and the attorney for a moment; it's clear that my lawyer is about to get his recess or a continuance to cajole me into taking a deal I've told him a hundred times I don't want. While I may not be savvy about court proceedings, I know enough to realize I don't have to put up with this. "Your Honor, I want to fire my attorney and represent myself." Yeah, I've heard the saying that a man who represents himself has a fool for a client, but that is the whole point if I'm to end up in jail for six months.

There's chaos in court while the prosecutor, the judge, and the joke of a defense attorney discuss the issue. In the end I get my way, although the public defender remains my legal advisor. The judge says, "Mr. Redhawk, how do you plead?"

"Guilty." I hold eye contact and ignore the disgusted sound Rafe makes.

The judge goes through the procedure of accepting and entering my final plea, then reads the charge and penalties before he passes sentence. "Given the injuries you sustained, I do not believe jail is the place you need to be. I hereby sentence you to twenty-four hours in jail and the loss of your driver's license for a year, and impose a six-hundred-dollar fine and completion of the substance dependency course. You may apply for a work permit driver's license if you need one. Failure to pay the fine or complete the dependency course may result in further fines and/or jail time."

He hammers the gavel and I'm left standing there, mouth agape. What the hell? He sentenced me to the terms of the plea agreement I just turned down. I hear Rafe chuckle as the bailiff places the cuffs on my wrists and gets ready to lead me away. My attorney mumbles something about this judge being lenient, and how lucky I am.

Actually, I'm not sure my luck can get much worse.

CHAPTER 5: RAFE
A Hard Challenge

I'm still chuckling as I get into the pickup and leave town—man, the look on Nate's face as the bailiff led him away for his night in jail! There'll be hell to pay tomorrow when he gets out, and the next few days will be full of fighting, but I am going to enjoy replaying that one little moment until then.

I swear, the longer he holds on to a destructive phase, the more the tricksters set him up for these traps. Thinking about this gives me an idea—one I'm sure will piss him off more, but I can't resist. I pull into the store parking lot and go inside. In the toy aisle I find a stuffed dog that is passable for a coyote, and my next item I finally locate on the novelty and souvenir shelves. I lift the acrylic orb and check out the spider from all angles. It's perfect! Nate wants to play with tricksters—I'll make sure he's reminded of them each time he makes a boneheaded decision.

On the way home I stop by the community center to see what activities are coming up around the rez and discover that aside from bingo and high school basketball games, there isn't a lot going on for the next few weeks. But the fall fair takes place at the end of the month, and its primary attraction is the Sunset Pow Wow. I snap a photo of the calendar and head for home. Other than Nate's dependency and medical appointments, he's got too much idle time unless he finds a job. I'm still trying to get him a position in the packaging department of the jerky factory, but it's anyone's guess if that will come together or not. I'll have to line up entertainment or projects if I'm going to keep him out of trouble.

After a peaceful night alone I prepare for the first of many fights as I wait for Nate to process out of jail. When he walks out, he looks pissed—doubtless because his attempt to avoid the rez didn't work out the way he hoped. The first thing he says when he gets in the pickup is to stop at the bar. He knows better; I say no, and the fight is on. We argue all the way home.

Sometimes dealing with Nate is like having a child—an oversized six-foot-two child. He even storms off to his room like a pouting teenager. I can't help it; I start laughing because I know what awaits him there. A moment later he's in the living room, waving the coyote, spider, and "Trickster Club" sign at me.

"You think you're real fucking funny, don't you?" He glares at me, but I'm still smirking.

I shrug and try to stifle a chuckle. "Well you're the one hellbent on hanging out with Coyote and Spider—figured you may as well keep them in your room. I'm sure they can encourage you into even more of a mess until you learn your lesson."

Nate's eyes narrow, and a jaw muscle twitches. While he may be on a kick about hating the rez, his heart is always with the people and our ancient stories—stories that are meant to teach. His beliefs are rooted in tradition, even though he's acting contrary to them now. But that's my whole point—he's out of balance, upside-down, and he knows it.

He sits on a chair and stares at the objects in his hands, then looks up at me. "I can't keep doing this, Rafe. The longer I live, the crazier it's making me, and I feel like one day I'll lose my fucking mind for good. Then you'll have to lock me away until I get old enough to die."

I sit opposite him and meet his determined gaze. "We need to get you healed up again, and you'll be fine, bro." It's not his physical injuries I'm talking about, but the emotional and spiritual wounds he's been inflicting on himself.

Nate shakes his head. "Not this time." A look I've never seen before settles in his eyes, as if the spark for living is dying. I thought he was in one of his moods, the kind he's always gotten over, but that look ... This isn't his suicidal or destructive gaze; I've seen those dozens, if not hundreds of times. This one screams, "I'm done." A lump forms in my throat as I study his face. What can I possibly say to comfort him or will encourage him to fight ... whatever this is?

"Shit ... this isn't like before. I can feel it." Nate's clutching his shirt, rubbing the spot over his heart like the pain is too much.

He recognizes it too, and now I'm getting scared. It's been months since his last drink, and he's not on any drugs. He's stone-cold sober saying this crap, and he sounds discouraged ... no, absolutely defeated. What does this mean for him with the years we have ahead of us? Is it possible to lose pieces of your Spirit, to die one small bit at a time? There's only one thing I can do, and I'm not sure it will work, but I have to try. I can't lose my brother like this.

One of the elders has agreed to help Nate, and I dial his number, hoping he's free to take Nate to the riverside camp tomorrow. When George says yes, I exhale heavily in relief. The old man says, "We'll greet the sunrise—bring him early enough for that."

Nate is scowling at me again, but he just looks beaten down, and I know he's not going to fight me on this. "Thanks, George. I'll drop him at your place in the morning."

The rest of the day he's subdued, but I know my brother well enough to let him have some space to think. As we sit down for dinner, I tell him what's on our agenda for the week: the sweat tomorrow, his dependency appointment on Wednesday, and a boys' basketball game Thursday night. Nate pokes at his food and nods.

"Don't let your enthusiasm get you too excited," I say.

"I don't need you entertaining me." He slams his fork on the table. "I'll do the sweats, go to my appointments, see the elders and healer, find a job, whatever, but I'm not going to games or other bullshit while we're here."

Now it's my turn to scowl. "Knock this shit off, Nate! You've gone from destructive to a damn recluse."

He stands up and throws his plate in the sink—I hear it shatter—and when he turns around, his face is filled with anger. "I told you ... I don't fucking want to be here! Thanks to you recommending the tribe's treatment center, I have no choice, but that doesn't mean I'm going to fall for what you're trying to do."

"And just what am I trying to do?" God, he's a pain in my ass.

Thumping his chest, he says, "You want to find the love of your life, go do it—alone. Leave me the hell out of it! I want no part of the split-tails on this rez."

I get up in his face, because this is total bullshit. "I'm trying to keep you out of trouble and keep you from getting bored. Once again I'm picking you up when you don't want to stand. Do I want a life? One that includes my soulmate? You can bet your stubborn ass I do, but you keep fucking up before I can make that happen. I get it. You don't want it, but damn it, bro, this is about my life too."

Nate scrubs a hand over his face, looks at me for a long moment, and then goes to his room. I start to clean up the dinner mess, including the plate he broke, and as the sink is filling with hot soapy water, he comes back out of his room with a bag over his shoulder. "Where the hell do you think you're going?"

"You want your life? You want to live on the rez? Fine, do it without me! You won't fucking need to worry about me anymore." He jerks the door open and looks back at me. "Have a nice immortal life, asshole. I'm done." The door slams behind him.

For a moment I consider going after him, but then I reflect on what he said and change my mind. Maybe our paths were meant to be different; maybe only one of us will become a guardian. It's possible Nate isn't destined to be immortal. My heart aches at the thought, but I'm tired of his bullshit too. Perhaps it's time to let him go. I call George, letting him know Nate won't be there in the morning.

I have no clue where my dickhead brother went; I only know that it's time I let him walk his path alone.

CHAPTER 6: NATE
Stuck

I trudge down the road toward town with no idea where I'm headed or where I'm going to stay. Hell, I'm not even sure what I want to do. I'm stuck, my life is in a stagnant rut, and I'm going to be buried alive if I don't crawl out of it soon. But I have no answers, and it may be too late to seek them. The cold night air seeps into my bones. I zip my jacket to block the wind.

A car passes me, then slows and stops; the passenger window is open, and I hear the driver ask if I need a ride. It's tempting, because I'm cold, but I honestly have no idea where I'm going besides nowhere. He asks if I'm sure when I turn him down, and I almost say that I'm not sure about anything anymore. Instead I nod and watch as his taillights disappear in the dark. It's the cold that finally pushes me to make a decision. I need to get out of the chilly night air and do some thinking.

Leaving the road, I cross a field and head for the mountains. It's after midnight by the time I arrive at a cut along the base of the cliff. After gathering dried brush and twigs, I kindle a much-needed fire and switch my boots for my well-worn moccasins. When the fire takes off and I can feel its heat radiating off the rock wall behind me, I set up my shelter and settle in for the rest of the night.

But first I pull out the damn stuffed dog and spider and set them where I can study them as I drift off to sleep. My brother is right about one thing; the tricksters are at play, and I'm falling into their traps.

My troubled mind decides that I need tormenting with more dreams—of her. Over the last few years the dreams have become more frequent, and so have my attempts to drown myself in alcohol. I want to pass out and not dream at all, or at least be too out of it to remember it later. What pisses me off most is that I never see her face. Her image is always out of focus, blurry, but I can tell enough to know she's Native. The dream doesn't hide her long, dark hair or the color I perceive her eyes to be—brown—and their almond shape set into her otherwise featureless face. In fact, if it weren't for who she is, I'd almost enjoy the dreams, because her shape suggests she's a knockout beauty.

I can already tell this dream is no different from the ones I have had dozens of times already. Her touch makes me hungry for more— I can feel the way my body and soul claim her as mine. We're always talking or laughing, but I never recall the details of what we talked about or found funny. She does seem to share my fondness for nature, as we're often outdoors. My heart swells with a love I've never known, one that leaves me yearning while I sleep and battling myself after I wake up. It feels so realistic, perfect even, the way her body fits next to mine, that sometimes I can't believe I'm alone when my eyes open. I actually feel empty inside because she's not there after all. Then I remember what she means for my life, and I shout at her to stay away and leave me the fuck alone.

Sitting up, I wipe the sleep from my eyes. I'd give anything for a bottle of bourbon right now. But that's why I'm here, isn't it? Maybe Rafe is right, and I need to get my shit together or at least figure out how the hell I'm going to get through the centuries of life still ahead of me. The rez is a double-edged sword—my salvation and my ruin. I become too disconnected whenever I'm away too long, but damn it, it's a high-risk location for me if I'm going to avoid meeting Mrs. Right-but-oh-so-wrong-for-me. I need to find the balance ... No, I stop that bullshit thought as soon as it starts. There is no balance; the risk never goes away, and the ramifications are too costly for my future.

A red-tailed hawk, my clan's namesake, screeches overhead, and I look up as it circles me, swoops down, and then flies up into a nearby tree. The hawk's head turns from side to side, as if it's trying to figure me out. "Good luck on that one! If you understand the mess that is me, why don't you let me know—I don't have a fucking clue anymore." It spreads and flaps its wings but doesn't fly away. I cock my head to the side. "Are you mocking me?" Without warning it swoops off the branch and dive-bombs my head. I duck just in time to avoid the collision.

Yeah, I deserved that ... I know it was sent to deliver a message to me, and I'm doing all I can to piss it off. But it seems this bird won't tolerate me being a jackass either. It flies up, circles, and charges me again.

"All right, I get it. I'll listen."

For the next hour the hawk sticks around as I try to puzzle its message out. It's been sent by the Creator, I know; it's also a guardian of our clan, or what's left of it, anyway. We lost track of our blood relations over the centuries, and there's no way to know if our descendant family died out or if they are thriving somewhere nearby or far away from here.

But by the time the hawk leaves, I know what I have to do. I put out the fire and clean up my campsite before heading down the mountain. It will be midafternoon by the time I reach my destination. Where I go after that will depend on what the elders have to say.

George is at the riverside camp when I arrive, and he looks up at me with knowing eyes. He's sitting outside the sweat lodge with a few other men I don't recognize—it's been decades since we last spent time on this rez, and these men may not even have been born then. But it seems their group came here with me as their focus, so I sit to join them. Aside from George there's one other elder, a stonebearer, a seer, and a healer.

The stonebearer takes the hot stones inside while I strip down; he'll also take care of the water needed to produce the steam. The other elder will lead the ceremony. Sweats have changed little over the centuries and never vary much from tribe to tribe, and it's moments like these I almost feel as if I've slipped back in time.

It's not until a cooldown period between sessions that I ask the seer about my life. The gray-haired man studies me for a moment before he answers. "Your path is long and unhappy, but you cannot win against yourself—who you are was decided a long time ago. You know what you must do."

I want to ask him to be more specific, but he speaks before I can utter a word: "Take the time to heal and dream—it will show you the way."

The heat inside the lodge feels good after being out in the chilly fall air. The moist aroma of the hot stones lulls my senses, loosening the tension throughout my body. A relieved sigh is my welcome to the relaxed state I've not felt for quite some time. So peaceful ... It's not until I startle awake, my heart beating like a trip hammer, that I realize I drifted off. A sliver of a dream tried to reach me, but I wasn't out long enough to grasp anything beyond a voice saying, "Keep running." Was that the dream message he wanted me to see, or rather hear? The words sounded sincere, nonthreatening, and I decide the message is clear—don't change what I've been doing. If I'm going to find a way out of this shit life, then I must live as I have for centuries and maintain my quest for death. A wry chuckle escapes me at the thought. Rafe won't like it one bit.

At the end of the evening, George drops me off at the trailer. Rafe is watching TV with his feet up and a beer in his hand when I walk inside. A beer? "What the fuck, bro, you holding out on me or just hiding it?" I drop my bag, walk quickly to the fridge, and grab a beer, but my brother is yelling at me before I can even shut the door.

"Drop it, Nate. I'm not fucking around." Rafe tosses his beer into the sink and clamps a hand around my wrist. I try to jerk my arm free, and anger flashes in his eyes. "You left, asshole, remember? I bought it this afternoon, thinking you were going your own way."

Prying my arm and the beer away from him, I go sit down in the living room and take a long, slow pull off the bottle, savoring the taste. Now, if I had a whiskey chaser or a double shot of bourbon, it'd be perfect. I hear Rafe slamming around in the kitchen and the clinking of glass for several minutes before he joins me in the living room, cursing. I'm surprised he's empty-handed. Closing my eyes to enjoy the flavor a moment longer, I'm caught off guard when the beer is suddenly snatched from my grasp. Rafe is moving toward the kitchen without looking back, and I leap up to catch him, but I'm too late to stop him from pouring it down the drain. Fine—I'll grab another from the fridge. But when I open the door, I find a surprise—my brother's earlier banging around was him emptying every bottle of beer into the sink. Now he's leaning against the counter with his arms folded across his chest. Son of a bitch.

"Damn it, Rafe. Are you seriously going to tell me that I can't have one beer until I get my license back?"

"As long as I'm paying for everything, yes."

My anger flares to match his. "You going to start telling me who I can fuck, too?"

"I never said you can't find bed dates, but you're going to do it sober and on my terms and my time since I have to drive you everywhere." My patience is down to its last frayed thread.

"Your terms? That's rich. Let me guess ... anything other than a Native split-tail is banned too."

Rafe walks past me and tosses the front door open. "You're being a jackass. But to clear this up: my house, my money, my rules. If you don't like them, then get the hell out!"

For a second or two I consider it, but I have nowhere else to go, and as long as I'm walking around with this damn halo screwed to my head, I can't even look for work. I reach past him and slam the door shut. Several minutes fall into the silence between us as we stare each other down. Rafe is the first to break eye contact when he turns toward the living room. I follow, but my gaze remains locked on the back of his head. Man, I want to deck him.

After Rafe cools down, he asks where I've been. I tell him about my night at the rock cliff and the afternoon at the sweat lodge. He seems surprised that George was waiting for me, but I let it go, my tone defiant as I tell him about my dream: "The seer suggested it would give me the answer I'm looking for, and it came while I was still with them. It said to keep running, and that's exactly what I'm going to do."

His eyes narrow for a moment, like he's considering what I just told him, but he says nothing—just nods and slumps back against the cushions.

We manage to get through the first two weeks on the rez without trying to kill each other—not that we can die at this age. I go to my court-mandated appointments, return to the sweat lodge, spend time with the healer, and attend a couple of basketball games with Rafe. Being at the games certainly gets us noticed, but aside from polite yet guarded greetings of welcome to the community, we've seen little from broads trying to come on to us. But now comes the hurdle I've been dreading. Tonight is the first night of the fall fair, topped off by the Sunset Pow Wow—designed to honor those in the tribe in their golden years who mentor and bring hope to the youngest generation. Don't get me wrong, I enjoy being at a pow wow; I just don't look forward to beating off the advances of single women looking for a man.

"Are you ready?" Rafe yells from the living room.

I finish braiding my hair and join him. "I'm only going without complaint because you promised me a beer."

Rafe shakes his head, mumbling under his breath as he walks out the door. It's a twenty-minute drive to the grounds, and there's a long line of vehicles waiting to get in. Tribal police are screening for drugs and alcohol, turning away those who have booze in their car or coolers or who are already drunk. Many pow wows are dry events now, and that's not a bad thing; in years past, the substance-impaired drove away families and those who respected the ceremonies, songs, and dances the most. I understood why so many of the people had become lost, but I hated seeing our ways disrespected. Rafe and I lived through what others can only relate to through history, and whether they realized it or not, they were on the verge of throwing away what so many of us had fought for and struggled to reclaim from the federal government. Without our culture we cease being a people. We should be proud of who we are and of the sacrifices our Ancestors made for us.

After we clear the checkpoint and park, Rafe takes the lead to find us seats. I manage to talk him into going to the top bleacher, though I want to crawl under the bench as the women begin noticing us. The heightened interest at pow wows often leaves me wondering if it's the curse that is alluring or if it's because we're new; this is one time when people drop their wariness of outsiders and are more open and friendly toward those who've come to watch or participate.

We're soon flanked by two small groups of women, and Rafe's all over it—checking them out, flirting back. There's three to my right and four to Rafe's left. Thanks to the fancy headgear I'm still wearing, the women all express curiosity about my injury and my health. Fuck, now they think they're the cure-all for me, and don't understand they're pure poison as far as I'm concerned. I've got no way out—so I choose to be surly and rude, making it clear that I'm not interested.

Rafe, on the other hand, is setting the hook with charm. By the time the opening ceremony and first intertribal are finished, the gals have done a little reshuffle. It seems one of them is winning the opportunity to have a more direct conversation with Rafe. Of course they decide to punish me by sticking the least appealing one next to me—a warthog has more personality than her. Too bad they screwed up and are making this easier for me. I'm fucking smiling inside.

"You're not as outgoing as your brother." The split-tail on the other side of the loser chick leans around her to address me.

I give her a cold look. "No, I'm not. I didn't come here to hook up with anyone." I jab my thumb at Rafe. "He did, so if that's what you're after, you may want to get in line on his side."

She gives me a dirty look and sits back to ignore me the rest of the night. My grin widens, and I find myself chuckling every time I catch her giving me the stink-eye.

When they announce dinner break, the chick Rafe spent the most time talking to goes with us to a food booth. We order the standard fair food: Indian tacos and fry bread with honey butter. I can tell by the way Rafe's leaning toward her and the not-so-accidental brush of his leg or shoulder against hers that he's interested in the gal, but I haven't figured out if it's for a good time or if he thinks she's the one. A part of me hopes she is ... I'm convinced that once he finds his dream woman, he'll back off and leave me the hell alone.

We take our food back to our seats, and the gal—no clue what the fuck her name is—looks right at me and says, "My cousin is arriving this week, and we're going on over to the Muddy Bottom

Pow Wow next weekend. She's not into dating either, but I was wondering if you'd mind if she comes along?"

What the hell did I miss while I was tuning them out? I look at her and back to Rafe, but he's staring at her like she's his last breath of air. Great, now I'm on the spot. "I don't do blind dates. If that's what this is, don't bother going there—you'll regret it. But if you and Rafe want an extra third wheel besides me, go ahead and bring her along." It's the most diplomatic way I can think to handle it.

"That's great! You'll really like her." She shakes her head and laughs. "I swear she's like the Pied Piper of men—they swarm her, whether she wants their attention or not."

Now I'm a little worried. If she expects me to run interference for her cousin, she's nuts. I want no part of her, the cousin, or any other Native woman. She isn't going to get any interest from me.

Rafe says, "We can pick you gals up Friday afternoon and pitch a tent when we get there."

The dinner break ends just in time to keep me from losing my mind—I can't take much more of this crap sober. The bribery beer Rafe promised for afterward has gone from calling my name to shouting it. I'm counting down the minutes until we can leave and I can find that cold one. At least the other chicks have decided to sit elsewhere now—I spot them on the opposite side. Unable to resist, I wave across the arbor at them, smirking. Now I have time to focus on the singers and the drums.

The steady, pulsing rhythm of the drums is almost painful until I feel my heart synch to the beat, and then I'm able to enjoy the way the singers' voices move me to other places and eras. I used to dance when we were younger, but then it was banned by the federal government—continuing those rituals meant harsh punishment, often by way of spoiled meat or not enough blankets to keep warm in the winter, and those leading the ceremonies faced jail. The government didn't trust or understand our traditions and considered them evil, thought they encouraged the people to rise up.

Our culture didn't fit their rigid ideas of assimilation, so they demanded an end to our way of life—for us to be like them, regardless of what this meant for us.

The only thing they accomplished was wounding a lot of people's Spirits and sending them on their final journey feeling broken and incomplete. Even Rafe and I didn't escape the sense of loss. For years we struggled alongside those longing for the rituals and activities that defined us as a people. Being prohibited from speaking our language and forced to cut our hair and wear clothing foreign to us was devastating, like being trapped in someone else's body, screaming to get out; I no longer recognized myself, and even my brother looked and sounded like someone I didn't know. I have never longed for death as much as I did during those bleak years.

When the bans were lifted decades later, many people no longer remembered with accuracy the original dances and songs, and too many from that time weren't around anymore to tell them. In some ways it's the same with the language ... dead, dying out, barely holding on, and a few lucky ones thriving. The people tried to adapt with the limited knowledge held by the storytellers, but I doubt they ever knew it wasn't quite the same.

I quit dancing when several traditional ceremonies were removed from the pow wows and new steps were invented that further led to competition dancing for certain types of dancers and styles. Common steps allow dancers with different tribal affiliations to compete regardless of geographic location—a concept I found interesting when it began, though it is something I still have mixed feelings about. The somewhat universal change saw a Warrior Dance evolve into the Grass Dance and Fancy Dance for men, which latter led to the Fancy Shawl Dance for women. Then Traditional Dance for men and women adopted modern regalia either in part or entirely as their steps, too, became universal. This I found necessary, or it would have made the brighter, bolder regalia of the other dance styles seem too flamboyant.

While tribe-specific song and dance still exist, they lack the broader pool of competitors since participation is usually limited. And that has led to the Intertribal Dance—a way to recognize and include everyone, critical for the acceptance and success of those gathered to watch, sing, drum, and dance. The Intertribal is the only dance where Rafe and I really belong, as our people have long since vanished.

I don't knock those who follow the pow wow trail or try to boost their income by dancing or drumming and singing, but it's just not for me. Maybe it's true what they say about teaching old dogs new tricks, because I'd rather see the old ways return. I miss ceremonies being shared openly with the people while we gathered to give thanks or to honor the Creator, the people, the warriors, our ways, and our lives; together the feast and dance had a much deeper combined meaning than they seem to now. But still I understand how important this remains to the people regardless of the changes over the centuries. I may want to avoid the rezes because of the one woman I never want to meet, but these people, this culture, will always be central to my life. They define who I am, the side of me I rarely show to anyone.

The night ends, and Rafe says goodnight to his new interest. We head alone to the back corner of the grounds, where we pitched a tent earlier. I'm surprised—I thought he'd go with her for the night or kick me out of the tent to bring her here. But he's in a good mood and we don't fight, even after we're settled onto our bedrolls.

Lying in the dark, I say, "So you like this one?"

"Yeah, I do. She's different somehow, and I think I need to show her a little more respect than getting her in bed right away."

A twinge of resentment mixes with the fear growing inside me. Maybe I'm not ready for Rafe to find his mate and move on without me, and now I can only hope he's wrong about her. He has to be mistaken ... wishful thinking, that's all there is to it. I shake my head, as if to reassure myself of how wrong he is, and roll over to go to sleep.

CHAPTER 7: RAFE
Waiting for the Wind to Blow

The rest of the weekend at the Sunset Pow Wow is great, mostly because Nate is giving me the space I need to explore my options. Aside from enjoying the music, dancers, and food, I'm having a good time getting to know Emily. She's wonderful, sweet and carefree, and something about her is different from any other woman I've met. The hollow, empty feeling that hits me on first contact with a woman—it isn't there with her. There's something more than physical attraction, but I can't quite define it. Something ... intellectual, emotional, spiritual? All three?

And yet if she is the one, this doesn't feel like I expected it to. Maybe I've watched too many crappy movies, but I thought there'd be some kind of aha moment, and that hasn't happened. The only thing I can do is give it more time, treat her well, and see if the answer comes to me. If it does and it's a yes, then I'll still be at a loss— no one has ever told us how we're supposed to claim our mates. Is it words that must be spoken, or a sharing of blood, like in fantasy stories, or something I need to do during sex? Or is it just a matter of falling in love and knowing in our hearts and souls? I guess I'll figure it out, or it will make itself known in time. Until then I am going to enjoy the flutter in my belly and the stupid grin she puts on my face.

At least Nate didn't run her off along with all the other women. Aside from that first night, he has behaved himself, and as promised I stop to buy him a beer on our way home. I don't think he's happy with me when I come out of the store with a six-pack, give four away to some dude on the sidewalk, and keep one apiece for him and me. I tell him to wait until we get home, but he has the entire bottle drained within five minutes. I have to threaten him when he tries to talk me out of mine. I've been dry for his sake since we moved onto the rez, and I deserve at least one beer for putting up with his shit.

The next couple of months fly by in a blur, but with some positive developments for Nate. The jerky plant hires him once the halo ring is removed, and though he's still a huge pain in the ass, he's having success with the dependency course—if you count that he's saying what they want to hear. I'm happiest he's spending time with those in the tribe who can help him the most. Whether he'll admit it or not, they could have a positive impact on him if he'd let them. But his attitude is one of resistance. The biggest issues remaining are my rules of no booze at home and no bars—I can tell he's plotting what he'll do once he leaves the rez, and I won't be surprised if he picks up where he left off before the wreck. Or worse—there's always that possibility with Nate. Shit, I wish I knew how to get through to him.

True to his word, he's refused even to look for a bed date since all the women we've met are Native. He's run off more than a few prospects, Emily's sisters and cousin included. I'm still seeing Emily, but it's not going anywhere, and I'm beginning to think she's not the one—something should have happened by now. I just don't get it. We're compatible, we enjoy each other, and we have great sex, but there's been nothing to signal that I'm immortal or a guardian now. So what the hell does this mean? The problem is deciding whether to break it off with her to continue my search or to give it more time and see if the elusive mate status makes itself known. Either she's the one and I haven't done something I'm supposed to, or she's not and I'm losing time looking for my soulmate. Fuck. Why can't I find anyone who kept better details about the thunderbirds? One, just one person to tell me what we need to know. Is that asking too much?

I finally try talking to Nate about it, and his only advice is to "dump her ass." Should have known better, but no one else in the tribe seems to have the answers either, and I'm afraid of what will happen if I don't find my soulmate. What if she has an accident and dies before we ever meet? Will that condemn me to a long life rewarded with death at the end? It's that thought that tips the scale and forces a decision.

After work that day I drop Nate off at home and drive over to Emily's house to tell her what I am. Two months is long enough, isn't it? If she needs to know before we can claim our mate status—if we've been doing it wrong all this time with the secrecy—my revelation will surely spark something. Won't it? But damn, I can't shake the feeling that this is the wrong way to go about it. She could freak out, think I'm insane ... or she could believe and blab it all over the internet, and that possibility chills me more. I have to do something, but my inner voice is screaming at me to be careful or this will be the biggest mistake of my life.

I pull into her drive, but I'm about to back out and leave again when I see her open the door. The way Emily smiles at me as I turn off the pickup makes me feel even more like a shit-heel. When she moves to hug and kiss me, I grab her upper arms and keep distance between us. "I hope this isn't a bad time, but there's something I need to talk to you about."

Now Emily looks worried, but she invites me in and closes the door behind us. "What's wrong, hon?"

"Do you know of the old thunderbird legends?"

"I think everyone knows the stories." Her face screws up into a half-confused, half-"are you serious" expression—wrinkled nose, curled lips, and one raised eyebrow. "If you're asking if I believe they're true"—Emily seems to be gauging my reaction, or rather figuring out the correct response—"then no, at least not the part where it suggests they're men sent to guard us. Thunderbirds are more like the dodos, a bird that's extinct."

I try not to, but I grimace. The more time goes by, the fewer people believe as our Ancestors did ... as Nate and I do. We are from a time when the legends meant so much more. Now reverence and respect have withered under the advancement of technology and humankind, and modern society has only a shadow of understanding of what used to be common knowledge and belief. Wouldn't my mate at least sense the truth? I remember the way she first reacted to my marks—she said it was an awesome tattoo. Keeping my disappointment and anger in check, I ask if she thinks immortals walk among us.

She laughs. "Do you mean like vampires and werewolves?"

Put like that, it seems stupid—even I don't believe in fantasy stories, and we've certainly never crossed paths with other preternatural beings in the centuries we've roamed the Earth. That's the moment doubt shakes me to the core. Has my asshole brother been right all along? I shake my head. "Never mind—that's not the reason I stopped by. The legends were more a sidetrack curiosity than anything."

"So why did you stop by? You seem upset." Uncertainty shows in her eyes—it's as if she knows I'm about to break things off, but won't believe it until it happens.

I fight to swallow the growing lump in my throat. She's not the first gal I've stopped dating, but she's the first one who makes me feel awful for ending it. I take her hands in mine and see a faint glimmer of hope in her eyes. "Emily, I like you a lot ..."

"But?" A frown spreads across her face.

I take a deep breath. "The situation with my brother complicates my life. You and I have had a lot of fun together, and I wish we could keep having fun—"

Tears well in her eyes, and she shouts, "Are you breaking up with me?"

Damn, this is hard. "I need to take care of my brother. We'll be leaving the rez soon"—I just made that decision as I said it—"and it may be years before we come back this way."

In a desperate move she squeezes my hands harder and clutches them against her chest as tears run down her cheeks. "Don't do this to us, Rafe. I'll go with you ..." Her tone is imploring. "I love you."

Damn it all to hell, I'm screwed. Now I have to be a bigger ass, and I don't want to hurt her any more than I already have. But I can't leave her clinging to us—it will hurt her more when she realizes I'm never coming back. "I'm sorry, you shouldn't ... I don't love you."

Emily shoves me back a step. "Get out! Get out! Get the hell out of my house!" She starts pounding her fists on my back as I head for the door. "You're an uncaring asshole, just like your brother. At least he has the decency to stop a woman before she ends up giving her heart away."

She doesn't know how wrong she is, but I'm not going to stick around and argue with her. At the door I half turn and say, "I'm sorry. I never wanted to hurt you." I walk away without looking at her or her house again, unsure if I just made the biggest mistake of my life or if this has put me back on the path to finding my soulmate.

On the way home I stop at the store for a half rack of beer. I know Nate isn't supposed to be drinking, and I've been a hard-ass about his constant demand for booze, but I need a drink—and there's no way for me to have a beer without letting him have one too. At least we'll be at home, and it's not enough to get either of us in trouble.

Sure enough, when I walk through the door with the beer in hand, Nate's eyes pop wide. His gaze travels from the beer to my eyes, and I see a mix of puzzlement and concern written across his face. He may be an ass nine times out of ten, but he's always there when I need him the most.

"What's going on, bro?" He follows me into the kitchen, obviously eager to hear why I've brought the booze home.

"It's my turn to fuck things up." I put the beer in the fridge, less the two I hold back, and hand one to him.

We go into the living room and sit down opposite each other. Nate studies me for a moment, taking a long pull on his beer. The sigh that follows tells me how good he thinks it is. "You gonna tell me about it?"

"Yeah." I take a big swallow myself, and I have to agree with him—it tastes good. "I went to tell Emily what I am and ended up breaking it off with her instead. Then she threw a curve ball that made the whole screwed-up deal worse, and I panicked."

"Okay, bro, you're talking in fucking riddles. Start from the beginning?"

Nate remains quiet while I lay out the mess I just put us in, as well as my fears that it could be the biggest mistake I've ever made. If I let Emily go and shouldn't have—

"Shit, Rafe, a gal sheds a few tears and you go soft and run away like a little girl." His eyes narrow for a moment. "Not that it will hurt my feelings to get off the rez, but where are we going to go? I've still got a couple of months before I finish the dependency course and six months until I can get my license back."

I take my head in my hands and squeeze my eyes shut. "You're one to talk about running, asshole." I draw a deep breath. Now isn't the time to fight, and he's not trying to pick one either. "I don't have a plan or a place for us to go, but we can't stay here or I'll look like an even bigger liar. I never wanted to hurt her … but there's no going back. I'd rather not see her again."

"You know the biggest hassle will be getting the court to sign off on me relocating." His brow draws down, and I see the shift in his expression—I'm almost certain what he'll say next. "We could lie low until I get rid of all this hardware, and then we can join the military again."

The warriors in us have never allowed us to sit on the sidelines long when it comes to fighting, and the likelihood of another world war is growing every day. The idea of signing up to fight is appealing, but something is holding me back—a feeling that now is not the time. I explain that as best I can, and though my reasons sound pathetic even to me, thankfully Nate doesn't push the issue. He trusts my instincts as much as he trusts his own. We agree to keep an eye on the unrest and fight later if we must.

"Jobs it is, then." Nate slowly strokes the length of his jaw, down to his chin. "If the judge won't let me go, then you'll either have to go without me or wait here until I can leave. But I swear, if you leave me behind, I will fucking hunt you down and beat the shit out of you the moment I get the hell off this rez."

Within a week we find a ranch that will hire both of us, but we'll have to leave the Flathead Valley and move to the small ranching community of McAllister, Montana. Some big-shot businessman owns the place, though according to the ranch foreman, Travis, the guy is seldom there. It sounds as if he's some crusty old geezer who's busy jet-setting around the world, taking care of his software tech company and construction empire like some Bill Gates or Donald Trump wannabe. Travis says that if we're hard workers, the owner is good about transferring employees to one of his other businesses if it's a better fit and there are openings. It's a nice carrot to dangle in front of us. The ranch work will get us by for the rest of the winter, but I'd rather do construction. I just hope the guy's businesses will go on if he kicks the bucket.

Nate is right about the court being the tallest hurdle; the judge isn't pleased, because the ranch's remote location means we'll need to travel to continue the alcohol treatment. A letter from a rehab center in the next nearest town to McAllister puts the judge's mind at ease, and he signs off on the deal.

Two days later we're packed and on our way eastward to the middle of nowhere, Montana. It's a welcome sight to see the rugged mountains again. When you live and roam as long as we have, you get to know a lot of country—though just as with many other places, time and civilization have left their mark. Gone are the days of wide-open, untouched countryside, even in areas like this.

So far neither of us has said a word for miles, content to let the scenery pass by. I don't want to know what Nate is thinking; I have enough of my own troubles. I'm still not convinced that leaving Emily and moving on was the right thing to do, but now that we've left there is no going back, and we can only hope this move gives us the chance to rebuild what Nate's wreck cost us. We want to support ourselves in the future—and the Creator knows we have a lot of future ahead of us.

It's almost dark when we arrive at the Cleary Ranch. Travis comes out to get us settled in one of the bunkhouses. The three bunkhouses were designed to hold up to two dozen people in total, though the one we're shown to is empty; Travis says we'll have it to ourselves until the peak seasons of lambing and calving arrive. Afterward it will empty out again until fall, when it's harvest time.

Nate and I want to unpack right away, but Travis isn't ready to cut us loose for the night. "Great timing, by the way—couldn't have planned it better if we tried." He smiles. "I didn't expect the boss back for another couple of weeks, but he got in earlier today. He's at the main house—come on up, and I'll introduce you."

We follow Travis to the ranch house, which is huge and appears to have been built recently. Everything is too new for my taste, but it's clear the old dude has money, if the quality of the wood and leather décor and the furnishings are any indication. A man with light-brown hair rises from his seat by the window and gives us a crooked smile as we enter. The quick once-over tells me he's a hired hand like us—he's in his mid- to late twenties and looks like the physical labor type.

"Hey, Matt, these are the two new additions." Travis points at each of us in turn. "Rafe and Nate Redhawk." Of course he gets us backward, as many do, and Nate is quick to correct him. Then Travis motions to Matt. "Rafe, Nate, this is the boss, Matt Wolfe."

What the hell? We accept his handshake and then sit down to be interrogated. Matt chuckles, fighting to keep a smirk off his face as he says, "Relax ... I'm not going to bite." For some reason he and Travis seem to find that humorous. There's an almost feral gleam that lights the boss's hazel-green eyes, and his antics don't fit the role of a successful business owner. Or maybe that's it—he's rich enough he can afford to be quirky. It makes me wonder what his story is and how he came into such wealth at a young age. I'm sure the guy can't be more than twenty-five, maybe twenty-seven.

We spend the next several minutes discussing our work experience and the construction jobs he may have available in the spring. "If things work out, I may have a dual-purpose job for you too. I'm looking at a ranch in northeastern Montana over the next few days. The sales flyer indicates it's an old place in need of some serious TLC." The two-bedroom house needs remodeling, he tells us, and the plumbing, wiring, and amenities will have to be upgraded. He also wants to enlarge the foundation of the main floor and add a second story with four bedrooms and two more bathrooms. "The barn and corrals will need to be torn down and replaced before they're ready to handle the cattle herd," he says. "If you want in on the start, you'll be able to help run the ranch and do the construction work too."

"Sounds like a good opportunity. I'm interested," I say, and look at Nate, unsure how he's going to react. Once he's free of his DUI restrictions, he may go on a multistate bender and not surface for weeks, maybe months.

He gives me a long look before shifting his gaze back to our new boss. "I'm in."

Matt turns his attention to the hardware sticking out of Nate's leg. "What's the story there?"

"Wrecked my bike a few months back. I'll need to find a doc here to remove it next week."

"Is it going to require a lot of downtime afterward while you heal? We start calving in the next couple of weeks."

I'm surprised the boss doesn't seem more upset that Nate needs time off right after he's hired us, but he sits patiently waiting for my brother's answer.

Nate says, "I'll only need a day or two. I'm a quick healer."

The answer seems to strike Matt as funny, and another short chuckle quirks his mouth into a grin. Just as quickly he snaps out of it and turns the topic back to the ranch, reiterating what Travis told us—he's away more than he's here, and at most he stops in one week a month, and not every month. I find that preferable to him being here full-time; something about this dude seems off, and I can't put my finger on what it is.

Still, when Matt invites us to stay for dinner, I don't see a polite way to refuse. A good-looking redhead with green eyes arrives and helps Matt cook a simple meal of potatoes, a green salad, and steak. They act like a couple—neither are wearing wedding rings, but it's obvious this is a long-term thing.

The steak is on the way-too-rare side for me, but I don't say anything. Nate, on the other hand, just gets up from his chair and returns his steak to the skillet to finish cooking it. I'm thinking he's going to get us on Matt's bad side before we take our first bite, but his girlfriend, Maria, laughs, speaking with an Irish or Scottish accent—it's impossible for me to tell the difference, but I'm sure it's one of the two. "He always forgets that most people don't like their meat practically raw." She rolls her eyes and swats Matt's shoulder. "I think you two will do well here. Matt needs workers who can make decisions without seeking his approval for every little thing."

"Good to hear ... I don't do well with someone hovering over the fucking top of me." Nate shoves another bite into his mouth, and the boss's gaze hardens. For a brief second it almost looks as if he is wearing eyeliner, but when I blink the only thing I see is Matt's stern expression. It seems Nate just blew it—I hope we're not out of the job before we start.

Matt says, "I don't care how you guys talk when it's just men around, but I won't tolerate that word in front of the women. Got me?"

Great, Nate is already screwing up by the numbers. "I gotcha, and it won't be an issue for me," I say, throwing Nate a dirty look.

Nate's fork pauses halfway to his mouth, and he looks between Matt and Maria. "Uh, yeah ... sorry about that, Maria. I'll try to keep it clean, but excuse me if I slip every now and then. I'm not used to being around women."

I choke at his blatant lie, and a mouthful of milk goes down the wrong way. The truth is, he just doesn't care at the moment what women think of him, and foul language is a good way to scare them off.

To my relief the conversation moves forward as if nothing happened. I'm glad Nate's personality may not cost us our jobs, so long as he can keep his language in check around women—seems we picked a good outfit to work for. Still, though Maria plays the perfect hostess and chats pleasantly about the ranch and how well we'll fit in here, these two just seem strange—the boss calls his gal witchy-poo, and she teases him with weird reminders about hairy frogs. I can't make up my mind if it's an inside joke or pet names like honeybun and sweetie pie.

I'm still mulling that over when Nate offers to help clean up the dinner mess. The redhead has a mischievous look in her eyes. "Thank you, but it won't be necessary. I'll have this taken care of in the blink of an eye."

Using the opportunity for an out, I thank Matt and Maria for dinner, saying we need to settle in and get ready for work in the morning. A part of me feels we've landed the best job we've had in a while, but the other side is launching flares, telling me to run. Something is coming. But what? As we walk back from the ranch house, I look over at Nate. "Is it me, or does it feel like we're suddenly waiting for the wind to blow?"

"I feel it too ... something about these people isn't fucking right." He glances behind us, as if he's making sure they're not following, and then he steps closer to my side. "Yeah, the wind is going to blow. I just don't know if it will be good or bad."

CHAPTER 8: NATE

Opportunities

Adjusting to our new boss and his girlfriend remains tense the first few days. They're friendly and likable enough—it's just that they're fucking weird. Is it because she's from Europe and they spend so much time there, or do they bring out the strangest qualities in each other? I swear they talk in riddles—or maybe they're trying to talk around something, unsure if they should say anything in front of Rafe and me. Of course, it's not much better when Matt is direct with us either. I know he's the boss and we need to follow his orders, but half the time it feels like the man is challenging me on some personal level, and it drives my fight instinct through the roof. When they finally leave to return to Venice, we relax for the first time since we arrived here. It certainly won't hurt my feelings that the guy is seldom around—I don't think I could take a steady diet of him or his crazy redheaded girlfriend.

There are two others working here besides me, Rafe, and Travis, both Montanans from the southwestern part of the state—making for a decent-size crew to handle the workload. The five of us fall into an efficient routine of feeding the cattle and sheep and preparing for the upcoming calving and lambing season. In preparation Travis sets Rafe's and my shifts and work detail separate from that of the other two, giving us little chance to get to know them. It's not something I'll lose any sleep over, though, since I get the impression they don't care much for Rafe and me.

There's always something to do on a ranch, even during the winter—fence repair, the corrals and barn to keep clean, and trips into town for supplies—and the sheep need shearing before they lamb, but we have most nights off. That will change once the first calf drops, and it won't stop until the last lamb is on the ground. A thousand head of cattle and half that number of sheep will make for a lot of extra work. We'll catch sleep as we can then, though over the next few days the additional hired hands will arrive and stay on until it is done, giving all of us a little downtime we wouldn't otherwise have.

I'd much rather have something else keeping me awake at night, but it's clear why Rafe hunted for a remote job; he's doing his best to keep me from running to the bar. I'll be without my license for a few more months, and until then I'm at his mercy. A situation grown beyond old and stale for me—it stinks worse than a calf with scours. At least Rafe has let up on his no-booze bullshit. As long as I don't overdo it, he keeps beer in the fridge and allows me a double shot of bourbon once or twice a week.

My other two favorite activities have been curtailed, since Rafe will only take me to community gatherings and my substance dependency appointments. Neither is conducive to seeking a bed date, and I swear, if I don't get laid soon, I am going to lose my fucking mind. Here most women keep their distance whenever we go into town; it's either because we're Native or it's the typical small-town bullshit. I'd never tell my brother, but this isolation is starting to make the fucking rez look good—at least there were willing women, and at this point I'd consider playing immortality roulette to see a little action.

About a week after the rods and pins are removed from my leg and just before calving begins, Travis invites me along for a late-afternoon run into town, and I finally catch my first fucking break—he knows I have a DUI, but he stops at the bar anyway before we head back to the ranch. It's Friday and a bit early, but a few people are already out for a night of fun. Travis says we're only staying long enough for a drink or two, though I'm hoping he'll change his mind. Near the end of my second drink I'm beginning to think he won't after all, but then a long-legged brunette comes in with a couple of friends, and she heads straight toward us the moment she sees Travis.

"Hey, Travis, been a while since I've seen you out and about." She smiles at him, but my attention is already drifting to the second brunette and the blonde next to her. The blonde is the friendlier of the two, though the brunette has a knockout body that I'd like to spend some time exploring.

Travis says, "Yeah, just been busy out at the Cleary place. Sheep are sheared ... we'll be calving soon. Figured I'd better stop by now, or no one will see me until spring." They both laugh, but the reminder that this may be my last chance to get laid for a while puts me in high gear. Checking out the other women, I try to not grimace. Pickings are slim to none, and these are my best options? I don't even want to consider the blonde, and the brunette seems too tightly wound for her own damn good. I have to convince one of these split-tails to be a willing bed date, or...

"Hi, I'm Nate."

The brunette looks at my hand as if I have something on it she doesn't want to touch. "I'm not interested."

Cold bitch. I'm scowling at her when the blonde steps in and grabs my hand to shake it. "I'm Bev, she's Amy, and the one talking to Trav is Lindsey."

Damn it, just my luck—the one I prefer doesn't want anything to do with me. Unless something better comes into the bar, it looks as if the blonde will have to do. "Hey, Bev ... that's not a name ya hear much anymore."

It works to get her talking, and she takes a seat on the bar stool next to me. Amy, the stuck-up one, heads over to the jukebox and plugs it full of quarters. At least she has decent taste in music—classic rock, a bit of country, no rap crap. Bev spends a few minutes talking about shit I don't care about, but I humor her ... I have to, or my dry spell is going to last even longer. When I finally see a few people move onto the dance floor, I ask her to come have some fun. She smiles as she takes my hand, though I'm beginning to doubt she'll offer anything but chatter; she keeps a respectful distance as we move to the beat. So she's not a dance-grinder, and I'm disappointed. Still, I can't give up yet—I'll wait for a slower song. I know how to work her kind.

Three more songs play before a slow one comes up, and then I draw her closer, keeping eye contact as I sing along, watching her every reaction. I'm not even sure if she's aware her body is drifting closer—it almost seems to surprise her when she lays her head on my shoulder. She jerks back, but I've got a good grip on her, and I hold her firmly against me. She relents, resting her head again as we sway to the music. Next I allow glancing contact between our hips, and soon she closes the space between us. By now there's no hiding what she's doing to me, or ignoring the way she presses tighter against me in response, and I smile. "Find something you can't resist, sweetheart?"

She laughs and smiles up at me. "Maybe." I give her a wide grin—she might give in to me yet.

I can tell Travis is a bit tipsy, but he's not paying attention to time, and I get the feeling he's looking for a little action himself. But then he notices it's near midnight—and he tells Legs that we can't stay much longer. Shit! I may need to get Blonde to offer me a ride home, because I'm sure she's not finished with my company yet, and I need a bit more from her too. But then Legs asks us and the blonde to come on over to her place for a while, and she'll make sure we're on our way by six in the morning. I could almost kiss her for the offer. One quick look at Travis indicates he's game.

Given it's a work night for all of us, we don't waste any time getting down to business when we reach Legs' house. As cautious and shy as the blonde was when we began dancing, I'm thrilled she's not holding back now. In fact she's become a raging octopus, with her mouth and hands everywhere on my body—something I'll never complain about. It could be weeks before I get off the ranch for another night like this one, and I'd be a fool not to make the most of it. Smirking, my anticipation rising, I strip her bare. Her body isn't great, but man, she's got some moves, and I swear she could suck a bowling ball through a vacuum hose. Thank fuck she's a decent lover. She gives as good as she gets, and although it takes some effort to push her over the edge, she doesn't up and quit. As long as I keep going, she keeps giving and taking. I can tell she's getting tired, but this split-tail understands how to please a man, and I'm fucking loving every moment of it.

It's after four in the morning when we drift off to sleep, and I swear that I've barely closed my eyes when Travis knocks on the door, saying it's time to go. Damn, I could use at least another hour. I thank the blonde for a good time and almost feel guilty that I can't recall her name; she'd be fun enough to see a second time. Maybe if I get desperate, Travis will tell me who she is. Until then, I'm not going to sweat it.

Breakfast is ready when we reach the ranch, and the angry looks Rafe shoots my way tell me he's going to grill my ass the first chance he gets. Sure enough, the moment we start feeding the cattle in the east pasture, he's all over me. I'm not going to put up with his shit today. "Let it go, bro. Travis made the decision to stay overnight when he saw a chick he knows. I'm just lucky it worked out for me too."

"I don't give a shit if you got laid; it's the other crap that matters." The knife in his hand slashes furiously through the netting on a three-quarter-ton hay bale. "Damn it, Nate. You're on probation—no bars, period! You're not supposed to be drinking!"

"Nothing happened, and I didn't get busted. Besides, what the fuck was I supposed to do? You'd have checked out your options too, so don't give me your hypocritical bullshit."

Rafe wads up the netting and glares at me—he knows I'm right. "I swear, bro, you get revoked or arrested again while we're here, and I'm going to let your ass sit in jail this time."

He doesn't talk to me any more than necessary for the rest of the day, and I don't give a shit. Last night was totally worth it. Maybe now I'll get through calving and lambing season without killing someone.

The extra workers fill up the bunkhouses over the next few days as calving season hits full stride. Travis splits the crew, with some working days and the rest nights. It goes much more smoothly than I expected, even when the sheep start lambing before the cattle are done. Though our boss shows up, he's only there for a few hours before he and Travis disappear for much of the next week. His girlfriend isn't with him this time—no one seems to act as if that's a big deal, so maybe they're on-off or in some kind of open relationship. She's sexy enough, and I'd tap that beautiful heart-shaped ass of hers if given the chance. When Matt and Travis return days later, the boss doesn't hang around, and he's gone again within the hour.

Matt seems to be an okay guy, but there is definitely something off about him, and what little I see, the less I want to know. Yet I still find myself paying extra attention to them both and I don't like what I'm noticing. They're secretive, they talk in private a lot, and their trips away don't gel. This time they claim they went cross-country skiing, but they left without ski equipment, and their single backpacks would only hold a couple of changes of clothing. So what exactly is our boss up to—drugs? Are they hit men? Is it some kind of cattle baron crime cartel? The work around here doesn't leave me a lot of time to dwell on the question, but it's never totally gone from my mind. Strangely, Rafe is less concerned than I am, although the situation rubs him wrong too. I keep feeling like I can't even turn my back on the boss, and I don't like being kept on edge like that without solving the problem with my fists.

I'm no nearer to finding answers when the sheep finish lambing three weeks after the calving is done. The bunkhouses clear out within twenty-four hours of the last lamb's birth, and once again it's Travis, the other two Montanans, and Rafe and me working our asses off to keep the ranch running smoothly. To celebrate a successful season with little loss and only a few bum calves and lambs, Travis takes the four of us out for a night on the town. Rafe is more than a little bent about the plan, but he has to keep his mouth shut if he wants to continue working here. I can't keep from smirking. He still spends the night trying to run interference on my drinking, but that's something else he fails at. It's difficult to be a hardcore asshole when you're in public.

I get a second opportunity at the blonde, and once more she tells me her name: Bev. I'm sure it will be forgotten again by morning. That's why all women are "sweetheart" to me—they think I'm being endearing, when what I'm really doing is covering my ass. It does piss me off when the stuck-up brunette turns a sweet eye and tongue on Rafe, though. What the fuck? We look the same, and she brushed me off without giving me a moment's consideration, but Rafe gets all the time he needs to decide how far he wants to go. I try to console my wounded pride with the blonde after she takes me home for the night.

Again she's attentive and willing to give as much as she takes. It makes for a fun few hours, but this time I sober up the moment she announces she's a thirty-second Crow thanks to some grandmother on her mother's side. Fuck! Fuck me all to hell. If she's not a wannabe Native, then I've been playing mate roulette ... and I need to leave before I'm screwed for eternity. But shit—it might already be too late.

She drifts off to sleep as if she didn't just upend my whole world. Stunned, I lie there, considering my options. There will be no waking up to her stiff, ratty hair and her makeup smeared in a macabre reminder of her efforts to look pretty the night before—I need to get the hell out of here before I insult this woman who, I have to admit, has been generous with me. She was great for a second hookup, but I won't be back for a third round to tempt fate. Three times lucky, my ass. Leaving her asleep, I dress and slip out of the house before sunrise, texting Rafe to let him know I'm heading back to the ranch on foot.

Rafe's already ahead of me—the brunette must not have put out for him either—and he says he'll give me an hour to close the seven miles between us, which means he will start walking again the moment sixty minutes is up. I know him too well. Snowflakes circle in slow, lazy patterns, but the intermittent sunshine breaking over the horizon takes enough chill out of the air to make it a good day for a run. I need to clear my head of the panic swirling through me. What if I set off some chain reaction, and the blonde shows up to claim me? I can't see myself with that woman for the rest of fucking eternity. I'm not sure I even like her. Sure, she's nice enough, but I can see those bitches of fate sticking me with someone boring and average like she is. Great sex won't make it all right either.

My mind is still in a snarl when I catch up to Rafe. I won't tell him about the way I might have screwed myself—not until I know if there's still a chance to get the hell out of this mess. Rafe, thankfully, wants to talk about work and the months ahead. I need the distraction. This crap with the blonde has me going insane.

Over the next few days I bury myself in our work, keeping my mind busy, but all the while I'm looking over my shoulder, expecting that damn blonde to show up. By the next weekend I find myself in the strange position of passing up the chance to go to the bar. I can't risk seeing her again. Rafe even asks me if I'm sick—though he knows damn well neither of us have been sick once since the fever that changed us. I'm not sure I breathe until Monday rolls around and she hasn't yet come looking for me.

Two weeks later I'm still jumpy, earning me a lot of ribbing—everyone notices I'm uptight. Then the boss man comes back into town and gives me something new to focus on. Just being around him gets my hackles up, and it's growing worse—I have to work really hard to portray myself as an easy-going ranch hand. With the exception of the day we first met, he hasn't threatened me, but it's like he's throwing off some kind of vibe for me to back down. It has the opposite effect—no one intimidates me, not even him. Hell, if it weren't for my strange reaction to the man, I'd even like him, quirky sense of humor and all.

Travis and Matt take another week away; again their excuses ring hollow and false. Unlike before, Matt doesn't leave immediately after they get back, but instead asks Rafe and me to join him for dinner. No surprise, we're fed steaks so rare and bloody that I swear they moo at us. I jab my fork into the meat to kill it and again return my steak to the frying pan to finish cooking it. I have no idea what he has against cooked beef. Matt ignores me and gets to the point of our invitation.

My insulting his cooking aside, it appears he's pleased with the work we've done over the last few months, and he thinks we'd be a good fit for the property he's buying up north. There'll be a lot of construction work to rehab the old ranch—and he still needs someone working the cattle he plans to run up there. With spring approaching, there are decisions to be made, and he gives us just a few minutes alone to discuss the offer.

"So what ya think, bro, should we go up north for a while?" Rafe looks hopeful. Translation: Native women, rezes, and mate hunting will make Rafe a happy man. Matt's second ranch is close to two reservations—Fort Peck and Fort Belknap—inhabited by the Assiniboine, Gros Ventre, and Sioux. They're good people we've sheltered with in decades and centuries past, but the more appealing aspect for me is the limited population on and off the rez. The small-town folks living between the two rezes mostly avoid the Natives as much as possible, but there are always a few willing—which means less risk for me. Given my near disaster with the blonde, I'm more than ready to get out of here, and the new area may offer enough choices for me to have fun, yet keep me far from any split-tail who could be my downfall. At the same time, the rezes will keep Rafe happy in his search for Mrs. Right.

Before I answer him, my thoughts turn to the escalating war. Recent events have tipped many nations toward a world war unlike any we've experienced in the past, and in some ways I'm itching to join in the fight. Barroom brawling and engaging in combat are the best distractive guarantees I'll ever have against an unwanted future. I know it's bad that alliances between countries have shifted, with enemies aligning together and turning on their former allies, but I can't ignore the opportunity it may bring to avoid something far worse—immortality. With sick fascination I've been watching as the superpower nations have deployed assets globally, and many NATO and UN countries have already joined the fighting. Air and ground assaults have touched six of the seven continents—even the US has reinforced their shores and borders, ready to protect them if need be. I have to know if Rafe is still content sitting idle amid what's happening in the world outside.

Rafe assures me the timing still isn't right but agrees we may need to get involved at some point. Accepting that we'll wait, I agree that Matt has a decent proposal—and it will keep us busy. "Yeah, bro, going north sounds good to me."

Matt is patient while we sort through our options, but the moment we accept the job, he starts issuing orders. He'd like us to head up immediately—he's sure the deal's going to come together and wants us to step in the moment it closes. "I'll put you up in a motel in Malta," Matt says. "You won't have to worry about expenses. I'll cover everything."

We end the evening and return to the bunkhouse. Rafe is tense, still waiting for me to object—I know him so well. But truth be told, it's not me he should be uptight about, it's our boss. "Anything still strike you odd about Matt?" I look at Rafe, wondering if he's noticed the peculiarities that I have about the man.

"Yeah, but I'm not going to lose sleep over it." He shrugs. "I mean, so what, he's weird. We get paid decent money, and he mostly leaves us alone."

I wish I could feel as blasé as he does, but Rafe has a point—Matt does take care of his employees, and he pays them well. "Then I guess we're headed up to the Hi-line."

Rafe smiles. "Yeah, bro, I guess we are."

Matt meets with us one more time before he sends us north, making sure we're ready to take on the responsibilities. He'll be in Venice, he says, but his realtor here will make sure we get the keys to the ranch at closing. "You two will be my leads on the project— if you need to hire local help to get the work done, just call me, and I'll arrange it. You're welcome to stay in the house, but if you'd rather rent something in town for more privacy, that's fine too. I expect it'll be a few months out before we have bunkhouses ready for anyone staying full-time."

"Sure, man, no problem." I still can't believe he's putting this much trust in us this soon. All he has is Travis's word for the work we've done over the fall and winter months here at McAllister. "You still want the new barn and corrals done first and the remodel on the ranch house after that, and then we're to start on the bunk-houses and other outbuildings?"

"Yep. I'll have credit lines opened at the local hardware and lumber stores as well as at the dehys or feed mills. As soon as the perimeter fencing is ready, I can arrange the first shipment of cattle, too, if you think you two can handle it." Confidence oozes from this guy in a way that is almost unsettling. He may be in his mid-twenties, but he acts like a man twice that age when it comes to business. There's something in his attitude that smacks of authority, even though I don't quite understand it.

Rafe says, "We can handle it. Just let us know if you want anything else done or if you change your mind about the order of work."

A lopsided grin spills across Matt's face. "The order of work might have to change if it doesn't stop snowing up there. It's a harsh country with severe winters, and spring may be slow in coming, but it will give you time to line out the projects for when the spring thaw starts." He doesn't know we're well aware of that area and its extreme weather—arctic cold in the winter and desert hot in the summer—and infamous mosquitoes. Legend has it that the fastest mile of railroad track ever laid was at Saco, due to the bloodthirsty swarms, and the town actually has a plaque boasting of it. I damn well believe it. In all our travels I've never seen an area with swarms as thick and vicious as those found in northeastern Montana—if ever there were vampires, they are it.

Matt hands each of us a bank debit card, promising to fund our base wages on the first of each month. He's about ready to leave, when he turns back with one more request: "Oh, and I need you to stop off at the Ford dealer in Bozeman to get the new one ton that's going up to the ranch on the Hi-line." He says the latter as if we've never heard of the strip of two-lane highway long known to those in the northern tier of the country as the Hi-line. I still remember watching from a distrustful distance as the crews laid the east-west rail line bearing the same name. The iron horse was quite a curiosity until it was completed in 1893, and settlers began following it to claim homesteads in the area—even though the land was already inhabited and claimed by the Gros Ventre, Blackfoot, Sioux, and Crow. Yeah, not a good time for many, including the white settlers, who found living conditions near impossible and the ground resistant to their crops.

Matt doesn't seem to notice the sarcastic looks Rafe and I trade, and he doesn't stop talking. "After you get up there, you'll need to take a day and go over to Havre and select a stock trailer. I'll make the purchase arrangement once you have one picked out. There'll be no need to worry about transport when we bring the herd in—already have a few bull racks lined out for that—but you'll need a stock trailer to take care of some of the veterinary needs."

I have to give it to the boss—he doesn't miss the smallest detail and is thorough to a fault, if there's such a thing as too much information about a job and its duties. But I won't knock it; we've had a lot of crappy bosses, and if he continues being this fair with us, I can try to ignore his quirks. Matt may be the one who can help us get back on our feet. As if he's been reading my mind, Rafe looks at me with a scowl. "Don't fuck this up, bro. This is the best opportunity we've had in years."

"Yeah, yeah, I know," I say, and walk away to resume working.

Chapter 9: Rafe
Blind to the Hands of Fate

Before we know it our relocation date arrives, and I'm nervous as hell. Nate still doesn't have his license back, and he's not holding a work permit driver's license either, but he's going to have to drive from Bozeman—where the new pickup is waiting along our route—to Malta. It's a three-hundred-mile stretch on mostly two-lane highways between the two, which means one long, anxiety-ridden day for me. I can't stop lecturing Nate, and he's getting more pissed every mile, but I need him to take the risks seriously. If he screws this up, it will be yet another setback for us. "Now is not the time for you to end up in jail, asshole."

"Back off, Rafe. I know how to fucking drive and I'm stone-cold sober, so unless someone hits me, the cops will never find out."

Maybe I shouldn't ride his ass so hard all the time, but he's the biggest reason we haven't gotten anywhere beyond surviving. Every time we build up reserves, Nate tears it all down with one of his bullshit messes. Just once I'd like to get ahead of where we are and not have to start from Zilchville again.

At the Ford dealership, I reluctantly hand the old pickup keys to Nate. His fierce scowl says plenty, but the "I told you so" will

come—and he will get even later. The salesman places the paperwork in an envelope after he confirms we're authorized to get the
rig for Matt. He seems as disinclined to hand me the keys as I was
with Nate, but finally he does, and we hit the road. Since I want
to set the pace, I pull out ahead of Nate, but damn, I'm hoping he
doesn't get in a wreck—not only could we lose our pickup, but my
bike would be damaged too.

It's late afternoon when we arrive in Malta without incident and
find the hotel. Given the town's size, it's not hard to do; the Great
Northern, or GN, as the locals refer to it, is on a street corner near
the junction of Highway 191 and Highway 2. There's not much
daylight left, so we make plans to locate the property—Wolfe's Den
Ranch, as Matt dubbed it—in the morning. Unfortunately that
leaves several hours of boredom that Nate is determined to kill
drinking, and trying to stop him is like standing in the path of a
tornado—he'll either twist around me or go right through me. All
I can do is follow along and hope he doesn't do something stupid.

The hotel lounge is dead, so he finds another bar just a couple
businesses away on the same block. This one isn't much better, but
with the size of the town, I doubt he's going to find a bar during
the week to give him everything he's looking for. Can't say I find that
upsetting. Nate hasn't let go of his self-destruct mode—he's only
been too isolated and controlled to resume it. This is his "told ya"
and payback all rolled into a one-man drunk-fest.

The locals give us a standoffish once-over but mostly ignore us.
I smile—that's strike one if Nate is looking for a fight. The bar-
maid engages us with typical bartender banter, and it's soon clear
she's not interested in either of us. The only other women here are
older and with their husbands or boyfriends. I smile again—strike
two. Nate slams down another shot and empties his beer. This is
one he won't strike out on, and I know he'll be blitzed by the time
I can get him out of here and back to our room.

It's near closing time when we finally leave the bar, and Nate is staggering; it's the most he's drunk in a while, and I'm sure he'll be hung over in the morning. I help get him ready for bed, and he passes out within minutes, much to my relief. A bonus of his current situation—no fights, no women—is that I can peacefully relax for the next few hours and may even manage some uninterrupted sleep myself.

Once I'm settled on the hard motel mattress, I reflect on the drive up. My mind kept wandering to Emily, and I think a part of me wished we were headed back to the Flathead Valley. Accepting this job has put more distance between us. I'm still uncertain whether I've done the right thing or whether coming up to the Hi-line was a mistake. But no—if I screwed up, it was the moment I ended it with her, and no amount of time or distance will change that now. Hell, Emily probably hates me after what I did to her. But if I was right to leave, then I have to keep looking, because she is out there somewhere. I'd never forgive myself if my soulmate needed me and I wasn't there because I was messing around with the wrong woman. Making her wait even one more day is an asshole thing to do. A Nate way ... not for me.

I use the quiet time to think about my woman, allowing my thoughts to drift over the long, fruitless search for her. Maybe this time will be different, and I'll be rewarded with her finally coming into my life. I'd like to think the odds favor it, but I know well the shadow of disappointment hovering over me if this turns out like all the other times before. I remind myself there's a decent chance with the proximity of the two nearby rezes. Belknap is the closer of the two, but I'll explore them both while we're here. As soon as we get a chance, I'll drag Nate along to check them out too. I can already hear the argument he'll give me, but I can't leave him unattended until the DUI mess is fully behind him. I can't risk him getting his ass in trouble again.

When morning comes, Nate is half-sick and fighting a head-ache. He's wearing his best hangover scowl, the one that screams it's a little too bright, a little too loud—hate self and the world too. Unsympathetically I wait for him to take some aspirin and drink a cup of coffee before we meet the realtor and get directions out to the ranch.

Forty minutes later we cross the cattle guard, and I take in the expanse of high prairie and low-lying hills. Trees are sparse, mostly clustered along a creek winding its way through the property, and the open ground, with its grasses and sagebrush, seems well suited to grazing. The remnants of hay fields speak to the overall run-down condition of the ranch, if the encroaching sagebrush is any indication. Matt wasn't kidding—this place needs some TLC. Ten thousand acres is a lot of ground, but it will offer plenty of work to keep us busy and Nate away from trouble.

After we check out the house and other structures, we explore what we can from the few roads that aren't snowed in. We're stand-ing on the edge of a hill, looking down into a coulee, when nostal-gia for an earlier time comes over me. "I'm glad there's places like this still." With the exception of fencing, much of the land has re-mained in a natural state—it's used primarily for grazing—and I imagine that if I looked closely, I'd find evidence of teepee rings. Unlike areas heavily changed by modern civilization, it's possible to see the countryside here as it was centuries ago.

"It's the closest we'll ever come to the freedom of the untamed land again." Nate's gaze is fixed on the creek running through the center of the coulee. The faraway look on his face is subtle, but speaks to the memories that are doubtlessly playing in his mind, as they are in mine. I watch his brows draw together as he angles his head—inspecting something in the coulee below us. "I think we rode through here a couple centuries back."

"We may have." It takes a few seconds, but then I see what caught his attention—boulders half-hidden in the sage brush, standing as silent observers over an ancient ceremonial ring. "I wonder if Matt will allow us a couple of horses to manage the herd or if he's providing four-wheelers up here like he has down at McAllister."

Nate shrugs. "Maybe we can get him to cover both. He seems generous enough."

I laugh and shake my head. "I still can't believe I thought he was some old rich dude. He got lucky coming into the inheritance—set him up for life." That was one detail we learned about our boss during the months at the Cleary Ranch. While he already owned a small construction business, everything else—the software company, the McAllister ranch—came to him when the original ranch owners, Josh and Lois Cleary, were killed. The man was his mentor, apparently. They had no kids and left it all to Matt.

Lucky son of a bitch. No one would say exactly how the couple died, but Nate's convinced they were murdered and believes it's proof of a mob or cartel connection. While I share Nate's curiosity about Matt, I can't go beyond accepting that our boss is a bit weird. Something is not right about that guy, and I wonder if we'll ever find out what it is. But I can live without knowing—as long as he keeps being a good boss.

Spring does arrive late this year, but we have a good start on the remodeling by the time the snow melts and the mud dries enough for us to switch to the fencing along the outlying areas of the ranch. The cattle will be delivered within the next couple of weeks, and the perimeter and cross fencing will need to be ready to contain them. While we're working on the fencing projects, two men arrive with a cement truck to set the forms and pour the new foundation for the addition to the ranch house. That will leave us trying to frame in the walls of the addition and finish the fence work before the cows arrive.

We make good progress on our ranch to-do list, and when we get the herd settled in, we establish a routine that balances the construction projects with the general upkeep of the ranch. Although there's work to be done seven days a week, I enjoy the occasional half or full day off whenever I need time for myself. Visiting the rezes is a big part of my off-ranch activity. It's always a struggle to get Nate to go, but I can out-stubborn him when I need to.

Of course, Nate goes out of his way to chase off any gal on the rez who dares to so much as breathe near him, but at least I'm getting the chance to meet the women here. Several prospects already show more than a passing interest in both of us, though that may change once Nate scares them away with his surly attitude. I shake my head, sighing. Some on the rez have taken to greeting us as the sun and moon twins. Even though we're nearly identical, it's easy for them to tell who is who—Nate's always scowling.

The months slip by, and we're kept busy between the construction projects and the five hundred head of cattle now on the place. The second-floor addition on the house is nearing completion, with the carpet, paint, electrical and plumbing fixtures, and bathroom tile work left to do. The main floor addition and remodeling were finished a few weeks ago. Cattle are the biggest disruption to the structural work—we've been checking on them more frequently than should be necessary, thanks to the big light-brown lone wolf we've seen lingering on the property. So far the wolf seems content to watch from a distance, but if he starts killing livestock, as the wolves in Montana tend to do, we'll have to deal with him. If we catch him in the act, we can shoot and kill him, but if he's sneaky—killing when we're out of sight—then we'll have to rely on Fish, Wildlife and Parks to remove him. As long as he is only passing through on occasion, we'll let him be for now. And that will allow us better chances for recreation.

There's a pow wow coming up that I don't want to miss. Like the county fair a week before it, the only way we can attend is to bust our asses doing the chores, head over before opening ceremonies, and come back to the ranch after it ends each night. It makes for a long day and a longer weekend, but I know it will be worth every minute. The more time passes on the Hi-line, the better feeling I have about being here, as if we're in the right place at the right time. It certainly helps that I have a few women in mind.

Nate, unhappy and ornery, disrupts my contemplation with his incessant efforts to provoke a fight as we drive to Belknap—a failing attempt to change my mind about going to the pow wow. I'm sure he'll do his usual pouting to drive women away, but I'm in too good a mood to let him spoil the night ahead. A gal I met at the fair and have texted and called a couple times since then is meeting me at the arbor, and I'm ready to have another good weekend with her. Kari's vivaciousness warms the coldest heart and invigorates those around her. While I can only hope she's the one, at least she's the first woman to offer me relief for my guilt over Emily.

After we park I send Kari a text to find out where she is—I don't want to wander around looking for her. She texts me back, saying she's in the bleachers, top row, on the east side of the arbor. Dragging my reluctant brother along, I find her and a couple other gals in the center of the bleachers. It's a good spot for watching the dancers, drummers, and singers.

The women have a blanket spread across the bench—a common way to claim seats are taken—and move to put a space between each of them as we climb up to join the group. "Fucking perfect," Nate mumbles behind me, and I laugh at him. It's bad enough for him when they sit to one side, but this arrangement is going to be torture.

Kari greets me with a kiss. "Hi, guys." She points at the two gals with her. "Shawna and Jolenthia." Her smile warms my heart—she's so open and friendly, and her upbeat attitude is infectious. We haven't had the opportunity to be more intimate than a kiss or hug, but I'm looking forward to the discovery process.

I grin, nodding to her friends. "Nice to meet you." I take the space between Kari and Shawna and suppress another laugh when Nate glares at me. He has no choice; he'll need to sit between Shawna and Jolenthia unless he forces the person on the far side of Jolenthia to move.

Shawna takes an immediate interest in Nate, flirting openly and touching him often in her attempt to gain a favorable response. It's not working, and I know it's going to blow up in her face if she doesn't back off and leave him alone. Nate's so tense, he's leaning a little more into Jolenthia each time he swats Shawna's hands away. Backed into a corner, or rather against another woman he doesn't want, leaves Nate one way out. It's going to get ugly fast.

The women are friendly enough and seem to dismiss Nate's attitude as if they think they'll cajole him into a good mood. I don't have the heart to tell them he's a lost cause—he'll make that point without me soon enough. I can tell he's trying to stay focused on the dancers and drum circles, but the women aren't taking the hint, even with his surly responses to the forced contact. By now Shawna has escalated to tucking stray hairs behind his ear while Jolenthia braces her hands against Nate's arm and shoulder, preventing him from falling into her lap. In all honesty it's mostly Shawna flirting with him; Jolenthia seems a bit shy, and aside from a quick hello, she's not said more than a few words. Even those have been mostly directed at her friends.

Out of the corner of my eye, I see Shawna stroking her fingers along Nate's jaw, and from his narrowed eyes and the ticking muscle in his cheek, I know she's crossed a line. Nate grabs her arm, roughly pushing it away. "Keep your fucking hands off me!"

"Why do you have to be such an ass? I'm just trying to offer you a fun time." Shawna's eyes are half-teasing, half-pissed—she's challenging him. Big mistake. Jolenthia, Kari, and I stare at the two. The tension is heavy, and I know Nate's about to shut her down for good.

He proves me right once again and uses a line I've heard him give before to blow off overeager chicks. He leans in so their lips are almost touching, and I'm sure Shawna is thinking he's going to kiss her, but then his voice lowers, sliding from seductive to increasingly more disgusted with each word. "I know you want me to pop the hood, see what's underneath, but I've already heard your bullshit engine run. You don't belong in a showroom, and I have no fucking desire to see whatever kind of nasty crap you think you have to offer."

Shawna turns beet red and her jaw drops open as Nate sits back, looking away from her. For a moment I think she's going to cry or bolt away from us, but instead she faces forward and remains quiet—she's not even talking to her girlfriends now. I sigh, knowing that had she backed off when he first told her he wasn't interested, he never would have gone for the gutter insult. Still, I wish Nate wouldn't be so harsh. His fear of Native women brings out the worst in him. Maybe I should have left him at home after all.

Now that Shawna is pouting and Jolenthia is even quieter than before, Kari and I have the opportunity for conversation that doesn't include the others. It may be cold of me, but this isn't all bad in my book. I like the way it feels when she holds my hand, and I'm considering how I can advance things between us. I'd like to keep seeing her awhile longer—there's a connection similar to what I felt with Emily, and maybe this time it won't be a false emotion. The hurdle we face is the rule Nate and I have about not bringing women home, period. But it's not like when we've lived in town, where everyone is close by. Between our responsibilities at the ranch and its isolated location, overnight romps elsewhere interfere with our ability to do our job. Not that it would hinder Nate much, since he always skips out on his bed dates as soon as the sex part is over, but I'm not him, and I refuse to live celibate just as much as I refuse to be like my brother. If I want Kari's overnight company, that means convincing Nate we need to bend the rules. Unfortunately I'm no nearer to solving the issue when the pow wow shuts down for the night and it's time to say good-bye to the girls.

I glance at Nate and recognize the look on his face. Shawna disappeared after dinner, and while he was a bit more polite to Jolenthia after Shawna left, the strain of the evening is etched on his face. I already know he's going to want to stop for a drink on the way back to the ranch. It will lead to another bullshit fight.

Chapter 10: Nate

Exceptions to Every Rule

It's useless—I've already lost the argument, but I'm not ready to give up. "One drink, that's all I'm fucking asking here." We have just under a two-hour drive back to the ranch, and I don't want to wait that long. I need something to clear my head.

Rafe keeps watching the road as he drives. "Forget it. Not happening, bro."

I punch the roof of the pickup truck. "Fuck, bro, I'm wound up like a spring about to break."

Now he looks across at me. For the longest minute he studies me in silence—almost like he's forgotten the road ahead and the fact that he's the one driving. Good thing we're on a flat, straight stretch, or he'd have us in the ditch. Finally Rafe draws in a deep breath, returning his eyes to the road. "I'll stop in Malta for one drink—one, got that? But you're going to have to give me something in return."

"What the hell, Rafe? You're blackmailing me to stop?"

"I want to make an exception to our rule while we live up here."

I know which rule he's talking about, and it's obvious what argument he'll make—things are different here, the ranch is too remote, and if either of us is going to see any split-tail action, we're going to have to bring them out to the ranch. Fuck. I don't like this, but I'm not sure we're going to have a choice as long as we're staying here. I agree to the deal, glaring at Rafe as if it's his fault for putting us in this position.

Truth be told, I've been considering it for a couple of weeks now, and after surreptitiously checking out Jolenthia most of the night, I find the idea appeals to me. I know that I acted like an ass, like I always do on the rez, but I did notice her. It was hard not to. Her pale complexion, dark-green eyes, and light-brown hair with its pink-dyed ends made her stand out in an erotic sort of way. For once I wasn't put off by the color in her hair either; somehow it completed her sexy little "can't have this" look. Her T-shirt and jeans accentuated her lithe figure, with those supple curves and well-toned muscles. She didn't look comfortable, and if I had to guess, I'd say she's not used to hanging around a rez. Thank fuck she's white, and at least she wasn't coming on to me like that Native chick, Shawna. That's one I wouldn't touch if you paid me.

A tease of Jolenthia's scent clings to my shirt, making my mouth water to taste her. I may have already blown my chance at her, though—she was quieter after I told off Shawna. Unless acting untouchable is all part of her game. Sometimes the gals who play hard to get are the ultimate in fun when they finally give in. I like the challenge she presents, and she'd make a great bed date, but she doesn't seem the type, and that's a problem because I don't date split-tails long term. If she hangs around the rest of the weekend, maybe I'll figure out the best approach. I need to find a way to bend her to my desire—to sex her up and throw her away afterward without a fight.

"Did you hear me?" Aggravation drips from Rafe's tone.

"Sorry, man, I was thinking."

He shakes his head, fucking treating me like a child again. Sometimes I can't believe we're twins or even the same age—Rafe acts far older than his appearance suggests. The wisdom he's gained over the centuries is always on full display, a silent reminder for me to stop being an immature jerk.

"I'd like to ask Kari to come home with us tomorrow night," he says. "If you're okay with that, we'll stop at the bar for a drink. If you're not, then we're driving straight through to the ranch."

A flickering thought suggests I could ask Jolenthia too, but I'm afraid she'd turn me down. Afraid? What the hell am I thinking? No, she's going to give in to me ... there's only one way she's going to blow me, and it doesn't include the word off. "Yeah, bring her home. It may be the only way we ever get laid around here. Now, stop at the damn bar. I need a drink."

We pull up to the curb, and I don't wait for Rafe to put the rig in park—by the time he locks the pickup and comes inside, I've already ordered a triple shot of bourbon and a beer. Rafe sits on the stool next to me and orders a beer too. I'm staring at the countertop, lost in thought again, and almost miss it when the bartender places the drinks in front of me. I slide him a twenty and grab the tall shot before Rafe can snatch it away. In my book, a shot with a beer chaser qualifies as one drink. It burns like hell, but I take it down in a few gulps. I close my eyes, hoping the booze will scorch through my messed-up thoughts, but it seems my mind is headed for confusion instead. I down the beer as fast as I can—we need to get out of here so I can top off this nightmare with the half bottle of bourbon waiting for me at home.

When we reach the ranch, I storm over to the liquor cabinet, grab the bottle, and head for my room. It doesn't matter how much I drink—all I can see is that pretty little gal with the pink-tipped hair. Fear creeps in again that she won't want me, and I try to shake it off. What the hell is wrong with me? I want to feel her pull me closer, not push me away. No, I want to sex her up in ways she'll never forget. I'll use every tactic necessary, persuading her to give me what I want, short of begging ... well, maybe that too. I will have her. I need to do this chick and get her the hell out of my system.

Just lying here thinking of her—the shyness and hint of inno-cence possibly hiding a wild side—has me trying to relieve the phys-ical tension, but Jolenthia as a fantasy is disappointingly unsatis-factory. Fuck. I hold up the bourbon and scowl at it—I should be well on my way to numb by now. If I didn't know better, I'd swear someone had watered down the booze. Rafe tried that once, but af-ter receiving a black eye and broken nose from me, he hasn't done it since.

Maybe it isn't even Jolenthia getting to me, but the strong at-traction between Rafe and Kari. I'm terrified I'm about to be left behind—I don't think he's ever looked at a woman like that, and if she's his mate, our paths may be about to part for good. There's no way I'll stick around watching him stay forever young while I wither away to old age. Yet the thought of not having him in my life crushes my chest to the point I can't breathe. My mind continues whirling in confusion, warring over need, want, fear, hope. I find the bottom of the bottle around three o'clock, and I know I'm hammered. But although I'm drunk, the numbness isn't there ... the bed is spin-ning, adding to the muddled mess in my brain. All I want to do is pass out, and even that seems to take a while.

When I wake, my head is pounding like a freight train is bar-reling through it. Déjà vu, it's Rafe banging on the door. "Come on, man. Get your ass out of bed so we can tackle the chores and hit the road."

It's been a few months since I woke to his bullshit, and it helps remind me what I'm running from ... and the fun I've been missing out on since my wreck. I'm two months away from getting my li-cense back. Then his control over my life ends, and I can return to doing what I like most—fighting and fucking. I'm long overdue for both.

Rafe bangs on the door again. "If you don't get your damn ass out here, I'm going to go without you today, take the keys, and dis-able anything not needing a key, including the tractors."

"I'm getting up—give me a fucking minute here." I haven't had a hangover since we first arrived in Malta for this job, and I can only hope it's done hammering me by the time we get to the pow wow. Otherwise it's going to be a long, miserable day with my head splitting in two.

Rafe got a head start on the chores, and it doesn't take us long to finish once I get out there to help. We're running late, though, and he's all sorts of bent about me being the cause. My head aches too much to fight, so I let him spout off. It's the fastest way to get him to be quiet.

After we arrive we find the girls in the same spot as yesterday, but this time there is no open seat between Shawna and Jolenthia, which puts me sitting next to Jolenthia and Rafe. I'm not sure how I feel about it, given my unusual interest in this split-tail, though now that I'm sober I suspect it might have been the booze fueling the hard-fucking fantasy of her last night.

She glances up at me as I take my seat. "Hi," she says, her voice timid.

I nod. "Hey there." In my periphery I notice Shawna shooting me a dirty look. Good. She got my message loud and clear—she'll leave me the hell alone today.

The event gets underway with a special tribute to our veteran warriors. The veterans are often recognized at pow wows, but times of war always bring our warriors' sacrifices closer to home for those on the rez. We stand in respect as the veterans present are honored and the Master of Ceremony reads a list of warriors currently deployed.

After a prayer and blessing for the troops, the veterans lead off the dance. Everyone retakes their seats, except Jolenthia. She offers to grab water for the group, and I can't help myself—I volunteer to go with her and bring back some food. I'm already kicking myself for this act of stupidity. This chick is a virus infecting every cell in my body. It's been way too long since I got laid. I offer to carry the bottles, but she declines. I can't believe I'm being a fucking gentleman—she's like an elusive walleye, refusing every type of bait I dangle in front of her nose. I'm still mulling that over by the time we reach the Thai food booth. Another plus in her favor—she's got to be the whitest white girl here. Most Native chicks would insist on fry bread or Indian tacos. Jolenthia places the order while I go next door to the Chuck Wagon and ask for a mess of fry bread. This time I get an assortment: some are covered in honey butter and others in cinnamon and sugar, and I even grab a couple plain.

Jolenthia hasn't said more than a few words to me, but as we head back to the bleachers, I catch her looking at me more than once— each time she blushes and looks away. Her interest, or at the least, curiosity about me feels good, which smacks of trouble, but her shy personality has as much of a draw on me as a good bourbon does. She's like a puzzle I have to solve or it'll drive me crazy.

"You're not from around here," I say as we sit down. I'm beginning to think I didn't get drunk enough last night.

Jolenthia darts a glance at me before looking back at the dancers. "No."

I want to grab her by the shoulders and make her give me more than a one-word answer. "Are you just visiting?"

"No."

You've got to be kidding me—this is like floating teeth on a horse. "Why don't you tell me a little about yourself." I smile at her, hoping it will encourage her to open up.

She bites her lip and looks at me for little more than a couple of seconds before her gaze falls to her lap. "I'm from Thermopolis, Wyoming. I met Kari there, and when things got bad at home, I came here to get away for a while. I'm staying with Kari until I decide what I'm going to do with my life."

There's a hint of sadness in the musical lilt of her voice, as if something happened that she doesn't want to talk about. I'm content letting her keep her secrets for now, but I feel compelled to get them from her someday. I freeze at that thought. Why the hell am I thinking of this chick as if I'm going to get to know her better? I glance at Rafe and Kari—they're nibbling on each other's lips and murmuring softly. Fuck. My gut clenches. Time with my brother may be running out. Looking at Jolenthia, I assure myself that it might be okay to spend a little longer with her if it means making the most of whatever time I have left with Rafe. I'll just need to be careful.

It's been over a century since I had any interest in knowing a woman, and the last one turned into an unforgettable friend. When it was time to move on, I found it hard to say good-bye to her—I knew we'd never see each other again. I've always wondered what became of her after Rafe and I left.

I glance again at Jolenthia and ask myself if I want to go through the pain of leaving a friendship behind once more. She looks like she needs a friend or at least a protector—her timidity may leave her vulnerable, and perhaps a male friend would help keep those who would harm her away. I scrub at my face. I'm not sure I like where this is going. I fall into silence as bittersweet memories flood in, bleeding my heart dry with the joy and sorrow they contain.

She was one of the most beautiful women I've ever seen, exquisite both inside and out. But while she was physically and spiritually strong, she had a tenderness, a kindness that wasn't common back then. Life was hard and short, and its challenges left many women jaded or beaten down—but not her. Catches Bird was the closest I ever came to being in a real relationship with a woman. There were times I would have accepted, no, wanted her as my mate, and yet somehow I knew she wasn't and never would be. I could have had her nonetheless, taken her as my wife, but there was no escaping the fact that she'd grow old and die long before Rafe and I would age another year. As much as I wanted her in the ways a man desires and needs a woman, I couldn't allow us to be more than friends—but that caused something in me to wither and twist until my heart hardened to stone. The day I said my final good-bye to her is the day I set my goal to grow old and die.

By dinner break I need to get away from Jolenthia—I don't like the way being near her is messing with my head. While the others go to get food, I slip away, telling them I'll catch up with them later. It takes me an hour to work past the raw emotions that Catches Bird always evokes. I don't want to go back at all, but in the same moment I don't want to stay away. *Jolenthia*. That refocuses me, and after dinner I head back to the bleachers, intent on getting her to go home with me tonight. It's perfect—Kari already agreed to come back with us, which makes it easy for Jolenthia to come along too.

But then I sit beside Jolenthia again, and I feel like an ass for wanting to make a bed date out of her. Even then I can't let this go—she may be as good as I imagine, and if so, I may have to consider bedding Jolenthia more than once or twice to get her out of my system. Damn, if I ever needed a drink, it's now. I need to fuck her and get all this weird shit with her over and done with. I remind myself we're making an exception, given our circumstances, and likely she won't want to come back to me any more than the rest of them. I can do this ... just like always. Fuck and run ... one and done. I'll never allow another friendship to shred what's left of my heart.

Drawing a breath, I lean closer to Jolenthia and lower my voice so Shawna won't hear. "Would you like to come back to the ranch with Kari and us tonight?"

She acts startled and looks around me to Kari before glancing up again. "Uh, I don't know."

Great. Not a yes and not a no, and I know better than to push her. I drop the subject and try to enjoy the rest of the night.

A couple hours later the women all leave for a bathroom break. I can't resist speculating whether it's to talk Kari out of going home with Rafe or talk Jolenthia into coming along. With the way my luck has been this weekend, it won't be the latter.

Rafe says, "You seem interested in Jo."

"Jo?" I try to play dumb.

"Yeah, Jolenthia. Kari says she prefers to be called Jo but doesn't tell people that when she first meets them."

Okay, that's good to know. Like one of those "only my friends call me such and such" things. Maybe I should try using it and seeing if it helps. "She's kind of different. In some ways she reminds me of Catches Bird."

Rafe gets a knowing look on his face, and a slight smile turns up the corners of his mouth. "It wouldn't hurt you to have friends."

And that's all he says about it. I let it go, because I can't fathom why I would want to go through that again. My earlier memories only reminded me it's not a path I'll willingly travel if I can avoid it.

The women return, and I notice Jo is sitting a little closer to me than she was before. I'm not sure what to make of that either. But it's getting late, and we have a little over an hour left until the pow wow ends for the night. I have to get her talking again. This is one of the most confusing situations I've been in for quite a while—decades or a century at least.

"Hey, Jo, would you like another water or soda? I'm going to go grab something."

Her extreme shyness is back. She doesn't look me in the eye. "Water, please."

I sigh as I leave the bleachers—she's not making it easy for me to figure this shit out. When I return to my seat, I don't say anything, just hand her a water and nod after she thanks me. If it weren't for Kari returning with Rafe tonight, I'd be begging him to stop at a bar again.

Shawna takes off before the last set of dancers start, and that leaves the four of us sitting there waiting for the end. The affection between Rafe and Kari suggests he's definitely going to have fun tonight. And me? Looks like I'm going to bed drunk and alone again.

After the closing we head toward the pickup, and I'm a bit surprised to see Jo walking beside me. Did the women park near us? But when we reach the pickup, Rafe opens the front passenger door for Kari, and Jo gets into the back seat. I blink hard a few times to make sure I'm not seeing things—she never said she was coming with us, and now here she is. I have no clue if she's along for the ride or if she finally decided she wants me. I shake my head and get in on the other side.

It's a quiet ride back to the ranch, with the exception of Rafe and Kari murmuring endearments to each other up front. My gaze keeps shifting to Jo—she stares out the window into the dark night. I want to unbuckle her and slide her next to me, put my arm around her, but she's not giving me any signs that she'd welcome my touch. For the first time I regret this rig is a crew cab. If it were a standard single cab, she'd be squished into my side or sitting on my lap, and I'd sure as hell be enjoying it.

By the time we reach the ranch, I'm feeling awkward and unsure what to do about the distance and silence between us. Unfucking-believable—this little gal has me acting like a teenage boy who's never been laid. Rafe and Kari seem content to ignore us and disappear into his bedroom within seconds of entering the house. Jo is still standing near the front door, and I'm at a loss to suggest anything. It doesn't help that I'm sober, but right now drinking seems like the wrong thing to do.

"Um ... would you like to come in and sit down?"

Jo nods and follows me to the living room.

"Do you want anything? Water, beer, bourbon, a snack ..." Every inch of me?

"No thank you." She sits on the opposite end of the couch, and I frown.

Three whole words and three feet between us. What the fuck am I supposed to do with this chick? Nothing ventured, nothing gained, right? I slide down the couch and close the distance between us, watching her reaction, ready to retreat if she's not receptive to what I'm about to do. She blushes and keeps her gaze pinned to her lap. I reach out and curl a finger under her chin to make her look at me. I can see conflicting emotions in her eyes—nervousness, fear, desire, and embarrassment. Only one matters to me. Leaning in, I brush a feather of a kiss to her lips. It takes a few seconds before she responds and kisses me back—but it's a start. I'm going to have to take it easy, or I'll run her off before I ever get her near my bed.

This weekend may not be a total waste of time after all.

CHAPTER 11: NATE

Heyoka

Each minute that passes brings Jo more out of her shell. We move on from just making out to heavy petting, and I know it won't take much more to get her to come willingly to my room. I still can't believe I'm about to take a woman to bed at my place, where she can find me later. But then I think of the way her hands feel on me, and I'm glad Rafe and I made an exception to our rule.

Regardless, if I don't get relief soon, I'm going to have to take matters into my own hands. She can always bring me back for a second round if she needs more time to decide. I pull back from the kiss. "Jo ... I want you." She meets my gaze, and I can see the indecision there, but it's waning. I feel my pulse increase. I kiss her again, encouraging her further: "I want you to come with me to my room."

She doesn't say a word, just nods. I'm not going to give her the chance to change her mind. I scoop her off the couch and wrap her legs around my hips as I continue to kiss her. Jo's fingers are tangled in my hair—she took the braid out over a half hour ago—and her kisses are passionate now. And damn, can she kiss! At my bedroom I pause, deepening the kiss as I open the door. I keep reminding myself to take it easy, not to scare her away. I lay her on the bed and slowly begin to remove her clothes.

To my surprise she removes an article of my clothing, somewhat awkwardly, for each one I take off her. It's my turn to feel nervous once we're naked, and sure enough, she crawls off the bed, gathers my hair in her hands, and lays it over my shoulder—she noticed my marks. I feel a finger trace the feather patterns. "These are different. I thought you had a lot of ink, but I'm not sure what to make of this."

Neither do I, and I'm not about to tell her what they are. My sole focus is easing her into this and not giving her any reason to back out. My need for her is raw, unfathomable, and must be sated before she leaves. Has it really been so long since I've been with a woman I could respect? Jo is ideal in so many ways. Aside from the dyed pink tips, she wears her hair natural, no nasty, stinky hair products teasing it into something it's not. I spent a large part of the day at the pow wow enjoying the way the wind moved through her long strands, which, like mine, nearly reach the crack of her ass. Her face is free of makeup, and her natural beauty shines through. Add those to her well-toned figure and almost innocent personality, and she's a woman that any man would desire.

Her fingers are tracing row after row of the feathery scars on the back side of my body—she's fascinated by them, I think. For some reason this doesn't upset me the way it usually does when a woman spends too long gawking at my marks. I decide it's her touch making the difference; it's wonderful, indescribable. She's either enthralled with them, or she's stalling for time. I turn to face her. "Jo, can I ask you something?"

She meets my gaze and nods.

"Are you, um ..." I'm suddenly self-conscious, because I never worry about these things where women are concerned. "You have experience, right? I mean, you're not a virgin?"

The flaming blush that colors her face and neck is my answer. Shit. I know she's willing, but I need to be even more careful handling her now. I tip her face up and tell her to look at me. When she does, I say, "It's okay—we'll go slow, and it will be memorable. I promise."

Jo swallows hard, and I ease us back into contact. A long, gentle hug leads to kissing a minute later, but I take my time touching her body and moving her to the bed. She has so much trust in her eyes, but I can tell that she's scared, and I continue going slowly. After I lay her in the middle of my bed again, I lie down next to her instead of on top of her. I need her to signal when she's ready for that.

What seems like hours later she finally pulls at my hips in a manner that suggests she's comfortable with me taking the next step. I roll her onto her back and move over top of her, keeping some distance between us at first. I bend my head down to kiss her as my body lowers over so slowly. Jo tenses when she feels me between her legs, and I give her more time to relax before I begin something I won't want to stop. Her hips roll, rubbing against my cock and making this incredibly difficult for me, but I try to distract myself with the sweet taste of her lips and the taut feel of her nipples and firm breasts until I notice her trying to line us up.

I see the anticipation mixed with fear on her face, and I smile. "It may hurt a little, but we'll go easy, and you can stop me whenever you need a moment to adjust to it. The pain, if you have any, won't last." She nods, and I can feel her body tremble beneath me. I about lose my shit right there. I've never felt this degree of passion for a woman before, but the need to make this perfect for her is sexy as hell and about driving me into a sex-crazed insanity.

We hold eye contact as we become one. Every now and then I pause until I feel her relax and start to move with me again. Instead of being demanding, the way I usually am during sex, I let her set the pace, and I follow her lead—which means I'm balls deep

inside her when I realize I forgot to put on a condom. Shit ... too
late now. It takes everything in me to hold back, but there's no way
I'm going to ruin this for her. I will take her over the edge, and I'll
be right behind her when she falls.

I'm not sure when my eyes close, but they do, and I'm fully im-
mersed in the sensuality of this beautiful woman moving beneath
me. I've forgotten how good sex feels without that rubber barrier.
Hell, for centuries there were no condoms, and sex was always un-
protected, but this is far better than I remember. I can feel her build
and climb higher, and I struggle to wait—I've never had to work
this hard to maintain control. Whatever she's doing to me, I don't
want it to stop. She's driving me fucking wild.

Then Jo's pace picks up, her breathing turning to heavy pants
as she clutches me tighter and tighter. I feel her climax, and there's
no holding back any longer. I intend to pull out, but I explode before
I can do that—and a sensation I've never felt before rips through
me. While my body is still reacting to my orgasm, it feels as if something is crawling or sliding under my skin. It's merely uncomfortable at first, but then my back experiences a searing pain that makes
my breath catch.

My eyes fly open. Jo is frozen beneath me with wide, horrified
eyes. I stare at her with equal terror as the slithering feeling under my skin finds its way to the surface, ripping open my back in
two painful tears. I can feel whatever was under my skin slide out
of what I now realize are slits where my skin has broken open along
each side of my spine, between my shoulder blades. I can't breathe.
I can't fucking breathe. Jo starts screaming and pushing against
my chest—she's trying to get away from me—and I can't move one
fucking muscle. I'm frozen with revulsion and disbelief as the pain
pushes me nearly to the point of passing out.

Her screams bring Rafe and Kari bursting into my room, but
I still can't take my eyes off Jo. Rafe is yelling something at me
while Kari tries to pull Jo out, and finally my brother tackles me,

knocking me away from Jo and off the bed. I feel as if he just ripped my body in half; my mind screams at the excruciating pain as I catch a glimpse of Jo fleeing my room. Rafe moves into my line of sight—his eyes are wide with shock.

Dreadful understanding rushes in, stealing the air from my lungs once more. He knows ... I know.

All I can do is choke out, "It wasn't supposed to be her."

CHAPTER 12: RAFE
Life Isn't Fair

I stare in stunned disbelief at my brother, but blinking doesn't change what I see. Nate is on his hands and knees, heaving labored breaths while he gasps and chokes out the same damn words over and over: "It wasn't supposed to be her." A huge set of wings rests over him, touching the floor. My mind can't grasp that this is real, but I know it is—I knew the moment I broke through that door. I'm at a loss what to feel or what I should even do.

He was on top of Jo—they'd clearly been having sex—and she was freaking out while he seemed frozen over her, with these giant wet wings dripping around them. It wasn't until I knocked him to the floor that the wings fluttered and gave a hard shake to flick off the moisture. They seemed to dry instantly then.

Nate's denial only elevates my confusion. I can hear Kari and Jo in another part of the house—crying, voices raised. They sound hysterical. My mind says I should go comfort them and calm them down, but my heart tells me to stay with my brother. A niggling instinct won't allow me to believe that the wings being out is the final step in this process. Whirling thoughts snarl and tangle around a couple of facts I can't ignore: Jo is what Kari is not. He has everything, and I have nothing. I clench my eyes shut, never loving and hating my brother more than in this moment. That son of a bitch! For centuries he's run from this, done everything he could to avoid it, while I've searched high and low, begging for it to come to me. Now here he is mated, changed, a guardian. A thunderbird. I want to fucking kill him for this.

It's my turn for hysterics—I start laughing and can't stop. Nate slumps to his belly, muttering once again, "It wasn't supposed to be her." I swear, if I have to keep listening to that, I'm going to gag him. Biting back the retort only drives my disappointment deeper. It was supposed to be Kari—it was supposed to be me, not him. It takes effort to hold those words back and push the thoughts aside. I need to deal with the situation as it is, not as I wish it had been.

My anger seems to have burned away my addled thoughts, and now I can think more clearly. Through gritted teeth I snarl at him to stay put. "I'll be right back, you son of a bitch."

I race through the house and find the women huddled together in the living room. Kari has Jo wrapped in a blanket, her arms around her, and is patting her back. "You're one too, aren't you?" Kari looks up at me as if I'm some kind of monster.

"Not quite yet. Until I do what Nate did, I don't get my wings or anything that comes with them."

"What does that mean? What did Nate do?"

I grimace when I notice the way Jo is trembling—she's in shock, and I might be about to make that worse, assuming what I say even registers with her. "They mated. Jo's his mate—the fates chose them. They were destined for each other." A bitter laugh bursts out of me in spite of my efforts not to be resentful toward Nate and Jo. I still can't fucking believe this is happening ... to him!

Kari looks simultaneously relieved and disappointed. "But ... we're not, right?"

Isn't the devastation etched on my face enough for her to figure that out without asking? I can't keep the scorn from my voice as I point over my shoulder. "Do you see any fucking wings sticking out of me?"

She flinches and turns red. I shake my head—I need to get a grip. "I'm sorry. That wasn't right, and I shouldn't have said it to you. It's just ... we've waited for centuries for this moment. I've always wanted it and Nate never has, and now he gets it while I don't."

"Centuries? What the hell are you guys?" Jo peeks over the edge of the blanket and Kari's arm. Her voice is so low I almost don't hear her.

"We're thunderbirds."

"Thunderbirds?" Kari's eyes widen. "As in the thunderbirds of legend?"

I nod.

"How ... old are you two?" Kari darts a glance at Jo and then back at me.

"We're about twenty-five, but we've lived for five hundred and fifty-three years—we don't age like you." The words have just cleared my lips when Kari passes out. I rush to pick her up off the floor and lay her on the couch. From the bedroom, Nate is screaming and moaning; I know he's in pain, but Kari and Jo also need to be handled carefully. Jo manages to go grab a cold, wet rag while I pat Kari's face to revive her.

When she comes to, she sinks as far as she can into the cushions. Mere minutes ago she couldn't get enough of my touch, and now she doesn't want me near her at all. I move back a couple of steps. "Kari, I need you to do me a favor, please."

She looks at me, and I'm not sure she'll do it, but if she doesn't, then Nate and I are going to have to go through this alone. "I want you to take my pickup and go back to the rez, find your healer and seer ... tell them what is going on with Nate. No one has ever told us what happens now or what comes next, and the way he's screaming, I think he needs help."

Kari sounds defiant. "I'll go, but I'm not leaving Jo here."

I really don't care at this point if Jo stays or goes, so I nod as I grab the keys from the tray on the counter. "Please bring your healer back here as quick as possible."

She sucks in a deep breath before asking me to get Jo's clothes from the other room. I hurry back into my brother's bedroom and find him still lying on the floor, sweating profusely. He's rambling on about a wildfire, the tricksters, a diversion ditch, and riding his Harley, which of course he still hasn't replaced. His wings are lifted and form an arc over his back, almost as if they are stroking his body. I'm going to have to get him into bed, but I need to get Kari on her way first.

Once I've collected everything of Jo's I can find, I take it out to the living room and wait while the girls go into the bathroom. They come out a few moments later with Jo dressed but not looking any better; her face is flushed, streaked with tears, and her eyes are swollen. I'm at a loss for words, but I feel I ought to say something. "Jo, I'm sorry ... What's happened here ... shit. We're kind of like family now, and I need you to come back when you've had time to think about this. Okay?"

She gives me a look of sheer terror, and something tells me it's not going to be easy to get her to come back. But what else can I do? I watch the women get in my pickup and pull down the driveway toward the county road.

Even if Kari is able to talk the healer into coming here, it will be after daylight when they arrive. Until then I've got to do my best to help Nate through this change. Inhaling the warm night air, I try to push my jealousy aside—my brother still needs me.

I return to his room and struggle to get him off the floor. He's so out of it that he's no help to me at all, but his wings are in my way, and other than grabbing him under the arms while facing him, I can't think of a way to pack him over to his bed. The pain I can see he's in tells me not to jostle him too much and to avoid touching his wings.

In order to get him on the bed, I have to fall onto it, pulling him down with me. Then I work myself out from under him as gently as I can while trying to ignore the fact that he's on top of me stark fucking naked. A part of me is glad he's not all there; the last thing I want is for him to remember this uncomfortable situation. It's bad enough that I will—and I don't give a shit if we did share the same womb for nine months.

After I have Nate as comfortable as possible, I fetch a large bowl with ice water and rags—he's burning up. I do what I can to lay the cold, damp rags over his body, but it's hard to keep up with since the rags dry out too quickly and I can't swap them out fast enough. When the ice melts and the water warms, I empty the bowl and start all over again. Nate moans, screams, cries, and whimpers throughout the ordeal. A few times he calls my name, but he doesn't seem to understand that I'm right here doing all I can to help him.

It's a huge relief when Kari returns a little after eight o'clock with not only the healer and seer, but another she introduces as an elder. I greet the two women and the man and show them back to Nate's room. Kari remains in the living room—I can tell she doesn't want to be here, but she has no way home unless I take her or she leaves when the others do. Jo isn't with her, which doesn't surprise me, and I'm beginning to think it was a mistake letting her leave. We're all in this together; if she is my brother's mate, that makes her my sister, and I've already let her down, whether she knows it or not.

Naomi, the healer, asks for as much detail as I can give her about our history and what we've learned from others over the centuries. She's obviously in over her head—this isn't something anyone today has knowledge of, and she's as much in the dark as I am about how to care for Nate. But at least she has healing skills, which is far more than I can offer him. The seer, Donna, observes the choices we make; she hasn't contributed anything yet, and I'm not sure she even needs to be here. The elder, Jim, does what he can to assist Naomi, but it's clear we're doing this blind. My brother is suffering for our lack of knowledge.

It's midday when Jim tells me to take Kari home, as Nate's fever and delirium may not break anytime soon. Kari nods curtly and without a word storms out of the house. By the time I climb into the pickup, she's already sitting there, her arms folded across her chest, staring straight ahead. Disgust and fear mar her beautiful face. Granted, I've accepted by now that Kari isn't the one, but I've never had to be around a woman who clearly regretted being intimate with me. I try apologizing, but she doesn't want to hear it ... she doesn't want to hear anything from me. We fall into an awkward silence for most of the drive. The slightly less than two-hour drive to the rez is long and uncomfortable. When I pull up to her place, she says one thing to me as she gets out of the pickup: "Forget you ever met me. I don't want to see you again."

What the hell can I say to that? In the span of a few hours, she went from liking me to eagerly participating in great sex with me to discovering I'm not entirely human. We have no future together—not that she'd want one with me now any more than I'd continue pursuing her. But her attitude sure proves that she never was the one I'm seeking, the one I still need to find. None of us would be in this mess if I hadn't run away from Emily—it's one decision I'm coming to regret, even if she wasn't the one either.

The drive back to the ranch seems twice as long as the drive out. My head feels as if it will explode from the tangle of thoughts that grows bigger with each new question I can't answer. Do we have to hide Nate from the public now, or is it time to let the world know what we are? Will the wings stay on display, or is it possible to tuck them back inside? Where does Jo fit in? Is she meant to be a guardian too?

I don't know what this means going forward—there are still too many unknowns. But worse is the shadow this creates over us.

What if I never get my wings, and I'm the one doomed to die of old age? What the fuck have I done to deserve to be punished like this? All of my efforts have failed, leaving me unworthy and denied entirely of this honor. Why?

My brother has disrespected the idea for centuries and done all he can to avoid it. Yet he's chosen? Rewarded? Fucking jerk doesn't deserve wings!

CHAPTER 13: NATE
The Past Fulfilled

There is something terribly wrong with me. Every cell in my body is screaming so loudly, I can barely think. I'm lying helpless on sweat-soaked sheets, chills racking my body as another set of violent shudders course through me, and the same three voices I've been listening to for who knows how long are still in a heated debate. The only voice I want to hear is my brother's, but before I lost the ability to talk, they ignored my earlier pleas, and now they act as if I'm not even here. If my body weren't in this state, with my back on fire, I'd be closing their mouths with my fists. Shut the hell up already and help me!

No, I can't muster a word or even move—those abilities abandoned me hours, maybe days ago. Instead I slip from the searing heat scorching my bones to a half awareness of the incessant bickering and then back into tormented darkness. Pitch black surrounds me again and again in a collision of confusing sensations. I feel fire engulfing my body while feathers lightly brush over my skin in a sweet caress, though I'm unsure if the feathers are cooling the burn or fanning the flames higher. Incredible agony rips through me, shredding tissue and bone and turning my insides into an intolerable molten mass. Death would be better than this, but it doesn't want to take me. No, it seems the fates have other ideas for my life, whether I want it or not.

A flicker of a memory comes to me, and my mind leaps to snatch it—I've been here before. Not quite to this degree, but it hurt like hell the last time too, even if this is worse, a thousand painful shades worse. Slowly I realize that the earlier episode was a piss-poor taste of what I'm enduring now. Then, too, I spent days slipping between darkness and a feverish, delirious reality. But I wasn't alone—my brother was there suffering alongside me, and our parents cried, prayed, sang, and waited as the healer brought us through it. I remember very little of what anyone said, but I retain a vivid memory of the ordeal, as well as the haunting aftermath my brother and I have lived with since.

We were ten ... it was five hundred and forty-three years ago that our lives started down this path, but after four centuries I gave up trying to kill myself. Since then I've longed to grow old and die as quickly as this gradual progression of life will allow. Old age is the only way to achieve it, and a big fat "if" hangs over that possibility like a storm cloud.

Rather, it did until now. All that belongs in the past, because I'm never going to grow old and die. Thanks to Jo ... Mrs. Right-but-oh-so-wrong-for-me. Fuck, was I ever wrong about cheating immortality. It was arrogant to believe I could sneak around the curse by avoiding the one sure thing that would freeze me in time. That is the very thing biting me in the ass now, and its teeth are sinking further into my bones with each excruciatingly painful hour that passes. There is no way to stop it—but that doesn't mean I won't mangle that bitch if I ever lay eyes on her again. She had to have known ... played me like a tool. I don't want her. I don't want this!

From outside the darkness, the sound of squabbling voices tells me this nightmare isn't over. My mind races, but I keep stumbling over one thought: it wasn't supposed to be her.

Finding the Right Path

It's been a week since I left Kari on the rez, and I've put forth a colossal effort to handle the ranch work by myself. Trying to keep things going around here splits my focus between work and Nate. His condition hasn't changed, and I'm beginning to freak out—this can't be the way it's supposed to go. Naomi, Donna, and Jim have come to the same conclusion, and they're reaching out to other tribes with thunderbird stories, hoping for a solution.

The problem is that the legends stretch from a couple of the eastern woodland tribes, across the plains, and to the Pacific Northwest. We can't even seek answers from the people we came from, because as our tribe died off, the few survivors were absorbed into other tribes throughout the region. It's doubtful their descendants can even recall the people the Ancestors came from; most don't even recognize our tribal name, Hachaath. The other modern Nootka tribes may not share the exact beliefs of our lost tribe either. Nate and I are the only ones left who truly remember, and even our memory is spotty, given the amount of time we have spent moving around as we slowly aged.

The first possible lead comes from a seer in Oklahoma whose tribe originally inhabited the eastern woodlands. The man has several questions that the three tribal members here can't answer; they have no choice but to put me on the phone. I swear the man is a proverbial question block, because it seems he never runs out of things to ask. He's run the gamut of diet, exercise, history, differences between Nate and me, and where we lived when we reached certain milestones, such as puberty or the loss of our virginity. I give him all the answers I can, but I don't see how any of this is helping. If anything, it's as useless as I am when it comes to ending Nate's transformation nightmare.

Afterward I sit in a chair in the corner of Nate's room, watching the ongoing torment. If it weren't for the fact that my brother can't die now, I'd be concerned that this ordeal was going to kill him. The agony, the delirium, the wings that have molted and grown back three times—it scares the crap out of me, and for the first time in my life, I consider that maybe it isn't such a good idea to become a guardian. This long life has been hard enough to experience, and I can't see the blessing in being made to suffer for days, weeks, possibly years or more. Thinking this was a great gift was a big mistake on my part.

The Belknap trio has gone back to the rez to get additional herbs and medicine, to do more research, and to talk with some of the other elders. I'm surprised we don't have a news crew on our doorstep by now, given how many have learned of Nate's condition ... or rather status as a thunderbird. Everyone swears to hold it to secrecy, but I'll be amazed if we can keep the public from finding out, and that in itself scares me. Not to mention that once it's out there, the news may chase off women, ensuring I never find a mate—or I'll be inundated with wannabes who treat it like a lottery winning.

"Damn it, Nate, I wish you'd come out of it. No one has a damn clue how to help you."

His body is trembling and flushed with fever, but for a brief moment his face clears and his gaze meets mine. As his eyes roll back into his head, I hear something, but too quiet for me to understand. "Nate?" I move over to the bed and sit next to him. "Do you know what you need, bro?"

He swallows hard but doesn't open his eyes. On the faintest whisper comes the word "Jo."

Jo? Didn't she already do her part? I don't understand if he thinks she can help or if he simply wants her because he recognizes that she's his mate. I call Naomi; she doesn't know either but is willing to go down another badger hole to find out. She promises to call me back later. Oh yes, let's take a century to figure this crap out, because watching my brother live in chronic pain is so much fun.

Sitting this close to Nate reminds me that it's been over a week since he showered—the overripe smell of his body is getting to be a bit much. Hygiene is way beyond his capability, though he'll shoot me if he finds out we stuck him in adult diapers. Since no one else is around right now, I decide to drag his nasty ass into the shower. The problem is that I doubt he'll fit into the shower stall with his wings out. The solution comes to me quickly, and I attach a Y hose connector to the washing machine water lines, add a length of hose to reach the backyard, and adjust the taps so the water won't be too cold or too hot. After laying out soap, shampoo, conditioner, a blanket, and a few towels, I go back to Nate's room and drag him out of bed.

He's lost weight in this past week, so it's slightly easier to maneuver him now than it was when I first picked him up off the floor. I wrestle him into position against the outside wall of the house, pinning him there as I open the sprayer nozzle. Too late I realize that I should have changed into shorts; my clothes and boots are going to be drenched. I do my best to hold him upright while trying to work the hose and wash and rinse his hair and body one-handed, which becomes a major challenge, as his wet wings seem to triple his weight. I'm soaked by the time he's as clean as I can get him. Drying him off is another interesting proposition, and I mostly leave him to air-dry on the blanket I've spread out on the lawn.

I strip his bed and remake it with clean sheets and blankets, then lug him off the ground and bring him back inside to bed. I'm hoping the shower helped; he seems a little quieter now, but it could just be a repeat of what he's been doing for a week now. Scream, thrash, moan ... reset ... whimper, cry, sleep ... repeat in T-minus twelve hours.

I glance at the clock on the nightstand—it's already two o'clock, and I still have a full day of work ahead. I leave him to rest while I try to get as much done as I can before dark. We're falling behind on our work, and I'm unsure whether I should tell Matt that Nate is sick or just keep hoping that the boss doesn't show up here anytime soon. When—if—I get Nate back on his feet, we're going to have to go double time to get back on schedule.

It's well after dark when I call it a day. Nate is still the same. Unsurprisingly, there's been no call from Naomi or anyone else from the Belknap trio. Too tired to cook dinner, I raid the fridge for leftovers—not much of that either. I'm putting my plate in the dishwasher when my phone rings. It's Naomi—I hope she has some news for a change.

"I talked with Jerry, the Peoria elder from Oklahoma. He had a bit of a sensitive question that I couldn't answer." I can hear a tinge of embarrassment in her voice.

Of course he did—the man never runs out of them. "What is it?"

She clears her throat. "Your brother was in the act of having sex when his wings came out ..."

That's common knowledge by now. Added to the whole fucking nightmare when Kari and I went into that room. I'll never forget the sight of Jo frantically trying to get out from under him and Nate lying there naked, incapable of moving. "Yeah, you've heard this before."

There's a long pause, and I'm not sure why. Then Naomi says, "Were they still coupled when you knocked him off her?"

What the hell? Where his dick was isn't something I noticed or gave thought to, and I doubt he can tell us. It's not something I particularly want to find out either. "Why does that matter?"

"Jerry thinks you may have interrupted the process. He spoke with a seer who has the gift of knowing—her senses are often correct. From what she described, it sounds like there may be a state of locking between the couple when they can't physically separate their bodies until the transformation is complete. If Nate was still in the midst of that when you forced them apart, he may be stuck in an incomplete or in-between stage."

Are they blaming me? "Are you saying we should have left him frozen and Jo freaking out like she was being raped?" That's messed up—I've done everything I can to help Nate. This is too much to believe. If she'd seen the terror and panic on Nate's and Jo's faces, I'm not sure she would have told them to carry on.

Naomi sounds exasperated. "It's the best we've come up with yet, and everything else we've tried has failed."

"What are you suggesting?"

She blows out a long, slow breath. "After my talk with Jerry, this was discussed with Jim and Donna. We think that Jolenthia needs to come back and finish what they started."

I about drop the phone, but I can't withhold a harsh laugh. Jo hasn't called, and when they tried to reach her through Kari, they learned that Jo had disappeared. How in the hell do they expect to find her and get her back here, let alone convince her to resume having sex with Nate? Aside from Jo probably thinking Nate's a monster—it's unlikely she'd want to see him, let alone touch him— I'm not sure he'd want to have sex with her either. Not after what's happened to him. Hell, he can't even give his consent. Wouldn't that be rape? "There has to be another way. None of us know where she is, and after the way she reacted, I doubt she'll ever come near him again."

"She has no choice. If the legend is true, they're mated. She won't be able to stay away forever." Naomi sounds confident, though somehow I doubt she is.

"If you think she needs to return, then you're going to have to get Kari to help locate her. It's their friendship that brought Jo up here to begin with." It should be Jo's choice, too, and not something they force on her—I can see all sorts of ways this could get worse than it already is. It doesn't take a genius to figure out that she's not going to talk to me.

Is there something else we're missing, or is this natural—and Nate just needs more time? I don't have any ideas, but if something doesn't change, I'll have to relocate Nate to the rez. I can't risk Matt showing up here and seeing my brother in the state he's in.

Three days later the Belknap trio arrives at the ranch, and to my surprise they have Jo with them. How did they find her? Scratch that—how did they talk her into coming back to the house? One look at her, and I can tell she doesn't want to be here—that's written in every feature of her face and in her tense posture.

I stand aside as they come through the door, and I don't miss how Jo keeps as much space between us as possible. She won't look at me either. How is she supposed to help Nate if she can't even acknowledge that I'm standing two feet away from her? We go into the living room, Jo sitting as far from me as she can get. She cringes and folds in on herself at the moaning noises followed by Nate's scream—his torment continues. I need to find out what they hope to accomplish if she's that reluctant to help.

"Naomi?" I look at her with questions in my eyes. Where do I even start?

She glances at Jo before her gaze returns to me. "We found Jolenthia in Havre, thanks to Kari. Jolenthia, understandably, didn't want to come back here. This has been quite an upsetting ordeal for her, as you can imagine."

"Then why did she come?" Jo still won't look at me; how much of that has to do with the twin factor or with her discovery of what we are is anyone's guess.

Donna says, "Jolenthia came because she respects the elders and the council—she's not here out of any consideration for you or your brother."

Whatever guilt I felt for letting her down and allowing her to leave when this first happened flies straight out the window. If his condition doesn't concern her, then she doesn't concern me. Regardless, it doesn't make sense that she'd care about the elders or council either. "She's not tribal." It's all I can say, because anything else will cause her to flee again, and Nate may need her.

Jim says, "Jolenthia is of mixed heritage, including Chippewa and Assiniboine. She has ties to family on Belknap."

No fucking way. The girl looks as white as white can be. In spite of myself I walk over to her and force her to look me in the eye. It's then I see it, or at least I think I do now that I'm looking closely enough. The cut of Jo's high cheekbones and the hint of dark brown, nearly black showing through the roots of her artificially lightened brown hair—even the almond shape of her dark-green eyes carry a hint of her ethnicity. How did Nate never see this? He was always so careful. I can't decide whether to laugh or cry at the absurdity. If Nate ever gets through this, he's going to have a stroke.

I walk back to my chair and sit down in defeat. "So, what now?"

"Now Jolenthia must choose a path, and in so doing she will either claim a future with Nate or doom him to this in-between stage, where he can never fully transform yet can never go back."

My stomach falls through the floor. The thought of my brother spending eternity or even multiple centuries the way he is now is unfathomable. It'd be far worse than taking a long vacation in hell. I look at Jo and wonder if she could be that cruel. Her arms are crossed, her fingers digging into her biceps as her chin tucks against her shoulder, fixing her gaze decidedly away from me. Her body language tells me everything I need to know.

CHAPTER 15: NATE
From Bad to Worse

I'm certain several days have passed now, though I don't have a clue how many, and I'm more lucid—even if the pain hasn't lessened. I'm slowly adapting to this new hell. At least the bickering people seem to have left, and Rafe is doing what he can for me. But no one seems to understand what is happening or when this fucking nightmare will end, and I'm beginning to think it never will. I need to find a way out of the pain holding me hostage.

The worst part is being unable to communicate my suffering, thirst, and hunger ... and my body's deep, unrelenting need for Jo. I'm not sure which is worse, the excruciating spasms when they ripped her away from me or the constant torture I've endured since. Why are they doing this to me? Why are they keeping her from me? I can think the words, form the sentences in my mind, but they fall apart before they reach my tongue. At least one of my needs has been met—Rafe will never know how grateful I was that he dragged me outside to shower. I was at the point where I couldn't stand smelling myself or the bed I've been confined to.

My raw anger at Jo has lessened somewhat, with one thought pounding its way to the forefront: Jo is my mate, and I desperately need her. But fuck! I want no part of her, and yet I may not have a damn choice; I can't get Jo out of my head. Every time I close my eyes, I see her. If I inhale deeply enough, I can smell her, and I can still feel the last moments I spent with her—the physical ache in my bones, the remnant of the way we merged together and then were torn apart, reignites the searing agony throughout my body. We shouldn't have been separated ... it wasn't done. And somehow I understand that this torment won't end until she comes back to me.

Then a vision of my salvation enters my line of sight—I just don't know if she's real or if I'm losing my fucking mind. I want to go to her and pull her into my arms, but I still have no control over my body. I try to will my arm to move, my fingers to reach, yet can't summon so much as a twitch. Teeth clenched, I try once more, drawing every ounce of strength I possess. And I fail again. Through hitched breaths my thoughts force a two-word sentence to my dead tongue—*Help me*. The words fall away like vapor. After a couple of minutes of struggling, I finally breathe out a single plea: "Jo."

In the doorway behind her stand Rafe and the ones I assume have been arguing over me. I need her. I need her to be real. "Jo ..."

She takes a hesitant step and waits a few beats before moving forward again. Damn it, let her be real. I will go insane if she's not. Halfway between me and the door, she looks back and says, "Can you give us some privacy?"

Rafe looks sick, and I can tell he's torn about what he should do. I try to plead with my eyes—he needs to understand that she's the only one who can help me. At this point I'd almost forgive her if she could just get me past this hell. "Jo ..." I'd bribe her with the damn moon—a house, a car, whatever price she'd demand—if it meant she'd come the rest of the way to me and end this torture.

My brother reaches for the doorknob and closes the door, shutting out those standing with him in the hall. It's just me and her now, but she's not coming to me, and I'm in horrible need of her touch—desperate for it. Only she can cool the fire burning inside me. I'm begging with my eyes, but she just stands there, and it's killing me. "Jo." She must know that I need her to end my torment.

She finally takes another step and then yet another, and my breathing quickens, but she stops just beyond my reach—not that I could move to touch her, regardless of how much I want to. I need her so badly, and the distance of this nearness is only causing the fire inside to burn hotter, blackening the marrow in my bones. "Jo!" The damn woman stays where she is and sits cross-legged on the floor. For the longest moment of my life, she just sits and stares at me. I can feel tears well in my eyes—I'm in so much fucking agony, and only she can stop it. My attempt to push words to my tongue fails again. How else can I make her understand?

Her eyes meet mine, and her voice is so soft, I almost can't hear it. "The others made me come back. They say you're like this because we didn't finish ..." She's wringing her hands in her lap. "A seer says we have to finish, or you'll be like this forever. That's the only reason I'm here. I'm not cruel, and I can't leave you like this, but ..."

What's cruel is her doing this to me in the first place.

Jo grimaces and looks away, then makes eye contact with me again. "I don't even know you. I can't be your mate or whatever this is supposed to be. I don't want you to suffer, but I don't want to be with you either."

A new pain radiates through me—one I've never felt before, but it's eerily similar to the heartache I knew when my parents died. "Jo ..." It seems to be the only word I can utter. Damn it, I need her. "Jo!"

"I just want to make sure we're clear about this." She stands and starts removing her clothes. "We'll finish whatever it is that we were supposed to do, but when it's done I'm leaving, and we won't see each other again. Understand?" She drops her bra to the floor, a fiercely determined glint in her eyes.

I feel more tears spill down my face, but I'm still unable to say a thing. My body aches for her touch, yearning for her soothing embrace as much as it craves to ... no, *must* unite with her and claim what is rightfully ours. I can't live without her. Not now, not ever again. She is mine. I'm hers. I must stop her from leaving me when we finish this.

But no—no. I don't want this curse ... her. Once she does what she needs to do, she can go. Fuck me, why does that seem so wrong?

Jo's movements are self-conscious and reluctant. I want to reach out and touch her, assure her that this is where she belongs, but no matter what I try, I can't fucking move. When she finally closes the distance between us and I feel her trembling hand touch my shoulder, I breathe in the first bit of relief I've had since she left. I still can't move, but she seems to understand, just lies down next to me, looking into my tear-filled eyes. It should be impossible to simultaneously desire and despise someone as much as I do her, yet it rips my heart out when I see the sadness fill her face and I know I can't do anything to stop it. Deep down I know that I can never agree to let her go from my life again.

Then slowly she wedges her body beneath mine. The more contact she makes, the more my body responds—a finger twitch, curled toes, a flexed bicep—and then my hamstrings tighten and relax. My cock hardens. Soon this will all be over. The scorching spasms ebb, and the fire starts to cool.

When she's squarely under me, I rest my forehead on hers, breathing her in, and my heart stills, untwists. "Jo, please." Unbelievable, I'm actually begging her ... I never thought I'd beg a woman for anything, let alone this. But if she knew how excruciating this closeness is, this inability to move my body to touch her, she'd wrap herself around me and never let go. I should never have pursued her in the first place. I know that now, to my regret.

I feel her hand slip between us as she guides me to where I need to be. Oh, her touch ... absolute perfection, an erotic healing balm, soothing and tantalizing. It seems to take her some effort to wiggle her body down under my dead weight before she's in position to take all of me in, but once she's there, my body seizes again, just as it did during our first encounter. Again I can't breathe—I can't move. My thoughts flicker between hatred and love, disgust and wonder. I find myself wanting, no, needing to look into her dark-green eyes, but unlike last time, Jo isn't looking at me—not even with a horrified expression. Her eyes are screwed shut so tight that I doubt daylight could penetrate her lids. I need her to look at me. I need to feel every bit of the connection between us. "Jo ..."

Desperation creates a new ache inside me as her eyelids clench tighter—she must look at me. In a dilatory manner her eyelids relax, and then her eyelashes flutter and slowly rise, but not quite opening. It's torturous for me, waiting in anticipation of what I might see. Will she release me from this prison? I have to know.

The slow lift of her lids gradually reveals the deep green of her eyes. I capture her gaze, and a moment later I feel something inside me shift.

Almost as if my body was frozen before, it now begins to thaw, and sensations other than pain return to my limbs. A cooling heat spreads, nerves tingle, and something indescribable builds inside me, soothing my pain-wracked body. It takes some effort, but I manage to bring my hands up to her face and cup it between my palms. "Thank you ... thank the Creator for you coming back to me."

Now it's her turn for tears, and I brush them away with my thumbs, wanting to take them away forever. I don't want her to hurt because of this—because of me. Not knowing what else to do, I press my lips to hers, hoping for one of her sweet kisses, but she refuses to respond. I feel the pang in my heart—my mate is rejecting me. It's not supposed to be like this. I need to fix it. But then, I'm not sure we should fix this; maybe the best thing she can do is get the fuck away from me when this is over. There's no forgiving her for what she's done. And yet I don't want her to leave me. The insane notion that she must stay by my side accompanies a possessiveness I've never felt before. It's irrational. I close my eyes, trying to push through my conflicting thoughts. Our bodies are locked together now, and the only thing I can think to do is follow my instincts and move. At least she responds to that; soon we're in the same rhythm and moving as one.

I'm not sure how much time passes, but I'm uncomfortably aware that Jo still won't look at me, she won't kiss me, and with her hands clutching the sheets in a death grip, it's clear she doesn't want to touch me. But she must. I wrap myself as tight to her as I can while our bodies build each other up higher and higher, and instinct propels me to lift us from the bed. My slightly extended wings beat a steady pace as we hover a couple of feet above the mattress. I know we will fall again together, and whatever happens this time, my physical torment will end.

What I'm not prepared for is that apparently this isn't a one-way street. Her arms wrap suddenly around my waist, followed a second later by her fingernails digging into my back. Warm blood trickles from the gouges she's leaving in my flesh. Jo screams. Her eyes are tightly closed, and her face is a contorted mask of pain and horror. Her skin ripples along her back, forcing me to readjust my hold. This can't be. No fucking way is this happening. Tips of wings come into view as Jo's back arches and bows while I hold her firmly against me. Her wings match mine in color. Did she know? Why would she hide this from me after what happened? Did she disguise her marks before? Body makeup, maybe, but why?

Mind whirling on overload, I struggle to process what is happening. I want to rub at my eyes, as if that will somehow clear my head or make sense of what I'm witnessing. Her wings give a hard shudder to clear the moisture from the feathers. She gasps, her deep-green eyes boring into me with such revulsion that I almost let go of her. But I'm awed by the sight of her. I sense her unasked questions too, though I can't find one single answer. No, Jo didn't have any marks like Rafe and I, but there's no denying the wings sprouting from her back.

I rotate us upward so that we're perpendicular to the floor, my arms secured low around her waist with my hands locked together at the small of her back to avoid her wings. She flinches, repositioning her brutal grasp so her fingernails are now digging into my shoulders—as though I might drop her. I will never let her fall. There's no room for either of us to fully extend our wings in this room, but her wings beat in time with mine. Her fear and revulsion are palpable. She's on the verge of hyperventilating, and yet our bodies are on the edge of release. In spite of myself I reach past her shoulder to feel the leading edge of her wing. It's so soft. Sexy as fuck. There are no words to describe the sensations coursing through me. I'm amazed and bewildered by what is happening between us, by this beautiful woman in my arms. Why did I ever fight this? How could I not want her now? For the first time in my very long life, I feel complete—whole. Home.

As my body comes down from the high of our union, I can feel another shift happening, the reverse of the moment my wings first exploded from my body. Instinct tells me to recline on the bed, and I rotate us again, hovering above the mattress with Jo on top of me. She instinctually increases the thrust of her wings to keep us from dropping onto the bed. My back arches, and I can feel that slithering sensation—my wings, starting with the wing tips, are once more going into a state of rest under my skin. Her wings beat in a slow, gentle rhythm, settling us softly onto the mattress.

Jo is going through her own completion, and I watch in astonishment as her wings slide back into her body. Did she know and deliberately trap me? Did she ever have a clue what she is? "Jo?" I look at her and shake my head to clear it. Why didn't I see the markings upon her? "Did you ..." What's the best question to ask?

She gives me a terrified look, and the moment our intense physical need for each other ebbs, she disengages her body from mine, scrambling off the bed, and gathers her clothes. Jo's back is to me as she dresses hastily. She was serious, then. She's going to fucking leave me! My heart threatens to shatter against my ribs. "Jo ... don't ... please, stay with me. We need each other."

Tears roll down her cheeks, and she refuses to look at me. A moment later she bolts out the door, and I don't give even a thought to clothes or whoever else may be here—my mate is trying to run away from me. I need her! She needs me. I reach the living room in all my naked glory, only to find Rafe and three strangers on their feet, their gazes whipping between me and the open front door. Without waiting for them to say a word, I run out onto the porch.

Jo is gone. She's nowhere in sight. I feel my wings begin to move. Within seconds they're freed again, and I give them a good hard shake to dry them before I take to the sky. I will get her back!

Chapter 16: Rafe
The New Reality

I'm dumbfounded when first Jo and then a very naked Nate dash out of the house. Then I realize that Nate's wings aren't visible, and I run for the porch, muttering, "Where are they going?" But when I step outside, neither is in sight, and the vehicles are still here. What the hell? I cup my hands to my mouth and holler for Nate and Jo but get no response. There's no way he could be out of hearing range already. On calm, clear days like this, with little wind, I can hear the whistle of a passing train ten miles away. I call for them a couple more times—still nothing. When I turn back to the house, I see the Belknap trio watching me, looking as confused as I feel.

Jim says, "Do you think Nate snatched her while she was fleeing and flew them off somewhere?"

It hadn't occurred to me that we'd be capable of flight; I'm not sure I've gotten past my shock that Nate has wings in the first place. Resentment swells again at the thought. That son of a bitch! Wings, a mate, and immortality. With anger boiling my insides, I look around again to confirm that neither Nate nor Jo is in sight. Damn it. My dickhead brother flew off somewhere, and I have no idea how fast or far he can go. I'm grounded here since my own bullshit wings are still lying dormant—for fuck knows how long, if not forever—and I can't even follow him.

"I don't see any other explanation." I'm thoroughly perplexed. What now? When will he come back? And if he does ... will Jo be with him, willingly or unwillingly? I don't think Nate would hold her against her will, but the mate bond could influence either of them or have other effects—good or bad. "Until he returns, what can we do besides wait?"

Naomi is quick to agree, and the three of them decide to leave—telling me to call if their help is needed after Nate returns. I have no confidence that will even happen. As they pull out of the drive, I scan the sky and the open countryside, but I see nothing other than the work I should be doing. I battle myself to get busy. I've always been responsible when it comes to a job, but now my anger, disappointment, resentment, and confusion have me heading for the house. Grabbing a bottle of bourbon from Nate's stash, I sit down and proceed to get drunk. Good thing he buys several at a time—I may need them in the days ahead.

As the alcohol clouds my mind, I try to put this whole mess in some logical order. I want a mate, he doesn't. He gets one, I don't. I ran toward, he ran away. I prayed and searched for years—sacrificed my dreams to keep us together. We are all we have. Or we were. The punchline is that my mate doesn't exist and the whole business about soulmates is total bullshit. How's that for irony? How did I end up with what he wanted? If I were Nate, would Jo have rejected me? I'm left with too many unknowns ... I can't think anymore. Nate is gone, pulled another one of his disappearing acts, and it may be years before I see him again.

I'm not sure what time it is other than well after dark when I pass out, and when I come to, the sun shining through the living room window sends a stabbing pain through my head. Great, I pulled a Nate, and I'm going to have to suffer through my day. I knew there was a reason I never do this shit. After downing a cup of hot coffee,

I head outside to get my day started. Once more I'm alone doing all the work, and as usual it's too much for one person to handle. Should I call Matt and make up some excuse for Nate, or should I give it more time and hope Matt doesn't show up here unannounced? The more time approach at least puts off the uncomfortable conversation, and considering everything else I'm sorting out right now, it would be best if the boss didn't get involved.

The next couple of days pass the same way, sans the hang-over—learned my lesson there—with me working alone and no word or appearance from Nate. The new corrals are almost finished, and I will have to ask Matt to hire someone to come help raise the barn. Sometime within the next day or two I also need to drive the herd to another grazing site, which will be a tough feat to pull off alone. But if Nate doesn't come back to help, then I'm going to have to move the cows myself or they'll overgraze their section of land.

My resentment ticks up another notch when the weekend rolls around and I can't take time off work to go anywhere. I hope that asshole brother of mine isn't getting drunk and laid, but with my luck he probably is, and I'm angrier than ever that I was doomed to live a long life alone from the start. All this time I thought the tricksters were messing with Nate because he was stubbornly running from this curse, and it turns out they were playing me too. I'd like to shoot a coyote right about now, but there's not one in sight. Hell, I'd even shoot at that damn light-brown wolf, but he's either moved on or is holed up somewhere. Wolves ... wise teachers, my ass. No doubt he's been sitting on the sidelines with Coyote, laughing his ass off at us.

Three weeks pass, and I resign myself to the fact that Nate's never coming back, that we were meant to take different journeys. I wasted centuries holding us together when I could have tried harder to find a mate—or at least done more to earn the honor of being a guardian. My D-list is growing: disappointed, discouraged, depressed, disillusioned, dysfunctional, distraught, disheveled ... don't give a flying fuck anymore. Worse, he's left me in the lurch with the work responsibilities, and I finally have to call Matt and request he hire a couple more men and send them my way. When he asks about Nate, I tell him my brother had to go out of town for a while to take care of a family matter, but will return soon. I'll have to think of some other excuse if that doesn't happen.

Matt is quick to hire new employees, and twenty-four hours after my request Larry and Brian appear on the doorstep, saying they're here to work. On the outside chance Nate does show up, I put them together in the only other finished and available bedroom; at least it has two single beds, otherwise one of them would be sleeping on the couch. We'll need to get started on the bunkhouses soon, though, as I'd rather be left alone outside of work.

Once they're settled into a work routine, I take a much-needed weekend off. This time I don't go to the rez—I know what a waste of time that is now—instead heading down to visit the nightlife in Billings and the strip joint out at Laurel. The strippers want nothing to do with a one-night stand, but I find a couple of willing bed dates at a small dive in Billings. Between throwing money at the dancers and getting laid, I manage to squeeze in three fights—two the first night and one the second. I get back to the ranch with a new D on my list: drained. Now I see why Nate wanted to stay drunk. Life is miserable when death is so far down the road that it feels as if the end will never come. This is my new reality, and I have lots of time to get used to it.

CHAPTER 17: NATE

The Chase is On

I can't fucking believe she ran out like that! I'm so focused on chasing her down—can't let her get away—that it's not until I'm high above the treetops that it dawns on me I'm flying. I'm actually flying! Fuck, what a head rush. A smile breaks across my face as I soar after her; she may have a head start, but I'm not letting her get away. I'll follow her to the ends of the Earth if I have to. I must convince her to come back ... I will make this up to her.

If I can catch her. Because shit, she's fast. My wings beat as quickly as they can, but I'm not gaining on her. I was hoping she'd be slower than me since she's female and smaller—if we're equals, this could take a while. I have to believe we'll tire at some point, because it's impossible for her to evade me for an eternity.

My wings pump harder, and I climb higher in the sky when she does. It's a relief to be less noticeable to anyone on the ground, especially with me flying naked. So far that's my only regret—she's clothed and I'm not. While a flying person is hard enough to explain, a naked flying man ... well, let's just say the last thing I need is to be the butt of fucking jokes about it. And I have no doubt Rafe will have plenty of bullshit comments after seeing me run out and disappear the way I did.

Flying people ... but are we still people now that we're immortal? If I ever fucking catch Jo, we'll have to find an elder and ask those questions. Yet there are other answers I need from her before these trivial issues are resolved. She needs to look me in the eye and explain how she hid what she was. I have to know whether this was a game to her, if she somehow knew what I was and set me up. But if she knew, why did she freak out like that?

It's getting dark when she finally descends, and I keep my eye on the slight gap where she disappeared into the canopy of trees. That's another perk I discover: my eyesight is sharper than ever before, and it seems that my hearing is more acute too. I'm still marveling over that when I get my first lesson on landing. Instinct tells me to use my wings to slow myself down, but what it doesn't tell me is that the space between the trees is too small to accommodate my huge wingspan and break my speed at the same time. Not that knowing this will help me now. I'm in a shitload of trouble. My left wing catches on a limb, and I start to tumble, hitting branches on my way down to the ground. There's not enough room to right myself or arrest my fall. A painful grunt expels a lungful of air as I hit the dirt with a thud, one wing folded uncomfortably beneath me. Damn it, that fucking hurt.

Hauling myself to my feet, I turn around and see Jo sitting on the ground, looking dazed and cradling a wing—doubtless she got the same lesson. Shit, I hope she didn't break anything. Her eyes are throwing razor blades at me, and I'm suddenly reminded that my mate doesn't want me anywhere near her or at all. In truth, I don't want her either, but despite myself I can't let her go. "You okay, Jo?" I take a deep breath as I approach her.

She tries to scooch back, but she doesn't lift her other wing enough to gain the ground she needs. The only thing she manages to do is trip over herself and fall backward. I kneel beside her and extend a hand to hold her wing while I look over her injury. She flinches and shrinks away.

"Let me look. We need to know how bad it is." I take the injured wing gently in my hands to inspect the wound, ignoring her distrustful expression. "It doesn't look like anything is broken, but you have a nasty gash and a few missing feathers. Do you heal fast?"

"I always have." But her eyebrows furrow, followed by a look of astonishment as she sweeps her gaze over me.

"Then this might be healed come morning," I say.

"You're naked," she says through clenched teeth.

"Really? That might explain why it felt a bit drafty while I was flying. Damn, Jo, you're observant." Her less than witty observation is ridiculous beyond measure. "You didn't leave me enough time to get dressed, and you're not much better yourself. Have you seen your shirt?"

She looks down and gasps. Yeah, that's what I thought. When she took off, she let her wings out without thinking about her clothes, and the force of the wings unfurling ripped the shirt apart, leaving the collar and sleeves holding what remains of the fabric in place. Given the bare flesh I see, I'm guessing her bra met the same fate. Jo tries to hold the shirt together and get on her feet, but she stumbles, exposing her bare breasts. When I reach to help her, she jerks away. "Don't touch me!"

Here we go. "It may surprise you, but I didn't want this either, and for centuries I did everything I could to avoid it. I had no idea you were the one. My dreams always showed a woman who appeared Native."

She looks down at the ground, quiet for a long minute. "I'm mixed," she says with a huff that seems to carry a hint of disgust. "I'm a pale Indian, thanks to white genes from a white parent." That doesn't make sense. Not that she's pale, but that I never noticed her Native traits, something I and many other Natives intuitively discern about others of mixed descent, regardless how different they are from the stereotype of darker complexion, dark-brown eyes, and black hair. "What tribe?"

"Chippewa and Assiniboine."

There are a few light-skinned, light-eyed people in both of those tribes, but Jo is as white as white can get, short of being a ghost. "But your hair, and ..." And I look at her—at the black roots of her hair and the shape of her eyes—from a different perspective, and I sort of see it. It was there the whole time, but her allure drew me in—I was blinded by the sheer beauty of her features, failing to really see who she was. "Fuck." I drop my head into my hands. "If I had known, I wouldn't have pursued you, but..." Even now I feel so drawn to her that I can't leave her alone, even knowing I should run as far from her as I can get. "You must have felt something too?"

Jo's eyes flash with anger. "Oh, I felt something all right. Try betrayed, hurt, repulsed, disgusted. And then to have to come back here .... the last thing I ever wanted to do was have sex with you again. But the nightmare didn't end there, did it?" Now her dainty finger is poking my chest, but it's not causing as much pain as her words. "No. Like a communicable disease, it infected me and turned me into a half-bird freak too."

"How old are you?" Shouldn't she be centuries old, like Rafe and I? This can't be ....

"I'm twenty-two." She sounds as if she's on the verge of hysteria. She looks it too.

"As in twelve months equals a year, twenty-two?" She gives me a puzzled look. So she wasn't a thunderbird before. Did I infect her, like she said? Is that even possible? "You never had any hint of wings or weird illnesses when you were a child?"

"I've never been sick a day in my life."

"Whoa, hold it right there." I grip her arms and look into her eyes. "That's not fucking likely. You had to have been sick at some point."

She looks away, her jaw clenched. I've hit a nerve, but whatever the problem is, she's not ready to share it. I drop my hands and take a step back to scrutinize her from head to toe. If she wasn't already a thunderbird in the making, is there something in her human genes that not only prevented illness but was designed to lure a nonhuman like me? Did the fates craft her as a trap? Now it's my turn to feel betrayed and hurt: I was tricked into this mess. "Look, it's getting late, and I don't want to fight. Let's just get some damn sleep. We'll sort this out in the morning."

"Provided you sleep over there"—she nods toward the tree fifteen feet behind me—"and I stay here."

It's obvious she doesn't want me near her, and the compulsion to take the cautious route here has me agreeing, even though what I want is to wrap her in my wings and hold her all night. I shake my head to clear it; a thousand thoughts and questions are parading through my mind, and the last thing I need is to pile in more by insisting she stay close to me. "Fine, but if you get scared or cold, tell me and I'll come to you."

I don't wait for her answer; I just stride to the base of the tree she assigned me and recline against the trunk, determined to keep my eyes on her. I shift uncomfortably against the rough bark—I'd much rather be in a soft bed or even have her ample breasts under me. No, instead I have jagged pieces of bark digging into my back. It's then that I notice my wings aren't even out anymore. I'm not sure when they retracted—I must be getting used to the way they slide in and out. For the longest time I can't close my eyes, afraid that if I do, Jo won't be here when I wake up. But then sleep catches me, and before I know it I'm cocooned in my wings for warmth and opening my eyes to daylight filtering through the feathers.

I pull a wing back and look in Jo's direction, wondering how she slept. My heart stutters and stops. She's not fucking there! I leap to my feet and look around the thin stand of trees, but I don't see her anywhere. What the fuck? Where the hell did she go? The only sounds I hear are forest noises and a chipmunk or two. Damn it! Maybe I should have throttled her when I had the chance.

I doubt that I can launch into the sky through the gap in the tree canopy, so I do another quick circle to find an area where the trees may be further apart. A hundred yards away the trees are thinner, but when I reach the spot, I realize it's still going to be a tight squeeze. My wings flap anyway, and I shoot into the air, just clearing the trees on my way skyward. I rotate, hoping to glimpse her silhouette in the distance, but all I see are other birds. I fly higher so that I can look further and scan more of the ground below.

She's out of sight. Now I panic, and son of a bitch, my chest hurts. I can't let her get away! She's my mate. We're meant to do this together. Not even the cold bitches of fate could be this cruel—give her to me just to doom me, then let her get away. Could they? No, no ... she's supposed to be with me. I can feel that truth in the deepest center of my soul.

A strange pulse moving through my head compels me to turn— I sense it's been there awhile, but I'm just beginning to understand it. At first I thought it was a lingering effect of my transformation, something like a hangover, but now I realize there is the faintest echo of her essence tied to it. When I'm facing the direction where it feels strongest, the pulse warms and settles into a strange thrum that seems to travel along my bones. It resonates loudly when I face north but drops to a barely perceptible sensation when I'm looking elsewhere. Could it be? So little is known about the thunderbirds, and I'm wondering if there's some type of mate sensor pointing me in her direction. I smile at the thought. If that's the case, then she can run—fly—but she'll never hide from me for long. The chase is on!

After the first full day of following but never catching Jo, I realize that I'm going to need clothes and food. She may have me chasing her, but I won't go hungry and stay exposed to the elements because of her shenanigans. While I may be immortal now, I can still get cold and hungry—surprisingly. Besides, being a half-starved naked flying man is insulting to my pride. I spot a clothesline full of laundry, swoop down, and land, but I don't take time to dress; instead I fly off to an area screened with trees, where I won't be seen. The jeans are a little loose on my hips, but they'll do for now. The muscle-cut T-shirt is open on the sides almost to my waist and big enough that I think I can wear it without tearing it to shreds or hindering my wings. The leather clothing of my ancestors was likely better for this condition—I could fashion and sew whatever I needed. Commercial clothes? Not so much of a ready solution.

My next stop is a little trickier, since I don't have any money on me and no weapons even to hunt small critters like rabbits. I circle high in the sky until I spot smoke from a backyard barbecue—smells like steak and probably chicken. I pause, hovering midair, thinking about the latter. Is it a bit too fucking weird if I still like chicken? I don't care ... I'm hungry. Whoever is cooking doesn't seem to be attending the grill. I land as quickly as possible, snatch a steak and a chicken breast off the grill, and head for the sky again. My stomach growls. I start eating the steak immediately while I fly to find a secure spot to hunker down until morning. I don't know how far ahead Jo is, but I'll let her have this night alone.

Tomorrow will be another story—she is mine, and damn it, she is going to get her ass home with me, where it belongs. Then a nagging voice tells me to stop being an asshole Neanderthal; if I want my mate, then I'm going to have to convince her she wants to be with me. But how in the hell do I do that, especially if she resists? Something tells me that flowers and chocolates will fail to impress Jo. I doubt she's the wine and dine type either, and sex clearly isn't the answer. What the fuck am I going to have to do to win her over?

I get up before sunrise so I can close some of the distance between us, and it pays off. Moments after the sun crests the horizon, I see her take to the sky about two miles in front of me. Today she will not fucking ditch me again! Unfortunately she seems to have other ideas, and I have to give it to her—she's not stupid. Her smaller frame and wingspan allow her to get into areas I can't, and she uses that to play an elaborate game of hide-and-seek all day. It's even more effective when she lures me to the ground to pursue her on foot into a heavily wooded area. She can just squeeze between the branches of nearby trees to fly out while I have to continue on the ground until I find an opening large enough to accommodate my wingspan. That tactic allows her to get beyond my line of sight again, and by nightfall I have to give up for the day.

For three weeks she runs my ass ragged as I chase her all over the western half of North America, much of which I recognize even from the air. Jo has zigzagged in and out of Canada, tried hiding in the Little Rockies, the Cascades, and the Rubies, and at one point led me through the Lake Tahoe area. She's fucking pissing me off now, and a part of me wants to beat her ass when I get my hands on her. Even for me that's a disturbing thought—it's one thing to be a jerk, an asshole toward women, but physically harming a woman is the last thing I'd ever do. My mother, or rather her Spirit, would never forgive me if I laid hands on a woman that way. But ... maybe I should seriously consider it just this one time. It'd be worth it. I try not to think of the irony that for centuries I ran from women, drove them away from me, and now here I am like some lovesick fool, chasing just one woman all over the damn place so I can convince her to come home and be mine. Man, if Rafe could see this shit, he'd never let me live it down.

Meeting of the Minds

Jo finally makes a tactical error, and it gives me the best chance I've had to catch her since that first day. She's flying low over the trees—probably looking for a narrow spot to go to ground—and she doesn't seem to notice the pocket of trees she's above opens into a wide field some distance ahead. If she follows the pattern of the last several days, she'll keep moving away from me. Lying in wait behind her is one tactic I can no longer use, since she learned that doubling back toward me gives me an opportunity to snatch her. It still irks me that she slipped through my hands when she pulled that maneuver more than once over the first few days. She was just fucking lucky, and as far as I'm concerned, her luck is about to run out, which means I need to be ready. Once she's on the ground and running, she'll be forced to decide whether to sprint across the opening—maybe hope I'm chasing her on foot—or take to flight.

I put on speed to reach the clearing before she does. There's a large pine with exposed branches near its crown, and I land on it to wait, confident I'll have her regardless what she does when she hits the end of the tree line. Twenty minutes later I'm not disappointed. She comes racing out of the woods, and for a moment I think she's going to dash across to the next batch of trees, but then I see her wings open with that first downward thrust. Jo has no idea I've already launched myself from the tree—and the distance between us is rapidly closing. I time my catch to come on the third downward beat of her wings so that I don't take a wing to my face or give her the chance to flog me, another nasty maneuver she's done a few times now to break my hold. My arms and legs are ready as I crash into her, and immediately I wrap them around her, pinning her wings to her sides as I climb higher in the sky.

Jo kicks, claws, and twists against my hold—I tighten my grip. "Damn it, woman, stop fighting me!" Of course she ignores me and does everything she can to pry herself loose from my arms, including retracting her wings in a poor attempt to slip through my grasp. I need to think fast. Surveying the land below, I recognize the Missouri Breaks in the distance—she's already lost, she just doesn't know it yet. Whether she realizes it or not, she was leading us right back home. I'm not sure I have the stamina to reach Wolfe's Den Ranch while wrestling with her midflight, but wise or not, I have to try. If I can get Jo down there, maybe Rafe can help me talk some damn sense into her, because she's just not right in the head. A persistent thought whispers that she's defective somehow, and given the massive screw-up this whole situation is, I can't help resenting her for it. I push back against the anger and hostility I feel toward her for doing this to me ... to us. If she had been born in a time when the people's legends were taken more literally, would she have fought me this hard? Or would she have been this way regardless of the era? What if my mate is broken and can't be fixed? That possibility leaves my stomach in knots.

A little over an hour later, I see the ranch in the distance, but I'll stay at a higher elevation until we're closer. I need room to dive after her if she manages to get free of my hold—she has already released her wings in a last poor attempt to break free or possibly in anticipation of bolting from me when we land. Weeks of built-up tension release when I spot Rafe walking between the house and barn as I start my descent. I'm not sure when I've ever been this happy to see my brother. I touch down right in front of the porch—I need to get Jo inside, where she can't fly off. Rafe is storming toward us with a half-concerned, half-pissed look on his face. I hope he'll be content to listen, because I don't need to deal with his bullshit on top of Jo's.

She's doing all she can to break free—bending, tossing her body into me, trying to kick or trip me. I don't wait for Rafe. Instead I haul Jo up the stairs and into the house. Her wrists are held securely in my hands, and they're going to stay that way until I can find something to bind them. Is it wrong that I'm kidnapping my own mate? By the time Rafe comes through the door, I have Jo in the kitchen, her wings tied to her sides with a piece of twine, and I'm cinching her wrists and ankles together with zip ties. She retracts the wings, but the twine is just tight enough that it doesn't fall away. I seat her on a kitchen stool and meet her glare. Yeah, this isn't going to be easy—she looks pissed all to hell. There's still the option of bending her over my knee and paddling her ass.

"Hey, bro," I say when I hear Rafe's footsteps behind me, but before I can say anything more, he spins me around and gives me a hard punch to my mouth. My hands fly up, one in defense position and the other checking for a split lip or broken tooth. "What the fuck?"

"What the fuck? Really, Nate ... what the fuck? You take off for over three weeks and then waltz back in here like it's no big deal and ask me what the fuck?" His arm draws back, but I stop this blow.

"Shit, man, chill out." I'm now blocking Jo from leaving, while with my other arm I'm holding my brother back from taking more swings at me. I don't need his crap, but I do need his help. "Look, it took me this long to catch her." I jab a finger in Jo's direction. "She's led me all over the bullshit country and part of Canada—I've been chasing her every damn day since we left. Now, if you're done for the moment, help me get through her thick skull so she under-stands sense."

Rafe darts a glance from me to her. Jo's eyes are blazing, as if she wants to kill us both. Lucky for me, that option is no longer on the table, but it does remind me that she may not be aware she is now more than likely immortal too.

Rafe looks toward the main entry. "Shit." He sounds worried. "We're not the only ones here now, bro. I didn't know what hap-pened to you, and I couldn't handle the workload alone. Matt sent two new employees up here about two weeks ago. They're out work-ing on the interior stalls for the new barn—you're lucky they didn't see you fly in."

I glance toward the door, then at Jo, and again at Rafe. Fuck. Without a word I toss Jo over my shoulder and take her to my room, her screaming her fool head off the whole way. I can hear Rafe fol-lowing me even over Jo's racket, though, and by the time I slam my bedroom door shut, I have her yelling at me and Rafe hollering at her to quiet down. Banging my fist against the door, I bellow, "Shut the fuck up, both of you!" I glare at them, silently daring them to open their mouths again. This whole thing is a nightmare. "Look, none of us were given a damn manual, and there sure as hell isn't a Thunderbirds 101 course out there to teach us this shit. We need to accept that it's not what I wanted or expected or what Rafe dreamed of, and it sure as fuck is beyond Jo's wildest imagination. But this is what we're dealing with, and running, yelling, or fight-ing isn't going to change one son of a bitching thing. Got me?"

Jo's body language screams that she'd like to rip me to shreds, starting with the removal of my favorite body part. Rafe, oblivious or deliberately ignoring her hostility, looks between the two of us. "Wait. You said you were chasing her all over the country? I thought you snatched her when you left here three weeks ago."

I blow out an exasperated breath as Jo averts her gaze, a muscle beneath her eye twitching. "Fuck no! We completed my transformation process, and in the middle of that I discovered there's something no one ever bothered to tell us, bro."

"What?" His brows furrow. I know this is going to blow his mind, but at least he'll get to learn about it before he experiences it firsthand.

"The way it works is that something happens during sex. Our mate sets off the change, and we're meant to stay physically connected until we complete that transformation. Then as we finish our part, it triggers"—I jab another finger at Jo—"our mate's transformation."

I can tell by the confused look on his face that what I'm saying isn't registering. "She fucking changed, Rafe! I sprouted wings ... she sprouted wings. I love her, and she fucking freaked and ran off." And I can't believe I just uttered the three words I swore would never come out of my mouth. The look on Jo's face tells me she caught them, and now she seems mortified on top of pissed.

Rafe spins to face her. "You have wings too?" I swear there's hurt wrapped around the incredulity in his voice. This must be a sledgehammer blow to his ego. It's not lost on me that this was his dream, not mine.

"Yes." Jo looks down at the floor, and I can see her withdrawing inside herself again. "He made me a freak like you."

While her words piss me off, they seem to set Rafe in another direction—he walks over and kneels in front of her. "Jolenthia, we're not freaks, and if you have any connection to your Native heritage, you already know that. This is an honor—there's not been a thunderbird guardian for the people in hundreds of years. I'm sorry my brother didn't know it was you or that you'd have wings too, but I'm telling you this has always been part of who you were destined to be, whether you knew it or not."

For a moment I think his pitch is getting through to her, but then even with her hands bound she shoves him back, sending him to an abrupt seat on his ass. "Honor? This is a nightmare that I can't get away from. I told Nate I'd help him complete his change, period. And this ..." She gestures wildly at herself. "This is what he does to me."

We hear a knock at my door, and I shoot Rafe a questioning look. A voice from the hall says, "Hey, Rafe, are you in there? We heard shouting ... is everything okay?"

Fuck, just what this circus needs is another clown. Rafe signals for me to grab Jo and wait here. He slips into the hall, and I hear him address someone named Larry: "Yeah, everything is okay. My brother just got back today, and we have a bit of a family crisis that has his wife upset." Wife? Jo is glaring daggers at me, but I shrug. What else can I do—technically Rafe isn't wrong, if she's my eternal soulmate. From the hallway Rafe is saying, "Why don't you and Brian continue working on the stalls and maybe the indoor runs and chutes for the rest of the afternoon."

"Sure, man, if that's what you want. I just wanted to make sure everything was okay with all the hollering going on up here."

I hear Larry walking away as Rafe reenters the bedroom, scowling at the two of us. "No more shouting, got me?"

We reach an uneasy truce and decide that Jo and I need to do some talking one on one. I still feel it's a little late for a discussion, but what can it hurt at this point? Rafe leaves us alone to figure this shit out, although he makes his feelings clear—like it or not, we are family, and that includes Jo now. I know him well enough to understand that he's not one bit happy about any of this, but he'll accept it for what it is.

After the door closes behind him, I get Jo to sit down on the bed and offer to remove the twine and zip ties if she promises not to run. She agrees, and I grab my pocketknife out of the pair of jeans that's been lying draped across the chair in the corner since the night of our first fateful encounter.

She stiffens when I crouch to remove the zip tie from around her ankles. "Jo, please don't do that. I'm not going to hurt you."

"You already have."

That burns my ass, considering that it took both of us to cause this situation. I slice through the twine as I mull over what she just said. It's doubtful anyone was more shocked than I was that this happened, and she had to have known she was at risk—I can't believe I was solely responsible for her transformation. There's no way she could be ignorant of what she is. I need to tell her the truth. "I've never given women a second thought or treated them with the respect they deserved. And I've definitely never wanted to go out of my way to make everything perfect for someone until I met you." I look at her, but she's staring at the floor. "I'm an asshole, okay?" I cut through the zip tie on her wrists, then kneel and begin gently rubbing the marks on her skin.

"But the hell of it is that I not only remembered your name ... I never called you sweetheart or asked if you saw something you liked. Maybe that should have been a big red flag waving in my face, a warning to run the other way, but I couldn't run from you. Everything about you captivated me, drew me in, claimed me as yours ... as if you were the very air I needed to breathe."

She'll never know how badly I wanted to avoid feeling like this about a woman, let alone allowing a woman that much control over my heart. Fuck, even admitting this to myself is hard. I wait for a long moment for her to say something, anything, but she keeps her gaze on the floor. I sigh. "Jo, I don't have answers to how this is supposed to work or where we go from here, but I know that we need to be together." I don't tell her that part of me may never stop hating her for saddling me with the one thing I never wanted. But I'll have to work on my resentment, because deep down I know I can't live without her—it would drive me insane. Damn, this bitch makes me crazy.

"Let me go." She says it so quietly that I'm not sure I heard her right.

"Let you go? We're soulmates, and I love you!"

Jo looks at me, and for once it's without hostility. "If what you're saying about all this is true ... let me go. If we're meant to be, it won't matter where I go, because I'll end up right back here with you eventually. But if you're wrong and we were only meant to help each other reach this point, then we won't make the horrible mistake of forcing ourselves into living a miserable life together."

I can't breathe again—her words sucker-punch me. Whether she knows it or not, she just ripped my fucking heart out and stomped it into the dirt. What use is a soulmate if I mean nothing to her? What is the point of all this if I'm meant to be alone? How am I supposed to find a way to forgive her if she won't meet me halfway? We both fucked up, and now we have to live with this—together, not apart. Not like this. But I'll lose her for good if I force her to stay. I blink against the rising well of tears and turn from her. "Go." I won't be able to hold the damn pain at bay much longer.

I hear her stand and move across the room. The doorknob clicks open a second later. There's a moment of hesitation, but I can't look at her—I won't. Then I hear the door shut behind me, and a few seconds later I see her walking down the driveway, out of sight of the barn. My heart falls through the floor when I see her take to the sky without ever looking back.

For the longest time I stare out that window at the empty sky, wondering where she will go and if she'll find her way back to me. The pain in my chest is a thousand times worse than when we were physically torn apart. Is this my punishment for trying to thwart the three sisters of fate and rejecting my destiny? Well, I hate to tell the cold bitches of fate this, but they win. I'm fucking done fighting them.

Same and Different

It's been seven weeks since that disastrous encounter between Nate and Jo, and the only thing I'm sure of is that life will never return to the path we've left behind. Seven weeks since either of us has been on the rez. Seven weeks since Jo destroyed my brother. I hate her for it. I don't like what he or I have become, and if I can't blame our cursed existence, I need to blame someone, and she'll do. For now. Our first taste of family beyond Nate and me, and it's totally fubar. It's cracked our foundation—I'm lost as to how we rebuild from here.

Nate doesn't drink anymore ... women don't interest him ... there is no fight left in him. He's not even looking for someone to fight. I'd always hoped he would quit those things, but not in this pathetic manner. I've never seen him like this. Shower, eat, sleep, work, and spend time alone—that's the extent of his life now. Hell, I can hardly drag him into a conversation beyond what needs doing around the ranch.

If this could be my destiny too—if my soulmate could hate me and leave without a second thought—then what is the point of my searching for her now? The irony is that I'm still out there looking, but I no longer care if she actually exists. As long as I find a woman to hook up with and then move on, I'm okay. Of course, it helps to

drink myself into a stupor every night so that I go to bed numb. I
don't want to see any more dreams; I don't need to be tortured by
what will never be.

Nate has warned me not to follow his lead on this, but the way
I handled it before was more wrong. I wasn't as cold and detached
as he was, but it wasn't much better to date women just long enough
to deepen their interest and then walk away, forcing them from
my mind so I didn't have to see the wreckage in my wake. I was so
determined to find my mate that I kept on looking, even though I
knew I'd wronged some damn good women over the years. At least
Nate's method was more of a pinprick—mine was a slice and slow
bleed. I can't help seeing this denial by the fates as my punishment
for hurting the women I did. It was wrong, playing with their hearts,
and I know that now.

Nate argues that it doesn't matter; we were both making a mistake by having sex without telling women what we are. I correct
him: what *he* is. My response pisses him off, and now I'm icing a
black eye while he insists I make some kind of disclosure before I
sleep with a gal. Yeah, I can just see that conversation playing out:
"Oh, by the way, I may sprout wings in the middle of it all, and if
that happens, just ride it out until you get your damn wings too."
I shake my head. That'd be one sure way to scare women off, but
Nate says that if my mate is ignorant like Jo, I'd be risking the same
result—heartbreak. He got part of that right. Jo is an ignorant
bitch. I know he misses her, but damn, I wish he wouldn't—she's
not worth all the pining he's doing for her.

I toss the ice from my glass in the sink and head outside to get
back to work. During the day, at least, I try to stay focused and do
my job. We are making good progress on getting the ranch into
shape. The bunkhouses are on hold while we complete the corral
system and the remodel projects on the house, but everything else
is coming together. It's still just the four of us—me, Nate, Larry,

and Brian. Matt maintains weekly phone contact, but he hasn't been here once since we arrived in March, and it's September now.

He's pleased with our progress yet dismissive of the wildlife issues. What the fuck? We're astounded by his seeming lack of concern for the predators and varmints inhabiting the surrounding areas. Whether it's badgers and gophers digging holes, grizzly bear and mountain lion sightings on the prairie west of this region, or the coyotes and wolf lurking around the ranch, Matt brushes it off as something nature will sort out. Every modern rancher or farmer we've known has taken steps to protect property and livestock from damage and loss. Not Matt. There's no figuring this guy out. But at least Matt's happy the winter wheat is in, and I agree that the first crop should be decent. The third cutting of the alfalfa and grass hay fields begins in a week. I glance at Nate, wondering if he'll insist on doing that cutting, and I'm surprised to find him staring at me. I can tell he has something on his mind.

"Hey, bro." Nate pauses as if to second-guess my reaction to whatever he's about to say. "Labor Day coming up. Want to go on over to Poplar and kill the long weekend there?"

My eyes narrow. Poplar's not some vacation hotspot. No, it's on the Fort Peck rez, and that weekend just so happens to be the last pow wow along the Hi-line in our area for the season. I don't even know why he wants to go, other than that it's safe for him now—there's nothing on the rez for him to run from. Still, I could use a break, and I know he could too, with the way he's been pushing himself—the son of a bitch has been working twice as long and hard as everyone else, and I'm certain he's doing it to avoid thinking of Jo. "Sure, why not."

We finish out the workweek and leave Larry and Brian to handle the spot chores while we're out of town for the weekend. The Poplar Indian Days is rather small in comparison to other pow wows, but it has a tighter community feel and seems dominated by family—I swear everyone here is related in one way or another, but I know that's not entirely true. The fall weather has a lot to do with this event being smaller. It's hard for those from outside the area to keep warm and enjoy the dancers and drummers.

To stay out of the wind, we opt for a couple of folding chairs right next to the circle. Nate and I don't talk other than settling where to sit and whether to grab any food or drink—but then again, we don't say a lot to each other anymore. What is there to say? My perfect fucking dream went bust, and his absolute nightmare became a reality. And at the heart of it is one woman—Jolenthia. She poisons us, divides us. The more Nate loves her, the more I hate her, and that further changes what we share as brothers. I can feel our closeness slipping away, and Nate either doesn't notice or doesn't care. Jo has destroyed us ... and yet life goes on without end. Well, no end for Nate, anyway. I'm sure at some point twenty, fifty, a hundred years or more down the road, this will be another half-forgotten part of our lives. At least I hope that I can forget.

I slouch down in my chair, letting the drumbeat pour through me, feeling the pain as the beats pulse and pull me into their rhythm. Behind closed eyelids I see the Ancestors dancing and singing a similar song in a wide-open field. I can feel Nate to my left and suspect his mind has also drifted back to an earlier time. The bygone era, when leather and feather were more than a Hollywood stereotype, is something we both miss. The old ways of hard living, surviving ... not enjoying excess in any form, but having only what we—

The trek through my memories comes to an abrupt halt when I feel someone touch my arm. My eyes fly open, and I see a pretty young gal in her late teens or early twenties standing next to me, smiling. "It's the intertribal—everyone should dance." Then she moves between Nate and me and reaches for our hands. "Come on."

I'm not sure why we don't resist, but maybe we're both too beaten down to try. We allow her to draw us to our feet and we join the others circling as the drummers sing. To my surprise the gal stays between us, and I wonder if she's afraid we'll stop and go back to our seats. I won't say the thought hasn't crossed my mind, but as my feet move to the shuffling and tapping steps—so familiar, ingrained in my soul—I feel a missing part of me return, a connection to life I've all but lost. Soon I can't resist grinning down at the girl dancing between us—I don't think she's stopped smiling at all. When the song ends, I'm definitely in a better place, and I'm glad she pulled me away.

The gal sits next to me when we return to our seats. "I'm Inaleah, Ina or Leah for short ... I answer to all three."

Her warm personality is too much to ignore—I'm actually looking forward to having a conversation with her. "Rafe, and that's my brother Nate."

"I remember seeing you over at Milk River Indian Days in July." She smiles at her recognition, and I struggle to keep everything from turning to ice inside me. That disastrous pow wow led to the whole Jo debacle and upended our lives.

I decide a change of subject is best. "So, you live around here or just follow the pow wow trail?"

Inaleah says, "I live over at Nashua, but I have family on Belknap and Peck."

"You're here with your family?" I already know the answer, but I wonder how many in this smaller gathering she's related to—it would explain her interest in outsiders.

She lists nearly twenty people while she points them out in the chairs and bleachers opposite us, and I'm certain that my assumption is correct—she is looking for someone outside her usual circle. Nate ignores her, but that's nothing new. He doesn't talk to anyone anymore.

"What about you? Are you from around here, or do you follow the trail?" Her lips lift into that infectious smirk again. Yes, I'm grinning back—I can't stay sullen in the face of such sunshine on this overcast fall day. There hasn't been anything to smile about since Jo happened.

"We come from an island in the Pacific Northwest, but we've been here awhile. Right now we're working on a ranch a little over an hour south out of Malta."

"Cool." Ina pats and squeezes my arm. She's the touchy-feely sort; many aren't, but I find it refreshing how comfortable she is with herself. "Maybe when I'm crossing between the rezes on the Hi-line, we can meet up for coffee or dinner or just say hi."

Did she just ask me out? I blink and look closer at her. She's pretty and outgoing, her long black hair is past her waist, and she has a decent figure from what I can tell under her bulky fall clothing. But she looks young, and I'm curious whether she's a bit too young. I don't do jailbait. "How old are you, Ina?"

She giggles. "Don't you know it's rude to ask a lady her age?" She winks, indicating that she's not really put-out—just teasing. "I'm twenty-four."

The breath I was holding escapes in a slow exhale—from her height and appearance, I would have guessed her to be closer to sixteen or seventeen. Now, if I play my cards right, she'll at least be worth a fun time in the sack.

We continue our friendly banter for the rest of the night, and the next day she finds me right before noon. While she flirts with me, she's still teasing and fun around Nate—she's noticed his attitude and seems determined to change it. She's also quick to pat, squeeze, or sweep a hand over our shoulders and arms, as if we're lifelong friends. For once Nate ignores the uninvited touch.

That afternoon, somewhat to Nate's displeasure, I make a point of ditching him to hang out with Ina for the rest of the day. We find Nate sitting alone during the nightly closing ceremony for the pow wow, and we're met with his scowl of disgust. Ina thanks him for giving us the day together before she bounds away, exuberant as ever.

Settling into our tent, Nate says, "So, what's the story with you and that split-tail?"

I shrug. "I'm not sure yet ... she seems nice enough."

Nate grumbles, "Just fuck her and get it over with already so you can run on to the next one."

I ignore his pointed barb, and though I won't admit it to him, that is exactly where my thoughts have been for the last several hours. It's just not possible with so many of the girl's family members around—last thing I need is a pissed-off father, mother, brother, sister, cousin, aunt, uncle, grandparent, what have you. My best chance is to talk her into paying me a visit on the ranch next weekend. I go to sleep formulating my plans.

Ina spends most of Sunday with me, and I learn she's more than willing to come out to the ranch. She works during the week at the medical clinic in Glasgow, which is only fifteen miles from where she lives in Nashua—and she has her weekends free. We arrange to meet on Friday evening for dinner, and from there I'll see where she's willing to go.

The week flies by, and before I know it I'm eating dinner at the GN with Ina in Malta. The date is pleasant enough, but admittedly I'm paying more attention to her body now that it's not hidden under a coat or sweater. It's not bad, not bad at all. Her small build is curvy and fit. I can tell by the way she's responding to me that she's a bit more than just interested, and that lines me up to enjoy her company tonight and tomorrow night. She'll go home on Sunday afternoon—which I'll be ready for. Depending on how it goes, I'll either see her for a few more weeks or brush her off for good before she leaves. Yeah, I've swapped places with my heartless brother, because I really don't care if she stays or goes after we're done. Worse is that I don't give a shit that I don't care, even knowing I should. I just can't find it in myself anymore.

Nate gives Larry and Brian the weekend off so Ina won't have to worry about being on an isolated ranch with four men. Not that

Nate would ever touch her; he's become a damn monk since Jo ran away. I don't think he's even looked at another woman.

When we arrive, Nate is watching TV, but he mostly ignores us. That suits me fine. I take Ina to the breakfast bar in the kitchen and offer her a drink. One drink leads to three and then to five, and I can tell she's getting a bit tipsy. "I think you shouldn't drive tonight and just stay here."

Her dark-brown eyes give me the once-over. "With you? Or are you offering me the couch?"

"With me, of course. Unless you'd rather sleep alone on the couch."

Ina laughs and walks over to put her glass in the sink. I'm leaning against the counter, taking in the sway of her hips, her mischievous smile, and the hungry glint in her eyes. Ina's tongue slides across her upper teeth. "I already had us heading for your bed at the pow wow last weekend."

Okay, so maybe I'm not the only one playing games here, and if she's on board with this, then there's no sense wasting any more of our time hanging out in the kitchen. I flex my fingers to motion her toward me. Without a moment's hesitation she takes my hand and follows me to my room.

Sure enough, Ina proves she is anything but shy when she rips off my shirt before I get one piece of clothing off her. The sensation of her fingers running over my abdomen is pretty damn good. Either I'm way overdue for this, or I've had more to drink than I realize, or this gal is about to show me the best time I've had in a very long while.

I wait until Ina has me undressed before I rush through removing her clothes. Not once has she paused to comment on my marks, but then she hasn't seen me fully from behind either. Just as well; I don't want to go through that meaningless discussion tonight. Ina's hands and lips roam over the front of me, but I pull her

onto the bed. There's no point wasting my time with a lot of foreplay. Once I roll the condom on—a modern necessity—I bury myself deep in her sweet honeypot. Ina is taking her own pleasure and
willingly allows me to enjoy her.

Then something happens, and for a moment I stop moving. She's
been gripping me so tight inside that I swear the condom came off,
and it might be loose inside her now. Shit—if it is, I'm going to
have to fish it out. But before I can voice my concern, Ina's urgency
builds, and the way she's writhing has me saying fuck it, I'll worry
about it later, and I make the most of every stroke. I'm not sure
what it is about her, but I lose my self-control, and as I hit that
peak and begin to fall, Ina goes wild and slams her body against
mine to find her own release a moment later.

While my body is pulsing with ecstasy, I have a vague awareness that something is crawling over my back. At first I think it's
her fingers, but then I realize that I can feel it on my legs, ass, back,
shoulders, arms. I cry out as my back rips open and my body locks
in pain. I can't keep my eyes open—I'm breathless except for the
short gasps that barely fill my lungs. Something like a million march-
ing ants moves up my legs and arms, meeting at the center of my
back—the epicenter of the most excruciating pain I've ever felt. I
finally meet Ina's eyes, and her face is a mask of wonder, confusion, and disbelief. I can't fucking believe this myself. Her hands
pull away as if my skin just burned her, but I suspect it's because
she can feel the unnatural movement under the skin on my back.

I want to tell her it will be okay, but I can no longer move or
speak. Then she goes to struggling, but I already know that unless someone forces us apart, she's as stuck in this moment as I am.
She's going to hate me. Unable to get free, she screams, and pre-
dictably that brings Nate to my bedroom. I can't see his face, but
I expect him to shut the door and leave, to wait this out. Instead
he approaches the bed, cups Ina's face in his hands, and shouts,
"Listen to me."

I see her eyes move toward him, and I know she's terrified by what's happening here—I'm only a step behind at scared witless, and I know what comes next.

Nate says, "You started this together, and you both must finish it together. Look over his shoulder ... watch." As if on cue, my wings unfurl, but all I can do is pant heavily through the agony. I don't know whether to be relieved or freaked out that Nate is kneeling by my bed while I'm in the middle of a sex act bonding me to my mate. "You must finish this! He won't be able to move until you get him past this phase. Once you do, the same will happen to you, and it will be up to him to bring you through it. Do you understand?"

To my surprise Ina says, "Yes ... but what ..." She trails off, like she's unsure which question to ask.

Nate says, "He'll explain it all when you're done. I'm going to go so you two can finish this in privacy. Okay?"

Ina nods, and I swear her breathing is as ragged as mine. This woman is nearly unflappable. Remarkable. I half expected her to pull a Jo, yet here she is riding out this unknown storm with grit and with determination to see it through. If I could, I'd kiss the hell out of her. I hope she doesn't change her mind and run when this is over.

It seems like an eternity passes before she moves beneath me again, and I realize my body is responding to her. I follow my instincts and give silent thanks to my brother for explaining this process to me and to her. It's too late now, but I realize he was right—I should have told Ina what I was before I ever took her to my bed. I offer a quick prayer to the Creator that I won't regret withholding this from her.

Ina's eyes are wide with wonder and fear, but thank all that is sacred, she is not screaming. Using my wings, I lift us off the mattress, and once Ina's wings begin to emerge, I rotate us perpendicular to the floor. My senses tell me that we've reached the zenith—I rotate again so that we're hovering next to the bed, with Ina on top of me. "It's almost over," I manage to breathe out. The sensation of my wings retracting is the strangest feeling, but I know that it will become second nature and I won't notice it much after this. As I settle onto the mattress, I watch as Ina's wings flex and curl and then retreat inside her too. How could I have been so foolish as to think my mate didn't exist? Is she here now because I gave up or because Nate and I were always meant to find our mates within a few months of each other? I may never learn those answers ... I only know the Creator has found a way to humble me once more.

A hundred questions flicker in her eyes, and her failed starts in trying to voice them aren't allowing her to put a single one forth. Placing a finger to her lips, I say, "Ina, we have a lot to discuss, and now we need to talk. Okay?"

She nods again, and I close my eyes in gratitude—our screwed-up little family just gained another member. I never expected she was the one, but now I know she is, and I will do everything I can to make her comfortable enough to stay.

Chapter 20: Nate
Fates are Mocking Me

I still can't believe what I saw, but I know it was real, and I did what needed to be done to help them through it. Whatever happens between Rafe and Ina, they have a better chance than I ever had with Jo. Just thinking her name lashes my heart again—it's bleeding out inside. I don't understand how my love for her can be so deep and intense while she feels nothing but anger, resentment, and hatred for me. What kind of cosmic fucking joke is this?

Sunrise is breaking when I step outside. Pushing my thoughts aside, I check on the livestock in the barn; we have a sick heifer and a wounded steer to deal with right now. After I make sure they're comfortable and have plenty of feed and water, I slip my shirt off and step into the corral run past the open doorway, turning my face to the sky as I feel for Jo. Whether she knows it or not, I've been stalking her every day since she left. It doesn't matter how often I tell myself I'm not going to do it again; I can't seem to override the need to protect my mate, and if I don't make sure she's okay every damn day, the pain becomes too much. I doubt she even knows, since I try to stay out of sight.

I shoot up into the air, climbing higher and higher until those on the ground won't think twice about the large bird overhead. The last thing I need is to be outed as a freak or to end up as a lab rat. My internal sensor points me to the rez, but instead of flying toward Kari's, like I expect, I find myself drawn to an unfamiliar ranch a few miles from her place. I land behind the silos to check it out. No one is outside, but I see a couple of rigs parked near the house. I'm sneaking up on the dwelling to peek through the windows when a blue heeler comes around the corner and starts to growl and bark. Fuck. If I run, it will chase. If I stand still, whoever is in the house will see me. There's little choice but to fly away. The screen door squeaks as I swoop toward the copse of trees along the creek near the barn. It'll be dumb luck if whoever it was didn't look up.

Landing just beyond the trees for cover, I look over the perimeter of the house; a shoeless and shirtless young man crouches near the dog, petting its speckled fur. Then I see her. Jo. I close my eyes as I draw in a deep breath, silently begging her to come back to me—but when my eyes open, a lump lodges in my throat and threatens to choke me. She's wearing nothing but a man's shirt, and her arms are wrapped around his damn neck. I have to grip the tree to keep from ripping the man the hell away from her. I'm struggling to breathe, my heart is twisted into a knot of permanent pain, and I realize that if I stay I'm going to hurt the man, maybe even her. There's no choice for me but to leave. I run along the creek until I'm well out of sight of the house and then take to the sky again.

My mind keeps replaying the bullshit scene, but now I hear the words she said the day she left me, that we'd keep from making the horrible mistake of staying together. This can't be right. She can't be with someone else ... damn it, she's my mate. Then I wonder if it's possible for soulmates to cheat on one another. Maybe she doesn't feel this same inexplicable pull between us. If not, does she even feel guilty? I let out an anguished cry that doesn't sound close to being human. Anger and hatred crawl through me, and once more I find myself wanting to kill her. I fly for hours, not paying attention to where I'm going or where I've been.

It's midafternoon when I spot Rafe and Ina flying in my direction, though they seem so wrapped up in each other that they haven't noticed me. What's abundantly clear is that he's not chasing her down to get her back. Fuck me. The last thing I want is to see either of them or the happiness they've found in each other. I turn and beat my wings against the air to gain altitude and disappear into the cloud cover. The cold condensation of the cloud as it collects on my body and wings makes flight difficult, but I'm not willing to drop down and have Rafe see me. I climb higher. When I finally get above the cloud, I have to work my wings twice as hard to maintain flight and rid my feathers of the frozen moisture.

I try to ignore that I can still feel Jo where I left her. She was perfect when she first came to me—innocent, pure sweetness meant only for me. Or so I thought. How long has she been seeing that fucking asshole? My heart sends another jolt of pain through my body. I need to get home ... I can't keep doing this.

When I reach the ranch, I find Ina standing with her arms wrapped around Rafe's waist and his hands on her hips. One look at them, at their happiness, makes it perfectly clear: the fates are mocking me.

"Hey, bro ..." Rafe looks at me. "Um, thanks for helping Ina understand." If he had listened to me, I wouldn't have had to.

I can only nod, because if I open my mouth, I'm going to say something I'll no doubt regret for the rest of my bullshit existence. Ina pulls away from Rafe and walks toward me—instinctively I take a step back. The sad, sympathetic look she gives me reeks of pity. "I'm sorry; I know this can't be easy for you."

Sorry. She's fucking sorry. How great is that? My gaze lands on Rafe, and I see the same look in his eyes. I can't take their pathetic sympathy. I need to get as far from here as I can. Turning away silently, I go to my room and pack a bag, then slide the window open and climb out. I wish there were a way to put the bag on my back, but I'm going to have to hold on to it as I fly. I have no clue where I'm going—only that I need to be as far from Rafe, Ina, and Jo as I can stand.

Turning southeast, I begin the long flight to South Dakota—the Badlands seem the best place to lose myself and not be found. Well, the only one who can find me will never come looking, and Rafe won't know where to start searching for me.

When I land two hours later, my arms ache from holding the bag so long. I'm in a remote part of the Badlands, and the rugged terrain—well away from the outer edges, where recreational wanderers could come across me—is the perfect place to hide. My mind goes on autopilot. I'm too numb to think anymore, and I'm so broken by grief that only basic survival matters now. Not that I can die ... no, I never will die, thanks to the fates. But that doesn't mean I need to live either. I can exist alone in this world, far away from everyone. It's probably best that way.

I gather the material necessary to build a temporary shelter and set up my camp. Before the winter snow comes I'm going to need a permanent shelter, but for now this will do while I prepare for my miserable life ahead. It's been so long since I've lived off the land that part of me welcomes this isolation. I'll have to hunt and smoke the meat and hides to augment my supplies for the winter, though at some point I may need to purchase a few staples; it's too late in the year to make cattail flour or find enough berries, roots, and herbs to round out my meals.

I start a fire to warm my chilled body but stare unseeing at the flames. My wings come out and wrap around me to provide further warmth, which I'm grateful for—it's a bit like carrying a down comforter everywhere I go. And the wings provide the only comfort I'm likely to have in the bleak years ahead. I'm not sure where my life went so damn wrong. My thoughts keep drifting over the more recent past—all the women I disrespected and tossed aside, the senseless drinking, and the running from something I never had a prayer of avoiding. The price I'm paying now by losing the only one who will ever matter to me seems excessive, but maybe I deserve it for all the crap I pulled.

For the first time in centuries I pull out my knife and slice my arms to release my grief while I sing in mourning. The Creator must hear my prayers. Jo must hear my heart speak to hers. I need to find a way past the shame of my mistakes to show gratitude for the gifts I callously discarded and now humbly seek to be returned to me.

I'm not sure how many days pass while anguish pours out of me in song, prayer, and blood, but when the snow starts to fall, I realize that I've still not built a permanent shelter and now I'm running out of time. I look down at the bloodstains on my jeans and the dried blood on my arms and hands, the wounds long since healed. My fast healing is even faster now—too bad the wound to my fucking useless heart will bleed forever.

When the sun rises, I scout for wild game; the hides and meat are a priority. My thoughts drift back to a day sometime after Rafe and I were struck with this curse, when I watched my mother prepare an elk skin for tanning. Rafe was off with Father somewhere, and I had stayed behind for a reason I no longer remember. But I do recall Mother's smile as she lifted her gaze to me. "Come, sit, and I'll show you. A day will come when you'll need to know how."

She had already defleshed the hide, removing the fat underlayer so it would not decompose, and had stretched it to dry a few days before. I sat beside her and eagerly took the elk antler scraping tool in my small hands. Mother put both of her hands over mine, extended my arms to their full reach, and with gentle but firm pressure pulled the tool downward to loosen and remove the hair.

A smile touches my face as I remember how my arms ached and were near-useless by the time I finished scraping off all the hair.

But I also recall my sense of pride as we moved through the progression of tanning that elk skin. That's when I realized how strong a woman my mother was—the elk hide was too heavy for me to lift after we washed it. I was not capable of wringing it out alone and watched in awe as she twisted it tighter and tighter. I helped her stretch it and tie it to the rack and then followed her lead in working the brain mixture, which she had already crushed and prepared, into every square inch of the hide. Afterward we took it off the rack to let it sit rolled up in a double layer of leather so it would stay moist overnight. The next day we cleaned off the brain residue, once more working the tool to further stretch and soften the leather, and later my mother had the hide thoroughly smoked to a deep golden color.

This hide would become new leggings for my brother and me. I wrinkled my nose when she said I'd also have to learn how to sew, but she was right; it was a skill Rafe and I needed long after she had taken the journey to our Ancestors. I can't stop chuckling now. Yeah, I've never been a fan of sewing; it's hard work pushing a bone awl and needle through tanned hide, and sewing a complete outfit is no easy process. Actually, it's damn hard work, but there's not been a year since Mother taught us that Rafe and I haven't made our own moccasins. It's still our favorite footwear—we only wear boots to work or when riding a motorcycle.

My gaze wanders over the herd of deer ahead of me, and I feel tears well in my eyes. Father may have taught us how to fish and hunt, but Mother was extraordinary and passed on so many of the valuable life lessons that sustained us for centuries. My deepest regret is that she had a normal human life span; I'd love for her to see Rafe and me now. I close my eyes, and for a brief moment I can picture the smile she would give when one of us made her proud. I'll never cease missing my mother.

It takes a few days, but my permanent shelter comes together, and the smell of meat smoking on the rack makes my mouth water. Near it are two hides; one is stripped of hair for tanning on both sides, and the other has the hair left on so that I can use it for warmth as the weather grows colder. I'm going to have to find a store soon, though, because I can't live on meat alone—and having some damn coffee would be great!

I have quit counting the days by the calendar; actual dates mean nothing to me anymore. The only thing I need to mark time is the passing of each moon. By its count I know when fall becomes winter and when spring will arrive. Civilization has changed so much that if it weren't for my memories, returning to this lifestyle would be almost impossible—so in a way I'm grateful that my memory is long. But I know that's a lie too. I'm not fond of remembering Jo. She haunts my dreams, just as she did before I met her, but it's worse now because I know what she looks like and how she feels, smells, tastes. The dreams are filled with my desire to have her in my life again, and my need leaves an unbearable hole in me when I wake.

Half my days now are spent shaking off the dream from the night before. Torn between extreme feelings—it's too close to the story of the two wolves fighting inside. Which one wins? The one I feed the most. The dreams nourish the good one, the part of me that wants to step up and fulfill my role as a thunderbird with Jo by my side. Good Nate envisions a strong and loving relationship with my mate ... the two of us working together to protect and help the people. The bad side is dark, violent. When it's at the forefront of my mind, I feel an overwhelming desire to rid myself of any good feelings, and I spend hours thinking how desperately I want to hurt and destroy Jo. My shadowed thoughts have run the gamut from staking her somewhere on a barren hillside to suffer, to pulling her feathers out one by one until she's plucked clean, then ripping the wings from her body. Bad Nate wants to take back this curse-gift Jo has saddled us with.

My deeper feelings toward her are just as wide ranging. I never thought it possible to both love and hate one person in such equal measure. The dreams embrace the love, passion, respect, adoration—but my daily struggle offsets my dreams with loathing, disgust, disrespect, resentment, and hatred. The warring sides have me lurching between unreasonable limits and without any middle ground for peace to settle within myself. That bitch has destroyed me in more ways than I ever thought possible. Worse? Every damn night and day are the same, and I know I'm feeding the wolves equally and not allowing either to win.

Even so, by the time the snow comes to stay, I have a decent lean-to built against a steep hillside that provides a good windbreak. I have an adequate supply of meat, too, and although it took multiple trips into the nearest town—it was impossible to carry all the groceries I needed in one flight—I have a sufficient store of canned goods and staples to last me at least a month. The biggest pain in the ass will be flying the trash out to the dump, but there's no way I'd leave it to litter my camp.

Yes, everything I need for merely existing is stockpiled, and I look forward to the long, cold winter months alone. If I can stay focused on survival, on living this simple life away from the people of this world, Jo in particular, then I may even find a measure of peace someday. For now I've got to keep up the bullshit lying to myself, or I'm never going to survive her rejection. At least I can feel resentment toward Jo for doing this to me, and that motivates me to live with this curse despite her.

But it's the moments I weaken and think of her ... no, miss her that are the worst. Damn it, can she even feel me? Could she find me if she wanted to? Maybe I have the wrong notion based on too many modern ideas of what a mate is. Maybe the only true mates are those from the animal kingdom—though I am part fucking bird. Then I remind myself that I'm also part human. It must be the human in her that is flawed or dominant. How else can she go on with her life without me?

CHAPTER 21: RAFE
The Good, the Bad, the Unacceptable

The days following our transformations are slightly overshadowed by Nate's disappearance, but I'm sure he is giving Ina and me room to discover our new abilities together. And it's been fantastic, almost indescribable. I have laughed and smiled more in these last several days than I have in the past five hundred years. From the rough landings to the faux arguments over who is going to shelter whom with our wings—I usually win that one—it's been a high point of an otherwise rough year. I still can't believe that for a few weeks I doubted I'd ever find my soulmate or believed I was doomed to be passed over for this honor. For all the crap Nate ever put me through, it's thanks to him talking me into going to Poplar that Ina found me, and for that I'll always be grateful.

It's hard for me to imagine what my brother's going through right now. His dilemma has me looking at Ina in awe—I could have shared my brother's fate. But I also suspect it's because of what she and I have that he went away and has no intention of ever coming back. As Ina and I settle into our new lives, my concern for Nate and our little family grows. The fall and early winter holidays have come and gone, and the new year is just two days away. Ina and I have both searched for him in ever-widening arcs, but no matter how much ground we cover, we've turned up nothing.

Ina assures me that Nate will come home someday, or we will find him. I'm not so sure of either. Unlike in my bond with her, I have nothing to tell me where he is or how he is doing. Am I doomed to go through existence with just one other? Are we not meant to be a family? While he can't die, that doesn't make me worry about him any less—particularly now, with the way the world is imploding on a global scale.

A few months before Nate left, several of the world's governments were ramping up for war, and since his disappearance that war has begun and grown in size and brutality every day. Granted, it's not the first war we've seen—more than I can count, especially if the wars against enemy tribes or the white man's wars against the Indians during the eighteenth and nineteenth centuries are factored in. But this one is different, even when compared to the widespread savagery of the first two world wars. More countries than ever are taking part, and even the United States and Canada are not immune to hostile action within their borders. We're lucky to be in this remote area—the thinly populated countryside leaves the old nuclear missile silos our greatest concern. I'm relieved there are none near Matt's property; that will keep us relatively safe from the fallout if any of those silos are hit by aerial assault, though if we're truly immortal, I doubt radiation will kill us. Regardless, that doesn't mean I want to experience getting my ass blown to smithereens.

So much ordnance has been dropped that there's been talk of munitions shortages—which may lead to the use of nuclear arms. That bit of unsettling news resulted in the loss of my two coworkers, Larry and Brian, who decided they needed to be closer to their families and left here days ago. It helped lessen my burden when Matt decided we could hold off on building the bunkhouses until spring. It's his hope the war will be winding down by then, and when it does it will be easier to find willing ranch hands or even transfer some of his construction workers up here to do the job.

Their departure leaves the house to us, which is fortunate, considering Ina moved in within days of our change—neither of us wants to live apart. Between the two of us, we're managing the ranch okay too, and I can see why the fates chose her to be my soulmate. I shake my head at that thought and wonder for the hundredth time how Jo can refuse to be with Nate. I really hate that bitch. She seemed so innocent and sweet, kind, even—I would have lost a bet if anyone had wagered she could be this cold and spiteful.

"You're thinking about them again, aren't you?" Ina doesn't look up from where her head is resting against my chest.

"Yeah." I kiss the top of her head. "I can't leave Nate out there alone for the entire winter with the war becoming more violent in this country. We're also supposed to have some role to play in protecting the people. It'd be nice if he were around to help us when we're needed."

She pulls back and looks up at me. "Maybe we should ask Jo to help us find him." I frown down at her, but she presses a finger to my lips. "She doesn't have to like him or even want to be near him, but she can take us to wherever he is and do it from a distance. It's not like we'd be sending her to talk him into coming back."

I can't fault the idea—other than that neither of us knows where the hell Jo is these days. Gone back to Wyoming? Moved on to another state? The thought of calling Kari makes me cringe—I've honored her request and have stayed as far away from her as I can. And letting her know I'm with my mate now seems more than a little cruel. But she would be the best source for obtaining information on Jo. Would Naomi contact her on my behalf?

The thought rolls around in my head for a couple more days before I make a decision and call the healer on New Year's Day. She sounds genuinely happy to hear from me, but when she finds out what happened with Nate, sadness seeps into her tone. "Give me a few days, and I'll call you back, okay?"

"Yeah, that's fine. I'm not going anywhere." My laugh feels as empty as the part of my life where Nate resides. Will I ever see that asshole brother of mine again?

Three days later Naomi calls back and says that Jo is willing to come out and talk with us, but the healer's not optimistic that Jo will be of any help. It seems Jo wants to hear what we have to say, or rather maybe listen to us beg, before she decides whether or not to help us find Nate. What choice do I have? I agree to Jo's terms, but I'm as nervous as a chicken with its neck stretched out on a chopping block when Naomi's car comes up the driveway the next day. Ina has to keep telling me to breathe and calm down. I don't want to calm the hell down—I want to rip the wings off Jo. She doesn't deserve to be one of us.

Ina must sense my hostility, because when the two women get out of the car, Ina deliberately stays between me and Jo.

I give Jo a hard look and nod, unsure what to say at this point. "Jo."

She glares back. "My name is Jolenthia. Only my friends call me Jo."

This is pure bullshit—she's my brother's mate, we're family, and I think that more than qualifies me to call her Jo. My tone is icy as I tell her we have a lot to discuss. "Why don't you come inside, *Jo?*"

"Rafe, don't." Ina places a hand on my chest. "Give me a moment alone with her, please?"

I look between her, Jo, and Naomi and give my consent by asking Naomi to come inside with me instead. There I can't quit pacing and then stopping every couple of turns to stare out the window at Jo and Ina. By the time Ina finally gets Jo to come into the house—it feels like days later—I've about worn holes in my moccasins. Granted, Jo doesn't come much past the door, and she refuses to sit down, but that's okay because the idea of sitting still sets my raw nerves on fire. I want to rip her apart, and with my newfound strength I don't doubt that I could. The problem is that she'd likely survive it.

Ina says, "I'm not going to go into what we talked about out there, but Jolenthia has agreed to at least listen to you."

I fail to keep the disdain out of my voice. "*Jolenthia* ... I don't know if Inaleah"—if she wants to play the full name game, I will too—"told you or not, but I've transformed and so has she. She is my mate. Nate is family. He's been missing for the last couple months, and with the way the war is spreading, we need to bring him home."

I'm not going to pull punches with this bitch. I take a threatening step toward her. "We know that you can sense where he is, that you can find him if you want to. The question is, are you so selfish that you'll refuse, or will you recognize the importance of his role as a guardian of the people?"

Jo looks down at the floor. "I'm not selfish." She lifts her gaze to me. "Your brother ... he did this to me. I never wanted—he took more from me than you'll ever know."

"It's all about you ... you, you, you, isn't it, princess? Have you given one thought beyond yourself?" I can't stop myself—I rush forward until we're standing chest to chest. "Let me tell you something, Jo ... my brother didn't want this either, and I could spend the next thirty damn days telling you everything he did to avoid it. But it still happened. Do you fucking hear me? It happened! Whether you wanted it or he wanted it, it's done, and like it or not, you two are bound. I can't believe that you haven't given him one thought since you ripped his damn heart out."

Ina grabs my arms, pulling me aside while she moves between me and Jo again. "Don't do this, Rafe." She shoves me back another step.

I point at Jo over her shoulder. "She fucking destroyed him, Ina." I've not been this angry in years, and I rotate away from her, punching the wall and leaving a big fat hole to patch later.

With her palms on my chest, Ina pins me against the wall. She gives me a look that tells me to stay put and let her handle this. I have to trust that she knows what she's doing, because from what I've learned about Jo, nothing would please her royal hine-ass more than if Nate ceased to exist—and I want to fucking kill her for it. Locking my fingers together behind my head, I go over to the couch to sit down before I put another hole in the wall. But if Jo so much as breathes wrong ...

"Jolenthia ..." Ina's approach is cautious, like she doesn't trust Jo either. "Regardless of what you feel about Nate, I can assure you that he really did think you were safe from becoming ... this." Ina unfurls her wings. Jo's eyes go wide, and her breath catches in her throat.

"I didn't know either, and if it weren't for Nate, I might have freaked out and run away like you did. But he talked me through it and explained what was happening when Rafe couldn't. I don't care what you think of Nate, but he's family. If you want to turn your back on all of us, fine. Just let us know where Nate is first. You may not care or want him in your life, but I promise you that Rafe sure in hell does, and I stand by my mate."

A long, pregnant pause settles between them. Jo turns and places her hand on the doorknob, and I hold my breath, hoping she could never be so heartless. Ina sucks in a sharp breath, clearly expecting the worst. Without looking at us Jo says, "I'll find him and let you know where he's at. Then you can go get him and leave me the hell alone."

CHAPTER 22: NATE
Unfinished Business

I'm doing well in my own little corner of the world. But I also know the rest of the world is not at peace. An increasing number of warplanes fly overhead each day, and I've heard the thumps and booms of ordnance exploding in the far-off distance, likely at Ellsworth Air Force Base outside of Rapid City. My thoughts drift more and more toward the purpose for which Rafe and I were born—to protect the people. Which people? Where? Our country is at war, but what is the role we're supposed to serve? The longer I am a thunderbird, the more I feel a sense of duty to something or someone, but I don't have a fucking clue where to begin. Once again I find myself wishing that our elders and storytellers had better recorded the first thunderbirds and the role they played in our history.

Instead I sit here pondering and never doing one damn thing about it. I lie to myself, say that we're not needed now anyway ... that this war will soon be over. Deluding myself is something I've become quite good at. It should bother me, but I find it calming to embrace anything but the raw, ugly truth. No, the war, like my mated-single status, is a fucked-up mess that robs me of any chance for inner peace. I have to have at least that much, or I'll lose what's left of my sanity.

With each sunrise I feel an increasing pull to reunite with Rafe, Ina, and Jo—we are meant to stand together, I'm sure of it. But I can't get past the overwhelming feeling that it wasn't supposed to be like this. The bitches of fate wanted us mated before we came into our full potential as thunderbirds—but while Rafe succeeded, I failed. How in the hell can I possibly fix that? Nor do I know how that alters my mission as a guardian. I miss the days of drinking, fighting, and fucking—at least that activity had life to it. Instead I spend almost every day huddled within my wings for what little bit of warmth I can find as I stay disconnected from the world, thinking ... All I do is think. I seem incapable of action, maybe because I'm lost completely on what action to take.

At least I'm getting better about keeping my thoughts off Jo, and the constant thrum of her in my mind is easier to tune out with every day that passes. I'm almost optimistic that eventually I will forget what that thrum is, and it will cease to hold any sway over me. Maybe it will disappear when the fates realize we never should have been together. Maybe in time I can find a way to face immortality and accept that those bitches destined me to be alone.

A noise catches my attention, but I don't lift my wings to look. There's nothing out here but me and the occasional eagle or hawk, both of which view me as a bigger predator and stay well clear of me. But then I hear something that doesn't make sense—I could swear someone called my name, and I know that's not possible.

"Nate?"

There it is again. I decide that it's a trick of the wind.

"Nate? Look at me."

No—that's the voice of someone I know isn't here. Still, I lift my head enough to glance over my knee, my feathers parting to allow me to peek through. I have to blink a few times to make sense of what I see. It looks an awful lot like Jo too, but I know it is not real—last thing she'd ever do is come looking for me. I put my head down and tighten my wings around my body to cut out the cold.

I feared it would happen sooner or later, and it finally has ... I've lost my mind, right alongside my worthless heart.

Then something grabs my wings and gently but firmly pulls them open. My head comes up again, and my gaze settles on the deep-green eyes that tore my soul in two. The last fucking woman I want to see. Is it too much to hope she'll take a knife and cut my heart out ... be done with it? No words come to my tongue—I just stare at her, wondering why she is here now. I attempt to curl my wings around me once again to shut her out, but somehow she ends up inside my wings, and the next thing I know, I feel her body moving between my torso and legs as her arms wrap around me. My own arms are held tightly to my sides.

"Nate?" I hear a slight hitch in her voice.

Something wells up inside me—anger, hurt, or resentment, or maybe some combination of the three. My wings fly open, and I jump to my feet, spilling her onto the snow-covered ground. Emotions roil off me in waves. "Go away. Leave me the hell alone! Just go away, Jo."

Her gaze drops to the ground, and I think I hear her say she's sorry, but I'm sure the wind distorted whatever she said. If she were sorry, she never would have left me ... never moved on to another man. And there's the match that ignites my rage and puts it in the lead. "Go back to your fucking boyfriend and stay the hell out of my life."

Jo looks as if I slapped her; her innocent expression doesn't fool me. I take a step toward her and push her back a few feet. "I. Said. Go. Back. To. Your. Fucking. Boyfriend!"

Tears well in her eyes, yet she manages to spew more lies without hesitation. "I don't have a boyfriend."

I can't contain a snort. "I'm sure you'll find another willing sucker. Go away."

That seems to rile her, and her hands come up, pushing me back a step now. "There's been no one since you. I haven't even dated.

You're like this constant shadow over my life! I can't even get away from you when I'm away from you."

I've got to give it to her, she's a fantastic liar—I saw her body draped all over that other guy. I just shake my head as I back up and then launch into the sky, hoping she'll get the hint and leave me alone. But I'm not that lucky; never am. No, she takes to the sky a half length behind me. She's yelling at me too, but I tune her out, not interested in playing her games. Jo is one sadistic bitch—I'll give her that. She must thrive on the pain she puts me through.

Whatever she's been flapping her jaws about finally comes to a stop—maybe the message is sinking in that I'm willing to play her game and let her go. Isn't that what she wanted? I refuse to look behind me and acknowledge her, though I can hear her wing-beats—I know she's following me. Then her wings go silent, and a moment later her body slams into me, knocking the breath from my lungs. Somehow she's managed to get her arms around my neck and her legs wrapped around my hips, hindering my ability to fly smoothly. "What the hell, Jo? Get off me!"

A frustrated growl precedes words pushed between clenched teeth. "Rafe begged me to find you. I could have just told him, but I came to see if you were okay, and I—"

"You what? Wanted to see if you could finish destroying me? I already got your message loud and clear. You don't need to keep coming around to twist the knife deeper."

The fast retort I was expecting doesn't come, and a moment later I feel a warm drop of moisture hit my neck. Then her arms and legs loosen, breaking the contact of her chest with my back, and as I twist around I see her tumbling through the air, not even trying to control her fall. What the fuck? I don't get this woman. The only thing I know with complete certainty is that if she doesn't start flying right, she's going to hit the ground awfully hard. "Shit. Damn you, Jo!" My wings pull tight alongside my body as I dive after her. She's going to be difficult to catch with the way she's plummeting, but I can't let her hurt herself this way.

We tumble and spin in a tangle of limbs, her head smacking my chin and making me bite my tongue. I manage to get ahold of her and straighten us out before we hit the ground—not my most graceful landing, but at least we're on our feet. She didn't resist, which is a good thing, or we would have crash-landed and both been hurt. Jo turns away from me immediately. I spin her back around. "What did you say?" When she doesn't answer, I grab her shoulders, forcing her to face me.

Without looking me in the eye, she says, "I only needed to locate you ... Rafe would have come." She looks defeated. "I needed ... I needed answers."

"Answers to what? You made your choice—you fucking left me, and you sure as hell didn't waste any time finding another man!" I'm shaking with rage, and the desire to hit something, anything, has my arms tensed and ready to strike.

Her head snaps up, and her eyes turn hard. "There is no other man! There never has been."

"Don't fucking lie to me!" My lips curl into a sneer. "I saw you standing there in his shirt, your bare ass hanging out. Your arms were wrapped around his—"

"What the hell are you talking about?"

I can't believe how credible her confusion is—she'd make a killing in Hollywood. Still, like a dummy I take the bait and play along. Without a second thought I tell Jo about my earlier stalking of her and the day I found her out at that ranch on the rez—what I saw. A strange expression comes over her face, and then she laughs. She's fucking laughing at me.

Jo shakes her head. "That wasn't me! You saw my older sister, Vivialena ... Vivi and her boyfriend. She's two years older than me, but everyone says we look like twins. That's one thing you should know a little something about. How many times have you been mistaken for Rafe?"

My body freezes in shock. How is that possible? I followed her signal there, and I didn't see anybody else. She grabs a wallet out of her back pocket, flips to a photo in the ID organizer, and thrusts it toward me. "I was there to visit her, not her boyfriend. See? Vivi and me. We've always emulated one another because we're that close—or were. I haven't seen or spoken to her since that day."

I stare dumbstruck as my hand closes over hers. Sure enough, the photo shows Jo and another gal who is her near double—they even have matching hairstyles, right down to the color. How the fuck didn't I notice it was someone else that day? There are no words that come to my mind or lips, but my silence seems to set her off again. "You're a real jackass, Nate! I should have just pointed Rafe in your direction."

"No. Wait." I grab her arm as she turns away again. Glancing toward the wallet she's folding to put back into her pocket, I say, "I didn't know." Yeah, it sounds lame even to me, but it's the first thing that comes out of my mouth.

Jo's eyes narrow. "That was my whole point when I left you! We're little more than strangers. And yet ... and yet you think we should live happily ever after for eternity."

I cradle my head in my hands, trying to find a clear thought or an appropriate word or two. Instead I fall back on my usual. "Fuck!"

She backs away when I move toward her, distrust heavy in her eyes. "Look, I know it was a mistake that I came, but I've delivered the message for Rafe." She motions over her shoulder. "You really should go home and talk to him or at least give him a call."

"No." I reach for her. "It wasn't a mistake. Come with me ... I'll get my stuff and we can go back to see Rafe. Then ..." I have to swallow hard to clear the lump that springs to my throat. "We need to figure out this shit, because we can't keep doing this ... either we make this work, or we leave it on good terms before we part ways."

There's no way I'll ever let her go, but she doesn't need to know that—she just needs to give me a chance and us the time to find our balance.

To my relief Jo agrees, and we head back to my camp to put the fire out and collect my bag of clothes. We're both quiet, but that's all right—I need to untangle the wolves fighting inside me. It's time to starve the bad one, and I know just how to do that: Commit to my mate. Show her the love I feel. I want and need her, I know that, but I'm not sure how to win her back—if I ever even had her to begin with. Every woman I've slept with has wanted more of me, but not Jo. Even in the beginning she came to me with some reluctance, and that quickly turned to revulsion. How in the hell do I get her back on a physical level, let alone an emotional one? That's what this boils down to—it isn't merely about sex. I never believed this much more was possible, and now I'm at a loss for what to do.

I realize the answer isn't going to come in the next few minutes, and it may not come at all if Jo and I don't resolve our differences. Are her thoughts and emotions as snarled as mine? Does she love me even a little bit? Do I have a chance with her? Does she want one with me? At the moment I'd almost welcome a quick one-nighter over this impossible challenge ahead. At least I know how to get strangers into bed. I just need to figure out how to win the one woman who walked out on me. Three ... four times, if I count the stunt she pulled a few minutes ago.

I'm no nearer to answers as we take to the sky for the return flight to Montana, but I'm glad Jo will accompany me that far. Still, she's reluctant to come in with me when we land in front of the ranch house a few hours later. I remind her that we can't keep doing this, and she agrees to stay for a little while. Even if she can only promise an hour at a time, I'll take it—as each hour ends I will find the words to convince her it's not time to leave.

Rafe and Ina look stunned when we walk into the kitchen, and Rafe raises an eyebrow, but the slight shake of my head tells him to leave it alone for now. Of course, I don't miss the fact that he is standing behind Ina with his arms wrapped around her waist while she's stirring something on the stove. The perfect happy couple, just what I wanted to see. Jo, somewhat hesitant, offers to help Ina prepare additional food, and I breathe a sigh of relief when Ina accepts the offer. Rafe moves next to me as the women bread a couple more cube steaks to fry and add vegetables to the green salad. I know he wants to go talk in private, but as long as Jo is here, I'm not letting her out of my damn sight. The moment I do she'll flee again, and I'm tired of chasing her down.

Dinner is a bit awkward—no one seems to know what to say—until Rafe ticks off the list of things done on the ranch while I've been gone. I find it odd that Matt hasn't shown up here at least once, but Rafe says the war has a lot to do with it. Seems our boss is stuck in Venice, holed up against the massive bombing campaign in Europe. Now I know that I've been out of the loop, because I'm floored hearing how much the global war has escalated during my absence. From the way Rafe and Ina are talking, it's going to get much worse before it ends. The warring countries seem determined to ruin every city in their enemies' territories, and people are dying by the thousands each day.

Rafe says, "I talked to the elders, and none of the rezes are immune ... their sovereignty is a threat to those invading this country, and some tribes are being punished for providing warriors to fight with the US military."

Young Indians have served with the American armed forces in every conflict going back to the eighteenth and nineteenth centuries, even if some of those involved in the earliest conflicts were no more than scouts. Nate and I did fight with the US in its global wars—we were meant to be warriors, and it seemed the ideal way to gain experience—but more often we fought to support the people against the federal government in past campaigns meant to wipe Indians out, manage them, or relocate them onto reservations, where they died by the thousands due to neglect and forced assimilation. More than once we were left behind on the battlefield when we took injuries that would have been fatal to anyone else, but even the worst injuries only left us incapacitated while we healed.

"What of us? Are we supposed to protect those on the rezes or all people?" I try to find the answer in his eyes, but I see the uncertainty there too.

"That's why I needed you to come back." Rafe looks at Jo. "If the legends are true, then we're supposed to be here right now—this has to be the time the elders and storytellers foretold, when the thunderbirds would rise. But it's a tall order for four of us to fill." His chin tilts in challenge to Jo—he's waiting for her to defy him. "That is, if a certain someone is going to step up and do what she was meant to do as part of this family. Otherwise it's going to be just the three of us fulfilling the legacy."

His point is well deserved, though I don't think Jo understands—or at least she pretends not to comprehend—just how important it is that we fulfill our role as guardians. I can see she's getting uncomfortable, but I'm not going to step in and defend her when she's the one who needs to make a decision. And Rafe is right. She's either with us or she's not. This bullshit really is that simple, regardless of how difficult the choice is for her to make.

The shy, uncertain Jo surfaces as she says, "I'm not sure what I'm doing yet. Nate and I need to talk and figure some things out."

Rafe slams his fist on the table, causing the dishes to jump and rattle. "That's right, princess, once again it's all about you. Family doesn't mean shit to you. People are dying while you keep on thinking, but you just go ahead, because you're more important than anyone else in this bullshit world." His chair slides back, tipping over as he storms out of the kitchen.

I saw the way Jo flinched at his words, and I sense they have a contentious history, but I'm not certain I want to learn the details.

Worse is that I'm not sure he's far off the damn mark, given what I've seen from Jo myself. What happened to the shy young woman who absolutely stole my heart and changed my world? It's no wonder I don't know what the fuck to do with her.

CHAPTER 23: RAFE

Strange Encounters

It takes me an hour to cool down—I regret Jo turning into one of us more than she ever will. My brother has been a dickhead during his destructive phases, but I'm not sure he deserves to be punished for all eternity with that woman. That's fucking harsh. I feel a rip in my heart every time I look at him and see the love and heartache pouring from his eyes. Why would the sisters of fate do this to anyone? I can't even blame this on a trickster, because it just feels evil.

Ina, to her credit, stays out of it and gives me room to work past the anger and rage. She offers to talk to Jo while the women clean up the kitchen, though she practically has to pry Nate out of the room. I know what he's doing—he's afraid Jo will run off again if she's out of his sight for a second. I have faith that Ina will stop her, unfortunate as that would be. I'd really like Jo to leave and never come back.

When Nate and I sit down in the living room, it's clear he doesn't want to talk about Jo. Instead we further discuss the operations and projects here on the ranch and then how and when we should do something as thunderbirds. Both would be easier to decide if we knew what exactly our role was supposed to be in all of this, or what was expected of us.

When the women join us, another awkward silence settles over the room. Ina tries, damn, does she try, to engage in small talk, but the unresolved matter of Jo is the damn elephant in the room, and her mere presence is sucking all the air out of the house. Nate's body language screams desire—he wants her so damn bad, it's painful to watch. At the same time I know that he's not going to do anything that might send her flying out the door. Now, if I were in his moccasins, I would have tossed her out already. But that is the whole point, isn't it? It's his path to walk, explore, live, not mine.

I'm relieved when Ina suggests we give Nate and Jo some time to talk, with the excuse that we have a project to wrap up for one of the new bathrooms upstairs. Her suggestion isn't a total lie, but it doesn't take long to put the supplies away—we had most of the tile, mud, and grout cleaned up before she started dinner. It's not until I'm lugging the last box of tiles to the hall storage closet on the second floor that she calls after me, "You okay?"

"Yeah." I want to scream, "No!" as I set the box on the floor. "That woman torques my ass in the worst way. I don't like what she does to Nate. Don't get me wrong, he more than deserves to have his ass kicked, but he doesn't deserve eternal punishment."

Ina pulls me into our room. "I suspect Jo isn't as bad as you think. She's hurting and confused, and she's fighting her feelings for him. I think she does love him and even realizes there'll never be anyone else for her, but sometimes a life-changing event can be hard to accept."

I know what she's trying to say, but everything about Jo sets me off. That woman is the one thing I can't protect Nate from. How is he supposed to go through eternity with her? It would have been kinder if the Creator had denied him a mate. "If she loves him, then she needs to be with him. No more bullshit. No more of her games.

She's selfish … everything she's done to him is out of spiteful self-ishness."

Ina pats the bed beside her. "Sit down, Rafe." When I do, she takes my hand and kisses my knuckles. "I think there's a lot more to this than just her reaction to becoming a thunderbird. Once she works through that, those two are going to be okay." Ina slips her hand into mine. "I haven't figured out what her story is yet, but I will find out."

I don't share her optimism, though I wish I could. "We'll—

"Rafe!" Nate hollers from downstairs, and I can hear the stress in his voice. Something isn't right, and for once I get the feeling it has nothing to do with Jo. Whatever it is has him scared. Without a second thought I run out of the room and leap down the steps, skipping two at a time, Ina hot on my heels.

Both Nate and Jo have their wings out and are facing something that shouldn't even be in this world. I skid to a stop next to them, my wings bursting through my shirt, and out of the corner of my eye I see Ina do the same. I blink hard; there's no way I'm seeing what's standing before us. It can't be real. "What the—"

"Don't know." Now that I'm at his side, there's a subtle shift in Nate's posture. He's ready to attack or defend if need be. "This crazy demon just waltzed in here like he owned the place. He waved me away and said I can't see them, as if he were some kind of *Star Wars Jedi*. But it's pretty fucking clear we can all see them."

I'm certain the four of us aren't suffering a group hallucination, which means we really are looking at a huge reddish demon with gnarled, pointed teeth and a crown of horns circling his head. And he's massive—the living room has ten-foot ceilings, and if they were eight, he'd have to stoop to fit.

If that weren't bad enough, the monster has dragged a woman in here with him. The brunette he's holding against her will is struggling to get free, but I don't think she's all there, because she's arguing with herself. It seems part of her wants the demon and the other part doesn't. Then she yells, "Zerbadiah won't hurt you—he's a good guy." Before any of us can reply, the woman adds, "No, he'll kill us all. You have to destroy him. Save me!" It's almost as if she read my mind.

"I don't want to hurt any of you. Just stay calm, and everything will be all right," the demon says as he adjusts his grip on the crazy lady, who is still writhing wildly.

I can see right now that the gal will be of no help; she's either possessed or too divided over her feelings for the grotesque beast to make sense. Without taking my eyes off the demon, I say as quietly as possible, "Well, bro? Any bright ideas, or are we just going to wing it?"

Nate says, "Real fucking funny."

Now, in all fairness I was going for cliché and didn't mean to toss out the pun. "Hum a few bars and fake it?" This isn't what I expected after all those centuries waiting to become a thunderbird. I thought we'd be battling Earth-type bad guys. My mind races over every legend and story connected to the thunderbirds, but I can't recall a single one that contains a demon or a lunatic.

"Not helping, bro," Nate growls through clenched teeth.

Jo takes a half step forward and glares at the beast. "What are you doing here, and what do you want?"

I should have anticipated Jo doing something stupid like this, considering the hellcat she is. Jo may not outwardly act like the strange woman, but inwardly they could be distant cousins from the looney farm. She fears and runs from things she shouldn't, then stands up to something she is better off not challenging. Nate's been stuck with a real winner there, all right.

The demon says, "I won't hurt you. I'm here with Matt."

Our boss? Unable to contain it, I let out a snort. I knew there was something not right about the man, but I'll admit I never imagined this possibility. Wait ... does Matt know what we are? Is that why we got this job so easily? Anger boils at the thought of our so-called boss possibly playing us for all this time. But if he were going to hurt us, wouldn't he have done so months ago?

"If we can just sit tight"—the demon inches toward the couch, pulling the lady along with him—"he and some of the others will be up to the house soon and can answer your questions."

"There's more of you here?" Ina's voice pitches up in terror, and I can't say I blame her. One of these demons is more than enough—I'm not sure even the four of us can take on a demon and win.

"They sent us ahead while accommodations are built for the others." The demon shrugs. "I expected you to be humans, not thunderbirds." An aha look crosses his face, and he whispers in the crazy woman's ear, "The lost thunderbirds ... the peace-bringer prophecy."

My eyebrows shoot upward. I heard what he said, and Nate likely did too, but it's the demon's recognition of us as thunderbirds that I find unsettling. "How do you know what we are?" Admittedly it's a stupid question, considering that our wings are on full display.

Self-preservation has my flight instincts winning the race against my resolve to fight. I barely contain a flinch when the front door bursts open and in walks Matt and some tall, pale-looking dude with dark hair and eyes. Doubtless the looks on their faces mirror my own—shock, mistrust, defensiveness. They're ready to fight. But so are we, and this could get ugly in quick order. I guardedly watch as my boss does a quick assessment of the four of us and the demon holding the brunette. Then he gives a sideways glance to his pale friend and moves between us and the demon, holding his hands out as if to keep the two sides separated. "Whoa!"

In the next instant his eyes seem different, with the green in his hazel coloring almost glowing. But it's what happens to his nose and mouth that's most disturbing. His face narrows, elongating into something resembling a canine or bear snout filled with long, deadly fangs. His words come out in a growl as he looks at the demon. "I thought you said they wouldn't see you?"

"What makes you think we couldn't see you?" Nate's glare is intimidating, but I'm not sure it's going to be enough against this group.

This situation is growing more bizarre by the second. Like tumblers on a lock, all the little oddities about Matt slide into place. He's not human, but what the hell is he—and why is he in league with a demon? I don't think any of us know what to do, because we're just standing our ground in a defensive posture, half crouching and with our wings ready to flog. What I wouldn't give for a set of talons about now.

The demon's red eyes bore right through us. "You didn't tell me your hired hands were thunderbirds."

The pale one steps closer to the demon. His eyes narrow as he takes in the sight of the confused woman in the demon's arms. Then a sappy, lovestruck expression settles on his face—something I've seen a lot on Nate's since he met Jo. Just what we need, another dysfunctional couple—they're all fucking nuts. Still, I get the sense that the man would fight to the death to save the gal, but if that's the case, why isn't he attacking the demon? The power rolling off the pale freak would make a grown man piss his pants.

"Thunder-what?" Matt spins toward us. "Rafe, Nate, you want to tell me what's going on here? What the hell are you?"

"What the hell are we? Fuck, man, what the hell are you?" Nate's fists clench.

Matt growls. "Nate, I've warned you before, that word won't be tolerated in front of women! You better check that shit and answer my question!"

For a moment he sounds like our *friendly* boss who scolded Nate when we first met, or at least the boss we thought we knew. But then I think back to his inside jokes and strange humor, like he really got off on knowing he was something other than human while those around him were ignorant. It kind of pisses me off, but it also tells me he's not a threat if we can come to terms here—Matt has proven himself to be more than fair in all our other encounters.

I step forward, trying to keep my voice level. "It seems we all have some explaining to do." It may not be wise, but I retract my wings—someone needs to give a little here, and Nate sure as hell won't until the others do. In my periphery I see Ina do the same. But Nate shifts position, and in reaction to the movement the pale man sinks into a fighting crouch, flashing a set of long fangs. Sharp, deadly claws extend from his fingers—his hands flex twice, as if readying to swipe. Whatever the hell he is, it isn't the same as Matt.

"Not a good idea, bro. We're a bit outnumbered here," I mutter.

Matt says, "Zerbadiah, take Ramira out of here for a minute or two while we get this powder keg under control." The demon nods and leaves, dragging the crazy woman with him. For a moment the pale one seems to consider following the demon out of the house, but instead he steps forward and takes a menacing stance near our boss. I get the strong impression these two have fought alongside each other before—and not necessarily against humans. A chill races down my spine. Fuck, we're not alone in this world, and the other supernaturals may be the very thing we're supposed to protect the people from.

"I'll have my buddy here put his claws and fangs away if you get your gal to retract her wings." Matt's words seem to bear their own weight, but Nate doesn't flinch under their power any more than I do. Matt dismisses the obvious threat my brother poses; in a steady, reassuring voice, he says, "Then you and I are going to put away our own special features at the same time. Okay? You on board with that, Nate?"

When Nate doesn't acknowledge the request, Matt says, "We don't want to kill you." This time his harsh tone is enough to prompt a response. They obviously aren't aware we can't be killed, but at this point I'm not sure we can kill them either. It'd be a vicious, brutal fight—the winner would be the one not lying in a mangled heap on the floor.

Nate gives the two men, for lack of a better word, a solid once-over before tilting his head enough to see Jo. "Go ahead, Jo. If that dark-haired guy doesn't change at the same time, the deal is off." The pale one scrutinizes Jo for a moment and dips his head in a manner that suggests he's willing to withdraw his fangs and claws. As if on cue, both lose their inhuman features—though Jo stares down the man, seeming ready to reverse herself if needed. Her mousy shyness is gone, and in its place is a steely determination that carries a hint of fierceness. I'm starting to feel like I'm trapped in an episode of *The Twilight Zone.*

"Okay, now it's our turn. You ready, Nate?" Matt's gaze never leaves my brother's eyes, not even after Nate nods his acceptance.

With all of us looking human again, it's a little easier to deal with the bizarre. For the first time, I realize that both Ina's and Jo's shirts have the backs blown out of them from when they unfurled their wings, and what's left covering the front doesn't leave a lot to the imagination. Shit. I move to somewhat block Ina from view—I don't like these men or whatever they are staring at my mate, and if they keep eyeballing her, I may not be able to hold back.

Matt whistles, and his typical good-natured humor resurfaces. "Boy howdy. If everyone can keep themselves under control, I'm going to have Dmitri"—he points at the pale, dark-haired one—"bring the other two back inside, and then we can all sit down to clear up this little surprise."

Before we can say yes, no, or go to hell, Dmitri is out the door and back seconds later with the demon and crazy lady. I want to question why the demon hasn't changed, but then I realize this may be his normal look. It takes a good deal of effort not to shudder at the thought. We've spent centuries believing we were the only preternaturals, and now I'm no longer sure what the hell is out there in our world.

The next several seconds go by like some twisted version of a Mexican standoff, with both sides staring one another down. I almost jump when the demon moves first to sit on the couch. He pulls the crazy lady down next to him, but when the pale one, Dmitri, sends him a sharp look, the demon takes his hands off her. What's up with this guy? He acts possessive, like a mate, yet the demon is clearly asserting some type of claim to the woman. Love triangle— or rather a devil triangle? Is Dmitri some form of demon too? Matt and Dmitri lock gazes for several long seconds before they too sit down, with Dmitri next to the brunette.

Without spoken agreement the four of us move at the same time to the couch opposite our unexpected guests. It gives me hope that we can be an effective team—a skill we may need sooner than expected. But I will protect Ina, no matter what.

Matt looks casual and relaxed, and if I didn't know better, I'd swear he'd just come to talk ranch business like he always did at McAllister. But like every other time before, he still feels off to me, and now I know why. He isn't human any more than we are. "Well, it seems that we've all been keeping secrets from each other. Not without reason, considering what we are." He chuckles. "But now that it's out there, I think we need to come to terms with this surprise and decide where we stand with each other. I like you two brothers, and you've been damn good ranch hands, but if we're going to be enemies, then this is where we part ways."

Nate, as always, has no filter. "We knew something wasn't quite right about you the first time we met, but I never saw this coming." I about want to deck my brother—Nate lacks the control for keeping his trap shut.

"Neither did I, so we're even in that regard." Matt looks from one to the other of us—point made, we all had something to hide.

But that doesn't mean I'm going to spill the beans on our whole story. I'm not sure I trust our boss or his strange group of associates. Who the hell runs around with a demon?

The boss's typical crooked smile flashes across his face. "I'll throw you a bone first." Dmitri darts a glance his way, but I can't quite decipher his expression. Perturbed? There's something about that character that screams deadly, and given the couple inches he has over us in height, I doubt he'd be easy to take down one on one. Not that it would stop Nate from challenging him, but it makes me think twice. I'm not saying he'd win—I'm saying I don't want to fight him unless it's necessary.

Matt says, "Introductions ... Dmitri, Zerbadiah, and Ramira and Eliza." Odd—Matt just introduced a woman who's not even here, but that is beside the point. He really needs to explain the damn demon. As if he understands our silence, he says, "Yeah, more about that in a minute."

Matt addresses his buddies first while the four of us maintain our silence. "Guys, these two, uh, men, are the hired help I told you about—Rafe and Nate Redhawk, who I never suspected were anything other than human." He doesn't miss a beat, swinging his focus back to us. "Want to tell us who the two women are? And what's the deal with the four of you?"

I'm okay playing this game if it gets us some answers. "This is Ina, and the woman next to Nate is Jo. We are—"

The demon, Zerbadiah, says, "They're thunderbirds, an in-between fae ... or at least part fae, which is why my glamour didn't work on them. If my suspicions are correct, they're the missing thunderbirds."

Okay, that's twice now he's called us fae, and he has my attention and evidently Nate's too—we both sit up a little straighter. What does he mean, we're part fae? If this guy is calling us fairies just because we have wings, he's going to have a fight on his hands, and I don't care how big and ugly he is. Another standoff silence grows as Nate and I measure the beast. I'm grateful for our years of fighting together, because we don't need to talk in order to read each other—we'll both engage within a split second of one of us making the first move.

The demon unexpectedly rises from the couch, which has Nate and I up in a defensive crouch before he takes one step. He shakes his head, seeming unfazed as he saunters away, saying he's going to notify a King Altheron and a few others. Zerbadiah says, "They must know we've found the thunderbirds at last." What I don't get is why they were looking for us, and what any of this can possibly mean. Is there a chance they can answer the questions we've asked for centuries?

"What do you mean, we're missing?" As hard as it is, I hold the demon's gaze. I have to know.

"They'll explain." Zerbadiah waves at Dmitri and Matt and leaves the room, dismissing us as if our question is beneath him. I wonder whether all demons are that cocky.

Matt acts like he didn't hear the demon. "So, we know what you are ... now it's our turn. I'm a mongrel werewolf—I used to be human and was turned, not natural born. He's a vampire, and she's ... well, the part you can see is a witch, but she has a vampire stuck in her head."

That confirms it. This truly is some bizarre *Twilight Zone* episode, because I swear he just used *werewolf*, *vampire*, and *witch* in the same sentence while in the company of a *demon*. But then the crazy lady opens her mouth, and I realize he claimed the witch has a vampire in her head. What the hell does that even mean?

The woman says, "Everyone seems to believe I'm some peacebringer who will save this world and the fae realms of Seelinara. But first I need your help to save me. I'm trapped in this witch, and her evil sorcerer uncle has my body locked away. If I die, both worlds are doomed."

She barely takes a breath and adds, "The only ones doomed are you and the rest of the putrid vampires walking the Earth. Well, them and the mangy werewolves too." That chick is way beyond off her rocker—she's sitting amid the wood debris of one that's completely shattered. The brunette needs to be in a psych ward—she's utterly insane.

But Nate focuses on a single word: "You know of Seelinara? This is just too fu—" He catches himself when Matt growls. "Too weird."

The front door opens, and the demon steps aside as a big man barrels past him, stopping a few short feet in front of us. The man barks an order that makes me think this must be King Altheron, and my mind whirls. King of what? "Stand!"

His demanding tone brings Nate and me to our feet, though to provide a screen for our women, not in response to his command. Seeing our defensiveness, Ina and Jo stand too, ready to back us up if needed. I'm really beginning to wonder if we shouldn't just get the hell out.

Then the king motions to a pale, unearthly-looking woman standing in the doorway—Milnea, he calls her—and orders her to read us. If it weren't for her youthful appearance—early twenties, I'd say—sharp teeth, and ethereal paleness, she could be some granola flowerchild left over from the sixties or seventies. She approaches us, and while I don't get a sense of danger, my curiosity is piqued when she places her hand over our hearts one after another. She says to the big man, "It's true, they're in-between fae—thunderbird hybrids." What is with this fae nonsense again? I can feel my wings twitch, ready to come out if I need them. The word has been tossed at us a few times now, and no one is explaining it yet, leaving me uncertain if they're hiding something or if we're more ignorant than I even thought possible.

Pointing at me and Ina, she confirms to the others that we're mates, then says we have good hearts and good intentions. Her assessment of Nate and Jo is spot-on—it's bad. "They're mates, but they won't accept each other ... and she's hiding something about herself, and doing it well enough that even I can't see it." She waves a hand, as if trying to clear away some invisible fog. "He'll be useless if she leaves, which could jeopardize the outcome of the prophecy." The prophecy? Are they talking about the legends our people told of our return? With their accents and appearances, how would they even know about us? There's not one Native among them, and Matt is the only one who even sounds American.

A younger, slender version of Altheron steps forward, inclining his head. "I'm Prince Dahliorn, the Unseelie king's heir apparent." He pauses to study Nate and Jo. Several uncomfortable seconds of quiet drift away. "We have a problem to resolve, so it appears."

Unease ripples through the room—Nate and Jo stand to confront the possible threat, while Matt and Dmitri lean toward each other in whispered conversation. At this point the only one not talking or moving is the newly arrived being that seems to be an angel, if his wings, chiseled features, and luminescent skin are anything to go by. But he appears just as menacing as the demon, and I'm struggling to wrap my head around how our boss has managed to get involved with just about every type of supernatural I've ever heard of. Shit, what's next? Pixies, sprites, and nymphs? I slide a sideways glance at Nate. His expression mirrors mine, and I'm fairly certain we're thinking the same thing: these people had better start making sense pretty damn quick, or we're outta here.

CHAPTER 24: NATE
Know Thyself

Up until now I've been mostly quiet while this weird bunch of characters settle in around us as if this type of thing is normal for them. Not for me—first I get Jo to come back to the ranch, and just as we start to have our first productive conversation, in walks this demon and turns the world upside down. Then our boss shows up with a whole fucking parade of who's what in the preternatural freak world, and although we're getting answers about some things, I'm not tracking the bigger picture of how the four of us fit into it. The vampire, Dmitri, impatiently drags a hand through his hair twice. If I didn't know better, I'd say he's as fed up as I am with all this crap. He's already asked—and been ignored twice now—if we can help free some split-tail named Elizabetta.

It gives me the opening I need, and I jump right in. "Can we get a few things cleared up?" My glare rakes Matt and his strange group before meeting the approving nods of Rafe, Ina, and Jo.

"What do you need to know?" Dmitri says, giving another glance at the chick between him and the demon. I swear the way he watches her is creepy, obsessed—total stalker.

I draw a deep breath. "Okay, first ... we're fae? Isn't that like fairies or something?"

It's the pale woman, Milnea, who says, "Yes, there are fairies, but fae have many species and subspecies just like beings on Earth. You're thunderbirds, considered an in-between species in the fae realm." Her explanation that follows shows just how little we know about ourselves and the world around us. She claims that unlike the Nephilim, born of humans and angels, the in-betweens descended from fae who mated with angels or demons. These pairings, she says, produced the first generation of Seelie and Unseelie, or light and dark fae; and when that first generation mated, the result was the seven immortal species.

Shit, now she has my attention. I still haven't accepted that we're immortal, but her explanation has me grappling with a truth I may not be able to ignore much longer. My raging inner battle has me only half listening as she further breaks down the in-betweens: "Three are Seelie and three are Unseelie, but only one inherited the dark and light genes of both—the thunderbirds."

I freeze, my thoughts screaming that this does not compute, even as Dahliorn says, "The in-betweens are revered among the fae."

"How can we be fae, then?" Rafe looks as confused as I feel. "You're suggesting we're part angel and demon ... I'm not following here."

Milnea gives us another smile, but I'd rather she didn't—that woman has the sharpest teeth I've ever seen. I'd lay odds she could put a piranha to shame defleshing bone. "The rarest life form in the multiverse, the Neraphilim, is the offspring of an angel and demon union. Thunderbirds come from the union of Neraphilim and fae."

What the fuck? Leave it to our species to be the standout freaks—light, dark, good, evil, immortal. But her explanation of our origin nags at me. "Thunderbirds are Native American legends, and we"— I point at Rafe and myself—"were born here to a people, to a tribe, that has gone extinct." I don't need to see Rafe's face to know this point was at the top of his list too.

The angel, called Nafurael, says, "You were born in this world, but the thunderbirds, like all other fae, first came from Seelinara. It's likely that you descended from one of the thunderbirds who lived on Earth before the veils between the two worlds were closed over six hundred years ago."

Rafe and I exchange an uneasy glance; this is getting too close to what we know of the people's legend and our long-lost grandfather. As if he's read my mind, King Altheron launches into a story that seems to tie into what we were told as children. According to him, Seelinarans lived freely on Enethura—Earth—until a sorcerer they call the evil one tried to destroy both worlds. The fae recalled the Seelinarans home, cut ties with Earth, and sealed the veils. If our grandfather, a thunderbird, was fae, then this explains why he had to go. But why did he leave our family behind? If what Altheron is saying is true, the fae tore families apart and left Rafe and me adrift in a world that had forgotten our origins and could never fully tell us who or what we are—something I've struggled with more than Rafe. Do they have any idea how much rougher that made it for us growing up different from the world around us? Of the difficulties and challenges that could have been avoided if they'd left even one of their kind behind? Fuck them!

Rafe nods toward Nafurael and Zerbadiah. "And where do they fit into all this?"

"Both chose to live on Seelinara," Milnea says. "Their kind have been among us since the fae came into existence. It's due to the celestials that fae have magic and special abilities." Milnea smiles, again with the teeth—it's enough to make a man swear off blow jobs. I cringe just thinking about it. "I'm an elemental who can call upon air and water." To demonstrate she chants something unintelligible, and the air in front of us shimmers and solidifies into a clear ball filled with water. Both Ina and Jo seem compelled to touch it, going so far as to pick it up and pass it between them when they realize it's solid. It's in Jo's hands when Milnea says something to release it, and the ball shimmers and then disappears without one drop of water being spilled.

And there goes the bottom out of the badger hole. Ina, though, seems entranced by the elemental's magic—she can't keep her big mouth shut. Her bubbly questions rub me the wrong way, and her easy acceptance of all this drives my resentment toward her a little higher. A mocking voice in my head suggests this is my punishment and Rafe's reward. Screw you, fates! My jaw clenches tighter as her questions become increasingly personal: Can we procreate? Can we get sick? What happens if we're injured or lose our heads? Does the mate bond form in love or create it? Fuck this. While we may need to know this shit, I don't like having it shoved at us all at once. And damn her for inquiring about the one aspect I'm trying to purge from my mind—fae having children with angels and demons. Because we thunderbirds descended from a Neraphilim, we have their dual magic inside us, which means we're part demon as well—and the unbidden images that conjures up are horrifying. I may do wrong, but I've never considered myself evil.

Ina finally says, "I don't want to offend you, but why would someone willingly mate with an evil being?"

Took her long enough to ask—no sane person would choose sex with one, as far as I'm concerned. Zerbadiah's red eyes flash a little brighter, and his disgruntled tone indicates he is offended nonetheless. He insists that only meritorious demons are allowed on Seelinara, those who have risen and been accepted into the celestial realm and are in favorable standing there. This sets off a brief discussion of good and evil, and both the angel and demon maintain that as sure as an angel can fall into evil, a demon can rise into righteousness. But at their core, light and dark remain, the difference between the two a simple matter of descent. Simple, my ass—nothing about this whole screwed-up mess is simple.

For the next several hours Matt's supernatural associates patiently field as many questions as the four of us can toss at them, but it's Jo who finally seeks the answer to how she and Ina were changed. That's something I've asked myself a thousand times, but I'm still unsure if I want to know. If I did this to her—if our curse had that power—then I have even more reason to hate it. This leads to additional confusion and some chaos when Dahliorn tells us that only the in-between can turn other fae into their species by mating—and that humans can't be changed. A sick, writhing feeling claws its way to my throat, cutting off my ability to breathe. With disgust and horror I look at my mate. Not human. What the hell is she?

Jo's already pale features blanch even more. "No, it's impossible." She keeps shaking her head, as if someone just gave her a terminal diagnosis. "I know my lineage, my family history on all sides. I'm human ... you're wrong."

Zorbadiah says, "Nafurael and I can tell you exactly what you are if you wish to know."

Rafe and Ina glance nervously at each other, but Jo never looks at me—her body curves away from me as if my touch could possibly do her more harm than it already has.

I hear Ina suck in a deep breath before she says, "Okay." Rafe nods as he grabs her hand in support. Must be nice to be them— Jo's still leaning away from me.

The angel and demon move the coffee table and have her step forward. I see Rafe tense as the two celestial beings place their hands upon her—the angel's hand over her heart and the demon's on her head—but after a brief minute their hands drop to their sides.

Nafurael says, "Your human side is a mix of Gros Ventre and Blackfoot, and your fae side, apart from the thunderbird, is efurrid—that is, a rock sprite. Seelie." He smiles at her. "One of our party, a sorceress named Alastrina, is also efurrid. If you like, she can tell you more about that side of your fae heritage."

I can see from the look on Ina's face that she's excited to learn this, and it's another stark reminder of the extreme difference between Rafe and me, and Ina and Jo. We're well past polar opposites—more like galactic opposites. Ina is part sprite, something cute and lovable, evidently. With my luck Jo will turn out to be some snakelike or goblin creature, cold and despicable. But what if they're wrong?

Rafe tugs on my arm—it's our turn to be tested. I'm astonished when Nafurael announces correctly that we are Hachaath and thunderbird. Should have asked instead, what if they're right?

Until this point Jo has kept as much distance as possible from the two celestial beings, but then she surprises me when she somewhat shyly steps forward, asking to be tested. The angel and demon place their hands in position over her heart and head, and a moment later they step back. One is smiling but the other looks concerned—and both exchange a glance with Altheron and Dahliorn. I almost feel sick when the demon opens his mouth to speak. This fucked-up night just keeps getting better and better. Jo wants no part of me, and she had to have known and hidden that she wasn't fully human. Now this? It'd be my luck if she turned out to be part demon—a darker fae. Sure would explain a lot.

Zerbadiah smiles with the ugliest gnarled teeth I've ever seen. Jo flinches, but I can't blame her—it's gruesome. My instinct is to put myself between her and the demon, but I hesitate, unsure I want to be between those two. Rafe makes the decision for me by grabbing my arm to hold me back.

Zerbadiah says, "You are special." He casts a glance at the king and prince. "She's of royal family blood"—he looks back at Jo—"but you're glamoured so humans see you as one of them and you believe the lie."

He pauses, but Jo's jaw is clamped tight. Shrugging, he says, "To humans you look Native, fitting with your story of being Chippewa and Assiniboine." He points at Rafe and me. "They see you as you are, same as they see me and the other Seelinarans."

So, not Native. I guess that explains why I never saw it when we met.

The room erupts, everyone trying to talk at once. My heart is pounding so hard it nearly drowns out the commotion around me, but then I see Jo sway. Damn it, I knew this was going to do a number on her. I leap forward just in time to catch her as she passes out. Someone suggests while I'm trying to revive Jo that perhaps she should be allowed to rest while our discussion continues, and seeing the almost unhinged look in her eyes after she comes to, I have to agree.

What I don't expect is that the vampire, crazy lady, prince, and elemental make the next few decisions for us. They inform everyone that they will take Jo to a bedroom and remain with her while these discussions continue. Reluctantly I agree, but when I see Dmitri move between us, extending a hand to Jo, I about lose my shit. No fucking vampire will touch my mate! Without thought I shove him away and pull Jo into my arms. "Mine!" I glare at him, and a slight smile breaks across his face as his head inclines in acknowledgment of my claim.

After he steps back I carry Jo up to my room and lay her on the bed. I only agree to leave her when the four of them reassure me that Dmitri will not touch her. My threat to avenge her may have helped a little, but I swear they seemed more amused than fearful.

Descending the stairs, I hear King Altheron saying something about thunderbirds' immortality and the Ancestors we may have living on Seelinara—and at that I stop cold on the steps. Is it possible our grandfather is still there? That revelation leads the discussion in another direction, and I feel like I'm getting fucking whiplash trying to keep up.

They begin to discuss when we should go and where the nearest veil is, but Matt returns their focus to what seems to be a bigger issue to him and Dmitri. "So if we're sending them to Seelinara, where does this leave us with trying to rescue baby vamp?"

Who the hell is baby vamp? Please don't tell me vampires can have kids—that's just not fucking right. Before I can voice that in a form that won't earn Matt's ire, Dmitri's tone becomes borderline violent, and I see the tension in his jaw and his fists curling at his sides. "We still need to find Guillermo and prepare Ramira to infiltrate his compound before we're going to be ready to rescue Elizabetta. That's assuming we can remove the sorcerer's belts from her and Dahliorn—it'll do no good to take her from that compound if Guillermo can use the belts to kill her."

"After being stuck inside that witch, I'd bet baby vamp would take the risk," Matt says. "But I'm inclined to agree with Dmitri—it may be too risky to proceed without the thunderbirds' help, and neither of us wants to lose Eliza."

Yeah, it's all as clear as mud, and now I'm not sure if Elizabetta is Eliza *and* baby vamp or if that damn witch has three vampires trapped in her head.

And apparently she is also connected to some fae prophecy that foretold of the veils being sealed, ending communication between Seelinara and Earth. The legend says a peace-bringer will find an ancient moonchild—an immortal werewolf—which apparently is rare, because most werewolves only live two or three hundred years. They believe this ancient werewolf is our boss, which means ... just how old is Matt? How many centuries has he lived?

According to the group, the peace-bringer was to find and return a lost prince, who they insist is Prince Dahliorn. The third leg of this prophecy is the thunderbirds ... us.

"What?" rings out times three. The looks on Rafe's and Ina's faces probably match my own bewildered expression. For centuries we grew up under the cloud of the thunderbird legend, and now they're saying we factor into some fae legend too? Fuck it, I need a drink. I go to the liquor cabinet and pour myself a shot of bourbon, downing it just in time to see Rafe and Ina reaching for one too. Of course the Seelinarans don't let this stop them—no, they keep on talking. I choke on my second shot when they suggest that the peace-bringer is the vampire trapped inside the witch. What kind of fucked-up world did I wake up in today?

Dmitri asks again about her rescue—he seems obsessed with the vampire in the witch's head. But then we learn why. She is his mate, and to my surprise, the queen of the vampire realm. Yes, that makes Dmitri a king, and now my mind is reeling in a new direction.

What started out as a long, lonely life has led us into a world—rather, into worlds—and realms we never knew existed. Fuck, we're over five hundred years old, and now we find out everything we thought we knew only proves we didn't know shit about the world around us. Then I realize all the stories and legends may be rooted in truth one way or another—and at this point I'd lay odds that if each one were traced back to its origin, we'd discover it was related to some long-ago fae from Seelinara. Rafe slumps onto the couch with his head in his hands. Ina stares blankly ahead. For centuries we sought the truth, and now here we are—information fucking overload.

That thought is still echoing in my head when Dmitri and Dahliorn enter the room, their expressions grim. Jo! I race toward the stairs, but they block my path, telling me to calm down. It's all I can do to keep my wings from unfurling as they stand their ground—the power rolling off them feels like a challenge.

"Jo is resting, but Milnea had to place her in a bubble when she tried to escape." Dmitri's matter-of-fact tone leaves the hairs on my neck standing on end—I'm envisioning Jo in something like the small water-filled orb the razor-toothed gal created earlier. My fists clench.

I try once more to push past them and find their physical strength matches their powerful auras. With seemingly little effort they grab my arms, hauling me back a few steps.

"Bubble? What do you mean, she tried to run away?" If they harm her, it may seal my fate to endure immortality alone. I yell for her again as my panic rises.

Dmitri says, "She wanted to use the bathroom to change out of her torn shirt, but I heard the window open, and when I busted through the door, she was about to jump out. I grabbed her in time." Rafe and Ina move in behind me—I hope it's because they have my back. But Dmitri barely acknowledges them. "After we placed her on the bed, Milnea created a bubble to keep her from running," he says.

I feel some gratitude that he stopped Jo from fleeing once more, but there's one detail I'm still missing. It hasn't escaped me that no one's mentioned Jo's nonhumanness since she left the room— I have to know what I mated with. "Supposed royal bullshit aside, does anyone care to enlighten me as to what the hell Jo is?"

Nafurael says, "Beyond inherently thunderbird, Jo is a sheridauk—an Unseelie in-between, the same as the king and prince."

That doesn't tell me a damn thing. "A *sher-eh-what?*"

"We're shifters, somewhat similar to the wolf, bear, and cat shifters in this world." But Dahliorn offers a description that paints the sheridauk royalty as four-legged animals nowhere near like any we've seen before. Then he adds that they too are one of the seven immortal species of fae. Jo's a four-legged animal? Something about this revelation upsets Dmitri, and in less than a heartbeat he flies across the room and grabs the Unseelie king.

Before Altheron can react, Dmitri has him by the throat, his fangs and claws extended. "You ordered us to find your son dead or alive. You lied to us and endangered my wife!" The tips of Dmitri's claws pierce the sheridauk's throat. It has my nerves jumping to release my wings, and I'm ready for a fight, especially if that Unseelie king shifts into whatever he is. Whatever Jo is, apparently—but I'll deal with that later. One look at Rafe confirms that if it comes to a brawl, we'll fight to protect each other.

Altheron's eyes flash red, and it appears he's going to shift, but when the vampire's clawed hand settles over the Unseelie king's chest—a clear signal he'll rip the heart out—the sheridauk ceases his struggle. But this capitulation is offset by the viciousness in his tone. "Fae cannot lie. I spoke the truth."

Matt joins in with his fangs showing, and he looks as torqued as the vampire. "Bullshit! We heard your threats and instructions"—he jabs a finger in Dahliorn's direction—"we were to protect him with our lives, but if he were dead, you wanted to know and you wanted him avenged."

The two kings are close in height, and even though Altheron's build is stockier, Dmitri easily shoves the sheridauk back a few steps. "You knew your son could never die."

I'd figured the vampire was one badass son of a bitch, and I have no doubts left now. He'd be lethal in a fight, and like me, he probably never loses—good to know if I ever end up on the wrong side of him.

"I. Did. Not. Lie." Controlled rage punctuates each word. Altheron gives a subtle shake of his head, and his eye color turns from red to light green. His gaze drifts toward Dahliorn before settling on the vampire again. "Had Guillermo corrupted my son and evil taken him over, Dahliorn would have been dead to me. He would have been cast out, added to the forbidden, and he would have ceased to exist in our lives."

This, as it turns out, is our first lesson on how tricky fae can be with the truth. These fuckers say one thing, knowing full well how it will be interpreted, and yet there may be a completely different meaning behind the words. In my book, twisted or manipulated truth is as good as a lie—but I'll admit the fae's duplicity has elevated the vampire and werewolf in my esteem.

Dmitri releases Altheron and rakes his hand through his hair twice, pausing to hold his bangs back. He and Matt appear to reach some kind of silent understanding before Matt urges everyone to retake their seats. The lopsided grin returns to Matt's face, but it seems to be meant for whatever passed between him and Dmitri. More secrets we're not privy to ... more lies? I'm going to start beating the truth out of these people, monsters, or whatever the hell they are.

He deflects from the confrontation by returning the topic to shifters—Earth-based ones. Matt tells us that our former supervisor, Travis, is part of his ragtag wolf pack. That explains their disappearing the week of every full moon, which I'll admit I never made the connection to. Why would I? I was stupid enough to think Rafe and I were alone in the supernatural realm. It's no wonder I didn't consider whether my boss was a damn werewolf.

I momentarily close my eyes, and when they open I pin Matt with a glare. Images of the lone wolf sitting watching us and the ranch come to mind. First visit, my ass—first two-legged appearance is more like it. "You've been here more than we were aware, haven't you?"

He shrugs. "I wanted to see how the ranch was coming along, and it looked like you had everything under control—I didn't need to disturb your work."

Rafe blurts out, "Shit. I'll be damned ... you're the light-brown wolf!" Real swift on the uptake there, bro. Matt simply nods, and I'm not sure if I feel relieved we didn't shoot him or if we should shoot him now on principle for spying on us.

The sheridauk prince, Dahliorn, speaks up: "I know we need the thunderbirds if Elizabetta is to fulfill the prophecy, but they must be ready to do their part. Jolenthia isn't."

I spin toward him—he is right behind me, but I hadn't heard or noticed him move that close. "What's that supposed to mean?"

"She has some dark things in her past which are making it near impossible for her to accept her heritage and her mate bond with you." Dahliorn's voice isn't cold or malicious, but it grates on my last fucking nerve. He's beginning to piss me off a hundred ways from Sunday.

"Then you need to back the hell off ... she just needs time," I say, but I already know it's not so easy as that. Something tells me her past is the poisonous cherry on top of her nonhuman shit sundae. I'm afraid to find out what these dark things may be, because I fear they will doom us to stay apart forever.

Dahliorn shakes his head. "Milnea and I can see past her denial. Jolenthia doesn't even realize what she looks like, and—"

"What the hell do you mean, what she looks like?" Fear creeps up my spine. If the earlier description of a sheridauk in its shifted form is anything to go by, my mate may be as hideous as that damn demon sitting across the room. Yeah, I'm fucking losing it at this point. Why in the hell did I get stuck with a whacked-out, lying, demonic-animal bitch?

"Someone has hidden her true identity, robbing her of knowing herself. She's never shifted with another sheridauk either, and we need to know why." Altheron nods in agreement with Dahliorn, and I realize they're acting as if they have some claim to Jo. Hell the fuck no. The younger sheridauk adds, "The fact she's part of the royal lineage presents a delicate problem for us. All of this must be resolved before she can fulfill her role as your mate."

Dahliorn's tone is commanding, and I've had enough. I take a swing at him, but he's surprisingly fast and ducks the blow. Matt and Dmitri move closer, their support for him clear. My brother, who should have my back, places himself between me and the sheridauk—he won't allow the fight that's overdue. Who is Dahliorn to decide my mate's future? It's becoming clear that Jo is a bigger surprise to Matt's friends than our status as thunderbirds, which leaves me wondering what the hell I mated with. Is her humanoid shape an illusion, or glamour, as the Seelinarans call a false appearance? I glare at the sheridauks. Every so-called answer only leads to more questions, adding to the unwelcome mystery surrounding Jo.

Dahliorn either doesn't see my look or ignores me outright. "I also agree that all of you should be brought back to Seelinara to learn your capabilities, magic, and natural skills before you join us in bringing the prophecy to fruition."

Rafe says, "What about our role as thunderbirds and our legacy to protect the people? What about our responsibilities here at this ranch?"

King Altheron waves Dahliorn aside. "It's a solid plan to return you to your other home world—you are of both worlds," he says. "You"—his hand sweeps across the three of us—"are so much more than you realize, and you can do far more than just flap your wings."

My mouth drops open as I stare at this Unseelie king and prince, who to an unexpected degree have become as valuable to us for information as any elder, healer, or seer has been over the past several centuries. It never occurred to me that we could do more than fly. But whatever it is better be useful, not awful, like the women laying eggs or something. My brain rebels against the flood of information we've learned tonight. This fucking curse! Enigmas, mysteries, unknowns, nothing being what it seems or should be ... We're not just freaks. We're freaks of nature, of the universe. And so far the details barely cover the surface of the iceberg they're exposing. At this point we know just enough to be dangerous and get ourselves in trouble.

We're in over our fucking heads.

CHAPTER 25: RAFE

Veascru Honda

It turns out Matt's group is here for the long haul—their place in Venice was blown up by missile strikes—and he announces this may become a somewhat permanent arrangement, or at least until the war is over. Their plans sideline all disagreements between Nate and me or even with Jo. If there's one thing we've learned, it's when to stick together, show a united front, and we and our mates will take care of one another first. At the moment Jo's still isolated upstairs, but I hope she gets the memo—or that one of us will have the chance to caution her later. Regardless of what she thinks of us, I can't allow her to reveal any weaknesses among our group. And I definitely don't need Jo's nonsense on top of the powder keg that is my brother. Pushing Nate much further will expose his volatility—nitroglycerin comes to mind. The fae are shaking that bottle and throwing sparks ... hell, the fuse is already lit. The tic in Nate's jaw, the growling at everyone, the furtive glances to check if I have his back, and the constant balling and flexing of his hands ... I know the signs, and it's not a matter of if, but when he will blow up.

It's selfish, but I'm grateful Ina isn't a mystery—no wonder everything went wrong for Nate from the start. Jo is a never-ending train wreck. The tricksters obviously aren't done messing with him yet, but even I know they need to back off and allow him some happiness in his life. Part of me wants to fix this mess, though the other half of me realizes there's nothing I can do, other than ride it out and help him when I can—and hope it doesn't destroy us in the meantime.

I'm still mulling over Nate's predicament as we head outside, where I discover how badly outnumbered we really are. Between the supernaturals from this world and those from Seelinara, I count somewhere between forty and fifty. While some of these beings may be considered minor league, the leaders and their immediate subordinates are clearly the all-star team of supernaturals. I'm still waiting to see if we're in the minors or majors, or if we have a shot at the top too.

To say the Druzhina—the vampire realm's elite enforcers of rules and punishment—are intimidating is an understatement. The power I sense in these vampires is incredible, but most remarkable is that some are more than a few hundred years older than Nate and me. Hell, even Dmitri and his queen, Elizabetta, have over a century on us. Together with the Druzhinniki—a similar group directly beneath them in the hierarchy—the eleven Druzhina help maintain order across the supernatural realms. The Druzhinniki, we're told, once numbered several hundred, but their ranks were culled during a recent war to get rid of a vampire who'd ruled their realm for a thousand years. And here I thought we'd been around a long time! I feel like we lived with our damn heads encased in cement—it's hard to imagine how all this could go on around us and we never knew it.

The Seelinarans present range from more sheridauks—the royal guard—to a mix of sprites, elves, an earth and fire elemental, an air and water elemental, and much to my chagrin, actual pixies. But it is the maxians who draw Ina's attention and in turn, mine. Maxians are magic wielders from this world, but like us, some are of fae lineage—hybrid offspring of fae and maxians. Matt's girl-friend, come to find out, is a wizard; that explains her humor at the McAllister ranch.

We also meet a warlock and the sorceress Alastrina, who is part efurrid like Ina. Yeah, my mate is part sprite—and even though she is now a thunderbird, the fae believe she can still use her efur-rid powers, though whatever those are exactly I'm unsure. It seems rock sprites use rocks, gems, and minerals with their magic, and they prefer to live surrounded by stone, which would explain Ina's rather large assortment of rocks. I chuckle in spite of myself—I helped her move her stone collection, and it numbers in the hun-dreds.

Ina whispers now, "All this time I thought the stones came to me for the records and dreams they contain, and now I wonder how many I attracted because of my natural magic. I can't wait to learn what I can do."

"I think we'd all like to fucking know what we can do," Nate's frustration matches my own. The long night of revelations opened up a world beyond our imaginations, and we were barely used to having wings at all. "Do you think our Ancestors in the tribe knew what the thunderbirds really were?" he asks.

I understand Nate's unspoken question: did they betray us by withholding knowledge? But I shake my head. "They had to have known something. How else could the thunderbirds have lived among our people and produced offspring?"

"I wonder when the knowledge was lost?" Ina looks at both of us, but it only reminds me that she was something more than mere human too—and obviously unaware.

"Who knows," I say. Not only was thunderbird history badly kept, but it seems the same is true for the efurrid, rock sprites. Yet I suspect the sprites influenced the Stone People legends as well.

Nate's eyes narrow. "Where do you think Jo fits into all of this? We don't even know what the fuck a sheridauk is, other than a demon-fae that shifts into some kind of beast." That seems to ignite something else, and he takes off toward the Unseelie king's royal guards. I find myself jogging after him—I know what he's going to demand.

One of the guards steps forward. "Thunderbirds," he says with a respectful dip of his head. "Is there some way I can be of service to you?"

Before Nate can say something that might cause tension between us and the fae, I jump in: "Will you show us what you are when you transform?"

The sheridauk nods and begins to undress, explaining that the king has forbidden them to use their full magic in front of us until we're properly informed of our capabilities—they don't want to risk triggering our own magic. Of course he doesn't elaborate. I swear I should have "clueless and don't understand" tattooed on my forehead. I hear Ina gasp when he starts to push his pants down, and when I glance in her direction, I see she's turning away from the man. When I face him again, he's nude, his body shuddering, and then he malforms. I blink, trying to absorb what I'm seeing. The humanoid form distorts and morphs, and his limbs take a four-legged's shape.

Glossy white fur erupts over his now sleek body, and scales or armor plates cover his throat, chest, and belly. His catlike snout grows large, thick fangs and razor-sharp teeth that look just as deadly as the long, stout claws on the toe pads of his feet, or rather paws. Lean muscle becomes bulky, similar to a bear's, but the body is closer to a wolf's. My eyes pop wide, and I find myself taking a half step in front of Ina as a layer of narrow spikes—inside a serrated trough that runs along his neck, between his humped shoulders, and down the ridge of his back—stand on end. They weren't kidding about these sheridauks having familiar yet distinct traits.

Talk about intimidating on steroids. There's no animal I can compare it to ... other than a beast ripped straight from the pages of a horror story.

Fuck, I wouldn't want to tangle with one of these things. Then I remember this is what Jo is too, and my gaze darts to Nate. He looks half-sick, and I can't blame him—Jo must have known she could change into one of these damn things. I recall the fae speculating whether she's aware that she can choose which form to take. Nate evidently didn't forget either, for in the next instant his wings are out and he's taking to the sky.

Zerbadiah says, "Will he come back?"

I shake my head, unsure if he just needs a few minutes to sort this bullshit out or if he's pulling another disappearing act.

"We must go after him." The demon's solid form vibrates, skin and bone turning translucent, almost vanishing, and yet remaining as he becomes foglike.

It's my turn to stare agape, struggling to comprehend how something that large in mass can dissipate into almost nothing. The moment the demon is a reddish vaporous cloud, he takes off after Nate. I'm still trying to keep my brain from short-circuiting. Ina's incredulous expression mirrors my own thoughts, and it takes us a few long seconds to realize now is not the time to contemplate what we just witnessed. Instead we release our wings and give chase.

Once we're airborne, I learn two things. Nate is a bit faster than we are—I can see the distance growing between us—and Zerbadiah is faster than Nate. Working our wings as hard as we can, Ina and I watch as the demon's mist settles over Nate, pinning my brother's wings to his sides. But he's struggling against the demon's hold and must be putting up quite an effort, because Zerbadiah loses control of their flight and they tumble out of the sky.

I barely register Ina's gasp as I go into a shallow dive in an attempt to reach them before they hit the ground, though I know I'm too far out—the low angle of my dive isn't going to give me enough speed. But I'm desperate to save him. Nate is writhing against Zerbadiah, which appears to be futile as long as the demon is in this half-mist form. My breath catches in my throat when I realize they're less than fifty feet from the ground. I'll never make it in time. While the demon may not be able to kill Nate, I can't bear the thought of my brother's body broken again, encased in medical contraptions.

Then to my astonishment, Zerbadiah's body solidifies as he rotates so that Nate is on top, and both hit the ground with a resounding thud. That son of a bitch just used himself to break and cushion Nate's fall. The impact doesn't seem to have any effect on the demon, though; he's still holding Nate even as he gets them both to their feet.

Ina sets down next to me, and we run toward the other two. "Hey, bro, you okay?"

Nate's still wriggling to free himself. "Yeah, I'm just fucking peachy. I'd be even better if I could get this big goon off my ass." His teeth are clenched in anger—I'd be rich if money fell from the sky each time I've seen that look on my brother's face.

A hauntingly raspy but echoing laugh rumbles out of Zerbadiah. "In the pecking order of the multiverse, young thunderbird, you'll find that greater angels and demons are at the top of the chain. You'll never outfly me or outmaneuver me. We'll consider this your first lesson."

I guess that answers my earlier question back at the house; if we'd tried to take him on in a fight, the demon would have schooled us like children. "Okay, we have him. Now what?" We need to defuse this before Nate goes batshit crazy and does something he'll regret.

"Now he goes back with us." Another hideous smile flashes across Zerbadiah's face. "The question is, will he come along willingly, or am I going to have to teach him a few more lessons before he makes the right decision?"

Ina places a hand on Nate's forearm. "Let's just go back, okay?"

"I can't. You saw that ... thing. Jo's one of them! I knew this was some cosmic fucking joke, and this proves it—the fates are spiting me for thwarting their plans." Nate is near full meltdown mode, but I'm again at a loss for the right words. An "I'm sorry, tough break, bro" wouldn't remove the fact that I'd be right there along with him if Ina were like Jo. One thing is certain; it explains why Jo acted the way she did. If I were in her shoes, I wouldn't want Ina to learn what I was either.

Zerbadiah makes a tsking sound. "You don't understand the rare gift you've been given. The seven immortal fae species are the only ones driven to find a true mate, while other, lesser fae may choose a mate but change their minds later and find another. Some, like the nymphs, are so sexually driven that they seldom take a mate longer than needed for procreating."

The demon turns Nate around, looking him in the eye. Fury radiates from my brother in tremulous shudders—I half expect him to have a seizure. Zerbadiah says, "But your bonding is exceedingly rare in our world. Only three other in-betweens have chosen their mates from within the seven immortal species. The power they wield together far surpasses what any other fae, angel, or demon can bring to bear; it is their lineage that produces the royal bloodlines. Those like you stand above all others when it comes to protecting the world, or in your case, two worlds."

Whoa, wait a minute. Did he just suggest that we are some shirttail relation to the Unseelie king and prince? Then I remember Zerbadiah's earlier insistence that Jo is of royal family blood. So is Nate's mating with Jo equivalent to marrying a cousin? I glance at Nate. If Zerbadiah expected his little pep talk to be well received, then he missed it by a damn mile. Unless you consider that Nate is ground zero for devastation—I can see it written all over his face, in his rigid posture, and in the wild look in his eyes. Damn, this is not going to be good. "Just calm down, bro ... it's going to work itself out."

"Calm the fuck down? Shit, bro, I have a mutant beast for a mate, who, by the way, hates me and may be related to us. And I'm supposed to just calm down and go with the bullshit flow?" Nate's gaze shifts from me to Zerbadiah. His voice drops an octave, turning harsh, gruff. "Can. I. Break. It?"

"Break what?" The demon appears confused, but I know exactly what my brother is asking.

"The fucking mate bond! She doesn't want me, and I'm not sure I want her anymore either ... I am absolutely certain the fates only stuck her ass with me out of some twisted desire for revenge."

The demon's form once more dissolves, losing body mass, but his words drift out as he changes. "You're eternal soulmates, two halves of one soul. There's no breaking what binds you. Your Spirit was forged and split between you both when you were created." And with that the ocher fog whisks Nate into the air and heads back toward the ranch.

I now understand my connection to Ina—even when we're apart, we are never truly separated. My eyes close as this knowledge settles in, and I'm suddenly humbled to receive such a gift from the Creator. Why me? Why us? It's disrespectful of me to question it, and I just as quickly offer a prayer of thanks to the Creator for reuniting the soul Ina and I were tasked with bearing. There are no words to describe the honor bestowed on us.

But then other questions filter in, and they are the ones I want answers to. My union with Ina is loving, natural, and welcome. Why must Nate and Jo's mate bond be so troubled? Do they have a chance to repair whatever went wrong between them, or are they doomed to spend eternity hating and running from each other, pushing each other away? I'm also unsure why Jo is being punished along with my brother. What did she do to deserve to share his fate?

I'm about to launch into the sky after them when Ina stops me. "Rafe, from what the others are saying, we're running out of time to help that vampire, Elizabetta, save both Earth and Seelinara. We need to help your brother and Jo come to terms with this. I don't want to know what happens to immortals when everything around us dies or ceases to exist."

Her words hit their mark, and I draw her into my arms. Ina may well be the compassion and brains behind our little quartet. "I love you, babe. Let's head back and see what we can do about getting those two to Seelinara."

A strange sight greets us upon our arrival back at the ranch. Nate and Jo are enclosed in a floating bubble together, and both look pissed enough to tear the world apart with their bare hands. I look at Matt, noting the amused quirk in his grin. If he finds this funny, then Nate fucked up again. "What's going on here?"

He laughs. "It was decided they needed a time-out, since they're vying for the problem child of the year award."

Man, this isn't going to go well once they're let out of there, and I know it. Shit, what a mess. Matt offers to relay the news to King Altheron that we're back, and as he walks away my focus is drawn to my brother. Nate has gone utterly still. Then he flashes me the "get me out of this shit yesterday" look, and that, combined with the bubble shimmering like glitter, is too much. I lose it, doubling over with laughter. Given the way he's already upset, I shouldn't laugh, but damn it, I can't stop myself. It takes a moment for me to regain composure, and when Ina asks me what's so funny, I about start laughing again. Looking Nate in the eye, I say, "Time to burst your bubble, figuratively, of course." I turn back toward Ina. "It seems Nate found a new trickster club member to play with. Jo's been messing with Coyote and Spider too."

The confused faces around me prompt an explanation of the Native legends about tricksters—Coyote and Spider in particular—and how they're meant to teach lessons through humor and contrary situations. "Both of them knew what they were hiding from each other when they met. Neither expected to be found out. That's what all this is—Jo's reluctance, Nate's love-hate—it's no wonder they can't make up their minds if they want each other or not. I think Coyote tripped them while Spider bit them in the ass, and now here they are, the butt of their own jokes."

"There's not one fucking thing about this that is funny, asshole," Nate roars, but I just laugh harder. He's lucky Matt isn't in earshot, or he'd be in even more trouble. And I'm lucky my brother's trapped in that bubble, or we'd probably be rolling on the ground in a fight.

To my surprise Ina laughs with me, and it's then that I know I pegged it in one witty swoop. I'm already wiping tears out of my eyes, when I see Nate and Jo turn their backs on each other in their tight little bubble, folding their arms across their chests. The childish act has me nearly on my knees—this may be the funniest thing I've ever witnessed coming from my brother.

Dahliorn puts an end to our moment of levity. "We really need to get you to Seelinara." He points toward four sheridauks and the two pixies gathered near us. "I'd like you four and one of the pixies to escort the thunderbirds to Seelinara. Guards, see that they are given appropriate homes near their kin, and Tavorell, carry the king's message to the palace. They'll need the best among us to start training as soon as possible."

That sobers me up, and for a moment I feel like a child again—others making decisions for me, and I have no say. But I'm smart enough to recognize that I'm out of my league here and am going to have to play by their rules for a while. I look at Ina. "We'd better go pack."

Dahliorn says, "That won't be necessary. Everything you need will be provided to you." He hands some kind of scroll to Tavorell, which is easily twice the pixie's height—but the little creature carries it as if it were weightless. Tavorell puffs out his tiny chest and winks at me.

A quick round of good-byes pass between us, Matt, and his strange friends. Then two of the sheridauks take position near the bubble and push it along, as though it's gliding on a cushion of air. Ina falls into step beside me, and clasping hands, we follow the first two sheridauks. Tavorell seems content to flit about, chattering up a storm as we head for the nearest veil.

The portal's location is another surprise; it's on the ranch and less than two miles from the house. The veil itself is on the side of a near-vertical hill in the same wide coulee that Nate and I recognized when we first arrived at the ranch. It boggles my mind how much of the supernatural world surrounds us and how we've lived so long ignorant of it. The elders and storytellers often said there were other beings and multiple rebirths of Earth that caused many of them to come or go. Aside from a few prominent legends, we considered much of it to be teaching lessons, and I'm beginning to understand we were wrong to discount those stories. How many hidden or forgotten beings are still here? We've been blind to this world—I am seeing it now with open eyes. And soon I'll be entering a world, a whole different planet, that I never knew existed in reality until six hours ago. I can't believe we're fucking doing this. I'm not sure what lies ahead, but reflecting on everything that has brought us to this point in our lives, I recognize two important facts. Being thunderbirds put us on a course to meet the fae long before Ina and Jo appeared; and we were destined to cross Matt's path too, since he proved to be the connection to the fae.

As our group comes to a halt in front of the steep hillside, one of the sheridauks turns to Ina. "Would you like to do the honors?"

She looks at us and then back at him. "How?"

He whispers something in her ear, and a strange expression settles on her face. "What does that mean?"

"Veascru nonda." The sheridauk tilts his head and smiles. "Welcome home."

CHAPTER 26: NATE

Grandfather's Father

The honey butter slipping off my fry bread is that I can't stop freaking out—yeah, I'm still having a hard time accepting that I mated with something that turns into a full-blown animal. Jo points out for the hundredth fucking time that I'm acting unhinged and have been since that damn demon returned me to Matt's ranch. Okay, so it wasn't one of my better moments.

Almost immediately my mouth overloaded my ass, demanding they keep Jo away from me, and next thing I knew, I was put into this bubble with Jo, with a little over a foot of space between us. Thanks to its shape, we can maintain that distance if we face each other and recline against the sides, but to keep from looking at one another, we're stuck standing back to back. Believe me, that's ten different ways worse. The contact has my body wanting to claim her, to wrap her in my arms and never let her go. My mind is fighting that urge, and I'm sure it's screaming at my rack of bones, telling it no fucking way is that ever going to happen again. Ever. I mean ... what the fuck? In what cosmic sprinkling of the imagination does a two-legged choose to mate with a four-legged? Wherever in the multiverse this is the norm, it's an alternate version of my life that I want no part of.

All I can think when I picture her body covered in fur is that she needs hair remover by the caseload—she must have to bathe in that shit every day. I know I'm being an ass again, but damn it, this is fucking with my head. I can't believe there's no way out of this nightmare—that demon must be wrong, or else he's fucking with me. How am I supposed to live tied to her for eternity?

And now we've been forced to come to Seelinara, and Rafe's little ray of sunshine, Ina, is the one who opened the veil that brought us here. She's acting like an exuberant child on a field trip, and Rafe hasn't stopped grinning either. I'm thinking the strange pressure that constricted and released as we passed through the shimmering barrier may have damaged his brain. He and I are going to have a long talk later—if I ever get out of this damn bubble.

I take note of our surroundings, and my eyes pop wide. This place doesn't even look real. Trees as tall as sequoias surround us, which by itself is okay, but it's their color that is unsettling. The trunks are green and overshadowed by a canopy of giant purple leaves. The forest floor is covered in all manner of thick shrubs and bushes along the well-worn trails. Even what I assume are animal sounds filtering through the trees are strange and unfamiliar to me. I usually feel at home in the woods and welcome the sounds of the critters that live there, but the unknowns of this place send shivers up and down my spine. How could such an opposite place be the sister world to Earth?

I look up ... at least the sky is blue and the clouds are white. So much for the holodeck on a spaceship theory I was working on. I'm still staring up at the sky when I'm knocked forward against the side of the bubble—and turning my head, I see feathers. "Damn it, Jo, what the hell are you doing?"

"Trying to get you away from me."

"Well, sweetheart, if you haven't noticed, we hardly have room for ourselves in here, so put your damn wings away."

She ignores me, and that just pisses me off more. I struggle to turn around and face her back, but once I manage it the spiteful side of me decides two can play this game. Only I don't think she's going to like how I play. I raise my hands, and on a silent three count I push off the wall of the bubble and pull her wings in and down as my own wings come forth and wrap forward around us.

"Get. Off. Me." Jo thrashes around, trying to wriggle free of my grip. I'm sure my wings encircle the bubble enough that those outside it can only see a ball of feathers now. If I hear one joke about being on the ball and getting it done, I'm going to knock someone out.

It's then I realize this might not have been the smartest idea I've had lately—the way her ass is moving against me is causing a problem. I murmur, "Fucking traitor." Of course Jo thinks I'm talking about her, and she spouts off, though she should know I'm talking about my dick. Through clenched teeth I say, "Unless you stop moving, we're going to do something we'll both regret." To make my point, I bump my hips against her.

She braces her hands on the bubble, pushing me back and drawing her knees up to further pin me to the opposite side. "Haven't you figured out that's what got us into this mess in the first place?"

That gets my dander up. "No, what got us in this mess is you acting all shy, looking too fine for your own damn good, and neither of us being honest about what we are."

I feel her deflate under the weight of the truth, and I know she's given up fighting me. But now I'm kind of liking the way it feels with her leaning against me, and the sexual side of my nature is filling my head with all the nasty things I'd like to do to her. Then it occurs to me that my body doesn't seem to care if she's a beast, an animal. I'm so disgusted with myself that I push her off me as I retract my wings. Her wings slap back as I release my hold, and I end up spitting out a mouthful of feathers—what a buzzkill.

"Just put your damn wings away." I turn my back to her as she retracts her wings, then say, "You can bet your sweet ass that when they let us out of this bubble, I'll be staying as far away from you as I can."

I swear she sniffles, and I have to fight the urge to turn and look. The last thing I need to see is her crying, because I already know what those tears will do to me. If I'm going to keep my distance from her, I can't let her reel me in that way. There must be someone on this damn planet who knows how to break our bond, and then we can go our separate ways.

Jo doesn't say another word, and I take to staring at the passing scenery as we travel along the forest path. Every now and then my line of sight falls across Rafe and Ina. They're holding hands and acting like they won the soulmate lottery and are now on a dream-of-a-lifetime honeymoon. Must be fucking nice to be them. I'm not sure if I'm jealous or just angry at what I ended up with for a mate. Either way, I can't take watching the perfect couple for more than a minute or two at a time. I wish we'd just get there already so I could get away from them and Jo.

Why did we come through a veil that seems so far from wherever we are going? My curiosity grows when I look up at the sky—the light is dimming. The sun, or suns—we haven't been out from under the trees long enough to find out—must be setting, as the shadows are now getting longer and the forest darker and increasingly ominous, with strange noises I can't identify. Then the evening shadows give way to full darkness, and to my amazement small twinkling lights illuminate the trail just a few inches above the ground. Whatever the lights are, they seem organic and reactive; they blink on within a few feet of our approach and go out shortly after we pass. This place has some freaky-cool wonders, but I wish it didn't. Enjoying Seelinara in any way is the last thing I should be doing—I need to get rid of Jo and get the hell out of here.

The miles and hours go on well after dark, and I can see fatigue settling in on my travel companions, but no one seems inclined to stop. The third time Jo sags against me and jerks away, I realize she's feeling it too, and no wonder—standing in the same place without moving is exhausting. But she's trying to fall asleep standing up, which isn't working out so well for her either. I let out a growl and turn around. Jo is facing away from me and has her hands on one side of the bubble in a poor attempt to stay upright. Without too much thought I grab her around the waist, then lean against the wall and slide down it, pulling Jo with me. When we're settled on the bottom of the bubble, Jo cradled in my lap, she tries to sit up, but within minutes she slumps back and her head falls onto my shoulder. She's out, and I wish that I were too, because holding her this way only puts my mind and body back in turmoil.

I'm not sure when I finally fall asleep, but the next thing I know, my lips are pressed to Jo's neck—which I'm nibbling. Fuck. Even in my sleep my body betrays me. Then I notice that her arms are folded over mine, and her slow, shallow breaths suggest she's relaxed, feeling safe in my embrace as she sleeps. We're far too comfortable sleeping like this for two people who don't want anything to do with each other. That's it, keep lying to myself ... that's what we're both doing, and I know at some point it is going to have to stop. But as long as she refuses to admit it, so will I.

I lift my head to look around, and another hot wave of frustration ignites my anger. You've got to be kidding me. We're in some sort of fancy bedroom with no one around, and still we're trapped in this damn bubble. What the hell is the point? Jo stirs, and I'm sure the morning is about to go from bad to worse. Sure enough, she doesn't disappoint; she leaps to her feet and starts yelling and screaming for someone to come let us out. I swear she's trying to break my fucking eardrums. Still seated, I ignore that her crotch is within inches of my face, and I bounce my head against the side of the bubble a few times in a futile attempt to vent my frustration.

But it seems to jar something loose in my mind instead, and I narrow my eyes as I replay what Zerbadiah said when he captured me.

"Together we wield power," I mutter, trying to sort out how that can help us—if it can help us.

Jo says, "What?"

I look up at her. "The demon said yesterday that together you and I have power that most fae don't, and I'm trying to think of a way we can access it, combine it, use it together."

Jo scowls, but for several minutes we talk about everything we've learned of our abilities. She has an advantage over me because she knew how to use her sheridauk side for years. I'm not sure which I resent worse—that she knew more about her abilities than I did of my own or that she has considerable experience using that other form. At the risk of sounding like a bad bar joke, I say, "So a thunderbird, man, sheridauk, and woman unite, and ..."

And nothing, because she's as stuck as I am. Then I get what I think is a brilliant idea, but I don't want to give her a chance to shoot it down. Without warning I stand up as fast as I'm able, wrap my arms around her, and kiss her hard. Jo reels back and slaps me across the face. "What the hell are you doing?"

I shrug. "I thought maybe if we played nice, it might burst this bubble. Guess I should have known better." Yeah, it was a stupid idea, but admittedly I'm getting desperate. I close my eyes and chant, "There is no bubble, there is no bubble." When I open my eyes, the bubble is still there, and Jo is looking at me like I've lost my damn mind. "What? It's not like your shrieking shattered it like fine crystal."

"Just shut up, Nate. You're driving me insane." She turns her back to me again.

"Welcome to the party bus to the looney bin—you drove me there weeks ago." This whole work together concept is never going to happen. My gaze sweeps around the room, and I get another harebrained idea, and like a fool I suggest it. Jo wants no part of it, so

I decide that I'm going to try it without her. I sway from one side to the other and get the bubble rocking; and the more it rocks, the more I throw my weight against the sides in an attempt to get it to roll. There's more than one item here with a sharp point—maybe we can pop the bubble if we angle it right.

Jo foils my plans when she uses her weight in countermoves to my own, which brings the bubble back to a wobbling stop. If I didn't know better, I'd swear she likes us being trapped in this damn thing.

It's clear that we're going nowhere until someone comes to get us, so I sit down again and lean my head back to wait. At least I'm right about this; after what feels like hours, one of our sheridauk guards ushers a tall man into the room, then leaves. The stranger circles us a couple of times before he stops and studies my face. He appears to be close to me in age—or more accurately, he looks late twenties in Earth years, but something tells me he's much older even than I am. He asks me questions about my family: who my parents and their parents were, if I know my ancestors' names, how old Rafe and I are, when we were born, and where we were born. I quickly answer each one, hoping he'll let us out, and after what seems like an endless interrogation, he finally smiles and touches the bubble. It disappears.

Then to my astonishment he speaks in my native language that all but died out along with the Hachaath, a language that even Rafe and I seldom use anymore. "I am your grandfather's father. When we had to return to Seelinara, I left him, another son, two daughters, and my wife behind." Deep sadness is entrenched in the lines around his eyes. "My brother and sister also left families on Enethura. It was always our wish that some of those children would be destined for this journey ... I so hoped to see at least one of them again." He looks down, brows furrowing, and I scrutinize his body language, trying to decipher if he's sad or simply disappointed.

But this man left a family—he had a choice, and he left. If he or any of the others had remained, Rafe and I would not have spent the centuries so lost. He could have prevented our suffering. He could have better prepared us, prepared me for the disaster of mating—maybe even helped me avoid it altogether. I can see the burden that decision caused, but I want to know why he made the choice. Someday I will find out. "What's your name?"

He looks up, and I see tears welling in his eyes. "Yes, I had forgotten—the Enethuran custom of knowing whom you're speaking to. Itturlo. They tell me you are a double son, but of the two you are in most need of your relations here."

"If you mean a twin, yes, Rafe is my twin, and he needs family as much as I do." I thought we covered this in his earlier batch of questions; either his mind is slipping, or we're losing something in translation. I fold my arms across my chest, feeling a bit self-conscious now.

"No, he fully accepts his journey and his mate. You, however, have struggled the most, and even now you reject the legacy left to you and the mate standing behind you. Your brother wants his family. You need them." Grandfather Itturlo's words grate on me because of the truth they contain. But I'd still rather solve the problem of this mate bond.

Then it occurs to me that he's talking about Rafe as if he's spoken with him. When did he meet Rafe? Seems my brother is a step ahead of me again—figures. "Speaking of, do you know where my brother is?" It's always safe to attempt a subject change when I want to dodge the hot seat, and to my relief it works.

Grandfather Itturlo smiles and nods. "He's been shown to a home among our kin, where he and Ina will live while we train the four of you." He answers my next question before I can voice it: "You were kept here because of the situation with you and your mate. That will be your first duty, repairing the damage between the two of you before you meet the rest of our kin."

Yeah, good luck on that. He has a massive pile of work ahead of him if he thinks he's going to fix what is wrong between Jo and me. I'm already regretting being here on Seelinara.

He leans to the side and looks around me—Jo must be trying to go unseen. Great. "It will do no good for you to hide," he says. "Now, come along, both of you; your first lesson begins now." Grandfather Itturlo walks out of the room, and Jo and I have no choice but to follow him, but that doesn't stop either of us from giving the other the hairy eyeball. I'm not buying her victim routine when she's the one who not only lied about what she was, but also likely rejected me to cover up her deceit.

When we get outside, I see an array of buildings, shops, and homes, but their construction is unusual, all natural elements— stone, dirt, living wood, and even what appears to be giant abalone shells. Grandfather Itturlo takes to the sky, and we follow him out of this town or village, whichever it is, and go a good distance beyond it. By the time we reach what looks to be a small shed in the middle of nowhere, the sun has climbed high in the sky, and my stomach won't quit growling with hunger. We haven't eaten since dinner the night before.

Grandfather Itturlo stops on the path in front of the shed and asks us to wait a moment. I have no idea what we're waiting for, but then I hear the sound of beating wings—and in fly Rafe and Ina with a group of about thirty thunderbirds. I suddenly feel smaller, less significant in the face of this many winged beings. When they reach us, they land and split into two lines leading to the door of the shack. What the fuck are they up to? Not even Rafe says hi, bye, go to hell—he smirks, giving me a knowing wink, and that makes me even more suspicious. Their wings stretch out, and they turn their backs to the walkway, forming a solid wall of feathers on each side.

"These"—Grandfather Itturlo motions at the lines of fae—"are your relations, both of you. Pass this test within seven days, and you shall meet them. Fail, and I'll have another lesson for you to try." He moves behind us, and with a hand on each he guides us forward. One of the strangers nearest the shack folds a wing and half turns as he reaches out to open the door. Jo's anxiety is written all over her face, but me—I just want to get this over with so that I can get away from her for good.

Without another word, not even so much as directions for the test we're about to take, Grandfather Itturlo pushes us inside and shuts the door behind us. I jump, turn around, and confirm it: he didn't come in with us. "Open this damn door right now!" What the fuck? Jo looks as perplexed as I am.

Several minutes of beating on the door, shouting for them to let us out, gets me nowhere—even with my temper and strength, I can't pry the door open. Then I pause to take in the room, and my jaw goes slack. In one corner there's a small cooking hearth, a single chair with a tiny table, and one set of dishes. In the opposite corner is what appears to be a closet, but closer inspection reveals that it's a box-style shower. Tucked into another corner is something that looks like a washbasin and toilet—no privacy. Worse, there's a single bed, and I mean a single bed, as in too narrow to sleep two people on their backs side by side. Fuck no. I spin around, only to find Jo already trying to get out the door. It won't budge, of course, and I point out how senseless this is, given that she just watched me rail against it and fail. Ignoring the stream of insults she hurls at me, I stomp over to the only window and try to open that, but fail once again. I don't see anyone outside, either, and after almost breaking a knuckle without cracking the glass, I understand it's obviously another waste of time.

Fuck. This shed is clearly set up for one person. It must be the fae idea of a joke, but I'm not laughing, and neither is Jo. She says, "Well, it's clear that this test is to see if we try to kill each other."

I glare at her. "We're immortal; I highly doubt killing each other is the test."

"I was being facetious." She returns my angry gaze in kind. "It's obvious they expect us to play nice."

Yeah, it is. And that ain't happening.

CHAPTER 27: NATE
Taken to the Shed

After arguing for a solid hour about whose fault this predicament is, we settle into silence and get lost in our own thoughts. I suspect they're just going to leave us in here for a few more hours and then let us out, and I'm content to wait. I sit on the floor with my back against the wall, and Jo does the same opposite me, putting as much distance between us as possible in this small space. Good thing too, or we'd probably come to blows. But then time keeps slipping past us, and the evening shadows grow. Neither of us has eaten all day or had anything to drink, and I'm at the point where I can't ignore my parched mouth or empty stomach much longer. I open the small cupboard next to the hearth—and discover a nice stockpile of food that looks like it would last for days. My stomach grumbles as I reach for a fruitlike orb similar to a red plum. Then my hope drops through the floor. "Uh, Jo ... we might have a problem."

"What kind of problem?"

I don't appreciate her tone. "Aside from you?" She gives me her razor blade stare—shocking. I stifle a chuckle and point to the cupboard. "There's enough food and water in here to last us a good week, but I can't touch any of it."

She pushes past me, but her hand hits the same barrier mine did. Now the panic is setting in. What kind of sick, twisted game is this? I lick my dry lips without relief. Jo's hand splays out across the invisible barrier between us and the food and water, and she tries pushing on it over and over—nothing happens. While she continues to push, I probe the outer edges, searching for a button or switch that might turn it off. Nothing.

"Maybe we need to push it together?" she suggests without a shred of confidence. At this point I'm willing to try anything, and I place my hand on the barrier above hers. Nothing. Damn it! I start to drop my hand, but the moment it makes contact with Jo's, our hands fall inside the strange cupboard. Startled, we look at each other and then at the contents of the shelves. I try to grab a jug of water at the same moment Jo reaches for something that looks like fruit. Again we're thwarted—it doesn't matter how we try, we can't touch a single item. Stumped, I withdraw my hand from the cupboard, and the moment I do, Jo's hand is expelled as if it were pushed out.

The absurdity of this place is getting to both of us. She frowns. I grin. Good to see we're still on the same page here—it's worked well for us so far.

"Any other bright ideas?" My scathing tone is half-sincere. I've never seen anything like this.

Jo shakes her head, and I can tell she's as frustrated and baffled as I am. At this rate we're not only going to fail this test, we're going to starve or become dehydrated. I move into the center of the shed and do a slow turn, taking in every last crevice of this funky setup. Then I think back to what Grandfather Itturlo said, and I don't like what comes to mind. I walk over to the chair, pull it out, and attempt to sit down. I say attempt because the moment I lower myself toward the chair, I find my ass on the floor.

"Hey, Jo, see if you can use this chair." Her back was to me while I tried, and I'm not about to tell her it wouldn't let me on it.

She looks aggravated as she yanks the chair away from me and tries to sit. Like me, she ends up on the floor. "Yeah, I was afraid of that," I say coolly.

"What? You're such an asshole, Nate!"

Ignoring her, I walk over to the bed and try to sit there. Same damn thing happens there too, but this time she laughs at me. I glare at her. "What the fuck is going on here?" I growl as I get back on my feet. We have a cupboard full of food and water we can't touch, a chair we can't sit on, and a bed we can't lie on ... I can't see the point of putting us in a fucking shack like this, and the gaping hole in my patience is rapidly filling with anger.

Jo blanches. I watch her face fall, and that sinking "not going to like this" feeling comes over me. I say, "Don't. Don't you dare. Don't even fucking go there."

"But—"

"Uh't." I hold a hand up and shake my head.

"But—"

"Uh't ... uh't-uh't!"

She closes the distance between us and places her hands on her hips, her nostrils flaring. "Quit being so pigheaded. I think we both just realized what is going on here, and it's clear there's only one way out of this stupid test."

"I say we go ahead and fail this one and see what they have for us next."

Jo lets out a frustrated snarl, stomps back to the wall, and kicks it before sliding down to sit against it. Sitting opposite her, I turn my head toward the only window. By now the evening shadows have given way to the dark of night, and I'm sure she's as hungry, thirsty, tired, and fed up as I am. It's going to be one very long week. But no—I refuse to believe they'd leave us in this shack for seven days without checking to see if we at least figured out how to get to the food and water. If I have to spend a full week in here with her, I'll likely kill her before the time expires. Or try to kill her—being immortal removes that option from the table. Guess I'll need to be content to wait for dear old granddad to fetch us in the morning, which I'm sure he will.

It's a great idea in theory, until morning arrives and no one comes for us. One look at Jo tells me she's either going to melt into a puddle of tears or lose it and attack me. It's that thought that spurs a decision—I know what she'll look like if she changes into her sheridauk form, and I don't want to see it. I stand up and stretch. "Okay, tell you what. Let's work together so we can at least get something to eat and drink. Deal?"

She jumps up and rushes over to the cupboard. I just shake my head. That was too easy—she must be more desperate than I thought. I place her hand on mine, and together we reach into the cupboard. This time, with our fingers entwined, I'm able to remove a jug of water. Our hands go back in for a second jug, some of the fruit, and a round cake or bread that smells nutty. I'm thinking we're good to go now, but once again it's not that simple. Neither of us can pick up anything we've taken out of the cupboard. We sit there scowling at the food and drink for several minutes, trying to puzzle this out.

I watch Jo cock her head first one way and then the other. She looks up at me and back at the offending pile of food and water. Then she wrinkles her nose and curls one corner of her mouth into an expression that screams uncertainty and disgust. "Um, Nate, can I try something?"

"I don't know, can you?" Yeah, my temper is pretty damn short at this point. This is driving me fucking insane.

"Knock it off and stop being an asshat." She scowls at me until I wave my hand in a "hurry up and get on with it" gesture. Jo swallows hard, and her gaze bounces between me and the food several times more before settling on me. "Nate, may I feed you?"

I'm thinking she's lost it, but I nod and shrug. "Yes, feed me, please." Whatever twirls her crank—I'm out of ideas.

We fill the goblet with what turns out to be nectar, not water, and pile a generous portion of food onto the plate. Looking up at the ceiling, I growl out a heavy sigh as we sit cross-legged, facing each other, with the plate balanced on our legs. Jo rolls her eyes at me, but to my amazement she picks up a piece of fruit and brings it to my lips. Excited, I grab her hand and attempt to shove a larger portion into my mouth. And I can't take a bite. Jo swats my hands away and tells me to keep them to myself. I fold my arms tight to my chest and glower at her when she suggests that's what I should have done when we met. I can't believe she's blaming me for this, not when she had a stockpile of her own preternatural secrets. She had to have known the potential risks—Rafe and I sure as hell did.

Once we stop fighting she's able to get the fruit past my lips, pushing enough of it into my mouth that—thank fuck—this time I can finally take a big bite. I could kiss her for figuring it out. No, no, and hell the fuck no! Scratch that—I am not going there.

But of course this whole lesson is layered in progressive steps that obscure its end point; after one mouthful I cannot take another. Evidently I have to ask to feed her, and when she says yes, she can take a bite of whatever I offer her from the plate. It works the same way with the goblet of nectar—we have to take turns, like five-year-olds on a damn playground. "Rewarded for playing nice. Maybe we'll find crayons and color rainbow unicorn pictures before naptime."

As the day wears on, we experiment with the furniture in the room. We can only sit in the chair if we're standing front to back and move together. It's the same, sort of, with the narrow bed, but that comes with its own built-in trick. The bed is not wide enough for us to lie next to each other on our backs, and if we lie on our sides, we must maintain contact—though simply holding hands won't do.

The moment we try moving to the edges, it's as if the bed detects the space between us and dumps us both on the floor.

By now darkness has settled in, and as neither of us wants to sleep together on the bed, we spend another long night in our spots against the walls. Today has been disappointing—fucking discouraging, actually. We believe we've mastered everything inside the shed—the food, drink, and dishes, the table and chair, and the bed—but we still can't leave. What the hell does this shed want from us? The fae and I are going to come to an understanding—with my fists—once we get out of here.

Day three starts with no one there to let us out, and the only thing we can do is repeat the process. Jo decides to take a shower this morning, and getting clean isn't her only motivation; I'm sure she wants a few minutes away from me as much as I want her out of my sight too. The toilet and sink have been the sole amenities we've been able to use alone—with one of us turning their back to give a sliver of privacy to the other—but Jo discovers the shower is one more twisted aspect of this shed. The narrow shower will not allow either of us to enter it alone, and I'll be damned if I'm going to shower together. I have no doubt that we'd have to wash each other, and that is something I refuse to do.

Instead of showering, we serve each other food and drink and sit on the chair or lie on the bed together. Nothing. I refuse to believe we must share a shower in order to pass this test. Jo suggests that maybe we need to eat at the table. Okay, fine, whatever. I just want out of here, so I agree to try it. Still nothing. The day passes slowly, but then evening shadows fall, and soon afterward night settles over the countryside.

"I think we're going to have to sleep in the bed." Jo sounds as dejected as I feel.

A groan rumbles from my throat. I'm afraid she might be right.

"Let's just get this done." I hear her draw a deep breath. "We'll sleep on our sides ... and you'd better behave yourself, or you're liable to come up with missing body parts."

At least she didn't recommend sleeping stacked one on top of the other. We stay fully clothed and make sure we're touching as we get onto the bed, though the uncomfortable proximity to Jo has me longing to sleep on the hard floor. To thwart my traitorous body, I make sure that Jo is spooned against my back—at least this way when a problem pops up, I won't be inclined to grind it into her. But the sleeping arrangement makes for a very long night, and my hopes that we'll be free in the morning are dashed when we discover we still can't leave.

Neither of us says much throughout the day, which is a bit of a reprieve—I'm done listening to her bitch and gripe about the situation. What is there to say that we haven't already argued and fought over? We go through the same routines, but I notice that as darkness settles over the land, Jo becomes more nervous. She fidgets, sighs, taps her fingers on the floor or herself, and casts combinations of pleading and dagger eyes my way. There goes my last frayed nerve—one more second of her antics, and I'm liable to gag and tie her with the sheets. "Just spit it out already, Jo." I know she's dancing around whether to suggest something that I'm not going to like, and she may as well get it off her chest.

"Do you think this test ... Is it possible that ... What if ... I mean, maybe ..."

"For fuck's sake, Jo, what is it?"

Her voice drops so low that I have to lean forward to hear her. "If it's not the shower, then maybe we're supposed to sleep naked?"

I freeze. Then I'm on my feet and pacing back and forth, my agitation growing with each turn. I jab the air with each word to make the point clear. "I'm. Not. Getting. Naked. With. You." There, I said it. Unbelievable. I never imagined saying those six words to any woman my body wants, but this is some seriously messed-up shit.

And we spend another night of getting nowhere, which leads to another long day of nothing. By nightfall I want to tear this shack apart but settle for punching the walls. Of course they don't break. "Fuck! What do they want from us? How the hell are we ever going to get out of here?"

Jo just sits there with her fingers laced together, hands on top of her head, her eyes closed. "We're not."

In a rage I attack the furniture—overturning the bed, throwing the table and chair across the room, and smashing the dishes. But when my rampage ends, the room somehow rights itself, putting everything back in place—even the dishes return to their unbroken state. Jo has that look on her face again, the one that says I'm an idiot. I flip her the bird; I'm an asshole, not an idiot. Her reply is the eyebrow arch telling me that I'm acting like a child instead of a grown-ass man. I swear, if I don't get out of here soon, I'm going to lose my fucking mind. But if we fail this test, I'm not sure I want to face a challenge worse than this one—this little honeymoon from hell is bad enough. With barely a rational thought, I jump to my feet and rip off my shirt. "Okay, fine. We'll sleep naked tonight. Take your damn clothes off."

"Say please." Her tone is curt.

"No." I don't wait for Jo's response—I tug off my jeans and boxers, followed by my moccasins. Several long tension-filled minutes fall off the clock as I stand facing the bed, sensing her gaze moving over every exposed inch on the back side of my body. Fighting the urge to imagine her fingers and tongue touching me everywhere, I squeeze my eyes shut and instead picture cleaning out barn stalls, shoveling manure, and laying down fresh straw. But then I see her naked on that straw. Damn her. "Please take your clothes off."

I hear the soft sounds of clothing falling to the floor, and a moment later Jo slides her arms around my waist from behind. Together we crawl onto the bed. I still haven't looked at her, but I sure as hell can feel the length of her naked body pressed into mine as her thumb strokes back and forth over my hipbone and along the right side of my V line. Damn it, she's causing a problem for me, and I really don't want to jerk off in front of her. I knew this was a horrible idea.

Keeping my back to her, I force myself to take slow, deep breaths and shut my eyes until I feel myself nearing the edge of sleep. I'm not sure how long I'm out, but the next thing I know, I'm waking up pressed into a warm body, my hips grinding against a firm ass that is meeting me move for move. My body stills. Jo's beautifully round ass. Fuck! I swallow hard, and my eyes fly open. We must have traded positions during the night. Then—oh, hell no! My hand is between her legs, my fingers in a hot, moist place I never gave them permission to go. My breath catches. We're not having sex, but we may as well be, with the way she's rolling her hips and rocking her ass against me. I try to ignore her hand slipping between us to stroke and tease the length of my cock, because if I think about— Fuck, I can't take this any longer. I quit. I surrender. Call me pussy-whipped if you want ... this is total bullshit!

I roll Jo onto her back, pulling her into the middle of the bed while I slide on top of her. She's not resisting one iota, and in fact she uses her body to eagerly convey acceptance of the open invitation—that she probably forged—and there's actually a smirk on her face. For a few long seconds we're both still as we look into each other's eyes. I see so many emotions reflected in hers, and I'm certain they're mutual, because I can tell it's not just me who feels raw and exposed in this moment. I see hope, fear, excitement, longing, adoration, and maybe guilt, worry, or shame—but then there's the briefest flicker of ... no, can't be. Jo's smirk falls away into a half-sad smile, and I see tears pooling in her eyes, and there it is again.

Love. In one bittersweet twist and lurch of a heartbeat, the pain of her rejection pushes a glimmer of my love for her to the surface. It's there and it's hers for the taking, just as much as it's there for me. I close my eyes and brush the faintest kiss to her forehead. In it is my unspoken capitulation, an offer to accept this, and now it's up to her to decide.

When my eyes open, I see her looking at me with amazement. Then her hands begin roaming over me—faster, hungrier, and with a need so primal that I can't ignore it or deny her. My breathing speeds as my body responds to her touch. She drives me into such a wild tangle of love and lust that I lose all self-restraint. In the next moment my hands and mouth frenetically explore every part of her body I can reach. Then my lips find hers, and that kiss breaks down the last barrier I've been struggling to hold in place for months. I want her. I need her. She is mine! Sliding between her legs, I align our bodies, and with her hands on my ass urging me on, I cross that line we've both been avoiding. Only this time we know it's more than a physical act of pleasure: we have claimed each other and will no longer deny the truth between us.

Over the next few hours our sexual and emotional hunger seem insatiable. For the first time since our transformations, my world feels right side up once more. My dreams for the future are nourished. I am no longer cursed. I press a feather-light kiss to her lips. "Shit. Jo ... you know there's no going back now, right?"

"I know."

"Damn it ... I love you, Jo."

I don't expect her to say anything in return. This is enough for now. But I feel her arms tighten around me as she pulls back until our lips are barely touching—and her words brush over my tongue on a breath. "I love you too, Nate."

My heart skips a beat, and I close my eyes to savor the words she just spoke. Nothing in my life will ever be the same again, and I don't want it to be, not now that my mate is finally at my side. I don't even give a fuck if we ever get out of this shed now, and if we do ... well, I guess that I'll be buying stock in a hair removal company and keeping her well supplied.

CHAPTER 28: RAFE

Fae Kin

To say Seelinara is incredible would not do this world justice. The magic of the fae is alive in this place, right down to the plants and trees and the beings that live here—the two-legged, four-legged, winged-ones, even the creepy-crawlies—all in an intriguing array of colors, shapes, and sizes that don't seem possible. But even among these spectacular beings the thunderbirds are a rare breed, and their total number is less than five thousand, spread across Seelinara and about a dozen different planets. If not for our limited numbers, we're told, the thunderbirds would protect more than these twelve planets. Yeah, I'm struggling to wrap my head around that little detail too—we really can travel to other places, but in a far more pleasant and faster way via the network of veils the Seelinarans created to access other worlds.

Even more exciting but also sobering has been the chance to meet our lost family and extended relations, who seemed guarded around us during our first few days in the village. Most thunderbirds are thought sterile due to the rarity of a mated pair having a child, and twins were unheard of until Nate and I. Some suspect it's merely nature keeping us immortals from becoming too many. Among the very few thunderbirds blessed with offspring, nearly all are single-child families, and that sets our grandfather's father's family apart—he has a sister and brother. It was a rare exception when they were born, and it hasn't happened again, or at least not until we came along.

It was these three—Grandfather, Uncle Rynuark, and Aunt Prania—who lived among the Hachaath six hundred years ago. Each of them took human mates, or spouses, rather, and found it easy to procreate; what they didn't know was whether any of their offspring would become thunderbirds, since their bonding did not change the human spouse. Although the thunderbirds eventually took new mates on Seelinara, none of them has had a child since. They placed all their hope in the children they left behind on Earth.

Grandfather says it was an oracle on Seelinara who told them of our coming, that the thunderbirds would rise again from one of their descendants. They just didn't know when or which one or even how many generations might pass in between. The more I learn about the past, the more my resentment over being left adrift fades. When I ask them why they left the instructions they did, Grandfather replies that the people needed to know to watch for us, but no one had enough information from the oracle to be more forthcoming. Our Thunderbird Ancestors didn't abandon us as easily or negligently as I once thought—Grandfather's wounded and apologetic eyes reflect the truth.

Grandfather, Aunt Prania, and Uncle Rynuark are shocked to learn that our dormant wings came at age ten. They claim no thunderbird has ever received theirs so young, which to these elders is even more stunning, considering there are two generations between us and them. They think it's because we inherited the active fae gene and our other relatives either didn't get the gene or it was dormant. Lucky us? Yet our aging doesn't quite match that of other thunderbird children, who age one year for every three years a human child gains. The math isn't tough to figure out—full thunderbirds reach adulthood in the length of time it took us to gain a single year of growth. If anything, our human genes should have allowed us to achieve adulthood and full transformation into a thunderbird within twenty to thirty years of our birth. It leaves me feeling like a science experiment that went more than a little wrong.

Our unique background has also given us a bullshit, almost god-like status among the thunderbirds, and I can hear Nate calling us fucking freaks again. He's already in for an ugly ride here, given his usual stubbornness and his reluctance to fully accept our gift. But the worst of it for him will no doubt revolve around Jo—and the little I've learned spikes my concern for Nate. The conversation I had earlier with Grandfather even rocked me to the core: Jo is in serious trouble and will face the Unseelie equivalent of a tribunal. Grandfather wouldn't tell me the nature of her crimes, only that they're heinous and that though her actions occurred on Earth, they fall under Seelinaran law. If she's found guilty, Jo will face punishment ranging from banishment from Seelinara to serving time at a location of the king's choice. Grandfather says the latter is often on another world, helping a troubled civilization under harsh conditions. It sounds similar to the Earth labor camps used to punish prisoners, but on a much longer scale of time.

No one plans to tell him and Jo in advance, because they don't want to risk either of them fleeing. Worse, Grandfather instructed me to keep this information in confidence, or I'll risk punishment too. I can sense the danger ahead, and I'll be smack in the middle of it with Ina. While the Seelinaran thunderbirds may be family, my loyalty remains with Nate; I know he can be a major pain in the ass, but he's my asshole brother, and I've always looked out for him, protected him. There may not be a fine line to walk, and any attempts to keep the peace are liable to singe my feathers. If I back the elders, Nate will accuse me of selling him out, and if I back him ... I shake my head. I don't want to contemplate the type of punishment these Seelinarans are capable of.

I need a break. I wander off to sit on a rock near a stream—the location speaks to me, soothes my Spirit—where I feel a connection to this planet. Rolling my head to stretch the tension out of my neck and shoulders, I try to absorb everything they've shared with me. The others respect my wishes to be alone.

I still have issues where Jo is concerned; she's caused so much strife in our newly joined family, shredding Nate's heart over and over. But my bond with Ina and her wisdom and ability to see situations from all perspectives have somewhat lessened my hard feelings toward Jo. Beyond Ina's influence I have my connection to Nate himself and the strong bond of brotherhood we've shared for centuries. Regardless of our fights or disagreements, we've been there for each other during the worst times. Jo has tested that to the limit—my protective instincts leave me wanting to shield Nate from her all the more—but I realize it's not just Nate who may need my protection, but Jo as well. For my brother, our family, I will do whatever it takes to keep them from harm.

Someone approaches me from behind—I smile, recognizing Ina's soft, moccasin-clad footfalls. When she steps into view, I greet her with a warm smile followed by a lingering kiss. "Hey, babe. How's it going with your efurrid training?" The Seelinarans aren't wasting any time in training us; the Unseelie king wants us returned to Earth as quickly as possible. Ina spent the day with an elder efurrid, learning about her natural magic.

"It's ... amazing. I can't think of any other way to describe how incredible it is." Ina's eyes dance with excitement as she grins at me. "You were right about the Stone People. It was the ancient efurrid that charged them with acting as record keepers and dream-givers for both worlds. Those from some native cultures learned eons ago that the stones held magic, even if none of us have ever really known or understood just what that magic is."

Wrapping her in my arms, I kiss her neck and rest my chin on her shoulder. "So what did you learn to do with your magic today?"

"I can cast spells to give stones, gems, and minerals a purpose—lock or unlock, hide or reveal, heal or sicken, and so much more. In time I'll learn how to create stones that can let us communicate with each other and even transport us from one location to another. The maxians on Earth have variations of those devices." My eyes go wide in a signal for her to continue. "From what my teacher says, the maxians back on Earth have their own natural magic. And the children of fae and maxians—the sorcerae—also have fae magic. Our worlds really are intertwined."

I say, "I can't believe how blind and ignorant we've been of the world around us. So much of this place is still very present on Earth, but few know about it or see it."

Ina moves between my legs and hooks her arms around my neck. "And what have you learned today?"

I tell her about my history lesson, which is part of the reason she found me out here, away from the thunderbird village—a small part. Contemplating the amount of trouble I'd be in if I told Ina about Jo's trial, I don't realize I've tuned her out until she nudges me.

"Is that all you've learned today, just history?"

Now I laugh; I can't help it. "No, but promise me you won't freak—I'll get enough of that from Nate when he finds out."

"Oh?" Her tone is cautious but curious. "Okay, I promise ... What is it?"

"It's not just our wings that we can bring forth when we need them." I pause to gauge how she'll react to what I'm about to say. "We can transform our feet into talons ..." Her eyebrows shoot up, and I have to stifle a laugh. Clearing my throat, I explain that with the transition our human vision also sharpens into the keen eyesight of a bird. "And we can sprout a beak that will break through just about anything or even rip an enemy to shreds." Apparently we can either stay in a partially transformed state or turn fully into a bird, but the latter takes so much magic that doing so can drain us of energy rather quickly.

"No way!" Ina pushes my shoulders back. "Get the hell out of here." She giggles, and I can see the wonder and excitement rippling across her face at the prospect.

"Give me a moment. It still takes me a little bit to command the talons to come out."

We both stare at my feet for several long seconds as I concentrate; I've only done this twice since learning about it, and I still fail more often than succeed. That, and I've noticed that unlike Nate and Ina, I have to work harder to use my abilities—they don't seem to come as naturally for me. I let out a sigh of relief when my feet transform.

"Oh my God. That's so cool! I can do that too?" She's practically bouncing up and down. I laugh again and tell her she can, and I'm sure an elder teacher among the thunderbirds or our uncle or aunt will train her to do the same. "You've got to show me your beak!" she says.

"Okay, but don't flip out on me, because my nose and mouth are going to disappear." After a minute of fixed concentration, I feel the warmth spreading—the signal that my body is accepting my will to change. But unlike with my initial transformation into a thunderbird, there is no pain. A few seconds later my beak manifests, and Ina squeals with delight, clapping her hands before she reaches up to stroke the feathers surrounding the beak now covering my face. Unable to resist it when she leans in, her face within inches of mine, I nip her just above the jaw.

She rubs at the spot, laughing even harder. "Whole new meaning to peck on the cheek."

"And henpecked," I say, earning more laughter from her. Man, I love this chick—she's been so accepting that she leaves me feeling like I can do anything I want to. No matter what kind of crap is thrown at me, with Ina by my side I'll always land on my feet.

Then her brow puckers. "You're right, Nate's going to have a shit fit and fall in it, and I'll bet Jo will be right there along with him."

My mood turns somber; Ina doesn't realize it's going to be even worse for Nate and Jo. She notices the shift, though, and places a hand on my arm, a concerned look in her eyes. Damn it, I wish I could tell her—I shouldn't be keeping anything from her. I sure won't promise to withhold information again.

Brushing my thoughts aside, I jump up from the rock and give her a reassuring smile. "Enough of this. Let's explore more of this wonderful world before we're needed back here to help prepare dinner tonight."

Ina flashes me a brilliant smile, and we let our wings out at the same time, taking to the sky. The new fae clothing has made this incredibly easy, as the magic in the cloth allows our wings to come right through without shredding or tearing the fabric. Uncle Rynuark claims we have the ability to cast fae spells to achieve the same result with our Earth-made clothes; that's something we'll learn along with our other training. I thought we'd spend a damn fortune replacing ruined shirts, and now we'll be able to wear clothing just like we did before. The best part is that the incantation can also be used on shoes, so we won't have to worry about removing them or running around barefoot if we bring forth and later retract our talons. I may never quite understand the magic behind it, but at this point I don't care, as long as it does its thing. Of course, I don't think Uncle Rynuark understands it either, because when I asked him, all he could say was that it's natural fae magic. Then he clapped me on the back and said, " *Veascru nonda*"—welcome home.

After a quick flight we return to help the thunderbirds prepare dinner, a custom shared by many Native people we've known throughout the centuries. Preparing a meal isn't a one- or even a multiple-person event; everyone who is going to eat has a role to play, whether it's gathering the heating stones, creating the different dishes, cooking or serving the food, or doing the cleanup. The tasks are rotated so no one is stuck with the same job day after day. Noticeably missing, though, are children, which makes all too real the fact that very few ever produce offspring. No one knows if that rarity will carry over to Nate and Jo or me and Ina, since three of us are part human and the sheridauks' ability to reproduce is nearly as rare as the thunderbirds'. Some say it's the curse of the seven in-betweens. Nate will feel vindicated—he was partially right.

Preparing and eating two daily meals together lends a sense of community and family to this village of thunderbirds, and I'm amazed how some humanoid customs seem universal, regardless of planet or species. Another similar custom is time spent together in the evenings telling stories, sharing the day's events, or talking of what needs doing the next day. The close-knit support is important, given the demanding role the thunderbirds play on Seelinara and elsewhere. Each day most of them leave the village to end disputes or capture rogues who would bring harm to the villages and towns they protect. It's not often their efforts to keep the peace fail—they maintain it's because of them that war is rare here. But sometimes bad intent and evil still find a way to hurt those living on Seelinara.

Such is the case of the Earth sorcerer everyone here refers to as the one born between worlds, evidently the same evil guy who has the vampire Dmitri's wife. It seems that this sorcerer has wreaked havoc on both Earth and Seelinara for centuries, and the last time he had a chance to strike at Seelinara, tens of thousands of fae died from his plague—known on Earth as the Black Death. He was the reason the Seelie and Unseelie royal courts cut ties with Earth and sealed the veils. The thunderbirds make it sound as if the sorcerer is worse than a damn cockroach when it comes to killing him too, and that's part of the reason we're needed now—and why so many fae have gone to help the supernaturals working with our former boss.

That partnership in itself is astounding, considering the ruling fae kept the two worlds isolated from each other for six hundred years. Somehow Matt, his wizard girlfriend Maria, Dmitri, and the sorceress Alastrina unlocked one of the veils, setting the renewed alliance in motion. Now the whole peace-bringer business has everyone buzzing. The Unseelie believe this peace-bringer is the vampire queen, Elizabetta, who is trapped in the witch's head—another thing the evil sorcerer is responsible for. All of it seems so fantastical that I'm unsure how much of it is true or how we're going to help, but I guess that's what we're here to learn. At the same time, I'm struggling to understand our role. I get that we have skills the others don't, and I'm sure we'll do well in battle—if it comes to that—but what makes us necessary, according to the prophecy? Greenhorns aren't usually assigned important roles, and we four newly turned thunderbirds are as green as they come. How can we hope to measure up against the experience of the elite supernaturals we met back on the ranch?

The critical portions of our training won't even begin until everything is squared away with Nate and Jo, and their experience here has been less than ideal. It seems our elders take it quite seriously when a newly mated pair fails to soar together. Grandfather decided they needed to be taken to the shed, which turned out to be a tiny shack equipped for one but spelled so that it takes two to do almost everything. At the same time it scanned the participants' pheromones for bond acceptance. Nate and Jo have spent almost a full week figuring themselves out—I know how damn stubborn Nate can be, and I've come to the conclusion that Jo is just as hardheaded—but Grandfather received word this morning that they finally embraced their bond, and he is going to bring them to the village today.

Yet here I stand nervously tapping my fingers on the rail, as if a bomb is about to explode. Too much can go wrong among the four of us if Nate and Jo continue destroying each other. We need to be strong together to be effective guardians, but this meeting has the potential to go badly in more ways than I can count, given what is awaiting Nate and Jo. The sheridauk delegation joining us for Nate and Jo's arrival is supposed to help the thunderbirds uncover whatever dark secret Jo is hiding, and that includes revealing her and her sister's sheridauk royal parents. Once that is resolved, they need to test both Nate and Jo to find out what abilities they gained with their bonding. I don't know what they'll find—good news for them is overdue—but if Nate and Jo are just getting their shit figured out, I can see this derailing their fragile start.

CHAPTER 29: NATE
The Monster Within

Neither Jo nor I are ready to leave the shed when Grandfather Itturlo comes for us, but I'll give it to the old man—he can be compelling, especially when he threatens to round up a few thunderbirds to drop the shed in some ice-cold bottomless lake. I have no idea if he's joking or not, but I'm not willing to find out. Instead we act like obedient children and fly after Grandfather Itturlo as he leads us to our new home in the thunderbird village.

To my surprise the dwellings are a series of networked treehouses with roof hatches to allow for direct flight or landing. We're told it's easier than launching or landing on the walkways or porches, which often have tree limbs obstructing access. I'll have to take their word for it, although I've gotten pretty damn good at landing after my time holed up in the Badlands—rugged terrain can do wonders for perfecting flying and landing skills. Now, if they want to follow me around for a day or two back there, flying in blizzard conditions, then we'll talk about tough landings.

Our new home is next door to Rafe and Ina's, and thank fuck for that. I need my brother close by in this strange world. The home itself is spacious—we could extend our wings at the same time in any room—and the twelve-foot ceilings throughout will make it easy to flex our wings if we wish. We're not given any time to try it, though; Grandfather Itturlo gives us ten minutes to shower and put on a clean set of clothes.

The fae clothing is different in style from what we're used to—leggings and tunics in a fabric that's something not quite leather or cotton but almost like a combination of the two. At least the clothing is comfortable, but I'm damn lucky I had moccasins on when we left the ranch. Rafe wore his work boots, and although he received the fae version of moccasins, I doubt it's the same, if the clothing is anything to go by.

Once we dress, we follow the overhead walkway to the center of the village, where we're to meet our relations at the community arbor. I think Jo is as nervous as I am ... back home, open and warm welcomes for those outside one's tribe don't usually occur unless it's during an event where several tribes are gathering, like a pow wow. And here it's not just meeting a new tribe but encountering a species we know little about. With no cultural knowledge, we may invite disaster if we do something to offend or disrespect these beings. Shit, I can't get my damn hands to stop sweating.

As we draw near I see fifteen thunderbird couples, plus Rafe and Ina. Off to the side stand three people who I suspect aren't like us—they have no wings on display, and there's a subtle difference in their clothing, comparable to someone wearing a business suit and someone dressed casually. They're the suits. The thunderbirds, contrarily, have their wings extended and are pumping them to and fro in greeting and welcome. No one told us what to do or expect, so we stand here looking like a couple of dummies, smiling at everyone.

Grandfather Itturlo nods at Rafe, and the two of them move together to greet the three other Seelinarans, who are still huddled in their isolated group. I'm not sure what they are—they're not displaying anything but a humanoid form—but I suspect that good or bad, we're going to find out.

It's then I notice Jo's sister, Vivialena, just beyond them. I squeeze Jo's hand and whisper that her sister is here. But where I expected a happy smile, Jo's face goes dark, and she scowls. Vivi doesn't venture past the group talking to Grandfather Itturlo and Rafe—nor does she look our way. This doesn't make sense. Jo said she hadn't seen her sister since the day I mistook Vivi for Jo—shouldn't they be happy to see each other? Something is really off between those two, for as close as they're supposed to be. Even Rafe and I know when to put aside our differences and stand together, but these sisters don't display a unified front.

I scan the fae surrounding us. Do they understand the concept of family as we do, or are they like Jo and Vivi? We're still standing in the middle of the arbor, with everyone staring at us like we're amoebas under a microscope slide. I feel Jo's hand tighten around mine, and I'm just about to say, "Let's get the fuck out of here," when Grandfather Itturlo approaches.

He grabs me in a forearm shake and greets Jo with a kiss to her head, then leads us to the thunderbirds lining the edge of the arbor. One after another we're introduced, but I'm not really paying attention to names or faces, and no doubt I'll have to ask them later who they are. My focus is on the three fae, who seem to be in some kind of heated discussion with Ina and Rafe. I've never seen Ina mad before, and her anger carries as much passion as her upbeat attitude. Apparently she's a little spitfire too. Whatever the fuck is going on can't be good if it has Ina riled.

Their argument comes to an abrupt stop as we draw nearer. I try to ignore that Jo is hiding behind me, and somehow I doubt her avoidance is a simple squabble with her sister. One more thing on my list of Jo mysteries. I give Rafe a questioning look, but the almost imperceptible shake of his head and firm set of his jaw tell me two things: he doesn't agree with these fae, and I'm not going to like what they have to tell me.

When we reach the group, the thunderbirds lining the arbor all drift away. I expected something more for a welcome, but it seems these extra guests have disrupted the introduction to our relations. Is this typical when outsiders crash a party here, or do they reserve this behavior only for those from Earth? Maybe they've forgotten how to interact with Earthlings ... or they've never liked dealing with us to begin with.

Grandfather Itturlo has me by the elbow as he makes introductions. "Nate and Jolenthia, this is Prince Wehlanth, second son to King Altheron. Crovek, sheridauk records minister. And Arlyntha, Unseelie Oracle of the First Order."

All this official-sounding crap is making me edgy. I'd like to know if Rafe's arrival in the village was this unsettling. I try to catch my brother's attention, but he's focused intently on Wehlanth, acting like he'd rather be anywhere but here. It doesn't help that Vivi still won't look at Jo, and Ina's glaring daggers at the Seelinarans and Vivi.

Grandfather Itturlo motions for us to enter a nearby building containing rows of seats and a platform at the front with a podium. Two long benches face each other on either side of the podium, and Jo and I are guided to the left-side bench with Vivi, Rafe, and Ina. I notice the sisters choose seats at opposite ends, neither looking at the other. No sooner do we sit than the thunderbirds enter and seat themselves in the rows behind us. Then Wehlanth, Crovek, and Arlyntha take the right-side bench. I know I've done nothing wrong, but this is making me feel like a fucking criminal.

After everyone is seated, Grandfather Itturlo says, "We are here for three purposes today. First, Jolenthia will be held accountable for crimes committed on our sister world, Enethura."

"What?" I leap to my feet, fists clenched, and move to block their view of Jo—I will protect her if they make a move against her.

Grandfather Itturlo gives me a stern look. "Sit down, Nate, or you will be removed until we're ready for you to be here."

Jo tugs on the back of my tunic until I sit, but I wrap my arm protectively around her. I can feel her whole body trembling. Vivi is still staring at the floor. Rafe appears twenty ways from Sunday miserable, and unease creeps up my spine. Whatever the fuck is going on here, someone needs to start talking and making sense before I tear this building down to get us out of here.

"Second, both Jolenthia and Vivialena will have the question of their royal sheridauk lineage resolved. We must know how these two came to be and how they ended up on Enethura long after the veils were sealed." Grandfather Itturlo is speaking to those seated in the rows, all of whom are watching this spectacle unfold. But he's not acknowledging the three sheridauks opposite us, and they won't so much as glance my way. Why not? "Lastly, we all know that Nate and Jolenthia's mate bond is unique because of their in-between status prior to mating. Due to their rare pairing, we must discover the full extent of their exchange of natures. Each will be tested on their ability to shift, revert, and alternate between the selection of their three forms."

Of course no one explains what exchange of natures means, and at this point I don't even want to know, because two fucking words are crushing all other thoughts from my mind: "three forms." And I about lose my shit right there, because I'm certain dear old grand-dad just implied that I can turn into one of those hairy, four-legged beasts. That ain't happening—not to mention that I still haven't even seen Jo that way and have no desire to.

I start to rise again, but Jo grabs my waist and forces me to sit firmly on the bench. I look down at her and see tears pooling in her eyes, and a mix of shame, fear, and guilt spreads across her face. A lump grows in my throat until I can't breathe past it. I don't understand any of this, but one look at Jo tells me she does. She's scared to death, which leaves me reeling—they are trying to take Jo away from me.

Prince Wehlanth moves behind the podium, looking directly at Vivi. "We have your sworn testimony of the events that took place on the nights of your sister's first three transformations. You have also testified to the events in her third and fifth years. Is that correct?"

"Yes." Vivi uses the same soft tone I've heard from Jo whenever she doesn't want to face something. Jo cringes, burrowing into my side.

My fight instinct increases with each tremble of her body. I jump to my feet again—I'm getting answers, or I'll shut him the hell up—but before I can take two steps, both Rafe and Jo have hold of my arms and are dragging me back toward the bench. Unable to make me sit this time, they grip me tighter to prevent me from lunging for the prince. For a long moment tension swells on a tide of challenge and anger as Wehlanth and I measure each other. The firm set of my jaw and my burning stare clearly convey my intent, and while the prince doesn't back down, he deflects by turning his attention back to Vivi after Rafe succeeds in pushing me down onto the bench. "Is there anything you want to add, change, or withdraw from that testimony?"

"I ... uh, I—"

Wehlanth's eyes flash red and return to their normal dark green. What the fuck was that? Vivi seems caught in the prince's gaze as she continues: "I ... I st-stand by m-my t-testimony ... it is complete."

Jo is now shaking so hard, I'm surprised the bench isn't vibrating from it. There's no way out of this building except for the door we entered through, and two thunderbirds are standing square in front of it. Then Wehlanth begins to read Vivi's statement, and my gaze whips back to the prince. According to her sister's testimony, Jo killed a boy on the night of her first shift to her sheridauk form. She killed another boy and a girl on her second change. The third change brought the deaths of two girls, and a shift during her third year ended with another boy dead. But it's the shift that happened in her fifth year that freezes me to my core—I can't breathe or swallow. Vivi claims that Jo killed a man, woman, and their two small children.

Without my even thinking about it, my arm withdraws from Jo's waist as I lean away from her, earning me a stern look from Rafe when my shoulder pushes against his. What the fuck kind of murderous monster did I mate with? Maybe I shouldn't stop them—maybe she's the one who needs stopping before she kills someone else. But my heart twists at that thought, even though my head is spinning. I may not be innocent, and I've certainly killed others in self-defense or during war, but never in cold blood.

Jo is full-out bawling now, and one of the thunderbirds approaches with a fae sedative that immediately hits her—within moments she's staring blankly, not moving or reacting at all. I feel sick to my stomach. I look again at Rafe, imploring him with my eyes to do something to get me out of this nightmare, but I can see he's as unsettled as I am. Only I get the feeling it's not because of the testimony that was read, but my reaction to it. At least I don't have Ina silently putting in her two cents where I'm concerned; her focus is on Jo, and her expression is part sympathy, part uncertainty. For once Ina and I are on the same page.

Prince Wehlanth says, "Jolenthia, you owe this body an explanation as to your actions detailed in the testimony I just read." I see the sheridauk's eyes blaze red again, and in my periphery I catch Jo's single nod. My own head keeps reeling. My heart is threatening to climb up my throat or beat its way straight out of my ribcage.

Jo says in a flat, lifeless voice, "I was alone at the park. I didn't see the boy until I was mid-shift, but my transformation completed, and next thing I knew, I was alone and deep in the hills outside of town. It wasn't until the next morning that I heard about an animal attack killing a boy at that park. I don't remember any of it." Well, small wonder—with the way she freaked out when I received my wings, and then again when she got hers, I have no doubt she went full tilt into panic mode when she turned into a mutant beast. Whether she remembers or not is another matter. Vivi is no help and still won't make eye contact with any of us. It makes her seem even more spineless to me, and I despise cowardice. The urge to throttle her is growing by the minute.

Whatever drug the fae gave Jo makes her comments sound devoid of emotion, chilling in its own way. I'm too stunned to do anything other than gape at her as she stares straight ahead, recounting the events in the same manner she might describe what she had for dinner yesterday. Is she really that coldblooded? Evil? I tune out most of what she says about her second and third shifts, other than her insistence that she has no memory of those killings either. If it weren't for the ring of truth in her voice, I'd think she was a bullshit liar. Would the fates stick me with a serial murderer? Just how sick and twisted are those bitches?

Jo's next words jerk me away from the questions swirling through my head. "I remember the boy from three years ago ... he was my boyfriend," she says without blinking. A lump lodges in my throat, and I sit up straighter, hoping to swallow it. If she's some kind of black widow, why hasn't she attacked me? Or will she someday?

Jo finally blinks twice, slowly. "We were going out on a movie date, but he drove to an isolated area instead. He wanted sex and I said no, but he grabbed me ... my shirt ripped, and I knew he wasn't going to stop. I tried to fight back, and he started punching me in the face ... and I knew. I knew he ... I shifted when I realized that, but I only meant to scare him ... I wanted to run away, but he pulled a knife and slashed my shoulder." Her hand moves up to her left shoulder, as if she's reliving the injury. Wincing at the echo of her pain, I move my own hand toward my shoulder before dropping it back into my lap. "Instinct drove me to end the threat, and in sheridauk form that meant taking his life."

Now all I see is fucking red, and it has nothing to do with that damn sheridauk's eyes. If the son of a bitch boyfriend weren't already dead, I'd be making him pay for touching Jo. Damn it! I want to hunt the fucker down, dig him up, bring him back to life, and kill him in the most brutal ways I know how. I'm so swept away by these emotions that it's not until Grandfather Itturlo is in front of me that I realize I'm standing, my wings have come out, and I have Jo clutched to my chest. Excited murmurs ripple through the room. "I said, back the hell off!" Those stupid enough to approach me had better stay away from my mate—if they harm her, I will lose it and will bring a wrath upon them like they've never seen.

Rafe joins Grandfather Itturlo, and now both are telling me to calm down. "Don't push this, Nate." Rafe places a hand on my shoulder, and I shrug it off. He steps closer, nearly touching Jo, and I move her to my side, blocking him with my elbow. Rafe says, "This is not the time or place for a fight, bro. Sit your ass down before you make things worse."

I shove him away—he's supposed to have my back, and at the moment it feels like he's on their side, not mine. "Get your head out of your ass, Rafe. Not all of us get a perfect fucking mate like you did." I motion around the room. "Do you think this is right? We don't belong here, and if you'd wake up, you'd realize they tricked us into coming here. That bullshit shack they stuffed us in for a week was nothing more than a jail cell, a distraction from this. They simply needed the time to interrogate her sister and put together this farce of a trial in order to take Jo away from me."

Preempting Rafe's response, Wehlanth says, "No one is going to touch your mate, but if you refuse to take your seats, I will have the thunderbird guards remove you from this building until a decision is reached in this matter." There's little doubt I can stand my ground in a fight, but I'd have to let go of Jo. I can't allow them to separate us even for a moment—and I won't leave her to face this alone. Grinding my teeth, I force my wings to retract just as Rafe mutters under his breath that I need to do as I'm told. Grandfather Itturlo gently pulls Jo from my arms and seats her on the bench, while I contemplate knocking Rafe on his ass. He's crossing lines that should never be crossed.

Once Grandfather Itturlo assures everyone that I'm under control, Prince Wehlanth instructs Jo to continue. The final and most heinous set of killings is like most of the others—Jo doesn't have any recollection of killing that family—but I barely listen. We may need an escape plan. Do I hand her over if they choose to punish her, or do I fight them and get her out of here? She's useless in her drugged state and will be no help to me—we're screwed either way. The only thing I know for certain is that this mate bond crap ain't for the fainthearted.

The prince sits down and the oracle, Arlyntha, approaches us and kneels in front of Jo. I thrust my arm forward to stop her from putting her hands on Jo, but Arlyntha sweeps my arm aside and says to Jo, "I'm going to read you now, but I need you to remain still and open your mind to me so that I may see these incidents. Do you understand?"

Jo presses tighter to my side but nods her acceptance. The oracle kneels and places her hands on either side of Jo's head. I about hold my breath the entire damn time. When Arlyntha lets go, she stands and addresses the prince. "We all know that a sheridauk youngling is most volatile during their first shift, due to the major changes their body experiences. It's for this reason that we assign two mature sheridauks to help a youngling through their first few shifts. Jolenthia had no such mentors. The boy was in the wrong place at the wrong time, and he was killed while Jolenthia was in the throes of transforming alone and unassisted. We cannot assign guilt for this death."

Prince Wehlanth says, "Crovek will enter blameless due to unattended first change for the boy's death."

I feel at once relieved and sickened. This isn't an interrogation—it's a damn trial, and she's been given no attorney or anyone else to guide her through the proceedings. Hell, neither of us even knew to expect them. I have zero knowledge of fae law, and for all I know, their punishments could be more barbaric than those on Earth. My mind is racing to find ways to get Jo out of this building and—if at all possible—off Seelinara before it's too late.

Jo seems to sense my intentions, because she clamps her hand around my wrist with a downward tug as Arlyntha continues.

"The next four killings over Jolenthia's second and third shifts were not her kills. These deaths may be attributed to coincidence and Vivialena's assumption that Jolenthia was to blame." Arlyntha speaks in a tone that is neither scathing nor comforting—it just seems cold—but she says the words I needed to hear.

My gaze darts to Vivi. She's staring at the floor, looking rather guilty herself, and she damn well should. She ratted her sister out to these fae. What kind of person does that? Jo's reaction to seeing her sister here makes sense now. But she said they were close ... and these incidents go back years. Why would they have a falling-out over them now? What could Vivi possibly gain with this bull-shit stunt?

"Noted. Crovek will enter innocent for these four deaths," Prince Wehlanth says. "And what of the boyfriend and the last attack resulting in a family's death?"

Arlyntha says, "The boyfriend died under the circumstances of his violent assault on Jolenthia. It is in our nature to end a potential deadly threat with fatal results." The oracle pauses, as if to allow her words to sink in.

The mere mention of the guy pulls my gaze away from Vivi and stokes the inferno blazing in my veins. I lean down, whispering in Jo's ear, "I'm not going to let anyone hurt you ever again."

The oracle says, "The final set of deaths were not Jolenthia's kills either and may also be attributed to coincidence and Vivialena's assumption of Jolenthia's guilt."

That bitch of a sister and I are going to have words when this is over. She'll be lucky if I don't skin her and nail her pelt to my wall. She accused Jo of killing innocent people, and from what I'm hearing, there isn't one that Jo's responsible for that can be considered murder. But how will these fae see it?

Prince Wehlanth nods. "Crovek will enter justified by assault for the boyfriend's death and innocent for the family of four. While blame can be assigned for two deaths at Jolenthia's hands, neither warrants reprimand nor punishment, and she is absolved of any wrongdoing in these matters."

Now it's my turn to tremble. Out of ten deaths, Jo bears responsibility for two—one accidental and the other well fucking deserved. Jo may turn into a beast, but she's no coldblooded killer. I breathe a sigh of relief and slip my arm around her waist, ashamed that I even considered she could be that kind of monster—deep down I knew her heart better than that. I scoop Jo into my arms. "I'm taking my mate home to rest." I couldn't care less about the rules of these proceedings, and I'm far beyond giving a damn. If I don't get her out of here right now, they'll have me on trial next for murder. "You can solve her parentage question and do whatever testing you need tomorrow. We've had enough bullshit for one fucking day."

Chapter 30: Rafe
Divulging Secrets

No one moves to stop Nate from leaving, and when he glances back before going out the door, I freeze. What the hell was that? I swear his eyes were glowing red. I shake my head as if that will help clear away the vision, but the look on Ina's face tells me she saw it too. It piles on to my confusion, frustration, and anger over this whole debacle—I had no idea that Jo's dark secrets related to murder, and I hate to think what might have happened if they had held her accountable and assigned punishment for either of the two deaths she is responsible for.

Most of the thunderbirds file out of the building, but Grandfather joins the prince, oracle, and records minister near the podium. I look over at Vivi, who's sitting with her arms wrapped around herself, tears sliding down her cheeks. "Ina, take Vivi back to our place and see what you can find out, including whatever else is going on between her and Jo. I'm going to seek my own answers from those four." I tip my head toward Grandfather and the others, noting their demeanors: Grandfather's worried, and Wehlanth's furious. Crovek is busy writing something. Arlyntha's studying me. Does she already know what is coming? The oracle gives me a small smile.

"You may want to check on Nate when you're done," Ina says. "I'll take care of her." She tugs Vivi to her feet, leading her toward the exit.

I watch them leave before I join the group by the podium and wait for an opening into their conversation. When they start talking about Nate and Jo's shared abilities, I say, "Does that have anything to do with Nate's eyes turning red?"

I'm half expecting them to deny what I saw, but Wehlanth merely nods. "That's why I didn't stop him from taking his mate out of here," he says. "If he's unaware of his full abilities or those abilities are still latent, pushing him could have led to a volatile transformation, his first shift into his sheridauk form. He likely would have injured anyone within reach."

"I've noticed your eyes turn red too."

Wehlanth instructs me to keep eye contact. "We sheridauks can influence mood," he tells me as his dark-green eyes turn a brighter, lighter shade. I feel suddenly relaxed. "And as you noticed, when our eyes glow red, we can compel."

"Compel what?"

"Someone to talk, share what they know, answer questions, follow a command or order, and in some cases take action." The prince lists these as if they are no big deal, but I find them a bit disturbing. Free will is sacred, and circumventing or interfering with another's free will can wound or scar their Spirit. We were taught this at an early age—I could never be as cavalier about it as Wehlanth seems to be. At least I know why Jo didn't hesitate to answer his questions during the tribunal proceedings.

"Why was it necessary to question Jo at all if Arlyntha could have retrieved the information without Jo saying a word?" I really need to understand what happened; it's the only way I can help Nate come to terms with what Jo was put through today.

Arlyntha says, "Fae cannot lie, but we're clever enough to skirt the truth or use truth to our own advantage. We needed to see if

Jolenthia's mating with Nate allowed any human flaws, such as the ability to lie, to cross over during their bonding. It also gave us the chance to see whether she would use her sheridauk or thunderbird powers to escape the stress of the confrontation."

"I think you need to consider finding some of your answers without involving Nate or Jo." I swear the damn fae like playing games with others' lives, but they need to stop messing with my brother. They have no idea just how little Nate will put up with—nor do they understand his propensity to go into fight mode. And that was before he possibly gained the ability to turn into a mutant beast.

Grandfather says, "We may not find them without those two."

"Bullshit. You have Vivi here—test her for the parentage and leave Jo out of that one." I'm not going to back down on this. I know my brother's limits too well.

Wehlanth says, "We will still need to confirm they are full-blood sisters, but you are correct that we can use Vivialena to determine their parentage, or at least half of it."

"Good. Now one other piece of advice." I allow my stern "take no fucks" expression to wash over each one of them. Time to dispel the notion that I'm a pushover who falls in line. "If you don't want to accidently force Nate into losing control, I suggest that whatever you have in mind for tomorrow, you explain everything you're doing and why, and you don't test either of them outside the presence of the other."

"Our ability testing is always done in a controlled environment with just the subject being tested." Wehlanth's tone is meant to end the discussion on this point, but today I'm not much better than Nate for playing by the rules.

"If you want to see just how violently explosive Nate can be, try splitting him from Jo for this. If there's one thing Nate does very well, it's fighting, and he doesn't need to be in a shifted form to inflict pain." What I don't tell him is that I'll be on Nate's side if it comes to a fight.

Arlyntha says, "Perhaps I should look into his life before we begin tomorrow, and we can proceed accordingly and in the safest manner to ensure each test's success."

It's a bit of a concession—I'll take it. "Now, if you're ready, I'll go get Vivi, and you can do whatever you need for her parentage test."

The sheridauk prince consents, and within fifteen minutes I have Vivi and Ina following me to meet the sheridauk delegation. Vivi tried arguing against it, but I threatened to throw her over my shoulder and haul her there. That's when she broke down and admitted that she didn't want to face them, in part due to her embarrassment over making charges that turned out to be false. It's safe to say she's learned a valuable damn lesson about leaping to conclusions, but whatever rift is between her and Jo is for them to sort out later. Right now my primary focus is taking some of this burden off Nate.

They seat Vivi on a bench, and Crovek pulls out some strange-looking device from a wooden case: one end looks like a pen or pointer, and the other end is an oval bulb. I watch with curiosity as he runs the pointed end down the length of Vivi's left arm. The device glows for a moment, and then a small, pearl-like ball drops from the elongated orb into Crovek's waiting hand. He frowns at it for a long moment, as if he's deciphering a complicated riddle. I'm not sure what we're looking at, because the marks on the ball are meaningless to me—I can't tell if they're symbols or letters or something else.

Finally Crovek looks up at Wehlanth and then hands him the ball. A dark look settles over the prince's face. He instructs Crovek to seal it in a box that only the king can open, and have a courier deliver it to Altheron immediately; the parentage issue will be handled by the king from here on out. I'm about to ask who, what, and why, but Grandfather places a hand on my shoulder and shakes his head no. Whatever this is must be big; Grandfather, too, appears shaken, and Vivi looks terrified. I can't blame her—the tension is enough to stifle the air in this bullshit room.

I lean over and whisper in Ina's ear, "I don't think this is going to be good news."

She doesn't take her eyes off the prince. "I'm afraid you're right."

After everyone else leaves, Ina and I spend an hour discussing the problem, but the best we can come up with is for me to tell Nate and let him decide whether to pass the information to Jo. I'm not looking forward to the conversation, but there's no way I can avoid it unless I'm willing to risk an explosion tomorrow when he finds out they're hiding something else.

We walk next door to Nate and Jo's home. Nate answers the door, and I can tell from the grumpy look on his face that he's still torqued about today's events. He turns and stalks into the living room. Ina gives me a reassuring smile.

"Hey, bro, do you have a few minutes?" I try to gauge just how upset he is so that I'll know what kind of nightmare I'll face when I tell him what happened. Whether he knows it or not, his reactions often make matters worse—it's no wonder we fight.

Nate scowls at me, not a good sign. "Why?"

I glance at Ina and draw in a breath. He's not going to make this easy on me. I ought to just thump him and drag him outside—I don't have the patience for his games. "Is Jo resting?"

"Yeah, why?"

Great, I'm dealing with the stubborn-ass side today. "Mind if Ina keeps Jo company while you and I go for a quick flight?"

"Why don't you just tell me what the fuck you want?" Nate folds his arms across his chest.

"Damn it, Nate. Don't make me draw you a bullshit picture here." My fists clench; it's time to out-stubborn him again. I give a pointed look in the direction of their bedroom—this place is almost identical to the one Ina and I have next door—and I raise my eyebrows as if to say, "Do you really want to do this here?"

Nate's eyes narrow. I know he understands the look, because we've learned to read each other extremely well over the past five centuries. "Fine, but this better be quick. I don't want to leave Jo alone where these vultures can pick at her."

"I won't let anyone in ... I'll keep Jo safe while you two are gone." Ina's tone is serious—she sounds like she means business, and I know Nate can trust her to protect Jo. I smile as I walk to the door— Ina is as tough as she is sweet. He has nothing to worry about. Still, it's hard to believe that after centuries of avoiding women or going out of his way to fuck and run, he is now so totally committed to one woman that they're practically inseparable. Ina gives me a quick hug and kiss, and again she promises Nate that she won't let anyone in to see Jo while we're out. That seems to relax him a little, but I know he won't stop worrying about Jo until he returns, and probably not even then.

No Easy Paths

What the hell is Rafe up to? Each mile we put behind us ratchets up my anxiety over leaving Jo with only Ina to protect her. The two women may be unable to defend themselves against the thunderbirds or sheridauks if they come for Jo again. Then I'll never find her—the magic of this place would challenge my ability to search for her without getting lost myself. A dozen scenarios tangle and snarl in my mind, and in all of them I lose Jo for good. Un-fucking-acceptable.

We're an hour out now, and I'm strongly considering turning back, when Rafe descends into a clearing near a waterfall. Like the rest of Seelinara, this place is stunning, but I have little appreciation for its beauty with all the other shit going on. I follow my brother over to a large boulder and brace myself for news that I'm sure I'm not going to like one fucking bit.

"Just spit it out, and let's get this over with. I need to get back to Jo." My patience is zero, and I'm still half-pissed at him for taking a stand against me earlier. Twice. Two times he sided with the sheridauks and made it clear he wouldn't have my back if it came to a fight—treated me like a child forced to sit in time-out.

304 *Rise of the Thunderbirds*

Rafe is blunt as usual, a sure sign that he's not real happy with me either. "I got Wehlanth to look into Jo and Vivi's parentage after you left, instead of waiting until tomorrow for them to spring it on her."

An icy chill runs down my back, but I wait for him to continue.

"It may not be good news."

Fuck, I knew we shouldn't have left the women behind. Afraid that if I move it will be to fly back to the village, I lock every muscle in place. Before Jo lay down this afternoon, she opened up to me for the first time since we arrived in the thunderbird village, and for once we didn't just talk to each other, we listened to what the other was saying. We'll need to do a lot more of that if we're ever going to get past our screwed-up start. But if her downcast eyes and soft, unsure tone were any indication, she's feeling more vulnerable than ever, and I can hardly blame her, now that I know the reason she hid being a sheridauk. The woman who raised them knew what they were but wasn't knowledgeable enough to guide them. Then after Jo's first shift and the death of that boy, she lived in fear of herself, and that fear fueled whatever tension already existed between her and Vivi.

Jo's words echo in my head: "So much of the last few years was a lie." Vivi led her to believe she was some out-of-control monster, and Jo was so afraid she'd kill again that when she met me she hadn't shifted in over four months. That's unnatural for a sheridauk, she told me; but she trusted her sister to know better, since she was older. Of course, the dead boyfriend was a whole other matter, and I told her not to feel a damn bit of guilt over killing that son of a bitch—the fucker got what he deserved. Hell, if she hadn't already taken care of the problem, I would be ending the oxygen thief's pathetic life the moment I set foot back on Earth.

Despite their disagreements, Jo's relationship with Vivi didn't take a bad turn until after I came into the picture and changed Jo.

Neither woman knew anything about our kind, and Vivi was convinced that Jo had become still more violent and dangerous because she had wings. The day I mistook Vivi for my mate was the day they stopped talking to one another, but even afterward the possibility and Vivi's insistence drove Jo further from me. She was terrified I'd find out about her sheridauk side and the people she thought she'd killed, and that I would abandon or discard her. While she never said it straight up, Jo clearly has rejection issues, and I suspect they trigger her to extremes: violence or depression and withdrawal. I admit her fears were warranted—hell, I wanted to break our bond when I learned she was a beast, and that was before discovering she'd killed. At least now, while I can't deny I'm still having issues over the whole four-legged–two-legged piece, I'm certain that by human standards we're both freaks. I just have to keep working on accepting the beast side of her nature. She may be deadly, but she's no serial killer.

I look at Rafe. "You'd better lay it on me."

"They sealed the results and are leaving this matter for King Altheron. No one bothered to explain what that means, but I didn't want you blindsided again."

Shit, now the identity of Jo's parents is being treated like a state secret? I swear the bitches of fate are getting off on messing with us, but I need to put a stop to the bullshit games going on here. I can't leave this for them to dump on Jo tomorrow. "Rafe, do me a favor?"

"Sure, bro, whatever you need."

"Find that poor excuse of a sister of hers and tell her to stay away. I'll let her know when Jo is ready to see her."

Rafe agrees to deliver the message to Vivi, and then he offers to bring Jo and me dinner so we can avoid the rest of the group. I can't thank him enough for that—if I had to put up with another evening of shit from those asshole sheridauks, I'd probably do something we'd all regret. Given half a chance, maybe I still will.

When I return, Jo looks so hopeful and afraid that I can't bring myself to reveal the full truth, or the little I know of it—she doesn't need that burden right now. Instead I brush the topic of her parentage aside as something that will be dealt with later, and I tighten my arms around her, unsure if it's to comfort her or me at this point. There are no easy paths ahead of us, it seems. More than ever I'm convinced coming to Seelinara was a mistake—of course, it's not like the damn fae gave us much choice. They act as if their prophecy is more important than our rise of the thunderbirds legend. Even I can see they at least intersect, yet their demands on us disregard our people and treat them as an afterthought. Hell, they treat us as if we're beneath them too. Rafe and I have lived through too many oppressed years already, and I'll be damned if they're going to walk on us that way. My anger boils, and I have to force myself to take a deep, slow breath—I don't want to upset Jo. I try letting go of these thoughts by burying myself deep inside Jo and her loving embrace. But when she drifts into a fitful sleep afterward, I lie there mulling over all the things I didn't tell her.

Shortly after daylight I wake to someone knocking on our door, and somewhat reluctantly I crawl out of bed to answer it. Neither Jo nor I had much sleep—not the best way to prep for the long day ahead. But it was worth staying up all night, at least where the sex was concerned ... I could have done without the rest. I'll probably catch hell for it later when she finds out I held back on anything I knew would upset her. Still, I'm not sorry, and if nothing else, making up could be fun. A snort of laughter escapes, and I work to stifle it. Doubtless we'll find other things to fight about in the future, but I have a growing slip of confidence we'll find ways to resolve them. I wipe the smile from my face before I open the door.

Aunt Prania's face lights up when she sees me. "You missed breakfast"—she's holding two plates of food on one arm—"and the others will soon be ready for the testing to begin. I wanted to make sure you and Jo had sustenance beforehand. You'll burn a lot of energy and magic by the time it's finished."

"Thank you, come in—stay while we eat, and we can talk." I step aside so she can enter, then excuse myself to get dressed. Her arrival is unexpected, though not unwelcome; she seems friendly enough, almost motherly. An echo of heartache is a quick reminder that I still miss my mother, even after all these years. Aunt Prania knew Mother's Mother, and she could share stories about her that will bring back lost memories for me, while giving Jo the opportunity to learn more about my family. That single thought lingers as I wake Jo and dress.

When we rejoin Aunt Prania, she's already seated at the table and staring out the window. A huge smile breaks across her face as she engages me in my native tongue; like Grandfather Itturlo, she remembers the Hachaath language. A mix of emotions rise within me, ruining my appetite with the bitter aftertaste of a lifestyle and people long lost to me and Rafe. I may welcome the return of those memories someday, and if Jo's willing I'll teach her the language, but since she doesn't know it, I keep our exchange brief and turn the topic to the testing the sheridauks have planned for us. Aunt Prania doesn't know the extent of the testing, but she assures us that our family will be there in support and that no harm will come to either Jo or me.

Her reassurances don't make me any less nervous—it's the not knowing what they'll spring on us that has me on edge. After the ambush of Jo's fucking farce of a trial, I don't trust any of these sheridauk bastards not to throw more curveballs our way. The nervous glances Jo keeps giving me don't make me feel one bit better either. It's nothing more than a reminder of how family helped get us into this mess to begin with.

Sure enough, after breakfast is finished Aunt Prania escorts us to the same building where the trial was held, with the same three sheridauks—Wehlanth, Crovek, and Arlyntha—once again seated on the bench to the right of the podium. My blood boils. I knew we shouldn't trust them, and yet here we are, lined up for more. We are welcomed with platitudes and promises of no surprises today—I buy that shit like I'd buy a bed full of rattlesnakes to sleep on.

Keeping my eyes on the sheridauks, I sit with Jo next to Grandfather Itturlo. Rafe and Ina are seated to his left, along with Vivi, of course. It must not bother these sheridauk assholes that Vivi betrayed her sister, and they clearly don't give a shit that I told Rafe to keep her away from us.

Once we're seated, Wehlanth moves to the podium and announces the purpose of today's gathering: to discover the full extent of the exchange of natures our mate bond produced. He goes on and on. Fuck, let's just get this done already—I could do with fewer speeches and more action here. Jo squeezes my hand, like she notices my rising tension and is signaling she'll have my back, same as I'll have hers. I can't keep disappointing her or letting her down.

Jo whispers, "You won't." I look at her, confused—I didn't realize I said that last bit aloud. I may be losing my mind, and no wonder, given what we've faced since arriving here. Sheridauk or not, as her mate I will never leave her side again ... not even after we get our asses back home to Earth where they belong. I don't care that they claim this is our world too—it doesn't feel like it, and I doubt it ever will.

CHAPTER 32: NATE
Discovering Our True Natures

The prince dismisses the other thunderbirds who gathered to watch unbidden, and after the extras clear out he announces they'll honor Rafe's request for a different approach to the testing. "Arlyntha will read you, Nate, and then we will decide how best to proceed."

"The fuck you will." I'm tired of these freaky-ass fae putting their hands on me. But before I can protest, the prince's eyes flash light green, and I feel a calmness wash over me, a desire to do as he requests. I sit there like a stooge as Arlyntha places her hands on either side of my head. I swear, once I learn about the magic I wield as a thunderbird, some of these sheridauks are going to get a pound or two of payback. One way or another, I will teach them a lesson about messing with me.

Arlyntha's expression transitions from concentration to amusement, then to sadness, embarrassment, and one look that I can only describe as leery. When she pulls away from me, she says, "His brother is correct about his volatile nature—he lives, loves, and fights with equal passion. Nate has been largely uninhibited in his behavior for centuries, and his two greatest highs are found within the pleasures of fighting and sex."

Just how much of my damn privacy did she invade? I would never give her or anyone else permission to dig through my mind like that. Granted, she's not wrong—I always have loved fucking and fighting—but it's not right to go into someone's head that way. And there are dark things in my past too, whether it's how we treated enemies during wartime, or the mean, ugly thoughts I've had about women who didn't want to accept that I was done with them after we fucked. I'm far from perfect, and I know well the scars hidden deep inside me and the wounds that will never heal—raw memories I've buried and never plan to share with anyone, not even Jo. Hell, Arlyntha probably glimpsed the heartbreak I have suffered since I left Catches Bird behind. The way the oracle just sifted through my mind feels as if she desecrated those memories and the most cherished years of my long life.

She says, "His skills as a warrior are formidable and shouldn't be taken lightly—he will be a risk if we force them apart for testing. But I don't believe it will be enough to just have his mate present for his test. I recommend his brother and grandfather be in attendance to help us subdue him without harm, if necessary."

So much for no surprises. What the hell are they going to subject us to that they have to fear my reaction? Prince Wehlanth seems to consider her recommendation a moment before he agrees, but against my wishes he includes Ina and Vivi in our little group. Then he calls upon an elemental to transport us to some other location.

Next thing I know, we're somehow moving within a pocket of air inside a raging torrent of water. The sound is deafening, but it only lasts a few seconds. When the water disappears, we are dry and standing in a clearing surrounded by forest. There are no sounds of civilization, and I'm unable to gauge how far we've traveled or even which damn direction we were taken. It'd be a challenge to find our way back.

Prince Wehlanth doesn't waste a half breath, quickly moving on to the first round of testing. First up is Jo's shifting ability for her thunderbird form, but I barely watch as she brings forth her wings without hesitation. Then comes the moment I've been dreading: Wehlanth instructs her to retract the wings and shift into her sheridauk form. No way in hell am I ready to see my mate in her beast shape, and from the manner in which Jo flicks her gaze at me, I know I've given my emotions away. Damn it, I've got to stop being so transparent when I'm around her, or she'll think I'm an even bigger asshole than she's already aware of.

I close my eyes and try to quell my reservations, but then I hear her say, "Nate, look at me." When I open my eyes, she's facing me again. Over her shoulder she says, "Prince Wehlanth, may I maintain eye contact with Nate for this test?" The timid, half-apologetic smile she gives me when she looks back tells me she caught my deer-in-the-headlights moment. Great. My attempt to return an encouraging smile probably makes me look constipated.

"You may." He inclines his head. "Shift."

Jo's body shudders, and her clothing seems to disappear at the same moment her muscles ripple and reshape her physical appearance. I recoil, stumbling back, and almost fall on my ass. Where an arm and hand once were, I see a fucking leg and paw. Nor does her face retain any resemblance to her human form; its shape is like the other sheridauk I saw, neither cat, bear, nor wolf, but some kind of strange mix, and yet not of those three. There's a hint of silver on the surface of her sleek black fur, almost the color of a silverback gorilla's coat, but the quills lining the serrated ridge along her spine are a reminder she's unlike any Earth animal. And the beast in front of me is my mate—I'm unsure whether to be sick or proud.

She looks back at Prince Wehlanth, and they seem to stare at each other for a long minute or two, but then Jo's head whips back toward me. Shit, what now? She takes a step and then another, pausing only briefly before coming the rest of the way to me. It takes everything I've got to keep from running—my flight instinct is threatening to override my urge to fight, a rarity that's only occurred a few times in my long life. Something I can't allow to happen now ... if I can help it.

Jo sits on her haunches and looks up at me, and after a few moments of watching her, I feel compelled to kneel at her level instead of towering over her. But I don't know if she's using magic on me or if it's our bond demanding I show her respect as an equal. Once I'm on my knees, I force my gaze to trail over her body, and ... she's beautiful. Deadly scary, but beautiful. Almost involuntarily my hand rises and strokes the fur along her snout, over her cheek, and down her neck and shoulder. The fur is incredibly soft. A wild thought flickers across my mind—it'd be exciting to feel her silky fur cuddled up against my naked body—my own living, breathing stuffed animal. It almost scares me that I'm not repulsed by the idea.

I lower my forehead to hers and say under my breath, "You're fucking stunning, gorgeous. I love you, Jo."

Her head pulls back, and I swear her upper lip curls into a grin. Then the next thing I know, her tongue comes out, and she licks the side of my face. I grimace, wiping the slobber off my cheek. "Seriously, Jo, that's just fucking gross."

Hurt is evident in her eyes, and her head droops. Damn it—I really need to get control of the bullshit flying out of my mouth. "I'm sorry ... I'm an ass, but I'm trying. Okay?" Jo nods, and I draw her into my arms, squeezing her tight to my chest. I'm one lucky son of a bitch that she's so forgiving of me, and I know it.

Prince Wehlanth breaks into our moment with another command. "Jolenthia, rise and transition directly to your third form."

She moves away from me and seamlessly completes the transformation from beast to bird—even her clothes reappear. I'll admit I was worried the others would see my mate naked, but Jo has no difficulty using her fae magic to keep her modesty. I'm awed at how adeptly she controls each aspect of her forms. Jo is remarkable; there's no denying it. And she's mine. Need and desire accelerate my heartbeat.

"Very good, Jolenthia." Prince Wehlanth turns to Crovek. "Record the results of her tests and rank her as intermediate for the upcoming sheridauk and thunderbird training. She still has a lot to learn."

The prince calls me forward next, and Rafe says, "Good luck, bro. You can do this."

I'd almost forgotten the others were here—they've been so quiet and still. That, and my focus was on Jo—another reason to be relieved I didn't make a bigger ass of myself during her tests. I take a deep breath and step forward, looking the prince right in the eye.

"Nate, we're going to have you shift into your thunderbird form, then back to human, and then we'll see if you can shift at least partially, if not fully, into a sheridauk. If you can, we will have you return to human before you do another shift into a thunderbird again." The prince's tone is matter of fact, businesslike. I'm still underimpressed by the man.

"Don't you think that if I were part sheridauk, I'd have known about it months ago?" Folding my arms across my chest, I give Wehlanth a hard stare.

This leads straight to another tense discussion with the arrogant fae. Arlyntha insists the exchange of natures happens upon the mating of two in-betweens. I think they're full of crap. If I had gained sheridauk abilities from Jo, wouldn't I have changed into a hairy beast long before now? It didn't take Jo more than a few minutes to become a thunderbird during our second sexual encounter. Hell, by that logic, I should have shifted into a four-legged animal the moment she sprouted wings.

The fae won't back down, and Wehlanth cuts off the argument by demanding I comply. Several long seconds escape while I size up the prince and decide whether or not to take him on. I could kick his ass in a one-on-one fight, provided he stayed in man form. If he shifted, though? Probably ... more than likely I could still put him in his place. The only thing stopping me is Jo's pleading eyes. Fine, I'll play their game, but I want it on my terms. "If I can shift into a sheridauk, why can't I go from that form to my wings like Jo did?" It's a ridiculous point, but I'm tired of being treated like a fucking child. I ought to buy a T-shirt emblazoned with "All grown-up and haired over—deal with it!" Maybe that would get the point across.

"Your magic levels are untested, and even if you gained the full ability to share your mate's first form, you might not have enough magic to transition directly between thunderbird and sheridauk, bypassing your human form. The last thing we need is for you to get stuck in some combination of the three—it could take days for you to work yourself out of that state."

Okay, that's more than a little unsettling. Bad enough being part bird freak, part four-legged beast. The image of me trapped between human, sheridauk, and thunderbird drives my desire to do as I'm told for a change. "All right, let's get this done."

"When you're ready, go ahead and take your first form."

I remove my shirt—it's not infused with magic—and a second later, my wings are on full display. The prince frowns, clearly still aggravated with me, but for what is beyond me. He looks at my grandfather. "Did you know his wings were this large?"

"I thought they'd be about the same as Rafe's, since they're twins." Grandfather Itturlo glances at Rafe and then back to me.

Turning to face Rafe, I say, "Brother?"

Wehlanth doesn't give him a chance to answer—he orders me to bring out my other attributes, and again I'm left looking like a clueless dummy. Grandfather Itturlo steps in, but this time he asks Rafe to show me. Disconcerted, I watch as my brother's face begins to change: The area above his upper lip elongates, seeming to absorb his mouth and nose. Feathers erupt from his cheeks and around his eyes, which are becoming more rounded, yet almond shaped. Rafe's lower legs thin; then his feet disappear as sharp talons take their place. I look up at the transformation of his head—damn beak included.

"What the fuck?" My mouth is wide with disbelief and shock. I ignore Ina's chuckle and her comment that we're just as much beast as Jo, though I suppose she's right—we're far from human.

Rafe laughs, or at least that's what I think he's doing, but it comes out something between a chuckle and a screeching caw. Then his normal face returns, and he's definitely laughing at my reaction. "While you two were being stubborn in the shed, the thunderbirds in the village were already teaching me about the thunderbird who lives inside each of us."

Okay, I'll admit it; I'm a little fucking jealous. It's certainly freakish, but Rafe and I have always been competitive, and I don't like it when he bests me. I didn't even know we could produce beak and talons, and now I want to see mine. With slight concentration I begin seeking them, and then I feel the familiar warm sensation that often signals the start of my wings coming out. Looking down, I see talons burst through my moccasins, leaving them shredded on the ground. My hands fly up to my face, and sure enough, there's a fucking beak.

Rafe punches my arm. "You're a damn asshole, you know that?"

It's my turn to laugh, and I realize that I sound as creepy as he did when he tried laughing in his extended thunderbird form. I will the beak away, a broad smile breaking across my face as I approach my brother and pull him into a hug. "Yeah, and so are you. It's why I love you, bro."

Once more the prince refocuses our attention. "I'm very pleased to see your natural ability to call upon your thunderbird, but we really must move these tests along. Resume your second, humanoid, form."

I do, and for the next several minutes he questions me about any changes I've seen since mating with Jo. I look at her, and she gives me an encouraging smile, like she knows something I don't. Mentally I run down the sheridauk checklist: shape-shifting—no, glowing eyes—no. I'm fucked, and I feel as if Jo somehow short-changed or outright cheated me. It's like I gave more of myself than she did, and I suspect her revulsion at discovering what I was probably allowed her to hold back. It's too late now, and in some ways that stings, but it's also a relief. I'm still not certain I'd want to be one of them.

"Let's just get on with this bullshit."

Prince Wehlanth says, "Third form. Shift."

I feel nothing and hope the expression on my face says I told you so. His eyes glow light green, and he repeats the command—nothing. Then his eyes turn red, and again nothing ... unless you count pissing me off. I dart a glance at Jo, but when I see her hopeful, almost expectant smile, I keep my mouth shut. If I'm being honest with myself, I'd admit that I'm more than a little disappointed and hurt she didn't gift me in return, especially considering that I didn't seem to hold back on sharing everything I had to give her.

The shuddering of Wehlanth's body pulls my attention from Jo. He's transformed into a huge black beast, and the spiky quills on his back are standing on end as he growls at me. That gets my fighting hackles up, and my wings come out—I'm ready to face the threat. "Bring it on, you son of a bitch." I lower into a crouch; from here I can either go on the attack or defend against his.

«I command you to stand down. Retract your wings!»

I blink hard, then tilt my head, tapping the side of my skull with the palm of my hand like there's water in my ear. What the hell? I swear that fucker just shouted inside my mind. Then his eyes glow brilliant red, and his voice comes through again: «Now!»

I'm unable to resist the compulsion and withdraw my wings—I'm utterly rattled.

I'm not given even a moment to contemplate whether I've lost my sanity before he's yelling again, silently, of course: «You will take your sheridauk form. Shift.»

"I don't fucking know how. I don't think I have one." The startled looks of those around me confirm that I may be losing my mind—they don't know who I'm talking to.

«Shift.» His upper lip curls into a snarl.

I just stare at him, unsure what to do. I feel nothing. I'm hearing voices. And I have one huge beast inching toward me in a threatening manner. Somehow the prince is preventing me from shifting into a thunderbird, and I'm not sure I can take him man on beast. I struggle to bring forth my bird, focusing harder. Nothing, not even the warm sensation just ahead of the change. That confirms it—the damn sheridauk is using his magic to block my abilities. "Fuck you!"

«Shift!» The prince's red eyes are boring a hole right through me. He takes two more steps, and now I'm calculating my odds of winning a fight against the beast ... not good. If I had a knife, it'd be in my favor, but like this?

Wehlanth growls at me. That's it—there's only one way to find out. Fists clenched, I lunge toward the prince. I may get my ass kicked, but I'll do as much damage as I can until he stops me.

A sudden tingle at the base of my spine bursts into something that feels like a lightning bolt moving through me. I'm so stunned that my thought process momentarily shuts down, and the next thing I know, I'm eye level with Wehlanth. What the hell just happened? Confusion, fear, and a swell of strange impulses propel me forward, catching the prince off guard and knocking him to the ground. I think he's as surprised as I am, because for a second his eyes retake their normal color. But then he stands to his full sheridauk height and releases a guttural growl that has me lowering my head in deference. Wehlanth springs forward and locks his jaws around my throat, taking me down to the ground. My instinct is to fight back, and that puts me on autopilot—I'm no longer in control of myself.

As my body writhes beneath his grasp, I become aware that I'm swiping long, sharp claws against his armored chest and shoulders. Claws? Then I see brindle fur, a mottled tan, black, brown, white, and gold. Fuck me. I did it—I changed into a sheridauk. Prince Wehlanth's voice booms in my head, «Stand down. Desist.»

I'm not feeling very rational at the moment—in fact, I'm scared, confused, and threatened, and I've had enough of this asshole. «Fuck you!» I push up with my legs and dislodge him from my throat, noticing the way his fangs grate against the protective plating on my neck. Without that armor he could have ripped my damn throat out. Now I'm incensed. I don't care who this bastard thinks he is; I fight to win. Leaping to my paws, I charge at him, snapping my jaws in an attempt to grab him by the back of the neck. That's a mistake—I feel his razor-sharp quills slice my tongue and lips. Then we're tumbling across the ground in an all-out effort to gain the advantage, and everyone else in the clearing joins in the fray.

Immediately I see Rafe and Ina with wings, beak, and talons in motion, and they're flogging, pecking, and raking at the sheridauks trying to take me down or pull me away from the prince. Grandfather Itturlo is far gentler; he swoops in and wraps his arms around a tan sheridauk, then flies away. Moments later he's back to grab another one. I haven't stopped clawing and biting every sheridauk I can—these fucking beasts need to learn a lesson about leaving me the hell alone.

My jaws lock around the snout of a black one with silver highlights, and I can feel my fangs break the skin. I shake my head hard and fast, side to side—I'm determined to rip the beast's head off. Its claws, raking at the armor protecting my chest, finally find their way to the softer flesh of my shoulder. Ignoring its yelping and whimpering, I bite down harder. Two other sheridauks bite into my haunches and try to pull me backward. I'm a fucking ball of pain and fury—someone is going to wish they'd never taken me on. I give another hard jerk, twisting my head back toward my side, and unbelievably, the head of the sheridauk in my jaws is still attached. What the fuck does it take to bring one of these sons of bitches down?

«Nate—stop, you're hurting me!»

It's Jo's voice, and her words hit me like a bullet train. Oh shit! I'm so out of control that I've fucked up again. Too late I realize the sheridauk I latched on to is Jo. At once I release her—I'm afraid to see the damage I've done to her face and body, but immediately I shift into my second form. I'm reaching for her when Wehlanth's huge black beast form crashes into me, and this time he has me by the soft tissue of my human throat. «I forbid you to shift. Retain this form!»

Unable to speak with my airway pinched off, I look up and hope he understands the pleading in my eyes, but the way his head is aligned to my throat, I suspect he can only see me in his periphery. Wehlanth begins to step back, pulling me into a sitting position but not letting go of my neck. I'm sure that my face is turning blue or purple from lack of oxygen. I feel Rafe grab my left arm—he's yelling at me to listen to the prince. That's a plum-peachy idea, but the problem is, I can't fucking communicate that I won't shift or fight back.

Then I hear Jo in my head again—she moves into my line of sight and my heart seizes, taking away my desire to keep fighting. Both sides of her snout are covered with jagged sores and puncture wounds. Blood oozes from them, dripping to the ground. She seems oblivious to the injuries I've caused, and my guilt expands as she lowers herself into a submissive posture before Wehlanth. «My prince, please stop.» Her gaze darts to me. «Nate, you need to concede. Just tell him you're done fighting.»

«Yeah, and how the hell do you expect me to do that when I can't spit one fucking word out of my mouth?»

It's Wehlanth who replies, shocking me to the core. «Because we can hear you—you've broken the barrier separating you from your sheridauk side, and its abilities are yours to command and control.»

Without even realizing it I passed their bullshit tests. My head is still tripping around that thought when Jo again pleads with me to relent. I signal my compliance, and the prince releases me and shifts back into his humanoid form.

Grandfather Itturlo tosses a set of clothes at me, and I reach for it, spitting blood and wiping my mouth with the back of my other hand. I'm now aware that I'm completely fucking naked and on full display. Ina at least has turned her back, but Vivi and Arlyntha aren't even trying to look elsewhere—no, their eyes are roaming every exposed inch of me, and they're acting like I'm the best damn eye candy they've seen in a while. Yeah, it seems I can still embarrass myself all to hell. Great, just fucking great.

Jo shifts back too, fully clothed, of course, and whispers in my ear, "You'd better get dressed before I'm forced to claw their eyes out."

Laughter ripples around us as I stand to dress and recover a little of my damn dignity.

Mind blown by the fight we had moments ago, I struggle to convince myself that it really did happen. I'm so absorbed in my reflections that I almost don't realize Jo is trying to get my attention. She says, «Babe, are you okay?» Her lips aren't moving. She repeats the question—without speaking—and rests a hand on my forearm, but I freeze, staring at her. What the fuck? One thing rockets past every other thought: I heard them in my head! I talked to the sheridauks with my thoughts. How the hell is that even possible?

Turning toward the other sheridauks standing together, I demand answers—out loud. They exchange looks among themselves, though no one seems willing to explain. But there is no way they're going to convince me that it didn't happen—and again just now with Jo. "Somebody better start talking right fucking now, and I don't mean inside my head."

Jo takes a step back and casts her gaze to the floor. Great, now she won't look at me either? My blood pressure ticks up a notch. Then Vivi clears her throat and asks Wehlanth to let her speak first. I don't care who goes first, as long as I get my fucking answers. And if she doesn't start explaining in the next two seconds—

"It's *mea'k spindalt* ... a sheridauk trait of speaking mind to mind," Vivi says. She seems to struggle to maintain eye contact with me, and I'm getting the sinking feeling that I'm not going to be happy about whatever's coming next. "I owe you an apology," she says.

Not quite what I expected. When I don't respond with more than a puzzled frown, she says, "I was wrong about many things. My sister, you, what we are. Jo tried to tell me that you weren't evil and that she felt no compulsion for violence when her wings were out, but I wouldn't listen to her. I was so scared for her ... what I thought she already couldn't control about herself. I couldn't believe it, not after knowing what we're capable of in our sheridauk form." She looks down at her feet. "But you ... I should have ... I mean ... it's just that she has full access to your thoughts, and I knew that, but ..."

My jaw drops open—snaps shut. I couldn't have heard that correctly. "What the fuck do you mean, she has full access to my thoughts?" My heart's already racing as I close the distance between us, stopping only when I tower over her.

Vivi glances at Jo and then back up at me, like she's deciding if she should run away or stay put and answer the damn question. I'll fucking hunt her down if she runs now. "I ... um ..." Vivi takes a deep, unsteady breath. Her hand is on her throat—I think she's worried I'll rip it out. "*Mea'k spindalt* ... Sheridauks have a natural ability to hear each other's projected thoughts, and somehow your mating with Jo unlocked your mind to her, even though you hadn't shifted to your sheridauk before." She quickly adds, "But I couldn't hear you until today. It was just something between you and Jo."

"When?" I lunge toward Jo, my hand jutting forward to grab her.

Her eyes get big and she steps back, barely avoiding me. "When what?"

My mind is whirling—I'm combing back through every horrible thing I've thought about Jo, and through all my deepest private thoughts as I struggled for want and need of her. Shit. My heart wrenches. Does she know about Catches Bird? "When did you start hearing my thoughts?"

I watch her throat bob up and down as she swallows hard. "Right after your wings came out."

Vivi reaches for me, grabbing my arm, pulling me away from Jo. "Please don't be mad at her. It isn't her fault—it's just something we can do. It's natural for us."

Mad? Shocked, appalled, betrayed, lied to, ashamed, enraged, and embarrassed would be spot-on. But mad? She knew. She knew I struggled between my love for her and my love for Catches Bird—how I resented that she'd taken the place of a woman who'd held my heart for centuries, that she'd claimed nearly all of my heart, leaving me just a sliver for Catches Bird. Jo knew—she fucking knew from day one how I felt about her, how fucking badly I needed her, how I hated myself for it. And still she ran from me, knowing it shattered me in ways I never thought possible.

Jo is already rushing toward me—she must have heard those thoughts too. Fucking fantastic. Urgency fills her voice. "It's not like that," she says on a breath as she reaches for my hands.

I jerk them away. Fuck, can they hear every thought going through my head? This is some twisted motherfucking shit. "Then tell me what it's like, Jo."

"It's only when you project your thoughts so strongly and when I'm not blocking you." She shakes her head vehemently and takes my hand again, which I promptly withdraw. "I can't hear everything you think. None of us can," she says. "It's only when your thoughts are unguarded and screaming loudly, and even then they're only projected toward those nearest to you."

"Like that's supposed to make this better?" I take a threatening step toward her. "You knew the pain and hell I went through, and you were content to allow me to drown in that heartache. Your rejection ate at my soul like a cancer!"

Wehlanth attempts to step between us, but I shove him aside. "Stay the fuck out of this. This is between her and me." Rafe, knowing me as well as he does, pulls the prince further away, telling everyone to back off and give us a few minutes. Great notion, just one huge problem—a few minutes isn't going to change one damn thing about this. And that's the bigger issue. Every fucking time I think Jo and I are moving forward, some bullshit thing comes along to show me just how wrong we are for each other. It must be karma, because it's clear to me that the fates chose Jo to punish me for the centuries of thwarting their plans.

Now I'm backing away, putting distance between me and Jo and Vivi. Jo's eyes go wide, fear coating each syllable as she speaks. "Don't ... don't do this, Nate. We are meant to be together, and we can—"

"Can what?" Now it's her turn to rush forward again, grabbing at me. We are chest to breast, but I manage not to grasp her, shake sense into her, even to touch her. "Keep tearing each other apart? Keep fucking lying until there's such a pile of betrayal between us that we'll never trust one another again?" I laugh ruefully. "Go fuck yourself, sweetheart, and stay the hell out of my head and my life." I don't wait for a response—my wings come out, and I fly away.

CHAPTER 33: RAFE
The Rock He Cleaves To

Jo's standing in the middle of the training grounds with a shocked and hurt expression, tears running down her bloody face. My sympathy for her is almost nonexistent. Nate's right about the cycle we're in, and it doesn't matter if it's me and him, him and her, or her and the rest of us—she brings a shitstorm wherever she goes, and the trouble never stays away long enough. I don't like it one bit. This messed-up supernatural version of a dysfunctional family is almost worse than no family at all. Well, at least Ina adds something ... but Jo? She is the capital D and syllabic emphasis in *dysfunctional*. Shit, even Ina's attempts to soothe me are failing—I want to throttle Jo.

Pacing back and forth, I try and fail to take Ina's advice to calm down. I wish I could, but this day has been an endless cascade of debacles, like the fates are itching to set Nate off in the biggest explosion Seelinara has ever seen. And they nearly did. At least he didn't maim anyone—even Jo fully healed from the marks he left on her during the testing.

"Ina, stay here and deal with her." I nod toward Jo, then address Wehlanth and Arlyntha. "If you're trying to make an enemy out of him, you're doing a damn good job." I warned them—they can't keep dumping on him like this. I doubt anyone realizes we were lucky he flew away. He was mad enough to kill—I've fought alongside him too many times not to notice. Unfurling my wings, I say, "I'm going after my brother ... and the rest of you are going to back off and leave him the hell alone for a while. That goes for you too, Jo."

Not waiting for replies, I launch into the sky. Nate's visible way off in the distance—I swear he's flying at full speed, which is still a bit faster than me, but not by much as I learn more about flying. He's a natural at it, I'm not. The only thing I can do is follow and hope I don't lose him as the distance grows slowly between us, though I'm not sure what I'll do when I reach him. I'm split down the center—I feel sorry for him, but now that I've left the sheridauks behind, I want to throttle him too. I'm sick of his drama—he brings so much crap on himself, and I'm dragged into the middle of it, whether I want to be there or not.

An hour later I see him angle down toward a clearing near a huge lake; I'm sure he recognizes it too as the one east of the thunderbird village. I circle over him when I reach the spot where he landed. He looks up at me, and even from this distance I can see his face is wet with tears. Damn it, can't he catch a single break? My teeth are clenched as I try to rein in my own anger—I don't like seeing my brother hurt, and aside from his botched transformation I can count on two fingers the number of times I've seen him cry. My heart constricts at the memories, because I cried then too: first when Mother took the journey, and again when Father joined her on the Blue Road.

After landing I walk cautiously toward him, trying to gauge what other emotions he may be battling, but I only sense anger and hurt wrapped around whatever disillusionment has rocked him to the core. Beating the hell out of him is off the table—he's a mess and needs my strength to get through this. "Hey, bro, what's up? You all right?"

A muscle in his cheek twitches—the tears are still running down his face. Then he shakes his head. Whatever this is, it's bad. I spot a large boulder near the water. "Let's go sit down and sort this out, okay?"

He stands motionless for another long moment before moving toward the rock. I join him and we sit in silence, my arm around his shoulder, both of us staring out at the calm water before us. I know he'll speak when he's ready.

My thoughts drift, which is easy enough in this place. Somehow the Seelinarans have managed to keep their world in a much more natural state than Earth, and yet they have technology humans haven't even dreamed of inventing yet. Still, it's not fair to compare the two planets—humans lack the magic and longevity of the Seelinarans to accomplish the same feats. The human race is young by comparison and hasn't developed a symbiotic relationship with the world around them; many don't understand the term "all my relations," and the Seelinarans do, even if they don't use that phrase. But there's a lot lurking beneath the surface of this planet and its inhabitants—and it's not all good. We've had little issue with the thunderbirds, but the other fae are underhanded and secretive in the way they deal with outsiders. Put them and my brother in the same setting, and things are going to go wrong.

Nate inhales deeply, ending my meandering thoughts. "I'm being torn in two," he says, "and it's getting worse every single day that Jo is in my life. I've never wanted or needed someone as badly as I do her, but she only ever comes close enough to rip my fucking heart out again and again. It never changes—lies, betrayals, mind games. Secrets."

A growl escapes me. No matter how badly I want to shield him from getting hurt, Jo is the one thing I can't protect him from. I regret taking him to that pow wow ... if I hadn't forced him to go, she wouldn't be in his life now. But there's no going back to change it. My shoulders slump. Once more I find myself thanking the Creator that Ina is nothing like Jo—if she were, I'd be as lost as Nate. "Do you want to tell me about it?"

Over the next hour I listen as Nate pours his heart out, and for once he doesn't hold back—he reveals the good, the bad, and everything from his raw, ugly thoughts to his deepest fears and purest desires. Nate accepts the gift we've been given and our purpose as guardians. He cares about the people, always has. He's protected them in battle, provided food and medicine, and helped those in need—and he wants to continue. I watch his face light up as he describes flying, the speed with which he can move, and the acute hearing and exceptional sight the transformation has given us. Immortality is his least favorite aspect—even now he doesn't want to live forever, but he understands it's an inescapable part of this. I know he'll adjust in time, and we certainly have a lot of damn time ahead of us. That is, if Nate and Jo ever settle their problems and don't tear us all apart.

What stuns me are the private thoughts that Jo must no doubt have heard, thanks to her ability to eavesdrop on his mind. During the days spent saturated in hurt and anger, Nate gave actual, serious thought to killing her, even plotting heinous ways to remove her permanently from his life. But he never has killed anyone in cold blood, and aside from accidentally injuring her during the testing, he couldn't live with himself if he deliberately hurt her. I suspect he'd rather permanently entomb himself before allowing harm to come to her. The mate bond is undeniable, and his love for Jo is ingrained in every cell of his body and Spirit. I know the feeling; Ina is just as much a part of me now, though without the nasty contentiousness Nate and Jo share.

The shed was a turning point for Nate, the moment he could truly embrace a future with Jo by his side. He feared losing her during the trial. Now this. I shake my head. While my brother ran from this path for over five hundred years, he has accepted there's no going back, no undoing this permanent change to our lives. But the relationship with Jo has confirmed the fears he's held for centuries, and he knows it risks tearing us apart as a family. I will fight against that too, even if it means helping him pluck out her feathers.

For now, if I can just decide where to start amid the wreckage of the latest Jo-storm, perhaps I can help him move forward. I've never failed him before. I'll even talk to Jo if it means we can put this behind us. "Maybe Grandfather or Uncle Rynuark or even Aunt Prania can help—they're all mated and have been thunderbirds their entire lives. They certainly know more about the different Seelinaran species than we do." Hell, they've had to live under sheridauk rule for hundreds, if not thousands, of years. They probably have all sorts of dirt on the Unseelie royal family. There must be something they know that will help Nate with Jo and the mind-talking connection—like how to turn it off.

Nate stands. "I'll be damned if I'll allow Grandfather Itturlo to lock me in with Jo again." He turns to look at me. "This conversation stays between us, got me?"

"But Nate, they're going to know something is wrong. Hell, they probably already do, with the hollering you did before taking off. Not to mention you likely amplified and shared whatever you were thinking but didn't say. They can hear your mind, remember?"

"I don't give a fuck what they know or think they know." He shoots me a hard look, one I know too well. He won't budge on this. "I'll play nice, let everyone think I have the perfect fucking life with my imperfect fucking mate. But Jo and I are going to come to an understanding, whether she likes it or not, and after we return to Earth she will stay away from me outside of our official duties."

I furrow my brows. I'm not certain how he expects to pull this off here, let alone keep Jo on some sort of professional working relationship after we go back home. Did he already forget how miserable he was when Jo refused to be with him? Fucking recipe for mate bond disaster.

I'm about to open my mouth, when we see what looks like a seal rise out of the water and approach the shoreline. It's the first animal I've seen here that is similar to those on Earth, and it's headed straight for us. But within feet of the water's edge, the animal peels its skin away, transforming into a naked human woman. Just when I think I've seen everything ... shit. What the hell is she?

The female smiles, draping the hide over her arm as she closes the gap between us and takes the last few steps out of the lake. Her gaze locks onto Nate. A come-hither smile spreads across her face. "Don't be afraid." Her voice is sweet, smooth ... alluring. She purrs seductively, "I listened as you spoke of the trouble in your life. I can help you." She places a hand on Nate's chest and looks up, waiting for his reply.

My internal alarms are buzzing, and the way Nate tenses, I'm sure his are too. He says, "Help me how, and what the fuck are you?"

"I'm a selkie." Her hand drifts down to his abdomen, and for a moment I think she's not going to stop there. She hasn't broken eye contact with Nate—she'd better not be using her magic on him. Nate seems entranced, though, and I'm liking this even less. "I know of a male selkie willing and desperate to take a mate. Bring your unwanted female here to the edge of the lake, and I'll have him waiting for her."

Nate's eyes narrow as he pushes her hand away. The half step he puts between them is typical of his fighting technique—stay within striking range but be ready and able to block. "That's it, just bring her here?"

Not what I expected him to say; I thought he was going to tell her to get lost. "I don't think this is such a great idea, bro." I'm not sure what this creature is up to, but it smacks of deceit.

"Mind your own fucking business." Nate grabs the selkie by the shoulders. "Answer me."

She shrugs off his hold and says, "All you need to do is upset her, which from what I've seen and heard won't be difficult to do. But make sure she is close enough to the water that seven of her tears fall into it. My friend can be quite convincing, and after her tears fall he will be able to claim her, regardless of your bond to her. She'll never be able to leave him or this place unless he frees her."

Now, I know this is bullshit, and I won't stand by and allow my brother to make this terrible mistake. It doesn't sound as if Nate could get Jo back if he changed his mind, and neither of us knows what would happen to their mate bond if it was tampered with. "Tell me something, selkie, are you the Seelinara equivalent of a trickster? You sure sound like Coyote and Spider back home— talk a fine line of bullshit, promise something better, and then let your victim suffer the lesson you bring?"

Nate looks so pissed that I almost laugh. "What, bro? She's feeding you a steaming pile of crap on a silver platter. You're only going to make things worse for you and Jo."

"I told you to stay out of it," he growls, looking back at the selkie. "When should I bring her?"

"Damn it, Nate! You're really going to be this fucking stupid?" The defiant upward tilt of his chin tells me all I need to know— yes, he is, regardless of what I say. It's the final straw. I've tried to keep my frustration in check, and I've gone out of my way not to make things worse since Jo came into his life, but this is his mess to deal with. For once he can go ahead and fuck up his future—I won't be there to help him clean it up afterward. I've got a mate to care for now. Ina and I deserve a chance at a good life together, and that's something we won't have as long as Nate continually drags me down with his bullshit.

I start to walk away but call back over my shoulder, "Jo isn't perfect, and she may even be wretched, but she doesn't deserve to be betrayed and discarded this way. If you do it, we're done. I will no longer be the rock you break yourself against." Then I take to the sky without looking back.

CHAPTER 34: NATE
Walking the Talk

Rafe's words echo in my head all the way back to the thunderbird village. I understand this is not the future or family he dreamed of—and that his grand vision of us doing this together is falling like dust to his feet. Even I know that this may mar our relationship forever, and I don't want that either. But I also know an eternity spent lurching from one relationship catastrophe to another will do even more harm to all of us—Ina and Jo included. I won't live that way, and Rafe and Ina shouldn't have to reap the consequences of the constant whirlwind that is Jo and me. I have two days to make a hard choice. I just hope Rafe keeps his damn mouth shut—then again, Jo may find out regardless, since she can hear my damn thoughts. Hell, for all I know, she heard everything that went through my head while I was talking to Rafe and to the selkie. Intrusive doesn't begin to describe the horrible lack of privacy— all beings should have the right to think freely. With my luck, Jo will be waiting to attack my ass when I reach the treetop village.

She did say strong emotions convey my thoughts, and I was pretty fucking wrecked by the time I reached that lake. If there is a limit to distance, she may not have heard a word, and then my

challenge will be thinking about this opportunity without thinking about it too hard. The selkie's offer is tempting—very fucking
tempting—but my damn traitorous heart is taking a lashing from
the mate bond at the mere idea of getting rid of her. Damn it all
to hell. I'm at war with myself, have been from the day Jo and I met.
And I have no idea which side will win—I only know that I can't
keep going on like this.

As the village comes into view, I try to let go of these conflicting thoughts and the decision I will have to make. Instead I deliberately focus on the conversation I'm going to have with Jo. No
more bullshit—she'd better be ready to reveal whatever else she's
hidden from me, or I will take the selkie up on her offer.

As I land on the catwalk, I see Vivi walking away from the house—
at least I won't have to put up with her crap or kick her ass out when
I get there. After I step inside, Ina rushes to assure me that she
didn't allow Vivi in to talk with Jo. I nod, looking over her head,
and see Jo sitting on the couch, staring at the floor. I can tell she's
been crying, though I don't know if it's because of me or Vivi or
because Ina did something to upset her. At this point I don't give
a shit. I tell Ina to leave. It's time to get this over with ... I want
to get on with my life.

When the door clicks shut, Jo looks up at me, and we maintain
eye contact while I take a seat opposite her—I need as much damn
distance as possible. Another planet would be ideal, but this will
have to do for now.

Jo says, "Nate, I—"

"Just shut the fuck up. I have a few things to say to you, and
you're going to listen, and then you're going to give me some damn
answers. Got me?"

She lowers her gaze to her lap and nods. Good. "This isn't working between us, and I know you already see that. We're going to
get past whatever shit they throw at us tomorrow, and then we're
going to knuckle down, finish our training, and get the hell off this

planet as soon as possible. When we're back on Earth, we will do our duty as guardians, but otherwise you will stay far away from me when we're not working."

"No." Jo shakes her head. "Don't you do this to us."

"There's no trust between us!" I stand, anger radiating off me in waves. "Shit, Jo, you concealed everything—eavesdropped on me and never said a fucking word. If it weren't for Vivi's big mouth, I still wouldn't know. Hell, you even blamed me for all of this, when you knew damn well that you weren't any more human than I was."

She jumps to her feet too, her hands clenched at her sides. "When was I supposed to tell you, Nate? When we were sexually coupled and disgust and rage poured out of your mind so thick it nearly choked me? Maybe in one of the many moments you wanted me dead? Or better yet, how about in the dozens of times you thought about holding me down and ripping my wings out feather by fucking feather?" Her eyes narrow with fury. "Was I supposed to waltz up to you with this announcement when you were considering beating my ass? Oh, wait, I know! The perfect moment was when you wished you could just fuck your way through a whole line of women to forget me—same as you did all the time before we met. Just when in the hell was I supposed to tell you without making this worse?"

My temper flares, partly with embarrassment and shame. I can't take back my thoughts—no one can—but like a thief, she stole them. She had no right to take a single one. "I never once said any of that to you. Not once, Jo. I never said any one of the vile things I thought, and if you heard them, you most certainly heard the thousand different ways I was breaking inside. You knew how I felt—and I'm not just talking about the bad shit."

"Oh yes, because those moments were so damn perfect too." She throws her hands in the air and walks away several feet before spinning back to face me. "Your manic moods ... by the time you switched to any form of kind or loving thought, I was lying in the wreckage of your hate. I'd just barely crawl out of that, and you'd slam me again."

The raw emotion has her sheridauk form rippling to the surface, and I can feel my own fight instincts climb. Jo shouts, "You're a complete asshole, Nate." Her head snaps up, daggers launching from her wild eyes—the look tells me she read my mind again. Damn her. "Really ... *I'm* a selfish bitch? You've never once considered that I have feelings too. No, most of the time you've preferred to believe I couldn't feel one damn thing and that I was incapable of love. Did you ever stop to think that you were the reason I never told you?"

Hell no, wrong answer—she is not turning this back solely on me. "We're done. I refuse to spend a fucking eternity having you rip my heart out day after fucking day. We'll find a way to get along well enough to do our damn jobs, but beyond that I don't want you anywhere near me." Yeah, I know I'm being a cold-hearted prick, but something has to give—I can't keep weathering her storms.

She wipes a tear away and sits stiffly in the closest chair. When I'm certain she is no longer on the verge of turning full sheridauk, I say, "What else have you lied about ... hidden? Better yet, how else have you used your mutant beast powers on me?"

Under her breath Jo says, "Even now you won't believe I feel any of this too." Her hands grip her knees and then still as she takes a deep breath and blows it out slowly. She swallows hard. "Hearing your thoughts is part of what freaked me out so badly when this first happened between us. I knew how you felt ... how this mistake was an immediate and horrendous regret for you." She looks away and draws another breath. "I knew what I was, but I didn't know what was happening to us, to you—it overwhelmed me, and your hateful emotions about did me in."

"Get to the damn point, Jo, and answer my question." I retake my seat, even though I'd rather remain standing. We have to settle this—time to stop running and avoiding the problem.

"I'm trying to! Give me one bullshit minute to explain so that even your stubborn-ass hide can understand." She glowers at me, and I scowl right back.

An uncomfortable silence forces the air out of the room as we stare each other down. For a moment Jo's eyes glow red, then light green, and I'm certain this time she's going to shift into her sheridauk form right here in the damn living room. I can feel my wings twitching under my skin, ready to come out and deal with the potential threat. But she closes her eyes and rolls her head like she's working out tension knots in her neck, and when her eyes open they are back to their normal dark green. "Sheridauks have the ability for mind-to-mind communication—*mea'k spindalt*, as Vivi told you. We hear each other's projected thoughts. Not all thoughts, just those we choose to send to someone else." She takes another deep breath, rubbing the palms of her hands on her pants. "Most of the time we mask our own emotions well enough that they don't bleed through to others. Strong emotions can allow private thoughts to come through, but we have the ability to filter them so that the words are muffled, muted. Weaker projected thoughts can be blocked entirely, and there were times I tuned you out because I couldn't stand listening to what you thought of me. But—"

"But you listened in anyway, didn't you?" I shift in my seat; part of me wants to hear what she has to say, and the other part is full-tilt screaming at me to get as far away from her as possible. "I had no fucking privacy, unlike you ... you completely shut me out and left. You can't say the same in return. Damn it, Jo, don't you get it? It's like reading someone's email or journal or listening in when they're on the phone. Private thoughts—which, by the way, means thoughts you and only you ever know—that's how normal people work through issues and make decisions. Not every thought is acted on or the emotion behind it etched in stone."

She closes her eyes a moment, slumping against the cushion. "Don't you think I know that? I was born this way. I've had years of Vivi in my head ... years of trying to block or ignore her private thoughts. We had no one to teach us how to manage these abilities. We had to cope as best we could." Her eyes open, and she looks defeated, but I keep my expression hard—I'm not ready to concede. Jo sighs. "And back on the ranch, the prince and king ... and here, the other sheridauks have access."

She averts her gaze. In truth, she's right—I never considered what it's been like for her, and my nobler side taunts me. Until we came here for that bullshit test, I only had her and not all the others in my damn head too.

Before I can form a response she says, "I struggled with the bond between us too, you know. I felt the same things you did. The pull, the need and want, the desire and revulsion. Yes, there were times I deliberately listened in on what you were thinking, projecting to me. But I needed to know if you were always going to hate me and resent me for what I did to your life."

"I don't fucking hate you!" The words are out before I can stop them. Shit. It's my turn to draw a deep breath. "I don't resent you either. But I swear, Jo, this is never going to work between us as long as the bullshit surprises keep coming. And it's a given that you already know all my secrets—even the ones you were never meant to hear."

"I didn't know how to tell you without making everything worse." She meets my gaze as she stands and approaches with slow, deliberate steps, then crouches in front of me. "You need to know that I'd never expect you to forget Catches Bird, nor will I ever replace what she meant to you. I love you, Nate, maybe even more because I've learned how deeply you can love others, and I don't want to lose you or spend my life separated from you. Being a sheridauk is what I am ... and I need you to accept all of me, not just the part that seems human, because I'm not human. And to a large degree, neither are you."

Her statement hits me hard; it's a harsh reminder of my struggle to accept what Rafe and I were destined to be ... of the role we're supposed to play in the peace-bringer prophecy. A role she complicated by sharing her nature with me, turning me into more than just a man and thunderbird myself. I'm as much of a beast as she is, if not more, considering my penchant for fighting. Everything about this feels impossible, yet my attempts to reject the truth—that I, we, are more than human, and we weren't meant to hold nine-to-five jobs—only invite more discord and bury us under a shit-ton of problems of our own making.

In my mind I hear the voice of a healer I knew two or three hundred years ago, a man whose words never left me. He said that I had to accept myself before others would and that I must learn to accept others as they are, because we are all precisely as the Creator intends us to be. He cautioned me that if I was going to talk the talk, then I needed to be ready to walk the walk, or I'd never find peace within myself or the world around me. His last words to me were "Walk the talk, always."

Reaching down, I lift Jo onto my lap and rest my forehead against hers. "You're right." I nod and press a kiss above her brow. "I'm sorry ... I'm not handling this bullshit very well. All I can say is that we both need to stop holding back. No more secrets. We can't keep hurting each other this way."

Jo agrees and plants a lingering kiss to each of my cheeks. When she pulls back, her intense eyes search mine, and I wonder if she's listening in on my thoughts again. But then without warning her arm rises swiftly, and she punches me hard on the jaw.

"Ow! What the hell was that for?" I roar in disbelief.

"If you ever—and I do mean ever—tell me to go fuck myself or threaten to leave me again, so help me, Nate, I will unleash my beast and rip every last feather from your wings, and then I will fly off and leave you grounded. You got me?"

I laugh in spite of myself as I pull her close and place a fierce kiss on her mouth. "I got ya, babe. It won't ever happen again, I fucking swear."

We spend the next couple of hours making love, and I discover that make-up sex can be hotter than hell—Jo is the best damn lover I've had in my long life. I doubt we'll learn how to stop fighting each other right away, but I'm grateful the Creator gave me the gift of a woman strong enough to put up with my shit. We might just survive each other yet. As for the selkie, she's the one who can go fuck herself. Jo is staying where she belongs—right by my side, always. I will never let her go.

CHAPTER 35: RAFE
The Time to Rise

Ina once again senses my disquiet and gives me the space I need to work through my conflicting feelings. If it weren't for her gentle strength, I'm not sure I could face Nate in the days ahead, and I'm beginning to think my relationship with him may be as damaged as Jo and Vivi's. I have no idea how we overcome this, and I don't like the new divisions that have grown between us here in Seelinara, let alone the way they're tearing apart our newly formed family. But within the unpredictable, ever-changing dynamics is Ina, and she's quickly becoming the glue that binds the four of us together. A chuckle escapes me now as I watch her move away from Aunt Prania and start walking toward me. Ina is always great at reading me and knows when I'm ready to talk.

I see a subtle hint in the quick tip of her head followed by her eyes looking upward, and without hesitation we launch into the sky and head for the area Grandfather has labeled my contemplation box. He's not entirely wrong—I have developed the habit of seeking this spot whenever I need time to think or be alone.

After we land Ina pulls me into a hug. She's waiting for me to say something, but I'm not sure where to start. We'll stand here all day until I do. My brows furrow as I try to untangle the words and emotions warring inside me. "Nate and I are all but identical in every way possible—shape, build, strength, intelligence, and much more—yet we clash and couldn't be more opposite in temperament and personality. If that were the only issue ..." I'm not sure where I'm going with this, but I don't want to allow jealousy into the mix. It's been difficult for me to accept that efurrids are mortal Seelies and not among the seven in-betweens like Jo and Nate and me. There was never a chance of my receiving Ina's nature, even though I was able to transform her to mine. Why does it feel as if Ina and I were ripped off, while Nate and Jo were rewarded? What makes them so special?

Taking a deep breath, I try again. "How can identical twins be the same and yet so different? How can one seem to be more than the other, and what does that say of the one who is less?"

Ina pulls back, looking up at me, then steps away and walks over to the boulder we often sit on. "You know our legends and beliefs," she says as I join her there. "You understand that in the greater circle of life there is a balance that is always maintained. There is no light without dark ... sky without ground ... good without bad ... sun without moon."

"That's the problem, Ina. My brother and I are out of balance."

She gives me an encouraging smile. "That's where you are wrong, hon. You and Nate are two halves of one whole—mirrored twins. You can't be the same in all things, because together you are balance, opposites. If you weren't, then there'd be no balance, as you'd have to occupy the same space, the exact role in life."

I shake my head. "I don't—"

"Can the sun and moon share the same place in the sky? Can the sky live on the ground or the ground live up above? Even light and dark can't be where the other is, and that is you and Nate. You balance each other—you must—or one of you would not need to exist."

Maybe Ina is right about Nate and I balancing each other out. I've often thought of Nate and I as polar opposites ... And that's when the aha moment hits. One word defining the answer I've sought for so long. One word that has always been there. One balanced meaning to explain the differences that at times have seemed unequal. *Polar.* The Earth's poles may look similar from the sky, and yet they are distinctly different in the roles they play in this world. They keep the Earth balanced. If I'm honest with myself, I can see it now; where Nate is more and I am less is reversed in other aspects of ourselves, and then I am the one who is more. In the end, we have balance.

I stand and pull Ina close, kissing her fiercely as my arms tighten around her. This woman has a natural magic, a wisdom that comes from a Spirit that sees far more than most ever will. "You're my strength in knowing when I'm weak in awareness. I never realized how lost I was until I found you. I love you, Inaleah Redhawk ... you are my everything when I am nothing."

Ina giggles and pushes me back a step. "I love you too, Rafe Redhawk, but I was nothing until you gave me everything."

Yes, the Creator knew what I needed in a mate, and she's the biggest blessing in my life. And while Ina continues her efurrid lessons and Nate and Jo learn about their sheridauk abilities, I will gain additional family time with Grandfather, Uncle Rynuark, and Aunt Prania.

It gives me one over on Nate, at least—I'm learning about our Ancestors and about Earth as our Seelinaran relations knew it before the veils were sealed. Their memories are sharp, surpassing my own, and I swear they haven't forgotten one detail of their lives, including their years with the Hachaath. They tell me stories of the Ancestors' way of life and the lost tribal ceremonies, and even correct me when I mess up the language. They'll never know how much I appreciate everything they have shared with me about the people who always held hope for our return. I feel reconnected in a way that I haven't been for a very long time, and it gives me hope that my brother and I will get ourselves back on good terms and even right the upside-down way our family began after Ina and Jo joined us. He may piss me off, but he is my brother, and I love him. We'll be strongest with a solid core to the four of us, and something tells me we'll need that strength to face whatever lies ahead.

Of course, in exchange for all I'm learning from my thunderbird family, I'm able to tell my grandfather, uncle, and aunt what happened after they left Earth, and each one goes through a period of mourning—they knew their spouses and most of their children would take the journey someday, but they weren't prepared to find out none of their children became thunderbirds until Nate and I came along two generations later. They also mourn the passing of the friends they made within the tribe, and the loss of the Hachaath people. Nate and I have always understood that we may be the only survivors who are nearly full-blood, but at least through us the Hachaath will live on. It's a humbling legacy for the thunderbirds, knowing that through them an entire tribe of people will never be completely lost to the passing years.

The extra time with my grandfather, uncle, and aunt also allows me to close the gap between my ability and skill level faster than I could have done on my own. They teach me how to adapt to my bird form, pushing me over the hurdles in areas that haven't come as naturally for me as they have for Nate, Jo, and Ina. Still, it takes me a full seven weeks before I'm ready to prove my wings in the combat training ahead. I will stand as a thunderbird in my own right.

The passage of time also lessens the strain on my relationship with Nate, and we're slowly reforming our bond as brothers, boosting my confidence that we'll bury the discord for good. Of course, Ina deserves a lot of the credit. That woman has gone to greater lengths than any one of us in ending our disputes, bringing us together. It's a trait that grew from her Earth family's influence, and

I understand now why her other family is tightly bound. The Creator or the fates had to have known she was exactly what our little family needed, and for that I will always be grateful.

The elders have begun teaching us about the unique roles thunderbirds fill on other planets, and how we may be of service beyond Earth and Seelinara. Indeed, many of the thunderbirds seem to think we're now at the top of the multiverse pecking order, right up there with angels, demons, and gargoyles, and that this somehow makes us unstoppable. The four of us agree that if we really want to get knocked on our asses, all we need to do is feed our egos and watch the sisters of fate smack us down. Thankfully Nate and I agree to tread on the side of humility and accept other preternaturals as equals, and our mates follow our example. It brings us a measure of respect and gratitude from the thunderbirds after we explain our unwillingness to invite that lesson into our lives—and how one of many reasons the tricksters exist is to teach through contrary and sometimes harsh lessons. The thunderbirds' acceptance of that wisdom increases our desire to introduce them to our other customs and beliefs too.

We start with stories and legends and work our way toward ceremonies, though without divulging our spiritual practices. Nate takes the lead in teaching them traditional dance, while I show them how to make a drum and play for them. Together my brother and I teach the fae—and Ina and Jo—how to sing, and in turn the Seelinarans teach us the same songs in the fae language. This is another first for Nate and me, and with each cultural lesson we give, we tie another knot strengthening our bond of brotherhood. It's the healing balm needed to repair our battered relationship— I can feel it changing us, moving us past the barriers that defined the contentiousness of the last few centuries. Will it last, or is it a one-off from sharing this part of ourselves with the thunderbirds? I'll learn that answer eventually.

Within days Nate takes this a few steps further and manages to talk our instructors into allowing us to paint our bodies and faces as we would for war or fighting. We receive a few surprised looks when we return to the village, but before long our fellow thunderbirds are asking us about meaning and application—and want to know how they can paint themselves for future battles. I'm a bit surprised Grandfather, Aunt, and Uncle didn't teach these things after they fled Earth, but they claim they held back out of respect for the Ancestors' reluctance to share this knowledge with outsiders.

Yet these thunderbirds are not outsiders—they are our extended family, and for the first time in centuries I have a sense of tribe again. Granted, Earth will always be our first home, but we belong equally on Seelinara and will be welcomed whenever we are here. Again I am grateful for the Creator making these two planets sister-worlds and forging a connection between the people of both. Nate and I are no longer alone on either world. I've gained a mate and a family and regained my brother and our sense of unity.

There are few times in life when one should look back, but this is one of those times. We drifted for centuries untethered to the world around us, never knowing if we'd ever truly fit in anywhere. The challenges we've faced were trying, sometimes heartbreaking, and it's yet to be seen what rewards they will bring to our lives, but there is always a gift to be found, even in the knowledge that the legends of our kind were true and not mere stories. I shake my head and smile. Ina and Jo too—they are the gifts the Creator blessed us with after we endured centuries alone in a world that didn't know we existed. They were the missing connection we needed to ground and balance us as individuals and as a team. In finding them we gained all that was missing or taken from us over time.

We are not a myth or a mystery. And soon the people will become aware we're no longer lurking in the shadows of ancient stories. It's a lot to live up to, and although we still have a long way to go in our training, I'm certain of this: We are real. We are united.

We have taken flight. And as thunderbirds we will rise as warriors for the people once more.

Coming Fall 2017

Redemption
Book Four of the *Nights of Shadow* series

Coming Soon ...

Book Two of the *Rise of the Thunderbirds* series
Read on for an excerpt from *Warriors* ...

Rise of the Thunderbirds—Warriors
Excerpt

My anxiety has built for days now that the path Nate, Jo, Ina, and I have been destined to walk lies directly in front of us. There's no going back—ever. I feel inadequate and can't understand why the three sisters of fate picked us for this journey, for the honor of being guardians. Not that I'll have time to dwell on it come tomorrow; from what they've described of our training, it will be like fae boot camp.

Nate and I have been through a few American military boot camps over the last couple of centuries, but everything on this planet is so different from what we've known on Earth that I'm not sure what to expect when our aggressive training begins. Aside from combat techniques, both with weapons and hand-to-hand, everything else will be new. Instead of five- or ten-mile marches, there will be short- and long-distance flying, along with flight combat and magic training.

We have a lot to learn if we are to be successful guardians of the people on Earth, which we've come to understand is all people and not just those of Native heritage. It's a damn tall order, but I know the four of us will do our best, and by the sound of things we'll have plenty of support from the supernatural community back home.

King Altheron has sent orders that we're to be readied to form an alliance with Dmitri and Elizabetta Markov, Matt Wolfe, Maria D'Arcy, the Unseelie Prince Dahliorn, and the Seelie Princess Milnea. The Seelinarans consider the ten of us a joint-world task force, since the fate of both Earth and Seelinara depends on the success of the peace-bringer, Elizabetta Markov. According to some ancient fae oracle, Elizabetta was fated to bring us all together. It sounds like a bad bar joke to me, considering what we are. I'm still trying to wrap my head around the fact that vampires, werewolves, maxians, fae, angels, and demons exist at all, let alone that we'll be working with them to save our two worlds. Seems they take this peace-bringer prophecy like it's an edict sent straight from the fates and the Creator. I'm undecided if it's true or not, but I can't fully discount it, since Nate and I are walking proof of one Native American legend. And there's no denying that my brother and I were always destined for this journey.

"You're awfully deep in thought. Are you going to lie awake all night?" Ina presses a kiss to my neck.

My arms tighten around her a moment before I tip her face up to mine and kiss her too. "It's tradition, don't you know? I don't think there's ever been a time Nate and I didn't stay awake the whole night before starting boot camp."

She chuckles and shakes her head. "Is that how you see the training we're about to get?"

"Yeah, babe, it is." My tone turns serious as old fears rise—injury, accidently killing an innocent person, being discovered for what we are. "They are going to teach us how to use our abilities for one reason—so we can fulfill our role as guardians. Warriors. That will mean engaging in the war when we get back to Earth, and it will mean fighting enemies we never knew existed. We will have to kill, and taking a life is never an easy thing to do or live with afterward."

Her brow furrows. "I hadn't thought of it like that."

I wish I didn't know either, but the hidden scars of past battles are haunting reminders that will not be ignored. Searching Ina's eyes, I see her curiosity and uncertainty and even a hint of nervous excitement for the journey ahead. I want to shield her from the dark, ugly realities as long as possible—now is not the time to push my ghosts out of the closet.

"Come here ..." I pull her on top of me and allow my hands to roam over her body. Ina is the balm that soothes and quiets my mind, and my thoughts of boot camp and war fade with each stroke of her fingers on my skin. "Let's not think about it," I say. "Instead we'll start a new pre-training and pre-battle ritual: spending the night enjoying each other in every way possible."

Playlist

for

Rise of the Thunderbirds—Flight

The songs in this playlist fit the themes and scenes of *Rise of the Thunderbirds—Flight.* They helped inspire me while I was writing this book; hopefully they will give you a deeper emotional connection to the story and its characters.

YouTube: http://tinyurl.com/o8hceoj

1. "Gett Off" by Prince [Nate's one-night stands]
2. "Night Vision" by Lindsey Stirling [Rafe's struggles with Nate]
3. "Spirit in the Sky" by Norman Greenbaum [Nate seeking to cheat death]
4. "Bad to the Bone" by George Thorogood & The Destroyers [Nate's fight scenes]
5. "Sundown" by Gordon Lightfoot [Nate and Rafe: duality of desire for a mate]
6. "Runnin'" by Adam Lambert [Nate in self-destructive mode; Nate's motorcycle wreck]
7. "If You Don't Start Drinkin'" by George Thorogood & The Destroyers [Nate hounding Rafe for booze]
8. "Need You Tonight" by INXS [Nate and the blonde in McAllister]
9. "Red & White (Driving Me Crazy)" by Northern Cree [Nate meeting Jo at the Milk River Indian Days pow wow]

10. "Closer" by Nine Inch Nails [Nate's fantasies of bedding Jo]
11. "Canli Opahkta Olowan" by Earl Bullhead [Nate and Rafe: pow wow reflections of the old ways]
12. "Black Velvet" by Alannah Myles [Rafe's slide into defeat]
13. "Broken Wings" by Mr. Mister [Nate chasing Jo]
14. "The Lightning Strike (What If This Storm Ends?)" by Snow Patrol [Rafe giving up on finding his mate]
15. "Heavy In Your Arms" by Florence and the Machine [Jo's rejection of the mate bond]
16. "Just One Arrow" by John York [Nate and Rafe: melancholy over a long, never-ending life]
17. "Earth Angel" by Northern Cree [Rafe's gratitude for receiving Ina as his mate]
18. "Sign of the Gypsy Queen" by April Wine [Nate escaping to the Badlands]
19. "Done All Wrong" by Black Rebel Motorcycle Club [Nate despondent in the Badlands]
20. "Blaze of Glory" by Jon Bon Jovi [Nate hitting bottom]
21. "I Didn't Mean It" by The Belle Brigade [Nate mistakes Vivi for Jo]
22. "Thunderstruck" by AC/DC [Thunderbirds meeting the other supernaturals as their world turns upside down]
23. "Stubborn Love" by The Lumineers [Nate and Jo struggling to accept and love one another]
24. "Radioactive" by Lindsey Stirling and Pentatonix [Nate and Rafe dealing with the fae on Seelinara]
25. "At This Point In My Life" by Tracy Chapman [Jo opening up to Nate]
26. "Arms" by Christina Perri [Jo revealing her hidden truths]

27. "Time Machine" by Ingrid Michaelson [Nate's desperation to undo mate bond]
28. "Excess" by Tricky [Nate losing it and being tempted by the selkie]
29. "Make Me Wanna Die" by The Pretty Reckless [Jo fighting back for Nate's heart]
30. "You" by The Pretty Reckless [Jo baring her heart and soul to Nate]

Acknowledgments

To my readers, I humbly thank you for buying this book. If you're familiar with both the *Rise of the Thunderbirds* and *Nights of Shadow* series, I hope you enjoyed the crossover between stories and the interaction of the characters. Let me know what made you laugh or cry or made you angry, but most importantly, whether you enjoyed the story.

And please consider writing a review for this book wherever it was purchased online. While I enjoy hearing what a reader likes or doesn't like about my characters and novels, I love it even more when a reader leaves a rating and review that helps others decide whether to read on or pass a book by. Share with other readers your thoughts about Nate, Rafe, Jo, and Ina—and of the worlds they belong to.

Special thanks to my beta reader team—Tony, Elaine, Sandy, Tim, Ruth, and Danielle. Your critical and complimentary input—and your enthusiasm and encouragement—helped make the final version of *Flight* possible.

My heartfelt thanks goes to my family, for putting up with me when I'm in serious writing mode and for all the times you have pushed me to follow this dream. I couldn't keep writing these novels without your support.

With gratitude I thank Leon Garcia for modeling for the *Rise of the Thunderbirds* book covers. His image is perfect, and I couldn't have found a better representation for Nate and Rafe. May the Creator always bless him and his beautiful Spirit.

Lastly, I once again want to thank my editor, Christina M. Frey of Page Two Editing, for all of her diligent and hard work. The spit-and-shine polish she helps me put on my stories allows me to present readers with good-quality books.

About the Author

Lianne Miller grew up in the mountains of southwestern Montana, in the Clark Fork River Valley east of Missoula. She now lives on the high plains in the northeastern part of the state, where she runs a horse ranch with her husband and an extended family member.

From riding horses to driving a semitruck and owning a small business, Lianne has worn many hats and labels, and she often claims to be a jack-of-all-trades and master of none. Now many of her days are spent writing and bringing to life the stories she began creating while raising her children. Lianne's books delve into judgment, tolerance, prejudice, and acceptance—challenges in both the human and the paranormal worlds.

Rise of the Thunderbirds is a crossover series set in the same preternatural world as her debut series, *Nights of Shadow*. Though these can be read as standalone series, reading both—starting with *Artifice, Vendetta,* and *Chaos* from *Nights of Shadow*—will immerse you deeper in her vision of Earth, Seelinara, and the shadow realms and will provide a richer understanding of the characters appearing in both stories.

For news about Lianne's stories and characters or to sign up for email alerts, visit her online world:

Website: www.liannemiller.com
Blog: http://apps.liannemiller.com/Blog
Facebook: www.facebook.com/MillerLianne
Twitter: https://twitter.com/_LianneMiller
YouTube Channel: http://tinyurl.com/owrvqhh